REVELATIONS

THE SOUL MONGER: BOOK TWO

MATILDA SCOTNEY

Revelations: The Soul Monger Book Two
ISBN: 978-0-6483191-7-7

Cover design by Beehive Book Design.

The past is never where you think you left it –

Katherine Anne Porter

CHAPTER ONE _

The Soul Monger!

Laurel's heart pounded. Darlen? Here? How had she not sensed him? Confused, Laurel looked behind for one last glimpse of Gabriel, but he was gone, separated from her now by the rapidly increasing distance of open space. Surely, Darlen couldn't be Gabriel's trusted merchant? But even as that knowledge spoke its truth to her, it did nothing to lessen her surprise at seeing her friend standing with the man who stole them from their lives all those months ago. A man for whom Helen always professed her hatred.

Darlen stepped towards Laurel, his voice hissing with urgency. "We don't have time for you to muse on my part in all this, Laurel. I need you to focus. Did Gabriel tell you how to infiltrate the fortress?" He gripped her arm, reinforcing that she must concentrate. A light sweat appeared on his forehead as he waited for her to answer. It was all happening so fast.

"Uh, Alisitrite." She choked on the word, dredging up the information from her clouded and confused brain. Swallowing hard, she looked him in the eye and took a deep breath. "Alisitrite. It's the only thing that can affect the fortress and only found on his home planet."

"Damn," Darlen spat, stepping back and running his grubby hands through his matted hair. This was not the news he hoped for. "Anything else?"

Laurel, still struggling with the sudden separation from Gabriel, the Semevalian female sacrifice and the significant presence of Darlen, now apparently an ally, threatened to plunge her back into confusion. Stay calm, she told herself, and allowed her senses to guide her. Darlen waited, but he didn't hide his impatience.

"I read the minds of the war council," Laurel said after a moment, wishing she had clarity enough to peer into Darlen's mind, but for now, he was out of her reach. Gabriel trusted him, and that would have to be good enough. "I know what the duke's next moves are."

Darlen turned to Helen. "We'll transmit to Harry and the League that we've recovered Laurel and ..." he made to turn away, but Laurel grabbed his arm. He peered down at her, his face creasing into a deep frown.

"Darlen, no." Laurel stepped closer as if she were about to reveal a dark, unmentionable secret. "Not the League. Just Harry." Darlen held her gaze. Laurel was a whole soul; he wouldn't ask why the League must not be told, she would have a good reason, and he would find out soon enough. "We need to get through the Miran Forin nebula and take out their communications."

"Just us?" Helen said. "How? We can't get through the nebula."

Darlen held up a hand to stop her, keeping his eyes on

Laurel's face. "It's okay, Helen, just Harry for now. We can get Eli, Marta, and Chloe mobilised. I believe Harry will trust your judgement, Laurel. The duke will be here in a matter of hours, so we must find a way to secure that mineral. Do you have a plan?"

Laurel nodded. "I need a datacache."

Darlen led Laurel back to the room where she first learned of the League and her new life. Mer, at the ship's controls, glanced behind as she entered, but with all Laurel had endured over recent months, he somehow seemed less menacing than before.

Laurel mapped a schematic of the palace on the datacache. "This is a direct route from the viceroy's chamber to the duke's throne room. Gabriel said there are compressed formations of the mineral embedded into the throne, three of them, and he says they require no processing or refinement, just securing to a warhead."

"How can you believe him, Laurel?" Helen cut in, her face twisting in disbelief. "He took you prisoner."

Laurel saw her logic, but Helen didn't know the whole story, yet. "Yes, but he also sent for Darlen."

Darlen glanced at Helen, who was trying to work out the connection. Darlen had given her very little information, only that they were rescuing Laurel, and of course, she'd insisted on coming along.

"Laurel's right. He's not the enemy. He's the solution."

"Okay." Helen crossed her arms. "Don't mind me."

"Attaching the minerals to warheads can be done on 100 moons," Darlen said, returning his attention to the datacache.

"Getting them might not be easy," Laurel warned. "And it's not the only part of the plan. We have to rescue Gabriel's family."

Laurel sensed Darlen's initial resistance, but he tempered that resistance with a feeling of expectation. It was not to be a priority; Laurel saw in his mind that first and foremost would be saving the League, but where for a moment she expected outright opposition, she sensed that if they could execute such a rescue, he would give her every support.

"I am acquainted with the viceroy," Darlen said, knowing Laurel might be trying to spy on his thoughts. "He has an eye for female slaves, so with you two, I've got an excuse for a visit."

"I promised Gabriel," Laurel said. "They'll sell his son to the Ferle, and his mother will become a chain slave. I can't let that happen."

Darlen stood unmoving. He had his own reasons for rescuing Gabriel's family, and he knew the cruelty of which the duke was capable.

"We need to get the mineral and knock out comms," he said at length. "Harry and the others will need to keep the Gartrya from the portals, but eventually, they're going to find out the duke is dead. We must rescue Gabriel's family before that, or the Primature Council will implement the Charter of Succession."

That surprised Laurel. "You know about the Charter?"

"Yes, but I didn't know of the duke's plans."

"And you see why we can't leave them there?"

Darlen always believed Laurel to be the strongest of

the whole souls, alongside Xavier. He saw it now, how she'd become so much more than she'd been in her previous life and felt a strange pride in the part he played, even though he doubted she would appreciate his feelings on the matter. Helen had made hers known constantly on the journey to Semevale 7. He nodded. Again, he knew it was wise to trust her.

"Whatever we do, we have to get rid of the viceroy," he said. "He holds the first key to the Charter and is our barrier to the throne room."

Laurel felt as though she now looked at a different man from the cocky, rude individual who brought her to this universe. She might have looked into his mind for the answer to her next question, but it seemed more right to simply ask.

"Darlen, what *is* your place in this?"

He gave a short, breathy laugh. "I don't have a place. I'm an innocent bystander."

"You appear to be neither innocent nor a bystander." Laurel pointed an accusing finger. "You rescued me on your ship, with a League cloak and Helen in tow."

"I was with Harry when Darlen arrived," Helen said. "He was coming to get you and said the informant had a way of releasing you. Darlen had the Semevalian woman with him." She held up her hands in defence. "I swear I had no idea what was going to happen until Darlen told me you were to be executed and that she was a substitute."

"Was that your idea, Darlen?" Laurel asked.

"Yes, I know Gabriel's history."

Laurel sat down slowly, ignoring Darlen's towering

presence above her.

"How could you?"

"How could I what? Know about Gabriel or to bring the substitute?"

Laurel shook her head, shaking off an urge to laugh or perhaps cry as she considered the smallness of the universe, how people could be thus linked. "Both," she said, looking up at him.

"The woman volunteered willingly—happily even," Darlen told her. "I don't believe we had a choice, and the duke will never know the difference."

Helen pushed Darlen roughly to the side to kneel beside Laurel and hold her hands in her own. "Oh, sweetie, we got you out just in time, didn't we? I dread to think what might have happened if Darlen hadn't seen that message."

Laurel didn't care to consider it in depth. "I would either have become a concubine or executed." She'd come so close, and now another woman would face that fate. "If the duke found out I'm a whole soul, he would have forced me to provide whole soul children."

Helen sat back on her heels in surprise. "How the hell would he manage that?"

"Gabriel. He's a whole soul."

Helen's jaw dropped. "I didn't sense that."

"He's unique, Helen," Laurel said, "conceived on Earth but born here of an Earth woman. His abilities set him apart." A ripple in Darlen's mind drew Laurel's attention. "How did *you* know about him, Darlen?"

Darlen pulled Helen to her feet and nudged her towards the control room. "Helen, send the message to

Harry. I suppose you can fly this ship?"

Helen shrugged. "I could probably work it out, but Mer's doing an okay job."

"Not good enough, Helen. I was going to tell Laurel of my involvement with all this while we've got the time, how I knew about Gabriel, but if you can't fly the ship..."

As expected, Helen was full of protestations. "Why can't you tell me too?"

"Because you talk too much and ask too many questions." Darlen towered over Helen, and she barely reached to the middle of his chest, but he couldn't intimidate her. Helen was a match for any man unless the bait was gossip.

"Okay," she said, backing down with a grin. "I can fly it. But stay right here where I can listen."

Darlen rolled his eyes. "That woman," he muttered as he swung a chair around to face Laurel. Mer attached himself noisily to his alcove at the edge of the control room with what sounded like a protest at being supplanted by Helen.

"I was born for soul mongering, same as my father," Darlen began. "The League believed they'd sealed up the Transcender nice and tight, but accessing it is in our nature; it reacts to us. I was young, and I'd only made a few trips. My dad gave up and retired when the League got in our way with their sanctimony and moral high ground." Darlen gave a short snort of derision for rules. "He didn't want a fight with the League, but me? I wanted more, so I took the closure as a challenge, one last trip, just long enough to pick up a couple more whole souls." Darlen's expression suddenly lightened, and the hardness left his eyes. "I only collected one—a woman. I'd seen her at the Louvre in Paris and couldn't believe…" He sighed, the dreaminess and longing in his voice at odds with his rough appearance. "The most exquisite creature I'd ever seen. Her eyes were extraordinary, grey, no—violet, and her skin, so fair." He inhaled deeply, momentarily losing track of time as he remembered, his voice fading before he recovered himself and returned to the moment. "Black hair, windswept," he smiled, "some of it tucked up under a hat—" Darlen demonstrated the shape of a hat with his hands before continuing, "the rest loose over her shoulders. Her figure was perfect, and the way she walked…" Darlen cleared his throat. "My response to her…was overwhelming." He leaned forward, his hands on his knees, the earlier tenderness now fleeing in the face of rage. "I found her again early the next morning, leaving an apartment building. The Gestapo had snipers positioned on a rooftop overlooking the entrance. I took her as the first shots rang out. They were going to kill her."

"She was in the French Resistance," Laurel said. "Gabriel told me." The story fitted together now, Gabriel's mother and Darlen, the sympathetic trader.

Still agitated at the memory, Darlen rubbed the back of his neck. "I gathered it was something like that. I couldn't let them kill her. I might not have found her in another timeline, and I didn't want to take the chance. She was…inspirational. Incredible."

The irony wasn't lost on Laurel. "You saved her so she could become a slave?"

Darlen looked down at his rough hands. "I'm guilty, I suppose. I was enchanted, filled with youthful passion. I knew I was unworthy. I spent long hours just watching her sleep in the variance chamber."

"Did you...?" Darlen understood the meaning behind Laurel's unfinished question. She referred to the practice of a Soul Monger impregnating an abducted whole soul female while she slept through the Transcender.

"I wanted to..." A sudden bashfulness, once again at odds with his demeanour, further softened Laurel towards him. "I didn't even try."

"Promise me you didn't do that to us?" Laurel prompted. She sensed he hadn't, but some verbal reassurance would be nice.

"Don't worry," he grinned slightly. "The League didn't want you pregnant. I didn't touch you."

At that, they both heard a faint "phew" from Helen.

"When I got back to Caltobar, my home planet, it horrified my father I'd wasted that last illegal trip. I told him I wanted to keep the woman, but he beat me within an inch of my life and, while I was unconscious, dispatched me to the black border to find quarter soul slaves for mining on Stipe Prime. When I returned a few years later, I couldn't find her. My dad had gone missing, so I supposed he'd gone off and died somewhere. Years afterwards, the only other living Soul Monger told me about a gig he'd been playing in secret for many years, and his father before and his father before, right back to way back when, pretending to be humble merchants. They took nectar and delicacies to an exiled royal family across the nebula, and of course, half soul and quarter soul slaves. He declared that when he died, I'd be the last one with the ability to pass through the nebula. He never said the Gartrya had their origins in League space, and it didn't occur to me to ask." Darlen shrugged. "He died, I took over the gig and his ship and given landing rights in the enclave. The duke and his aides received me well. I picked up from conversations they were plotting war, but I assumed they had some dispute with another system.

"One day, returning to my ship, I noticed a woman walking in the garden. Beside her was a man in his early twenties, a boy of about eight and a young woman who favoured the duke in looks. I hurried towards my ship because it's not permitted to look upon the royal family. I stopped in my tracks when their conversation reached my ears."

"Why?"

"They spoke French."

Laurel understood.

"Yes," Darlen said, reading her expression. "As I said when I first woke you on the ship, I understand many Earth languages. The woman looked at me. It was her—older for sure—but no less enchanting. And the young man, I felt him go straight to my head… his thoughts struck me with a 'phhht', like a slug between the eyes. He was right there in my mind. It wasn't hard to guess he was a whole soul. He watched me as they passed by. I saw his eyes…" he screwed up his face. "I would never have produced a child with his looks. I've got a face like a spikit's arse."

"What's a spikit?" Helen called out.

"Looks like a camel," Darlen called back.

"Oh," Helen replied. "I see that."

Darlen rolled his eyes again, and Helen threw a mischievous grin over her shoulder.

"You took Gabriel's mother in the hours after conception," Laurel said.

Darlen nodded. "That seems to be the case, but I didn't check for pregnancy after variance. Obviously, once I got banished, my father did."

"They killed the Soul Monger who sold her to the duke," Laurel told him. "They followed his ship and destroyed it in a fight while the duke was trying to learn how he navigated the nebula. Could that have been your father?"

"It's likely," Darlen said without emotion, "seeing as I heard he went missing soon after he sent me to the dark border. He didn't cross the nebula often, but he must have known about the Gartrya gig and decided to trespass on the other Soul Monger's patch to get rid of the woman."

"What are these 'beads' Gabriel used to contact you?"

"In every communication through space, microscopic beads break away from the stream, tiny echoes. Think of it this way; a puddle of water on the ground is a conversation. What happens if you drop a rock in it?"

"It makes a splash?"

"Yes, it smashes the conversation and the little droplets that fly up contain tiny echoing shards of what was said. If those little droplets were the communications beads, they usually get ignored because they are unintelligible, fragmented echoes, partial copies of the whole. All communications frequencies have them, but Mer picked it up when he was purging the comms cache. He recognised the language. French."

"Gabriel's mother?"

"I guessed. Because they're beads, which makes them of limited duration, I only made out one word of any use. Invasions. In no time, I heard of the raid on Semevale 7, but the League played it down as nothing more than a disagreement with half-soul miners. I suppose I was still in shock from seeing her again, and I stayed out of it. Then I picked up another bead; it gave a number, fifty thousand, also in French followed by another bead, more cryptic, but I managed to decipher it to an invasion of Semevale 8. This time, I informed the League anonymously. They were too late, under-prepared, but they at least were able to place a military presence on the planet. After that, each time I got a bead, I tipped off the League. I eventually realised the Gartrya were exiles or banished from the League; I didn't know why. It made the League's complacency even harder to understand. They speak of altruism, of an all-embracing society, but they seemed to choose not to embrace the Gartrya."

"We made the same observation," Laurel said. "Canon Akkuh makes the decisions there."

Darlen looked unimpressed. "Canon Akkuh? He's an idiot. I never trusted him. Before the war started, I transmitted a communique to the League from the duke. Akkuh tried to block it."

Laurel nodded. "He did block it. It was an overture from the duke and had Akkuh acted on it, the League may not be at war now. I'm willing to bet he's been the one to filter all your messages, including the information that the

Gartrya are former members of the League."

Darlen shrugged. "I didn't know what was in the first message. I just transmitted it. I didn't even know why the duke was contacting the League, seeing as there was no way across the nebula. The communication was passed to me in the early days of the duke preparing the lifeform and just before I saw the duchess, so I didn't particularly care. I was always more concerned with getting away from the duke's forces, who constantly tried to identify how I came and went through the nebula. But it was a helluva lucrative gig, so I kept going."

"How you get through the nebula interests me too," Laurel said, "but we'll come to that. I'd like to understand why you are helping the League. Your homeworld isn't part of it. Why did you respond to Gabriel's message this time?"

"The League's been a stable influence in the region for aeons. Soul Mongers, traders, and cartels might be the galaxy's low life's, but while we stay away from the League, it doesn't interfere, but it does offer help when regular folk need it. Many of us wouldn't want to see the League fall."

"That's not the only reason, though…?" Laurel avoided looking into Darlen's mind, but the answer is undeniable when a man wears his heart on his sleeve. Laurel heard the words and felt his sadness.

"I couldn't bear a war where she might be hurt."

With his response, Laurel allowed her opinion of him to thaw. Here, in the interests of helping the League, of making her understand his role, he'd shared a secret he'd carried with him for over thirty years.

The sensitivity and emotion of the moment went right

over Helen's head. "That's all very interesting, I'm sure, but I don't understand why we have to destroy the fortress," she called over her shoulder. "Eli says there's no-one there."

"There are thousands of troops, Helen," Laurel told her. "If we kill the duke, the throne falls to his daughter, and she is pro-League."

"Well, get Eli to blow him out of the sky; he should be easy to spot."

"His ship is covered in the same stuff as the fortress," Darlen said. "And from what Laurel says, they'll hold Gabriel responsible for the duke's death."

Laurel stood and pulled up an image of the nebula on the starchart. "We need to get through the nebula at a point they can't detect us."

"If Darlen knows a secret passage," Helen suggested, "we can use that."

"I don't have a secret passage, Helen. I go through wherever I want. The nebula doesn't affect me."

Helen didn't seem surprised. "I always thought you were inhuman."

"I'm human, Helen," Darlen retorted, "I'm just not human like others."

"Okay, touchy bum. So, how are we going to get through?"

Darlen looked at Laurel. He knew she knew, but their secret looks meant too much delay to get an answer to suit Helen's liking.

"If you are making any sense of what he's talking about, Laurel, tell me, or I'll read his mind."

"No, you won't," Darlen said, "you're too busy flying

this ship."

Helen wrinkled up her nose. "I've been in your mind before, and it's disgusting."

But before Darlen could react, the ship's sensors diverted Helen. "Harry's responding. Eli, Chloe, and Marta are rendezvousing with us. They have a plan to take out the connections and satellites holding the creature in place once Darlen gets us through the nebula. When the comms go down, the lifeform is bringing our guys across." Helen looked directly at Laurel. "Harry's not informing the League."

"We have a few hours before we reach the nebula, Laurel," Darlen said. "You look tired."

"I was injured trying to escape a few days ago." Laurel did feel tired; perhaps weary was a better word. "I've had a few sleepless nights since, but I feel fine."

"Rest. I'll wake you when I need you."

"They might blow us up before we get to Gartrya," Helen said as she relinquished control of the ship to Darlen and steered Laurel from the room. "You still haven't told us how to get through the nebula."

"They won't shoot at us, Helen. The palace knows my ship well."

"Just the darling of the universe, aren't you?"

"That's me," Darlen grinned. "Make sure Laurel sleeps."

Helen's mind was loud and bursting at the seams, and her questions spilled out into Laurels head, preventing her from resting. But they were a distraction, even though she didn't answer them. Laurel didn't want to think about extracting a weapon that would kill Gabriel, and she couldn't dwell on alternatives with Helen so close, but she also knew that try as she might, there could be no alternative, no compromise. She thought of Gabriel's final words, and sadness settled on her like a heavy mantle.

"It is far better that one single soul perishes; than entire worlds continue in fear."

CHAPTER TWO _

Three League scouts stood by at the nebula. Marta was first on board, sweeping Laurel into a tight embrace. "We knew you weren't dead, but we were terrified."

Eli's greeting was typically more moderate, with a simple, murmured, "It's good to see you." But his relief was palpable.

Chloe wept, trying to speak through her tears. "Sorry," she choked. "You frightened us."

Laurel smiled and hugged her tight. "I wasn't badly treated, and I'm fine now," Laurel sighed. "I'm happy to be back."

But Helen still had a burning question that needed an answer, more important in her view than the reunion. "What I want to know is—" she wagged a finger in Darlen's face, "how you get across the nebula?" Her question firmly delivered, she stepped back to await his reply.

Darlen didn't answer, just tipped his thumb at Laurel, inviting her to go first.

Helen jabbed Laurel in the arm. "Okay, Laurel. You obviously know. Spill!"

"Alright," Laurel began, "I can't speak for Darlen, but

we, I mean whole souls, can enter the nebula. It won't harm us."

"What?" A chorus of voices and incredulous faces greeted her statement.

"It doesn't affect us." Laurel raised her shoulders. "I don't know much more than that."

"Who told you?" Helen demanded, giving voice to her scepticism. "That whole soul at the fortress?"

Marta, Chloe, and Eli looked at each other, bewildered. A whole soul at the fortress? But Helen wasn't concerned with her friends' amazement. "He works for the enemy, Laurel. You can't trust him!" She ignored Laurel's telepathic comment that Gabriel was a friend and not the enemy.

Darlen interrupted her. "No, Helen. Whole souls can enter the nebula, same as me, and just in case you're wondering, I am not a whole soul. Now, to avoid alerting the Gartrya communication relays within the nebula, we will be entering from my planetary system. It brings us out on the other side in the Bazire Sea."

"Bazire Sea?" they all chorused again.

"Yes." Darlen opened a starchart and showed them the sloppily mapped area of the nebula's distant side, no doubt carried out by the Soul Mongers on a quest for business. "It's devoid of anything apart from space-dwelling creatures, which are hostile but easy to squish if you've got a good aim. We'll travel up the border of the nebula once we get through, then across to Gartrya." Darlen pointed at Eli, Chloe, and Marta. "You three are taking out the comms on the Gartrya side?"

Eli nodded. "That's the plan," he confirmed. "Once

they're down, the lifeform is bringing five squadrons across, then Marta and I will head for Gartrya. Harry's sending a couple of engineers to disable the relays that are imprisoning the lifeform; by their calculations, they should only have to dismantle those on the Gartryan side entry point to free the lifeform. It seems the relays inside the nebula were to force the lifeform back and forth, so we won't have to tackle those."

"Are you sure we won't come to harm?" Helen didn't trust Gabriel's word; she didn't trust Darlen, even though he seemed to be a friend now. She could only content herself with Laurel's assurance.

"Gabriel is on our side," Laurel said, catching the seed of her anxiety. "I believe we are safe." And because Helen trusted Laurel above anyone, she would also trust her word.

It took three days to pass through the nebula. Widespeed precipitation slowed their progress, the saturation becoming less dense as they travelled deeper into what Darlen called the nebula's heart. To Laurel, it seemed less like a heart than an artery where she felt life flowing through the still yet unknown length of the nebula, its mystical colours weaving their fascinating threads through immense clouds and enveloping wayward mists. Filaments of undefinable shades filtered their way through the hull, and fiery bursts of light appeared at the ship's edge. Dusty shapes and tree-like structures hovered momentarily before being swept aside. Not one of the whole souls felt any ill effects, even from those parts of the nebula that drifted through the bulkhead. The experience invited considerable debate as to why they were unharmed, but even Darlen didn't have an answer. They just had to accept they were not like other humans, and despite all that had gone before, to them, it somehow confirmed their uniqueness.

Passing through from League space would have been more direct, but Laurel knew with the Gartryan communications intact, it would have been too much of a risk, and she took some time to consider a plan to rescue Gabriel. Each time she came to the same conclusion. They couldn't do it without jeopardising Gabriel's family.

Helen spent her time in the nebula cleaning the ship and washing the nasty artwork from Mer's face. She was manifestly relieved when they exited the nebula and travelled up through the Bazire sea without running into any of its native nasties.

On reaching the edge of the Bazire Sea, Marta, Chloe, and Eli stealthed their ships and headed towards the communications relays, staying within the nebula margin where they could avail themselves of normal widespeed but remain undetected. Helen, Laurel and Darlen would continue the journey to Gartrya in open space. Their goodbyes were short, not one of them willing to consider that the plan might not work, and they would never see each other again, or if they did, it would be in a Gartryan prison or as slaves to the duke.

"It's got oceans!" Helen exclaimed as the planet came into view. "Like Earth."

"It's a mix of swamp and desert mostly," Darlen said, pointing out the topography on his starchart. "It's not like

Earth at all. The environment is much more hostile."

"I think it's pretty," Helen said, tilting her head to the side.

Darlen glanced across. "Earth is far nicer from orbit."

"Yes, well, we're never likely to see it again, are we?"

Darlen ignored her sarcastic response as a shaft of light made contact with the ship. "That's their main sensor," Darlen said. "It analyses the markings of the ship. It knows me, so don't worry. They'll let us in."

"Do they know we're aboard?" Laurel asked.

"Yes, they can tell how many are on board, but I'm a trader; I've brought slaves here before. They'll assume you're for sale, and they don't know we know the duke's not there."

Laurel had an idea. "Helen, do you remember shielding those kids from the blast at our first battle?"

"Of course, I've done it a couple of times since as well."

"Can you do it at will?"

Helen screwed up her face. "Kind of, but if I do, I can't use any other empathic skill at the same time, and it seems limited to a few metres."

"Are you and others around you at all visible when you do it?"

"Um, no, I don't think so, and I can't maintain it for long."

"Some of them will know we're here, so we can't use it to hide, only cover that which has not been seen," Laurel said, paraphrasing Gabriel's words.

"If it helps." Helen was still unsure, and Laurel sensed

she felt some pressure. "I'm not sure I'm reliable."

"We're all taking chances," Darlen said. "The palace compound has guards stationed at the enclave exterior and within the palace grounds. Get out of those clothes; uniforms won't be easy to explain away. There are some of those short gowns in the back; they're the ones I always use."

Darlen brought the ship down in the grounds. They saw half a dozen guards approaching from the viewport, looking relaxed and friendly, as if Darlen were a welcome guest. He sat the two women in seats and placed anchors on their wrists, attaching them to the sides of the chair.

"Don't be indignant, be submissive, and don't talk," he warned them, throwing Helen a meaningful glance. "The anchors are for show only; they're not locked, so follow my lead."

Darlen released the ramp, and the guards boarded, greeting Darlen with slaps on the back and loud voices. The men glanced at the women, but they were more interested in the floral bottles and boxes Darlen had stored. They helped him unload before informing him the duke was away at war but would alert the viceroy that the merchant was paying an unscheduled and most diverting visit.

A single guard led the trio along the path and around the rear of the palace. Laurel kept her eyes cast down after Darlen threw a warning glance. She must not make eye contact. Even so, Laurel built up a picture of the palace. The building was only three floors high, its exterior uninspiring in faded yellow-washed stone. A terrace ran the length of the second storey where the stone fretwork hinted that in its heyday, it would have been gleaming white and glorious. Now, the stone was chipped, flaking, and covered in moss. The gardens were barren of flowers and plants, and several skinny, dog-like creatures slunk about growling, at them, at each other and anything that provoked them.

"We're going to the ground chambers," Darlen whispered. "The viceroy is the duke's righthand man, the most senior member of the Primature. We'll get nowhere unless we take him down. He makes the rules on acquisitions. Laurel, you'll tempt him. Helen's too skinny."

For once, Helen didn't need to be told to be quiet; it occurred to her that perhaps this time being too thin might be a positive thing.

CHAPTER THREE _

The guards left as the viceroy welcomed Darlen, leaving Laurel and Helen standing obediently to the side, alert to their surroundings but still with their eyes cast down, waiting for a signal from Darlen.

The short, thin, and richly garmented viceroy raised his hand to his forehead in a formal greeting. "Alas, Merchant, the duke isn't here. He goes to fight a holy war."

To Laurel's surprise, he spoke broken Seera rather than his native language. "We didn't expect you, my friend. It has been a while. The war goes well for the duke, but we have only meagre rations for us here, so there will be no banquet! I suspect our men out in League space eat better than we do. I've sent many of our troops out to the far side to get provisions for us here, and even traded with the Ferle, so we don't starve."

He had a robust laugh for such a diminutive frame, and Laurel felt disgust and bitterness rising in her throat. This man had no right to laughter, to any kind of joy when he had the power to deliver Gabriel's family to an awful fate and engaged without conscience in the trade of young people to that race of cannibals.

"Tell me, my friend," the viceroy said. "Do the Independent Systems yet support the war? I believe the League are attempting to conceal it?"

Darlen feigned indifference. "I'm afraid I have no information for you, Viceroy. I seldom return to my own system these days. I pick up most of my merchandise from outlying systems. I have little reason to go back."

"I see." The viceroy gave Darlen a conspiratorial smirk. "I believe the duke will give you a good reason to return. You might not be aware the duke plans on restoring the Transcender when he is victorious? An army of whole soul slaves would have seen an end to this conflict by now."

"I wasn't aware, but it is good news," Darlen grinned. "I understand Soul Mongers have little to do these days."

"I thought there might be none left."

"There are a few," Darlen lied, "getting on in years, but they will be happy to reaccess the whole souls. They brought a good price, especially the pregnant ones. One or two often filtered down to us humble traders. It would be good to build up such an enterprise."

The viceroy indicated to Helen and Laurel. "Too much to expect these are whole souls?"

Darlen laughed. "Hardly. I picked them up from Okalaka, pretty much on your doorstep. Their previous owner died, so I got them cheap."

"The duke won't take field slaves, Merchant, but he will still invest in his appetites." The viceroy laughed, then approached Laurel and caressed her cheek with the back of his hand. He lifted her hair to his nose and sniffed, then examined her face, his eyes hooded, his beaky nose too close. Then he ran his hand down her body, dropping his fingers between her legs, lingering there before reaching around to squeeze her buttocks. Laurel didn't move a muscle. The viceroy barely glanced at Helen.

"The large breasted one will persuade him," he declared, turning back to Darlen, "but he won't pay much. Are they pregnant?"

"Nope, I've tried. Tried with them both but nothing."

"Well, I won't take the skinny one. You might be able to trade her on your homeworld or keep her for yourself if she is to your taste. She would be too thin and old even for the Ferle. The other one can attend the duchess when the duke has finished with her. He proposes a speedy return here and the relocation of our people back to our rightful home. Won't be long now, eh? eh?" The man laughed and gave Darlen a good-natured punch on the shoulder. Darlen, a compelling actor, laughed along with him.

"Is the duchess in attendance?" he enquired casually.

"She is, Merchant, come sit." The viceroy led Darlen to a bench. "The duke sent his son to the war."

"He sent his heir to fight?"

"Of course, he must fight beside his father."

"Well, I'm sorry there aren't a few more guards," Darlen said, pretending disinterest. "Not so good for business. My arrival was unheralded, and I apologise, my lord, I could have sold a few more bottles—" his next words scoring a hearty laugh from the viceroy, "and earned a couple of nights off the skinny woman with the guards."

"I am sorry, but we are down to less than two hundred guards in the enclave, Merchant. Not many pickings for you."

"On the contrary, Viceroy…" Darlen smiled evilly, his eyes narrow as he leapt to his feet, sweeping up the smaller man by the throat in one large fist and lifting him easily into the air. "Very good pickings." The viceroy's legs kicked wildly as his hands flew to his throat, desperately clawing as Darlen squeezed his miserable life from him. A trickle of yellow fluid trailed down the choking man's leg, staining the floor as his body relaxed. Darlen shook him, drawing a final rattle from the viceroy's throat.

"He's dead," Darlen announced as he dropped the body to the floor, looking around for a suitable hiding place for the corpse.

Laurel and Helen disengaged their anchors.

"You could have shot him!" Helen looked in horror at the viceroy's swollen blue face, the violent death only enhancing the still stunned expression.

"The guards would have detected the discharge of a weapon," Darlen said as he dragged the body to a curtained nook. "We need to get out of here."

Laurel had no time to reflect on Helen's sentiment. Choking the viceroy was cleaner; a weapon would have left pieces of bone and skin and blood splatter. She looked around. There was a smear of urine where Darlen had dragged the body, but it was already drying so it wouldn't leave a trace. She took the viceroy's small personal sidearm and shoved it in her belt, then helped Darlen cover the body with rugs and cushions. Leading the way, Laurel allowed her memories of Gabriel's descriptive stories and diagrams to run like an interactive map in her mind. Darlen and Helen followed close behind.

"The throne room's this way." She made to break into a run, but Helen grabbed her arm. "Stay close to me," she whispered urgently. "If I can do the invisible thing, it may help."

Running along a cold corridor that fell smartly away into underground apartments, it turned out that Helen could indeed do the "invisible thing" as they passed several guards unseen. Laurel hoped they wouldn't come across the guards who received them when they first arrived, or their cover would be blown. As they headed towards the throne room, Laurel became aware of a strong female presence, curious, alert and alone, tracking their progress telepathically from one floor above. Laurel knew this must be the duchess, but she had no way of identifying Gabriel's son, who could be anywhere in the palace. But first, they needed to secure the Alisitrite gems. Then they would turn their attention to rescuing the duchess and Marcel.

The corridor had several well-lit passages, but Laurel knew precisely which direction to go. The throne room was just as Gabriel described, the furnishings drab and neglected, and the interior walls dirty and dilapidated, a memorial to the duke's fanaticism and confidence that he did not need to maintain this stronghold. But Laurel wasn't here to critique the interior decorating. Above the throne, the spectacular deep blue gems, faceted and burnished to a rich gleam, sat nestled in deep bowls—the only grand feature in the entire chamber.

Removing the gems from their seating proved difficult. Laurel concentrated all her strength on levering them free, she even tried twisting them, but they wouldn't budge. Knowing it was only a matter of time before someone discovered them, Darlen took the viceroy's sidearm from Laurel and sliced the cups holding the gems. The gems, roughly the same size as soccer balls, were surprisingly heavy. As Darlen detached the last gem, an alarm sounded.

"They've detected us. We need to go."

"That's the only way in." Helen looked around as the sound of yelling and footsteps reached them. If these guards were the same ones who'd seen them earlier, Helen couldn't protect them. But Gabriel had considered this very scenario. Laurel headed towards the far end of the chamber.

"There's a secret exit behind the throne."

Laurel found the entrance, but it appeared to lead deeper underground.

"Wouldn't the guards know about this?" Helen asked, even at her height, she had to duck to go through.

"No, only the duke and his advisors."

The tunnel was barely bigger than crawling space, virtually airless and full of choking dust; they had to roll the gems before them so they could use both hands to crawl. It was a tight squeeze for Darlen, who had to lie on his belly and wriggle through, but they eventually emerged outside the palace walls into dense undergrowth. They slithered up an incline until they found an unhindered view of the palace and Darlen's ship and where they could remain undetected, at least for now. They heard sounds of shouted orders and running from the compound. It would seem the guards believed they were still within the palace.

"Maybe we should have stayed and fought," Helen

whispered, although no-one was around to hear. "Now we have to get back to the ship, and we're on the other side of the palace."

Darlen shook his head. "We're fine here, for now. It looks like most of the exterior guards are diverted to the threat within the palace. They'll know it's me that's breached security. We might need to stay hidden until the others arrive, assuming they do. Let's hope they've managed to disrupt the communications."

"That could be days. We can't just sit here and sunbathe," Helen hissed. "What if the guards blow up your ship?"

"Helen's right," Laurel said. "To get these minerals to 100 moons, we need your ship. It doesn't look guarded."

Darlen poked a retinal optimiser into his eye and surveyed the palace grounds. "No, it doesn't, not yet, but we still have to get past the guards, and that won't be easy." He grinned. "But the ship's got repulsive fold-back shielding. If they blow it up, it'll blow them up back and the palace with it."

Helen threw up her hands. "That's just great! We'll be well and truly stranded." But her concern just brought an infuriating chuckle from Darlen.

Laurel agreed they had to get to the ship, but she had another worry. She couldn't filter out Marcel's location. She even had difficulty sifting through intent, not sensing a single benign thought from the direction of the palace other than the whole soul, whose presence was powerful. For his part, Darlen knew this was at the forefront of Laurel's mind. That she'd made a promise. He pushed his concerns away and rolled onto his side to face her.

"We'll get them if we can," he said. "Otherwise, I'm sorry, but we'll have to leave them behind. Delivering these minerals to the 100 moons is our priority. With the viceroy dead, and if the others have been successful in knocking out those comm lines, they should be safe for now." Darlen placed a reassuring hand on her arm. "We won't abandon them. We'll come back as soon as we deliver the minerals."

They stayed hidden by the undergrowth, watching for either an opportunity to move or for signs of Marta, Eli and Chloe, which would mean the portal entrance communications and jugular relays were disabled. Darlen estimated at least an eight-hour journey between the nebula and Gartrya at widespeed even if their plan went without a hitch, and that would only be the two scouts. It might be several days before Harry arrived with reinforcements. The afternoon sun burned, and their throats became parched as they waited. Even Helen didn't speak, but she conveyed with nothing more than a scowl how she hated the feeling of her tongue adhering to the roof of her mouth. Darlen took it in his stride.

"It'll start to cool off as evening draws in. Later you'll be pissed at freezing your nuts off, but we can get some moisture off these shrubs then. If we're here in the morning, we might need to find somewhere else to lie low." Darlen bobbed up his head, raising his hand to stop any reply. "Wait!"

A flurry of action from the guards gave them the chance to jump the dividing wall to the palace grounds.

Darlen translated the shouting voices.

"They've found the viceroy." Darlen alerted Mer to be ready to leave as soon as they were aboard.

"Can't Mer come and get us?" Helen tried to snatch Darlen's d-com, but Darlen wasn't letting go.

"That would tell them exactly where we are."

Helen didn't think of that, so she followed as Laurel and Darlen took off towards the palace, using low walls and hedges to hide their progress. The guards didn't see them, but they were still too far away from the ship, and they didn't know which of the exterior guards saw them when they first arrived, so Helen's cloak might have limited effect.

Laurel lay flat on her stomach, peering around a corner as she tried to take stock of the situation unfolding in the palace grounds, desperately wishing she had a retinal optimiser and a wrist lick. The Viceroy's sidearm was a short-range weapon, powerful enough but not meant for combat situations.

Darlen whispered urgently from behind the opposite wall. "They're congregating near the ship, and they're wearing arm canons. They've realised I'm in on the assassination, and it looks as if they've analysed the shielding capacity. It'll take them a good while to figure out the harmonics though. I pieced it together from different technologies."

"I don't care what you say, Darlen," Laurel whispered back fiercely. "I'm not leaving without the duchess and Gabriel's son."

Darlen didn't respond. He activated his d-com, instructing Mer to transmit a sensor sweep of the ship's perimeter and advise him of guards and artillery. A dozen bramble droids rolled in to join the soldiers. "They may have originally thought we had another means of escape, but they must realise now we'll be coming back for the ship after all." Darlen wriggled from his position, making to head off. "We need to divert them. Let's go back over the wall and around to the other side."

Laurel didn't move. Together, she and Helen faced off Darlen. Seeing their united front and realising he needed them, he grunted. "Okay, can you locate the duchess?"

"Above us—" Laurel looked up, trying to gauge the duchess's position, "but she's moving. I can't tell where or in which direction. I can't pinpoint the child."

"Is that her?" Helen pointed casually to a woman, her long hair flowing, wearing the enemy's one-piece uniform, who strode purposefully along the upper terrace. Her expression grim and determined, she sported a knuckle band on her left hand, which she fired from all ports, a hand blaster in her right hand cutting down several soldiers at once.

Darlen looked up. "That's her," he exclaimed. "Let's go!"

"What's she doing?" Helen grabbed Laurel's arm. "She's firing at the guards!"

Laurel scrambled to her feet. "She's creating a diversion." She hesitated as the sense the duchess knew who sent her reached her mind, but in that same instance, Laurel also felt the presence of Gabriel's son, as the boy's grandmother communicated his closeness. Laurel tried to direct her thoughts, using the French that Gabriel taught her at the Fortress. The duchess understood; she would get herself and her grandson to the ship.

The trio ran just as the guards overcame their astonishment at being fired upon by their sovereign lady. Those who fired back deliberately avoided hitting her until a senior guard yelled in rapid Gartrya. The firing stopped for only a moment, then returned, this time not considering the status of the woman upon whom they fired. Laurel, Darlen and Helen had no choice but to join the battle. Helen and Darlen both had wrist licks, but Laurel had to make do with the clumsier sidearm. Even in the confusion, the duchess immobilised several guards before she was hit. Laurel saw the weapon slip from her hands and reeling from the impact of the shot to her shoulder, Gabriel's mother pitched over the terrace and crashed to the ground below.

Darlen was the first to reach her, pulling her behind the low wall. A young dark-haired man vaulted the terrace, narrowly missing being taken out by weapons fire, and landed beside them, the duchess's sidearm in his hand. Helen didn't wait to see the outcome. She grabbed Laurel and Darlen's gems and sprinted for the ship, hoping against hope she was invisible to at least some of the guards. Even so, she fired off her wrist lick to cover herself for those who could see her. She made it safely as Mer momentarily took advantage of the troop's diversion to drop the shield and admit her. Helen fell flat on her face and dropped the heavy gems the second she made it up the ramp. As they rolled into the ship, she briefly wondered how she ever got the strength to run so fast, carrying those three heavy gems.

The blast stunned the duchess, but her shoulder wound was little more than a graze, so shaking her head firmly, and with the guards and bramble droids advancing, she took the weapon from the boy and, with Laurel and Darlen's help, got to her feet.

For many minutes, they kept the guards at bay, but there was no opening for them to make a dash for the ship. For Mer to bring the ship across now that their position was revealed would mean lowering the shield yet again, and with the minerals on board, Darlen was reluctant to order Mer to rescue them. Several guards made it up to the terrace, giving them the advantage of firing down on the group. The duchess and Laurel took out the bramble droids, and Darlen concentrated on the soldiers on the terrace. But they were surrounded. Several soldiers jumped from the boundary wall. The low walls Laurel and the others were using as shields would only obstruct them from getting a good view for a few moments more. Darlen took a graze to his face that momentarily dazed him, and Laurel covered Marcel with her own body to protect him. As the enemy guards moved closer, Darlen signalled Mer to leave for the 100 moons to get the minerals to the League.

Above the melee, two League scouts flew low and scattered the palace ground forces. The viceroy had said there were around two hundred guards in the enclave. Laurel sensed far less now, but news of the fight would have reached the squadrons the viceroy deployed elsewhere to forage for food, which meant they would be back to engage the League scouts.

They took their chance as the League ships distracted

the guards, running for Darlen's ship as it hovered, ramp down. Darlen took out two cannons as Mer dropped the shields to allow them on board. Laurel lifted Marcel and tossed him to Helen, then jumped onto the ramp herself. Darlen slid up the ramp, holding onto the duchess as she too scrambled aboard. With the ship hovering, it wasn't so easy to make it into the interior, so with them still on the ramp, the retracting mechanisms automatically overrode Mer's attempt to close. Laurel reached back to grab the duchess and pull her onto the ship, as soldiers wearing lethal tack guns and arm cannons gathered below. A shot rang out, and the duchess collapsed forward, blood spurting from a wound in her back. Marcel yelled, and together they grabbed the duchess to haul her out of harm's way.

As Laurel lifted her, the sound of gunfire became distant as the older woman's head dropped back. She looked into Laurel's eyes, gently searching. Gabriel's mother was exquisite, her mouth small and perfectly shaped, her nose pierced with tiny jewels and delicate chains at each nostril, signifying, Gabriel told her, membership of the noble house. Her skin was smooth and unlined, and in her wide, intense violet eyes, Laurel saw the world of sadness she and Gabriel shared, but also the sanctity of the love mother and son held for each other and the boy, Marcel. In that sacred moment, Laurel knew she was right to come here.

Death found Gabriel's mother lying in Laurel's arms, and as her spirit fled, she looked into Laurel's mind for a glimpse of her son. Beside them, the boy sobbed.

Between them, Darlen and Laurel dragged the Duchess's

lifeless body on board. Mer closed the ramp, but another shot slipped through before it shut.

Laurel didn't feel the fire in her chest or the tack as it entered her lung, only realising something had hit her when she sank back into Helen's arms. There were sounds all around, but so distant. Helen called her name. Another voice, younger, more youthful, wept and became ever more removed. The stench of burning flesh wafted upwards, and someone pushed something against her chest. What was it? Rags? A hand? Her mind drifted towards pain. She couldn't go there. God, she was tired. Why use the effort to think? Why even try to breathe? Random thoughts wandered in; the last time she saw Gabriel, the lake at the park near her apartment in Chicago, the one that iced over at the first sign of winter, her collection of old books that brought her so much pleasure. Strange, she hadn't thought of those books since coming here. No matter, care left her, worries faded, slender, familiar threads of colour wove in and out of her thoughts, and she thought she raised her hand to touch them, to allow them to take her where they might. She read somewhere what a beautiful thing it is to die. Dear Aunt Lucy's face swam into the colourful fronds, and strong arms buoyed her as the last sigh left her body.

CHAPTER FOUR _

Laurel woke to a physician in League uniform leaning over her, a MedAid by his side and a full-body pandroscope recording her vital signs.

"Ah," the physician smiled, waving the MedAid away. "Welcome back. How are you feeling?" Laurel struggled to sit up, confused. She'd been on Darlen's ship, and they'd rescued the duchess and Marcel.

The physician placed a hand on her shoulder. "Not yet, Laurel," he said, "your lungs are damaged. They have a temporary repair, but one of them will need replacing when you get to Mentelci. I'm sorry."

It came to her then, Gabriel's mother in her arms, the weeping boy, and the searing pain in her chest from a ground-based tack gun. And now, she would face the grief of her failure to save Gabriel's mother. Laurel closed her eyes.

"Did everyone else get out?" she said, her voice rasping, the effort of speaking bringing on a painful fit of coughing. "Are they okay?"

The physician gave her a broad smile. "You'll be glad to know your shipmates are fine."

"How long have I been here?" But the coughing started again. She felt parched, and the physician helped her to take a few sips of water.

"You're well hydrated, but it's normal for your throat to feel on fire after an injury like this. Don't try to talk too much if it irritates your vocal cords. To answer your question, you've been here for two weeks."

"Where's here?"

"100 moons. The transport arrives from Mentelci soon, and we will transfer you to a medical facility there."

Laurel nodded weakly and managed a murmured, "Thank you."

"It's us who should be thanking you," the physician said. "The information you gained during your imprisonment at the fortress directly affected the outcome of the war."

Laurel shifted her head so she could look directly into his eyes, hoping for a glimpse into his mind, but even the thought of attempting telepathy was all too overwhelming.

"It's over then?"

He nodded. "These seven days."

And then Laurel felt the weight of what transpired settle on her. She became aware of her damaged lungs and the pain in her body, but most of all, her heartache. They destroyed the fortress, but it meant Gabriel was also gone, and she didn't save his mother.

"What about the boy?" she asked the physician, "the one in Darlen's ship? And the woman?"

The physician tilted his head. "I know nothing of a boy nor a woman."

"We rescued the Gartryan duchess and her grandson." Laurel steadied her breathing, willing herself not to descend into a fit of coughing. "They were with us, on Darlen's ship. The palace guards fired on us. She was killed."

The physician looked confused. "I'm so sorry, but there were only two people with you," he said, shaking his head. "The merchant who brought you here and one of your colleagues, a female who elected to stay here with you. Darlen delivered the minerals to the engineers, and you to the infirmary. He placed you in one of his variance tanks, bypassed your breathing and stopped the bleeding. His quick actions saved your life." He patted her hand. "I wish I could help. Perhaps your colleague may be able to fill in the gaps, or possibly Commander Harry when he recovers."

"Harry?" She hadn't given him a thought, but now she felt a rush of concern. "What happened? Can I see him?"

The physician laid a reassuring hand on her shoulder. "He is to be evacuated to Mentelci. You can't see him as he is in an induced coma to help him recover, and I assure you, he will." He considered his next word. "Eventually."

Laurel allowed what little empathic sense she had returning to reassure her the physician spoke the truth and was convinced of Harry's recovery. She let his kindness and her senses soothe her fears. "Doctor?" She wanted to ask him about the fortress. "Can you tell me…" but a familiar and very welcome voice cut in.

"It's destroyed." Eli stood in the doorway, and with a warning she must not sit up, the doctor smiled and left them alone. Sitting beside her on the cot, Eli squeezed her hand. There was sadness behind his smile and even had Laurel had the strength to delve into his mind, he knew something he would not allow her in to share. She assumed it was to do with the end of the war.

"Tell me, Eli," Laurel said, needing the details of how they destroyed the fortress, and of Gabriel's last moments. She prayed he didn't suffer. Prayed that somehow through the bonds the two had forged in their time together, he knew his son was safe.

"When the duke exited the nebula," Eli said gently, "the lifeform remained long enough to take five scout ships, along with Harry and as many troops as we could squeeze in, into the nebula to wait while the Gartryan side relays were disabled. Xavier went with them. After Marta and I mounted that surprise attack on the palace, and you were injured, Darlen brought the minerals here; the engineers mounted them on three warheads. I was the obvious choice to go to Semevale 7 because I could get through the ordnance network. I sensed the whole soul even before I struck orbit. Laurel, I saw he wasn't an enemy. He communicated with me." Eli tapped his head. "He gave me the exact coordinates of where to strike and the distance to fire from so the fallout wouldn't injure me. It was suicide for him, but he had such…" Eli shook his head, searching for a word that would go far enough to describe Gabriel's last moments, "…dignity."

Eli knew Laurel could easily read his mind if she pushed it, even in her weakened state, but he'd pondered this ever since the destruction of the fortress. "His very last thought, Laurel," he said, leaning forward, his voice low, "was of you."

Laurel felt her eyes fill with tears. She'd been prepared, of course she had and knew Eli would be the one they'd send, but she wished it could have been her, to have one final moment with Gabriel, to hear his thoughts, to tell him his son was safe.

A few minutes later, Helen arrived and sat on Laurel's other side. Eli diplomatically ascribed other duties requiring his attention as he left the two women together, giving Helen a small, sad smile that Laurel missed.

Laurel was glad for Helen's presence. "I wish we could have told Gabriel we saved Marcel," she said as Helen combed Laurel's hair with her fingers. The rhythm soothed her, and slowly, her sadness found a place to settle. "Where did Darlen take them?"

"As far as I know," Helen replied, "that lad you threw on board is still with Darlen. The kid didn't speak the whole time we were together. His grandmother's body is on Darlen's ship as well; Darlen took them with him when he left you and the minerals here, just in case the fortress didn't get destroyed. Even so, he's keeping them with him until they install Gartrya's new duchess."

Laurel smiled. "Darlen's full of surprises, isn't he?"

"He is," Helen agreed, "and I hope Gartrya gets its act together. Otherwise, that young lad will end up as the surrogate son of a Soul Monger and stuck with the life of a trader."

"Better than the life the duke had in mind if he'd discovered Gabriel's plan." The thought made Laurel shudder, they'd saved the boy from a terrible fate, but now, he'd lost his father and grandmother. It was a lot to take in, and it would have been a blessed relief if Laurel could have buried her face in Helen's shoulder and sobbed her heart out. In her mind, she did just that, but her body remained still, unsure of how her damaged lung would react to an outpouring of grief such as the one she was storing up. Helen, so reliably unreliably perceptive, smiled.

"You fell for him, didn't you, chick? That Gabriel?"

"I kept reminding myself he was my jailer," Laurel said. "But he told me everything about the reasons for the war, the minerals, the layout of the palace."

"Darlen confirmed the old woman was Gabriel's mother and the boy his son; loyalty leverage, I suppose."

"The duke kept their origins a secret from his people because of his love for the duchess—his obsession with her. You heard the story; Darlen fell for her as well. There was something different about her, Helen, different to us, something more." Laurel recalled the vividness of the woman's eyes. She lifted her hand. "I'm rambling. It's just I felt a whisper as she passed."

"Darlen took it very well," Helen said. "If he hadn't told us, I would never have known he was in love with her. What I don't understand is why the duke kept the duchess's origins a secret. Why bother? They were a slave society."

"The duke saw her as a prize, I suppose." Laurel had wondered about this herself. "And then when Gabriel came along, to save face, he passed Gabriel off as his heir, and knowing no different, the people believed Gabriel would inherit the throne. The duke had a plan in place that if he died, Gabriel would be branded a traitor, and his mother would become a chain slave—whatever that is—and his son sold to the Ferle."

Helen's face twisted with disgust. She'd heard the stories about the Ferle.

"Gabriel had a biotracker," Laurel said, "so the duke would know if he left the fortress. He couldn't escape."

"Then we couldn't have rescued him, anyway."

"No." Laurel made a small, helpless gesture with her hands. "There were too many variables; we may not have rescued his family, we may not have successfully dismantled the communications, and the lifeform itself may have chosen not to help us."

"Eli would feel bad about blowing up your lover."

"Helen…" Laurel sighed at Helen's comment.

"Hmmm…?" Helen wasn't in Laurel's mind, but she had a knowing way about her right now.

Laurel didn't plan to pursue the subject; there were other, more pressing issues. She dropped her voice to a whisper. They were alone, but this was too important for anyone to overhear.

"Helen, I learned a few things about the League while I was in the fortress. They weren't innocent in all this." She leaned closer, wincing at the pain in her ribs. "I need to get more information."

Helen also leaned closer until she and Laurel were almost nose to nose. "The League? In what way?"

"Do you remember Darlen mentioning the message he sent, the one he didn't know the contents of?"

"The 'beads'? Yeah, I remember."

"In that communique, the duke demanded the League restore his planet and mineral rights to him and his people.

Canon Akkuh must have been on alert once he received a message from the other side of the nebula."

"Because he didn't know Soul Mongers can enter the nebula?"

"That's right. He also didn't know whole souls could either. Centuries ago, his family were responsible for genocide on account of a rare mineral found on the duke's origin planet. With the population gone, the Canonical family declared the planet their property and took over the compensation rights of the mineral."

Helen wrinkled her nose as if detecting a bad smell. "If his family had secrets, that message must have put the wind up him."

"I bet it did," Laurel agreed, "but at that point, he didn't know the Gartrya had discovered a way to bring their forces across. Akkuh didn't tell Congress about the message. He still hasn't told Congress."

Helen shook her head. "If he did, he'd have to admit the sins of his family. He won't do that."

"Don't you see, Helen? His family have held this secret for centuries, but now, Canon Akkuh's silence directly influenced the war. If he'd informed Congress, come clean and not swept it under the carpet, so many lives would have been saved."

Helen gave Laurel's words a moment's thought. Laurel was too sick for all this intrigue and far too emotional, and Helen still had more bad news to deliver, and she wanted to say it before Laurel got her telepathic wind back and went into her mind.

"We're all going back to Mentelci," she said. "Harry's

the best one to help you find out, and judging by your whispering, what you found out isn't common knowledge. But he needs to get better first."

"The doctor told me he's in a coma."

"I think they did something to save his leg. I'm not sure; he had heaps of broken bones in his back. They did some stuff to him, and they're going to do some more stuff on Mentelci. I think he's out of danger, though. They've got stuff to do to you as well." Medical terminology and anatomy weren't Helen's strong points.

"Is the League going to help relocate the Gartrya?"

"I don't know, but we freed the life form." Helen wriggled around anxiously, hoisting up her feet onto the bed and crossing her legs, then flopping them back down again to the floor. Her mind was open; Laurel felt the tug, but directly she was in, she retreated, gasping, one hand flying to her mouth and the other supporting her painful ribs.

"Laurel, I'm sorry," Helen said, taking Laurel's hand and lifting it to her bosom. "We couldn't tell you because of your injuries."

A tear rolled down Laurel's cheek, then another, but she remained in control, waiting for Helen to continue.

"After the others disrupted the signals between Gartrya and the nebula, they picked up a communication, a sequence of algorithms needed to free the creature; it probably came from Gabriel, but they learned that disabling the relays wasn't going to be enough. The lifeform took Xavier and Harry and a few troops across the nebula. Xavier did that invisible thing same as I do to hide them from the enemy sensors." Helen shrugged. "I didn't even know he could do it. Once the enemy comm towers were down, the troops went through to relieve Marta and Eli and secure the palace. The creature took them through the nebula in hours, far quicker than it ever conveyed the Gartryan troops. That's how they got to Gartrya so quick to help Marta and Eli, but you were gone by then."

"What happened?" Laurel already knew, but she needed to hear it.

"Eli came back to help, and he and Harry input the final data into the relays, but the creature didn't dare move. The Gartrya set a line of explosives, like a string of pearls around the portal's perimeter, in the event someone found a way to disable the relays and to stop the lifeform entering Gartryan space. The pearls had a reflective cloak to hide them. Harry reckoned the explosives were set after the informant last passed through the nebula; otherwise, he would have mentioned them to you." Helen paused for a moment. She knew what happened, but it was so hard to relate. "The only way to free the lifeform was to find and extract each pearl manually. All four went out into open space, Chloe, Eli, Harry and of course, Xavier, because the lifeform trusted him. They wore those space suits or whatever they're called, and they got most of the pearls to a safe distance to detonate inside a containment field."

And now would come the awful part. Helen wished with all her heart she didn't have to be the one to tell Laurel, but she was, and Laurel was sitting on the edge of her mind, seeing her thoughts unfolding as Helen related what Chloe had told her.

"The creature reflexed from its confinement. Part of

it—some kind of tail—had been coiled for all the time it was in captivity flipped out involuntarily and hit Xavier, tearing his suit to shreds and slamming him into the nebula. Harry reached out to grab him but got caught when one of the pearls exploded, which knocked him into the ship like a missile, then he rebounded straight into Chloe who saved him from floating out into space."

"We lost Xavier?" Of course, they had. Laurel saw it the moment she stepped into Helen's mind.

"Even whole souls need to breathe in the nebula," Helen said miserably.

"I can't believe it."

"The war is over. Xavier would be glad of that."

Yes, Laurel thought, over, just by wiping out one maniac. An image of Canon Akkuh drifted into her mind, with a warning that the war was not yet over. Helen saw it.

"Well, World War Two ended when Hitler died because there was no-one to follow."

"I think he suicided when it was clear they lost the war."

"Whatever, people followed him, and now the Gartrya can follow a better leader."

A better leader? What constitutes a better leader? Laurel suddenly lost her courage. There was still so much to do. Gabriel was sure of Shumuyi'beh's wisdom, but even whole souls can be mistaken about people. Look at how she judged Darlen initially, how she judged Gabriel.

Tears spilled onto Laurel's cheeks. All this could be such a waste. "What if Gabriel is wrong about his sister?"

"He isn't wrong," Helen soothed. "Darlen sent me a

message. The lady who will be the new duchess was distraught when she found out the old woman was dead but happy we saved the boy. She plans to make overtures to the League for acceptance, provided we can conduct an evacuation across the nebula."

"Where are the others?"

"Marta and Chloe are on Semevale 8; it's pretty messed up there."

"Will you be staying with me?" Laurel asked, her voice small and tired, suddenly feeling she didn't care what happened to her, provided they lost no-one else.

Helen settled herself on the cot beside Laurel and snuggled her into her arms. "I'm coming back to Mentelci with you, sweetie. You need looking after."

Laurel did need looking after and who better than Helen, a natural—as Helen described in her own terms, "looker after-er". Being so close to her best friend, and with the weight of all the weeks of fear and loss, Laurel finally turned her face into Helen's shoulder and wept.

CHAPTER FIVE _

Laurel's first view of Mentelci planetside was through a medical facility window. Intrigued, she found herself unable to wait for the day when she would be strong enough to explore her new world. When that day finally came, recovered from the surgery to replace her damaged lung, she could properly reflect on the newness of her life. She enjoyed the new experiences now part of her everyday world; food, fragrant with spices and so much more varied than the few easily constituted, and dull fare supplied to the troops, with exotic names and aromas that would tempt even the fussiest appetite. Then, there were words like 'planetfall', 'planetside', 'widespeed,' and the various planetary systems' names. She'd used those words daily during the war, but now, she got to examine them, feel them roll off her tongue, taste the intricacies of her strange new language. Laurel loved the form and structure of language, particularly ancient civilisations, and wondered if that was where her future would take her. This society didn't need nurses, so maybe Laurel would indulge in her other passion: ancient worlds and languages. Congressman Bela had visited with her and asked that she consider her future on Mentelci.

The League were prepared to consider any proposal. Laurel didn't mention what she knew about Canon Akkuh. There was little solid evidence to support the claim, but her knowledge of his deceit cast a cloud over her pleasure in her new life. It needed resolving, and now, Canon Akkuh's dishonest dealings were fast becoming Laurel's priority.

Having seen Mentelci only from space as a yellow planet, she assumed the air would have a lemony tinge or hue. Since leaving the medical facility and the restricted view from her room's expansive glass windows, Laurel learned Mentelci was a world of beautiful, majestic cities, vast oceans, and abundant wildlife protected within sanctuaries called Wind Field Seas. The city precincts buzzed with people from different worlds, who brought their art, cuisine, and fascinating cultures. True, everywhere appeared bathed in a golden light, like Earth on a sunny day, but unlike Earth, Laurel never felt unsafe or threatened as she wandered about, even late at night, when the near moon of Imbri cast it's comforting rays across the land.

Following her release from the medical facility, the Protectorate, the section of the League that concerns itself with the physical welfare of the treaty planets and their inhabitants, assigned Laurel and Helen an apartment together. This new home, sumptuously furnished, luxuriously carpeted, and equipped with the most up-to-date technology, towered above the bustling galleria, with views out across the Wind Field Sea. At night, through the window, Laurel loved to watch the ghostly moon Imbri chase away the sunlight as it rose to guard the night.

Laurel's first thought, once properly mobile again, was

to visit Harry. He'd asked for her, and Laurel was eager to see him now that he was allowed visitors. Chloe, Eli and Marta were still on active duty assisting the cleaning up on Semevale 8 and hadn't yet made it back and despite regular visual interaction transmissions, Laurel missed them desperately.

Harry hung suspended from a contraption that looked suspiciously like a scaffold. A pandroscope stood vertically just a little to his left and behind, probably to stop him from checking it. Laurel's own experience in hospitals reminded her doctors made the worst patients. Suspended in a tight brace, Harry's torso and legs disappeared into a blue forcefield that further stabilised his lower limbs, keeping them immobile and his upper body upright. His hair was long and a little untidy, but he looked good for a man with a severed spinal cord. True, he looked bored and uncomfortable, but overall, surprisingly well. His familiar smile greeted her, making Laurel want to rush into his arms and give him a big hug, but she knew that wouldn't be advisable under the circumstances. It was just she missed him and all her friends.

"Laurel!" he gasped. "You look incredible!"

"Replacing a lung does wonders for a girl," Laurel laughed as he carefully reached out for her hand. She knew he was as relieved to see her as she was him, but a second later, as his fingers curled around hers, the sense of something more profound came to her. She'd felt it before, by the stream on 100 moons before she left for the fortress.

"I heard about Xavier," she said, gently withdrawing

her hand.

Harry nodded sadly. "Yes, the creature bonded with him. Chloe had little sense of the lifeform but claimed it felt sorrow when it realised what it had done. She said it followed Xavier into the nebula, but I was unconscious by then."

"I gather the current duchess has opened a dialogue with the League?" Laurel hesitated, "Are you okay to chat? I don't want to tire you out."

"I'm desperate for any diversion you can offer, Laurel. I eat standing up, sleep standing up, pee standing up…" He stopped when he saw Laurel's grin. "You know what I mean. This is it for now. You can chat away."

"Just wondering about what's happening with the new duchess. Helen and I are out of it now, but you're still military for a few more weeks. I thought you might know if the duchess has made any overtures to the League?"

"Apparently so," Harry said. "She didn't waste any time with her request to relocate within League space, establish a colony on one of our uninhabited planets and start over."

"What does the League say?" Laurel guessed it wouldn't be as straightforward as just granting asylum or accepting refugees. She felt Canon Akkuh might be a stumbling block.

"That she isn't forthcoming as to why her father declared war on us," Harry said. "I reckon she knows but isn't saying."

Princess Shumuyi'beh wouldn't tell the League the reasons. How could she accuse the Canon of ignoring the duke's warning? Or of exposing the League's ancient sin of genocide? Princess Shumuyi'beh believed the League offered a fresh start for her people, where slavery would not be tolerated and where every person would be safe from species like the Ferle. If the Canon thought his family's secrets were to be made public, there was no way they would admit the Gartrya. It had to come from someone else. Laurel felt an urgent need to tell Harry what she knew. It couldn't wait.

"Harry, I know the reason behind the war."

Harry tilted his head. "You do?"

"Canon Akkuh ignored a warning from the duke."

"How do you know?"

"The informant." Laurel found a high stool and sat in front of Harry. "The man who contacted Darlen? It was him who told me about the gems and how to get around the palace. And he told me about Canon Akkuh receiving a communication from the duke, either a threat or maybe an invitation to open a dialogue; I don't know which. Darlen verified it was him who transmitted the message."

Harry gave her a wary smile as though he expected her to deliver the punch line of a joke. "You've got it wrong," he said. "The League had no prior knowledge of the Gartrya."

"I'm not wrong, Harry." Laurel dragged her seat closer, looking him directly in the eye. "Centuries ago, the Gartrya inhabited a planet within the League, Inikamara. It wasn't a treaty planet at first. The League helped them during a catastrophic poisoning, evacuating many of their people, but a civil war followed. Later, the duke of that time and the

League fell into a dispute about a mineral on the planet. To gain control, the Canonical family sent the remaining inhabitants into the nebula."

Harry listened in silence, then snorted a laugh. "What a lot of nonsense, Laurel! If they made an overture, Canon Akkuh would have responded appropriately and advised the League." He studied her for signs of a prank, then scoffed. "Someone's feeding you fairy stories."

"Harry, no." Laurel insisted he listened. "Canon Akkuh knew about the threat. Xavier never trusted him from the outset."

Harry was stubbornly loyal to the League, so she pushed her thoughts into his mind where he could see for himself that she was in complete earnest, that this was no prank.

"Okay," Harry said, "why did Darlen never mention he'd transmitted a message to the Canon?"

"He didn't know what was in the message, Harry. And you and he don't exactly get on," Laurel pointed out. "Darlen's been trading with the Gartrya for years, and other Soul Mongers before him. He suspected the Gartrya was exiled, but he didn't know the League banished them." Laurel shook her head, and Harry was momentarily distracted by how pretty her curls were now, tossing about and falling over her shoulder. Her expression cured him of being fanciful; he must never forget she could read him. But these instincts, this knowledge supplied by the informant, were hard to swallow, although faced with what appeared to be Laurel's absolute conviction, he had no choice but to listen.

"And you believe this story?"

"I do. What is important is that Canon Akkuh rejected the overture even though he must have realised that someone was crossing the nebula. Whether he knew it was Darlen…well, I don't know that, but remember the League wasn't aware of the lifeform, so he thought his family secret was safe. The information must be documented somewhere."

"His secret? There's another secret apart from the communication?"

"Yes. The mineral you use in medicine."

"We use many minerals and compounds, Laurel. Which one?"

"Epo'negra."

Harry nodded. "It's found on Norik. I've never heard of this Inikamara."

"Then Norik is Inikamara."

"That's absurd, Laurel." Harry let out a short laugh. "It would mean the League was responsible for genocide and Canon Akkuh guilty of war crimes."

"I know." Laurel clasped her hands together. Harry was listening, and she couldn't lose him, not now. "They uprooted an entire civilisation. The duke wanted what was legitimately his birthright returned to him. Unfortunately," she sat back, she had to concede the point. "He was a psychopath."

"And you learned this in the fortress?" Harry was sceptical, that wasn't unexpected, but he no longer dismissed what Laurel said.

"When I was captured. I only spoke with one person,

a man supposed by the Gartrya to be the duke's heir and successor."

"He was the enemy, Laurel." Harry thought it a reasonable point. "Could it be he was feeding you lies?"

"No, the duke's heir was the informant."

Harry fell silent. They'd received useful information from what appeared to be a single source within the duke's ranks, and that same source had contacted Darlen with a plan to rescue Laurel. Canon Akkuh had denied Harry and the whole souls leave to attempt a rescue. Harry wondered what went through Canon Akkuh's mind when he finally discovered Laurel was not only free but had also used information from a Gartryan source to end the war. Harry concluded the Canon was probably highly anxious in case she spoke up.

"The informant was a whole soul slave paraded by the duke as his heir," Laurel explained, wanting Harry to have the complete picture, "while privately treating him as a slave, using his mother and child as a lever to ensure his loyalty."

"Wait, the duke's heir is a whole soul?"

"Yes, but he died when the fortress was destroyed. He wasn't on their side, believe me."

"I wondered how you found out about being able to enter the nebula. I thought it was something Xavier discovered. So, this man told you?" Harry knew he'd been too quick to judge. Laurel was no fool, and if this informant was also a whole soul, perhaps she was right to trust him.

Laurel allowed herself a small smile as the last of Harry's scepticism and disbelief faded into guarded acceptance. His convincing might need a touch more tweaking, perhaps with hard facts if she could find them, but already, he was on her side.

"You know, Laurel," he warned, "if we ever prove this, the Canonical family will come under intense scrutiny." He took a deep breath; the ramifications scarcely bore thinking about. "They've done so much for so many civilisations. If this happened soon after the formation of the League, it could have just been a miscalculation of an undeveloped and naïve society?"

"A miscalculation?" Laurel spluttered. "Genocide is never a miscalculation."

"I meant only there may have been mitigating circumstances." Harry tried to calm her. Trust him to say something inflammatory. "If what you say is correct, and I have a few doubts, the Gartrya need to be restored to their homeworld. The League's Constitution states unequivocally that any resource deemed suitable for common use is to be shared, and the owners compensated. It's at the very heart of League doctrine."

Harry felt a weight descend on him as he reflected just how well it had worked. He'd trusted the League all his life, defended it, worked for its advancement, and now…

"When did this compensable law come into force?" Laurel asked.

"I don't know." Harry attempted and failed a shrug. "It's always been there. The League is ancient, but its fundamental laws haven't changed in generations."

"I don't think 'always' goes back far enough, Harry. The treatment of these people dates almost to the creation of the League. It's possible the treaties at that time were more informal."

"There is a government historical archive," Harry said. "I have clearance. Maybe there's a reference to this incident."

"Buried deep enough so no-one would find it?"

"Perhaps, but this is ancient. There may be a datacomp from someone in government."

"A datacomp?"

"Yes, a compilation file, a journal. Citizens loved to keep records, and some are preserved. Lesser officials may have made reference, but reform legislation will affect legal compilations, so the original content or intent may be unrecognisable. But if we can find something less formal, we can bypass Canon Akkuh and take it straight to Congress. They may be prepared to make reparation to Shumuyi'beh and her people, and they can deal with the Canon as they see fit."

"The Canonical family's historical crimes won't be common knowledge," Laurel said, making a mental note to investigate a few of the public files for clues. "I'd say Canon Akkuh didn't reveal the message from the duke to anyone in Congress, not unless he has any Congressmen in his family."

"Yes, he does."

"Well, they may be keeping the secret as well. Is there anyone else we could take the information to?"

"There's the Protectorate. Under Congress, they have authority over mineral rights, trade and commerce of all treaty planets. We'd have to have pretty solid evidence to get them to hear our argument, though."

"I realise you're taking a leap of faith, Harry. I trust what Gabriel, the informant told me. He sacrificed his life to end the war and to ensure the safety of his family."

"I have faith in you, Laurel, but the proof of this remains to be seen, and…" Harry winced as he lifted his arms, "as you can see, I'm in no position to mount an investigation."

"I understand," Laurel smiled. She needed his expertise, but he was in no position to offer it. She would have to wait, so as a diversion, she pointed at the contraption holding him.

"You look uncomfortable, dangling there, like a puppet. I'm expecting any minute you're going to dance a jig!"

Harry looked at his force field and brace prison. "It's not as uncomfortable as it looks. And I'm lodged, not 'dangling'. The brace supports my whole body and protects from any compression of my spine, allowing the spinal cord to heal."

"I know your spinal cord got severed."

"In two places," Harry nodded. "I've only got three healbots in right now, the others have already exited, so it's well and truly on the mend."

Laurel stood and checked out the pandroscope. She'd noticed a rise in heart rate and a tiny spike in adrenaline when she discussed Canon Akkuh, but it was showing normal status now.

"You're showing twenty-three per cent neurological deficit in your lower limbs," she said, "but your muscles are pretty good. A bit flaccid here and there."

"Thank you, doctor!" Harry laughed. "They deliberately placed the pandroscope out of my sight so I wouldn't keep checking it."

"I guessed as much, but that's what friends are for. I can only read the obvious bits, anyway. How long will you be in this thing?"

"Another week. Then I've got to start walking. I reckon I'll be out of here in a month or so."

"That's good news; the others arrive back in two days, so I expect they'll be up to see you. We have a meeting with Congressman Bela to evaluate where we go from here. Then, we'll attend an accelerated learning program. And…" Laurel's eyes lit up, "Congress has promised us a vacation. After that, I know Eli and Chloe plan to stay in law enforcement. They're presently submitting their applications, pending their further education to qualify."

Harry already knew that. "And your plans?"

"I haven't got any." Laurel shrugged slowly, a hint of the dreamy in her voice. "I wake up to the Mentelci sunrise, and I find myself filled with wonder. I watch both moons rise at night and feel that same wonder." She sighed, then smiled at him. "It's beyond anything I ever imagined, but I worry about Helen. She seems the most lost of us all. Marta's going to check out her options in commerce when she gets back, but Helen just stays in the apartment. And to answer your question, I guess there aren't any nurses here. I have considered linguistics and studying the ancient civilisations I've researched on the treaty planets, but I'm just not sure."

"You could become a physician." Harry had been

planning on suggesting this to Laurel almost since they'd first met. She would be a perfect candidate.

"How?" Laurel laughed. "I wouldn't know where to start. Besides," she pointed to the pandroscope behind the bed, monitoring Harry's vital signs, "the technology is beyond me."

"You could start at the beginning."

Laurel gave the matter a moment's thought. It sounded appealing.

"It's an idea. I'll speak to Congressman Bela."

"It will keep you in the capital for a couple of years." Harry again took her hand, but this time, he lifted it to his lips and kissed her fingers as he added, "Which is where I'll be based. I'm not going back to the constabulary."

This time, Laurel didn't remove her hand from his.

"You know," Harry said softly, "I hoped we could get to know each other a little better. There are lots of worlds out there, lots of opportunities. I plan to explore as many as I can, but to be truthful, Laurel, I would prefer we explored them together." He drew her closer, close enough to place a tender kiss on her mouth.

It didn't seem to matter to Harry that she didn't return the kiss. At that moment, it was impossible to gauge what she felt. Losing Xavier was still painful, and the loss of Gabriel. It always seemed Harry had a grasp on his feelings, such a grip on life. That's why he could think of giving, of offering her love even after what he'd been through. But for Laurel, she wasn't at that place, so instead, she smiled.

"I just want you to get well, and I promise I'll consider what you said about a career in medicine."

CHAPTER SIX _

Several days later, the League of Treaty Planets held a memorial service to honour Xavier with a commemorative plaque erected within the Halls of Congress. Canon Akkuh addressed the entire council, speaking of Xavier's empathy with the lifeform and how he had paid the ultimate price in honouring the League. He didn't mention the actions of the whole souls, of Harry and his squadron, which brought a decisive end to the war. Congressman Bela gave a beautiful, tear-provoking eulogy in which she praised Xavier's sacrifice, selflessness, and courage. Watching Canon Akkuh was difficult for Laurel, knowing what she knew. Her sense of outrage ran deep, and she wanted to stand and scream that he spoke of honour when he had none.

Because of Xavier's death, Congress agreed they would undertake no formal celebration of the whole souls' contribution. Instead, they held an informal reception with representatives of Congress and the Protectorate. Laurel hated doing it, but she took a surreptitious look inside Congressman Bela's mind and, to her relief, found her new friend hid nothing incriminating. The same went for Congressman Ips and Congressman Sella. It seemed the most senior members of the Congress were innocent of any knowledge of Canon Akkuh's family secrets and his deceit. Besides Helen and Harry, Laurel didn't tell the others, fearing she might involve them in a conspiracy too huge even for her to expose. She struggled with the fact but knew she had to wait until the dust settled, bide her time, and wait for Harry to recover.

The Protectorate inducted all five whole souls into an accelerated learning program. Eli resented being torn away from piloting, but the carrot the League dangled considerably influenced his decision to cooperate; a position in Outer League law administration, which meant not only flying scouts but any ship the Constabulary assigned him. Chloe soaked up the learning programs like a sponge, Eli struggled most, and Helen was the annoying kid at school who constantly sought to distract the others. Marta, with her ingrained ability to focus, breezed through the lessons, as did Laurel, who had to admit, learning about the League and its history, its society, varied cultures, languages, and trade was hugely satisfying. She came away from the program invigorated and appreciative of her newly acquired learning. Besides those figures she knew were traitors to everything it stood for, she saw for herself the leaders were dedicated people from all walks of life and many worlds, who each proclaimed their "half soulness" and "quarter soulness" like a badge of honour. Laurel grudgingly allowed that she might credit even Canon Akkuh with many outstanding acts of altruism and sacrifice for the benefit of League members, but she would never lose sight of what his lack of action cost the Semevalians.

While the League considered their various applications for new careers, the whole souls transferred to Leyis, an Earth-like world with green hills, brooding mountains and a diverse ecosystem and society. Their accommodation's resort-like surroundings were abundant with fruit, wildlife, sea, sand, and sunshine, nestled in a paradise of sandy coves and soaring, shrub-covered cliff-faces that towered above natural windows and rock-like bridges framing an azure sky. Wiks and colourfully plumed bird life shared the trees and plants in complete harmony. The entire world was a garden paradise. Or, according to Helen: Bali.

Ru and Forik, local people, were their guides. Knowledgeable, hospitable, and kind, Ru was young, exotic, funny and able to create incredible beach barbecues from local produce, which she cooked under the sand. She and Eli developed a mutual admiration from the moment they met. Forik, the husband of several wives and father of many children, worked on his fruit farm for most of the year, taking pleasure in showing visitors his glorious and peaceful planet. He knew the best locations to relax and enjoy sport and wildlife, or if the silence became too much, he knew where they could find entertainment and the company of others.

In such tranquil surroundings, released from the chaos of the war and frenzy of accelerated learning, the friends had time to reflect and come to terms with their grief at losing Xavier. It hit Chloe the hardest. While the others talked about their future aspirations and their shock at losing one of their number, Chloe reverted to the tearful girl they first met on Darlen's ship so many months before. She refused to speak, spending hours wrapped in a blanket on her bed, weeping, refusing food, and only accepting drinks when Laurel or Helen coaxed her. A League physician attended and confirmed the spindle, implanted behind her ear to repress grief response and allow her to focus on the war, had now absorbed. Chloe would have to deal with losing her family, her old life, Xavier, and her fears for the future. Rejecting any comfort or offer to share her grief, Chloe closed her mind even to Laurel. Concerned, Laurel contacted Asde, still serving as a League soldier until his return to law enforcement. Asde's commanders permitted him to come to Leyis and remain until the whole souls returned to Mentelci.

Within moments of Asde's arrival, Chloe was clinging to him, weeping for her little brothers, her parents, the family dog, for Xavier, for her school friends, for having the whole souls who she knew loved her, for losing all those people in the war. It all came out, and a day later, although Laurel knew Chloe's grief would never leave her, she saw she was already finding a safe place for it to settle. When she noticed Chloe and Asde walking together on the beach, Laurel breathed a sigh of relief.

As their time on Leyis drew to a close, Helen and Laurel stretched out for the last time on the sand. Before them, an expanse of wonderfully calm blue ocean stretched out to a far distant horizon. Above, tall trees created a perfect canopy to shade them from the sun. A group of wiks dusted up the sand as they went past.

"I like wiks," Helen said, rolling her head lazily to

watch them as they twirled by. "They remind me of bees."

Laurel followed her gaze. "They carry out the same purpose, I suppose, except they don't sting."

"I heard that on some worlds," Helen said idly, "not treaty worlds, they capture the babies to put in cages and give as gifts because they produce brighter pollen when they're stressed. But they die quickly in captivity."

"I've never heard that. How cruel!" Laurel couldn't imagine separating a baby wik from its clan. She'd seen how wik babies behaved when they got left behind. They simply inverted and sat on the ground like a miniature Christmas tree until an adult wik rescued them.

"Yes, but it's—was, a slave society." Helen allowed her head to roll back so that she could see Laurel. "Old habits die hard."

"You can't compare wiks with humans, Helen. Besides, we kept birds in cages."

Helen nodded, shielding her eyes as she watched the wiks spinning up the cliff face, disturbing a flock of noisy birds as they went. "Do you miss sex?" she said, her abrupt change of subject taking Laurel by surprise.

"Helen!"

"Just asking. I thought maybe you got laid since you got here. Harry, perhaps? Or the guy at the fortress? You fell for him." Helen didn't demand an answer, just turned her gaze on Eli walking along the sand, his arm over Ru's shoulder, Ru's arm around his waist. They were laughing. "I reckon Eli has. He and Ru seem to have something going."

"Good for them." Laurel had no interest in her friends' sex lives or lack thereof. She knew Helen sensed her disinterest but carried on nevertheless.

"I wonder about Chloe and Asde," she said, her mind not really on what she was saying; it was still away somewhere with the wiks. "She's still a kid in so many ways."

"She's nearly eighteen, and I don't think it's our business, Helen. Besides, Asde's a good person; he won't take advantage of her."

Helen shrugged and gazed out over the ocean. "It's not just sex, I miss. It's other stuff. Vacuum cleaners. Do you miss vacuum cleaners? And television. I miss watching telly and eating a cheese sandwich and having a beer."

"I don't think about it, Helen." Laurel was used to her friend's vacuous ramblings. "I didn't drink beer, and we don't need vacuum cleaners." But she decided to compromise. "I liked television, though."

Helen wasn't listening anyway. "I used to do baby lamb chops in my sandwich maker. They smelt divine. I grated nutmeg and rosemary on them." She sighed at the memory. "Did you like lamb chops, Laurel?"

"I'm a vegetarian."

"Oh, of course, you are. I might become a vegetarian. I haven't fancied meat since Darlen made that comparison between his face and a spikit's arse. That's what they have as meat here, isn't it?"

"Darlen's face or a spikit's arse?"

"You know what I mean." Helen sighed again. She was missing little details of home. Now she had the chance to think; Helen was homesick.

"Do you reckon Marta's having sex?" Helen said after

a few minutes silence. "Some of those big, tall guys on 100 moons fancied her like mad."

"She's very striking," Laurel answered, "but I don't think she's encumbered by those kinds of needs."

Helen swivelled her head around, eyes wide.

"Really? Do tell."

Marta had only mentioned her sexual orientation once in passing, that she considered herself asexual, and she didn't care who knew it. Still, Laurel cursed herself she'd mentioned it to Helen of all people. She was committed now, so she tried to play it down.

"Only that she said she tried it once, didn't care for it, and consigned it to trash."

"Wow." Helen couldn't believe her ears. "Pete, my ex, he was a prick, but he was great in bed."

"There's more to a relationship than great sex, Helen."

Helen rested her head and closed her eyes. "I dunno. Right now, I'd settle for great sex."

Laurel grinned. "What's with the fixation, Helen? We're going back to Mentelci soon. You'll meet someone; you're pretty and funny. Don't worry." Laurel didn't doubt she would. Someone as unique as Helen would be snapped up in a heartbeat.

Harry didn't wait for a single day to pass after their arrival back on Mentelci before he turned up at Laurel and Helen's apartment, where all the whole souls were preparing to disperse to their various accommodations. He was walking well, without aids, and looked to have put on a bit of weight. He'd also sorted out his sandy hair from the untidy mess it was in the medical facility. It was still spiky, only longer and not yet at the point where it laid down neatly on his head. Helen teased him about using him as a toilet brush, but he didn't get the joke. He couldn't because toilet brushes were unheard of in the League, and he didn't see the connection with spiky hair, even though by League standards, Harry was noted for his sense of humour.

After the greetings and hugs, he drew Laurel to the side and proposed a walk to the Galleria, the broad, paved area that stood between the glorious Wind Field Sea natural reserve and the entrance to the capital.

"I drew a blank in the public archives," he told her when they'd settled at one of the many pavement cafes. "I examined the government archives here, as well. There's nothing."

"Gabriel wasn't lying."

Harry sensed defence. He held up a finger so Laurel would see he hadn't finished. "No, I don't think he was. I tracked down Darlen. He said I should believe you and what this Gabriel said. Besides…"

He was taking too long, so Laurel impatiently prodded around Harry's mind.

"There *are* hidden records?" Laurel just knew it would come to this.

"Yes, Laurel," he sighed, his pleasure in discovering this information stripped from him before he could even utter the words. But Laurel was on a mission, and he was learning that patience was not always her greatest virtue. "Hidden, but not from you. I think one of Canon Akkuh's ancestors extracted them."

"Would they be destroyed? Something so incriminating?"

She shared the thought with Harry, then pulled back, realising what she was doing was at best rude and, at worst, invasive. Harry was her friend. She shouldn't be reading his mind and asking telepathic questions unless it was essential. Harry accepted her withdrawal, waiting for her to sit back and allow him to explain, the corners of his mouth lifting to show he was glad of the courtesy.

"I spent my rehab time with my dad," he said. "He asked about the whole souls and the war, and I mentioned the League's possible historical interactions with an extinct race called the Inikamara. I can't hide my thoughts from him either, but he gave me a clue as to where they might hold the information. Somewhere the League won't want us snooping for these particular files. I doubt Canon Akkuh would want this secret seeing the light of day."

Laurel wondered about those files. If they were hidden from the general population, why wouldn't they be hidden from her? She wanted to know how Harry's dad knew, so she allowed Harry the floor.

"When I was a child at school," Harry continued, "Dad became interested in the history of the League. He's quite an expert, and he has a brilliant memory. His mentors directed him to the universities and their libraries, so I thought he might have come across a compilation referring to a possible banishment in the early days of the League."

"Was that wise? We're treading on shaky ground here ourselves."

Harry shook his head. "He won't say anything. He was only looking at the history of the founding of the League.

He liked political ideals and the structure of society, and that was his interest, building up a picture, finding his place. There's a library in the old city, in Upper Temple, attached to the Canon's residence. There's a public zone, but here's the thing; Dad says it has archives below it." Harry nodded mysteriously. "Sealed archives."

Laurel knew the area. The Canonical palace was built partly over a water catchment. "I went to Upper and Lower Temple during the accelerated learning," she said. "We didn't go into the library, though. Has your father seen these archives for himself?"

"No, but he's an empath. He knows they're there."

Laurel understood. "That's why they can't hide them from me." She looked out to the Wind Field Sea. This was a possible lead, somewhere to start. "We need to get in and see the records," she said, turning to Harry, her amber eyes bright and determined. "Break in if we have to."

But Harry's enthusiasm didn't meet Laurel's expectations. Instead, he lowered his voice and looked around. "I was afraid you'd say that Laurel, but before we get caught and tried for treason while we're working out how to *commit* treason, bear in mind this crime is historical. Exposing the Canon may destabilise the League. We could make a confidential submission to the Protectorate or even to Congressman Bela, tell them what you know. As a whole soul, they'll listen to you."

For Laurel, too much was at stake. With nothing to support her claims, the Protectorate would likely question her motives for making an unsubstantiated allegation against the most prominent family in the League.

"No." Laurel's face set with determination. "Hard evidence would be better, and besides, Harry, it's not historical anymore. The duke's quest for restitution and Canon Akkuh's dismissal of the communication dragged it into the here and now."

Harry scratched his head. He knew she'd come up with a counterargument. She was good at that, and he was beaten even before her next words.

"I'm just saying we can't know this and ignore it, Harry. Canon Akkuh kept the petition to reconcile a secret—that makes him directly responsible for a war that killed countless innocent people. It's been over three months since that war ended, and what's been done about the Gartryan petition to resettle?"

"Not much," Harry had to admit. "I'm not privy to the details. Even with the League knowing whole souls can safely transport the half and quarter souls across the nebula, nothing is in place for the five of you to bring that about. It is possible Congress aren't convinced the Gartrya are no longer a threat; that Duchess Shumuyi'beh won't suddenly declare war once she gets a foothold. Interestingly, I hear there is opposition to her petition to resettle in League space from some factions on Gartrya itself. They're going to hold an election. She might get deposed."

A challenge to an ancient autocracy? What a turn-up for the books. The duke would turn in his grave, hopefully. Laurel had a sense this turn of events might work to Shumuyi'beh's advantage. "Some will follow her even if the League doesn't agree to resettle them," she said. "It might be cleansing for their society. I doubt they have the means, or any fight left to conduct a civil war if there is any division."

"Let's hope it doesn't come to that." Harry tapped his finger on the table to bring them back to the matter at hand. "If we're going to take this risk, break into the archive and get this hard evidence—" he closed his eyes for a moment, "if it's even there—we have to bring Canon Akkuh's treachery to the Protectorate's attention in such a way he can't run and hide."

Brave words, Harry thought as he tried not to think of the consequences if Laurel and the informant were wrong. Either way, he wouldn't let her do this alone. "We'll go to the library. If you can sense the archives, we'll find a means to get in."

Laurel had made up her mind. They only needed to finish the planning. "What's the security like?" she asked as soon as he finished speaking.

"Oh, well, there's none in the library save a couple of Constabulary patrols. They've guarded the residence for a few months even though the war never got as far as Mentelci."

"The war?" Laurel's eyebrows raised slightly in question. "Or since the whole souls arrived?"

Harry's look was sobering. He hadn't thought of that, but yes, Canon Akkuh posted guards at his residence around the time Laurel went missing at the fortress.

"In that case, we have to be careful you're not recognised. It's going to be risky." Harry considered just how risky. "Perhaps we should get Marta or Eli in on this."

"No. We'll ask Helen," Laurel said. "I did tell her, but

I think she's forgotten. She may be able to shield us."

"Helen?" Harry screwed up his face.

"You don't seem keen?"

Harry shook his head. "No, Helen's great," he said, "but she's..." he looked around. "She's loud. If we're breaking into the Canon's residence, we don't want to attract attention."

"That's not fair," Laurel scolded. "She rose to the occasion on Gartrya, and she knows when to be serious. She'll be fine, and we need her abilities, so don't look at me like that."

CHAPTER SEVEN _

Laurel, Harry, and Helen met to discuss the next stage of the plan. Despite Helen's poorly developed empathic and telepathic skills, she sensed enough to know this was important. Too important, she thought, for her to participate, and even before either Harry or Laurel spoke, Helen wondered why the others weren't invited. Laurel's comments to her back on 100 moons had long since evaporated.

"Helen, do you remember me telling you about Canon Akkuh knowing why the war started?" Laurel said.

Helen nodded blankly; she remembered something. Laurel could duck inside her mind and dredge up the missing info if she needed it.

"Harry's discovered there's an archive below the Residence in Upper Temple. I believe we'll find the evidence we need there."

Still, Helen didn't make the connection. "Why are you telling me?"

"Because we need to get into that archive and locate the evidence." Laurel opened her hands in invitation. "You can shield us."

It wasn't sinking in. Helen just stared at them both. "Why do you need shielding?"

"Helen," Harry responded, with more patience than he felt, not worrying too much because it was unlikely Helen was anywhere near his thoughts. "It's not common knowledge there is an archive there. It's the ideal place to hide any records. We don't know where else to begin. But no-one can see us, and no-one must know. What we're planning is highly illegal."

Helen's eyes darted from right to left and back again. She might not be the brightest bulb in the chandelier, but she knew treason when she heard it and finally came to understand the weight of what Harry and Laurel proposed.

"You want me to help you break in and steal government documents? Laurel, what if we get caught?"

"It would be riskier just Harry and me, but with you…" Laurel encouraged that little spark of interest she saw in Helen's mind. "It would be difficult for them even to see us."

Helen scrunched her face in thought. "What if the shield doesn't work? It doesn't always."

"You made it work on Gartrya."

"I was scared," Helen replied in a matter-of-fact tone.

"Well, as Harry says, this is highly illegal," Laurel pointed out. "That'll probably scare you enough. I'm willing to take a chance. That war could have been so easily avoided, Helen. We can't let the Canon get away with what he's done."

Helen looked at Harry. He nodded silently. If the two people Helen admired most in this universe needed her help, she would willingly give it.

"Okay. If I can help. I'm not much good at the other stuff, empathy, telepathy."

"And so far, none of us have shown your ability to hide people," Laurel smiled, satisfied. "I believe my telepathic senses will be enough."

"Helen?" Harry asked. "How does it work? I've speculated about it since the time you saved those children."

Helen waggled her head, giving her cloaking ability some thought. "I'm not sure," she decided. "I've only been able to work it out in the last couple of weeks. I can't do it like this, sitting here with you two, being normal, but if I get an adrenaline rush or become angry or frightened, even happy, I get the sense of being just behind my body, propelling it forward. I can't stop it from happening, but now, I can control how long it lasts. Dunno where it comes from."

"Are you aware of your body while you're like this?" This was the first time Helen allowed herself to be engaged about the ability, and Laurel wanted to take advantage.

"Yup. And talk and move around, but it's like I'm working a puppet."

"I wonder how it protected the children from that blast on Semevale 8?"

"No idea. It didn't happen when I got punched in the jaw and shot," Helen ruefully replied. "I wish I had it on Earth. There were a few people I would have liked to disappear."

"If it works for us now, we'll find a way into the residence," Harry said. "There's a carnival in the Upper

Temple in two days. We'll go; the carnival may serve as a distraction if we're poking around. Another problem might be accessing the vault. The Canon most likely keeps the combination either in his head or under his mattress, but if it's just a door, I can pick a lock."

"You're very optimistic, thankfully," Laurel smiled. "Helen, you're sure you're okay with this?"

"If you need me, Laurel, I'll do my best."

Laurel had visited the Old City only once during the accelerated learning program with Chloe, Marta, and Helen. Built in the early years of the League on the banks of the Ponsecki, a broad, crystal-clear river, the city was divided into two levels, Upper and Lower Temple. The Lower Temple buildings were crowded together and composed of bright, shining steel that reached towards the sky like a jumbled mixture of spears and old-fashioned artist renderings of space rockets. Each tower was multi-hued, with a metallic base underpinning the colours. A few towers exhibited an attempt at artistry and aesthetics, but to Laurel's eye, each one bordered on the garish. Although the exteriors were not to her taste, Laurel recognised, as a former amateur student of ancient cultures and antiquities, that as edifices, the structures echoed the discernment of a long-dead society. Many showed signs of remodelling, perhaps to bring them into the modern age while still paying homage to the forefathers who built them. Lower Temple contained the entertainment districts, retail sections, bistros, saloons, parkland, just like any city on Earth. It even had seedy areas that attracted merchants and the shadier offworlders from systems outside the League.

Habitation areas in Lower Temple made the best use of the views across the river to sweeping fields and magnificent mountain ranges in the distance. The Ponsecki stretched into forever under a golden sky, its waters shimmering like a river of jewels in the day and reflecting the ghostly image of the near moon of Imbri at night. On their visit with their tutor, they'd travelled across the river and into the foothills to Upper Temple, where they had a superb, elevated view over Lower Temple.

"Manhattan dressed up for a carnival," Marta had said, referring to the colourful spires and shiny building fascia. Laurel lost count of the times she'd travelled across to Manhattan from Brooklyn, and over time, paid no attention to the view. Perhaps if someone sprayed metallic paint on the Manhattan skyline and polished the buildings, Laurel might have agreed with Marta, but as it stood, Marta's comparison failed to move her one bit.

Upper Temple, built on the foothills overlooking its less salubrious counterpart, sported cobblestoned streets, magnificent houses, museums, a few tumbledown yet preserved-for-posterity buildings, and lovingly tended parks and gardens. For centuries, the Canonical family held the official seat of the League. The Residence stood at the pinnacle of Upper Temple, overlooking the city and sweeping views below and partly built out into one of the many tributaries which ran from the mountains behind Upper Temple to feed the Ponsecki. Laurel believed she had never seen a building on Earth to compare with the Residence. It simply took her breath away, not just its appearance but the sense of what it represented. History seeped from the stately gothic-looking walls, and Laurel felt if she listened closely, the voices of ancient politicians would have reached her with their wise words, overseeing generations of galactic treaties and laws. The windows, broad-based, wide and culminating into elegant, uniform arches above, were undiminished by the faint blue glow of a forcefield. A narrow moat filled with climbing floral vines and shrubs adorned the lower levels. The main doors, immense, ornate, and guarded by a pair of armed League Constables, sat above wide steps flanked by a manicured terrace garden. It was here that an enlightened League made the judgment to end slavery and close access to the Transcender. And here, yet another decision came about, made in desperation, to allow a Soul Monger through once more. Captivated by the charm and elegance of the building, Laurel felt a sense of satisfaction that as a monument to the Canonical family, it was built long after the decision to commit genocide on Inikamara. Therefore, its beauty remained unspoiled by the evil of those founding fathers of the League.

"Well?" Harry whispered.

Harry, Laurel and Helen stood across the street from the Residence. Music and laughter rang through the air as the carnival reached full swing.

"Your dad was right, Harry," Laurel whispered back, even though there was no way anyone would have heard them above the noise. "It's underneath the residence, but the archive extends out to under the tributary. I don't understand why I didn't sense it when I was here before."

"I can't feel a thing." Helen looked around, beginning to twitch and jiggle her hips. "All this music. I just wanna dance."

"Be serious, Helen," Harry hissed before turning reproachful, "I told you so," eyes to Laurel, who ignored him. Nevertheless, they were whole souls where, Laurel suspected, whole souls might not be welcome. Not if the Canon found out.

"Yes," Laurel echoed. "Don't draw attention to us."

Helen left off jiggling and fell to grumbling instead. "I like parties."

They'd only arrived as evening drew in, using a public shuttle from the capital to avoid any identifying vehicles, and at once got swept up with the crowds. The mood was happy and boisterous, and if Helen could control herself, they'd just be another three faces in the crowd.

Laurel tried to attune her senses to evaluate an easy entry into the vault. It wasn't so easy in a carnival atmosphere, and feelgood-hormone-saturated brains left the revellers thoughts unguarded, allowing random voices to waft in and out of her mind as they jostled past.

"Helen," she said, giving up on her struggle for control. "Do you think you could shield us while we get through the front door?"

Harry shook his head. "No, that won't work. The doors open from the inside; even the Canon has to be admitted by a member of his staff."

"Really? How peculiar." Laurel forced herself to laugh as a crowd of merrymakers thrust the trio apart as they made their way past. One good-looking man lifted Helen into the air and spun her around, calling her "gorgeous" in Seera. Helen looked giddy and smug as he put her down, and she sighed wistfully as he continued on his way.

With the option of the main entrance closed to them, Laurel needed an alternative. She moved closer to the tributary, where it was darker and quieter and where she could collect her thoughts.

Helen watched her. "You didn't have a plan, did you, chick?" she declared, not needing to read her mind to know Laurel was flying by the seat of her pants.

It wasn't a question, certainly nothing that required a response, but Laurel suddenly held up a hand. She turned her head slightly towards where the Residence's outer walls met the tributary.

"Do you see that wall, Harry?"

He glanced discreetly in the direction she indicated. "The river barrier, do you mean?"

"Yes." She leaned close to him and drew the giddy Helen in as she dropped her voice. "It's angled with the library. We need to get over it and find a way into the building."

Harry took another glance. "That might be the only way in."

"We'll get wet," Helen whispered. "Besides, the moon is reflecting light in the water. Someone's bound to wonder what we're doing wading through the river."

"The water's low this time of year, Helen," Harry responded. "It might be a bit muddy."

Laurel was too busy evaluating how to get over the wall

to be interested in Helen's concerns. "The wall doesn't appear to have any downlights, but it's quite high. What do you think?" She looked at Harry for his thoughts.

"I think it's a stupid idea," Helen sniffed before Harry could reply. "We'll get caught, and you'll be left to explain to Canon Akkuh why you're hunting him down."

Laurel pursed her lips. "Helen, you said you would help us, not bring down a curse on our heads."

"I am helping. I think we'll all end up in prison."

Harry glared at her before turning to Laurel. "I told you she would be a problem."

"Oh, you did, did you?" Helen faced him, hands on hips. "Well…"

"Stop it, you two," Laurel snapped. "We're going over that wall. Shut up, Helen. You too, Harry."

Casually, they edged their way into the shadows, and once they were out of sight of the carnival, Helen used her irritation with Harry to summon up her cloaking ability. There was some reflection of the moon and the coloured carnival lights on the water, but they were sure the occasional ripple the invisible trio made as they waded through wouldn't draw attention.

"The wall's too high," Helen said, taking another opportunity to grumble.

"We can climb." Laurel pointed upwards. "The entrance to the vault is on the ground floor, and the vault is directly below us. I know we're close. Once we're over the wall, I suppose a window in the Residence on the tributary side will still have a forcefield?"

"Probably," came Harry's reply through the gloom. "I can deactivate a window easily enough, provided there are no guards. Are you able to sense if there are any close?"

"Yes, street area and a few on the upper levels." Laurel scanned what she could see of the Residence. "What I wouldn't give for a retinal optimiser. The guards aren't on high alert, so I guess the Canon's not here." She hesitated, attuning her senses to the immediate surroundings. "The area behind the wall is deserted."

The ground underfoot changed from soft grass to sludge as they skirted the tributary. Getting close enough to the wall meant sloshing through mud, so Helen kicked off her shoes, and being the lightest of the two women, Harry lifted her onto his shoulders to peer over the wall.

"I can't sense anything while I'm doing the shield thing, but it looks deserted," she whispered loudly. "There's a whole row of windows, though, all with forcefields. Are you sure you're going to know which one, Laurel?"

"Yes, and I can't sense any guards patrolling this area. Harry, shove Helen onto the top of the wall."

"I haven't—" Helen wailed, but a tap on the calf from Harry shushed her, "—got any shoes on," she finished with a whisper.

Laurel saw Helen's shoes as they became slurped up by the mud. It was too dark to rescue them, and it might distract Helen from maintaining her cloak, so Harry gave Helen a shove, and she lay perched on top of the wall.

"I'll give you a lift up, Laurel," he said, propping against the wall for support. "You and Helen may need to pull me up." Laurel stepped forward, and the mud sucked a shoe from her foot. She discarded the other one as Harry lifted her.

Helen and Laurel held onto Harry's arms as he scaled the wall. They waited, relying on Laurel's telepathy to assure them no guards were in the vicinity and that they hadn't been detected. Laurel just hoped Helen could maintain her cloak. They dropped down the other side and ran across the small lawn, pressing themselves against the Residence wall.

"We're almost above it," Laurel whispered, not sure whether their voices could be heard while Helen shielded them. She looked down as she sensed the vault metres below her mud-caked feet. The window to her right glowed with an active forcefield. "That's the window we need to get through."

"I can deactivate the field," Harry said, then added with a note of caution, "but I can't reactivate it behind us, so someone will eventually notice it's down and come looking."

Laurel waved away his warning; they'd got this far, but the lighting was better this close to the Residence, and she didn't want to delay just in case Helen's cloak failed. "We'll have to make good use of the time we have, then."

Harry took a palm-sized Constabulary-issue datacache from inside his shirt and entered a sequence. The forcefield faded, and he smiled at Laurel's puzzled expression. "All law enforcement officers have one of these," he said.

"You're not in law enforcement anymore."

"I omitted giving it back on discharge," he grinned. "I thought it might come in handy. See? I'm not such a company man."

Laurel climbed through the window, reminded she once unjustly accused him of being just that.

"Sorry," she said. "I take it back."

An unexpected sight greeted them as they climbed through the window. Unlike the polished, contemporary styles of the interiors Laurel encountered elsewhere, here soft drapes hung from panelled walls, elegant furnishings and ornaments, carved seats, and tapestried cushions were all meticulously arranged. Paintings rested on scrolled easels and the whole place smelled of dust and age. She turned to Harry.

"I've not seen anything like this since I arrived. Not even in the museums. It looks like old Earth. Possibly seventeenth and eighteenth century."

"It's impressive," Harry agreed.

"These must have been taken from the Soul Monger's forays to Earth." Laurel could see no other explanation. "It seems slaves weren't the only things they prized."

"Perhaps," Harry agreed as he examined the elaborate drapes. "Can you sense the entrance to the vault? We need to get out of this hallway."

"I'm still hiding us, Harry," Helen said, then stopped, "I think, but they'll be suspicious that someone is in here."

Laurel and Harry both turned to her, and Helen pointed to the floor. Muddy smudges led from the window. "I don't know why they're not hidden," Helen said. "Maybe bits of mud fell off our feet. Sorry, I don't have any special mop and bucket abilities."

Harry grabbed a rug to throw over the offending dirt.

"They won't notice," he said, doubting his own optimism. "Laurel?"

Laurel stared thoughtfully at the wall. Slowly, she extended her hand. "There, that's the entrance."

Harry looked to where Laurel pointed.

"It's just a blank wall," he said as he produced a tapered pin from his pocket.

"What's that?"

"A universal key. I got it during a raid on one of the cartels. It's programmable for numerical sequences, but it will fit an old-style, encrypted lock a datacache can't decode. There's got to be some kind of numerical assembly to get inside, and I thought, between you and this, we can access the vault. But Laurel," he raised an eyebrow, "you're pointing at a wall panel."

She shook her head. "No, that's it."

Helen tapped the panels. "There's no door."

"This is it." Laurel was determined; she was exactly where she needed to be. "The entrance is somewhere there."

For Laurel to say so, there definitely must be something. Harry couldn't see the entrance, not even when Laurel lifted a slender velvet drape to reveal a panelled wall behind, no different from the others.

"Try your key, Harry."

"On what? There's nothing there."

"There is, behind these panels."

Harry waved the spike around like a magic wand. Nothing.

"We must be missing something," he declared. Harry

was on edge, desperate to get out of the corridor. He thought he heard a noise and peered about them, but Helen laid her hand on his arm, reminding him that to all intents and purposes, they were invisible. Laurel didn't move. She seemed calm, and he took assurance from the two women that for now, at least, no-one knew they were there.

Laurel saw beyond the panelling. "This is it. I'm certain," she said, too immersed in the images playing out across her vision to nurse him through any fears of discovery. A sequence of symbols, unlike Seera or any language she'd come across since arriving, loomed and receded before her eyes. "The key won't work if it's calibrated for League mathematical sequences," she said, looking up at Harry. "These are glyphs."

Harry stared at the key, realising it was most likely useless. "How do you know?"

"I'm not sure. Can the key be modified? I could describe the forms to you."

"I can resequence the key, but I don't know if it'll run to glyphs."

"The sequence is changing as we speak. I'll describe the characters. As they change, program them into the key, it may be a code we can interpret."

Laurel described the characters to Harry, but they shifted too fast and even when she got inside his mind, he was too slow to record them. She took the key from him, and after a moment, a single sequence dropped into Laurel's mind. As it did, the door clicked open, and together, the three stepped behind the velvet drape into history.

CHAPTER EIGHT _

Stepping through the entrance to the vault, they waited as the panelled door closed silently behind them. The trio heard each other's breathing, even Helen's tummy rumbling, but all around, there was only darkness. For Harry, there was no way of knowing if they were on the edge of an abyss or landing, so he waited for Laurel to see if she would move forward. Even she hesitated, allowing the atmosphere to settle into her senses. Laurel sensed Helen's shielding no longer covered them, and she almost heard the grin in Helen's voice.

"It's not as if anyone can see us in this darkness! But that cloaking thing's handy, isn't it? I really could have used it a few times back on Earth if I'd known about it."

"I feel the same way about telepathy, Helen. What do you sense here?"

"Nothing, but that's not a surprise. It stinks!"

"My senses feel, I don't know…expectant." Laurel sniffed the air, ripe with the stench of stagnant water. "As if there's more here than we came to find."

The three blinked as an automated light belatedly responded to their presence.

"Thank God for that," Helen said, peering down a dimly lit stairwell. "I thought we were going to have to pick our way in the dark."

A noisy air recycling unit churned into life, covering them in dust particles. Helen covered her mouth and nose as they listened for any sign that the noise might have alerted the guards. But there was no other sound than that of the stale-smelling air recycler stirring up the atmosphere. Laurel led the way down the steps. As they went deeper, her sense of water flowing above them became stronger. At the bottom step, a passageway opened out before them.

"The tributary is right above us," Laurel said. "This is absolutely the place. Look, there's an entrance."

Harry felt around the walls, "It's the only one and not hidden like the entrance above."

It surprised them the door yielded no resistance. A simple sliding mechanism activated by a wave of the hand. No authorisation was requested, no imprint; it was simply unlocked.

"The Canon must be very confident of security down here," Helen said, flapping her hands at the even more concentrated dust that filled the air inside the vault. "God, this place is a mess. Doesn't the Canon have a cleaner?"

The vault was as Laurel had seen in her mind, untidy, dusty, ancient, but with perfectly preserved scrolls and bound volumes. Nowhere else since arriving had she seen books. A broad study table sat in the centre of the vault, with an equally sizeable old-style Visual Interface like the one at the fortress, only bigger, suspended above. Centuries of knowledge lay in random piles around the vault's rock floor; some appeared undisturbed by the ages. All they needed to do was locate the ones showing the most recent signs of use.

As she looked around, intrigued, the sense of rifling through an ancient resting place, a mausoleum, and scouring its mysteries came to Laurel. Still, she also felt like the archaeologist she once considered becoming, uncovering strange and forgotten artefacts. This place held the League's history; it was no wonder the residence above spoke so strongly to her.

The vault, not particularly large and constructed from natural rock, held indentations on the walls stuffed to bulging with datacaches, datafiles, old Visual Interfaces and texts. Many looked as if they'd been removed and thrust back in when the contents were not what the seeker desired. Laurel turned full circle while Harry and Helen waited, then Helen pointed out a handprint where someone had swiped a fine layer of dust from the centre table.

Harry followed Helen's gaze. "This is a fairly new platform. Maybe whoever installed it left that handprint?"

They knew that wasn't the case. Whoever was going through these archives was there recently, knew the access sequence and might return.

"You can do that shielding at any time, right?" Harry asked Helen, just to make sure.

"Mostly," Helen answered, making a non-committal shrug of one shoulder.

"Mostly?"

"I told you, I'm not reliable."

Laurel interrupted. "It wouldn't matter. There's barely

enough floor space for us, let alone anyone else. Remember, even if they can't see us, we are still solid; they'd know something is here."

"They might think it's a ghost and run screaming back up the steps!" Helen found the idea hilarious and dissolved into a fit of giggles.

Harry pursed his lips in disapproval. "I told you she wouldn't take this seriously."

"You are, aren't you, Helen?" Laurel defended her friend. She pushed Harry towards a high alcove set with stone ledges. "Let's get started."

But the piles of scrolls and books piled up on the ledges, and the datacaches balanced precariously one on top of the other seemed daunting. Helen grumbled that they should have brought dinner with them, and as they began their unearthing, Laurel agreed she had a point. This would take a long time.

"I didn't expect to find written works, Harry," Laurel said as she sifted through a pile of dusty tomes laid out on the floor. "They're like old books we have on Earth. I'm scared of touching anything in case it disintegrates."

"It'll just add to the dust," Harry said, patting his hands and sending a puff of dust into his face. "Don't worry, this place might look messy, but these vaults preserve pretty well. There's a few in the Constabulary Headquarters, they're like this but not so dusty, and that's probably to do with the age and disuse of this place." He took the volume from Laurel's hands. "Books do exist, but I've only ever seen one or two."

Clearly, the early craftsmen constructed the

bookbinding with an eye on preservation; a virtually invisible metal seam ran through each page, linking it to its cover. It was impressive workmanship. Laurel picked up another book and turned it this way and that to make sense of the pages, but the words meant nothing to her.

"Do you recognise the language, Harry?"

Harry placed the book back on its pile. "It's not written in Seera. It might be a language that predates."

"Can we activate the Visual Interface? There might be a catalogue of the files here."

Harry shook his head. "The guards might detect the signal, but—" his green eyes lit up, "I brought this…" Harry held up his still active military d-com. "I disabled the tracking component, so we can use it to try and translate earlier League dialects, but it will be limited. And we're going to have to search for the records ourselves."

First the datacache, then the translation key, now a d-com. "You have a problem returning government property, don't you, Harry?" Laurel grinned.

"Aren't you glad I do?"

With nothing left but to sift through the piles of scrolls, books and documents, Laurel got to work. Many of the scrolls were of a silken-type fabric, but it was the first time she'd seen anything that resembled paper. In each case, the handwriting was exquisite, and nothing appeared printed, making each edition an original. Harry started at the top of a stack of datafiles, applying his d-com to analyse the texts, but met with little success. Laurel sat on the floor and methodically worked through the scroll tubes lying around. Her mind told her the information was tantalisingly close, but after a while, she began to doubt and question that it was just her overwhelming desire for justice clouding her judgement. She leaned back her head and rotated her shoulders to ease the tension.

"This will take forever," she groaned as Helen flopped down beside her, her muscles also stiff from sitting on the hard floor. Harry was having none of it. He was not comfortable with the magnitude of his decision to help Laurel, but he was here now to find the evidence and find it he would. He was not in the mood for complaints.

"Well," he said, "we don't have forever, Laurel, just tonight, and we would be wise to be out of here by daybreak." Harry eyed the dusty handprint. Laurel knew he was uneasy, but she sensed no-one in the vicinity, and the festival was still in full swing. It didn't seem the guards had discovered the deactivated window either.

"I wonder what this is?" Harry held up a small rectangular stone. "I've never seen one of these."

Laurel scrambled to her feet. Helen stayed leaning against the wall, watching them. This enterprise was exciting at first, but with all these books and stuff, it had taken a decidedly dull turn.

"It was right at the back of the old data compilations," Harry said. "I don't think anyone has touched it in centuries." He held the stone up to the light. "The inscription looks ancient, definitely not Seera." Harry examined the stone, shaking his head, but Laurel noticed markings etched into the face of the stone. Her voice became an excited whisper.

"You're right. This *is* ancient, to my world as well." She

looked up at Harry, the amazing discovery making her heart pound. She ran shaking fingers over the markings. "This word here, it says 'Exodus'."

"Exodus?" Harry raised his eyebrows, waiting for her to explain.

"It means 'to leave'."

Helen appeared beside them; maybe this adventure was showing promise.

"Do you think this is what we're looking for?" Harry tapped the stone on the table, an established technique for activating out-of-date datafiles, but nothing happened. Acting on instinct, Laurel took the stone from him. "It's not a datafile. Here, let me see."

The instant it touched her, a vibration rang throughout her body, the stone warmed in her palm, and intuitively, she held the stone at arm's length. That same intuition told her Harry was right; this was from an age long preceding any history and technology known to him.

"I must have softened it for you!" Harry said quietly, awestruck as light and movement pulsed from the stone, forming itself into a holographic page covering two-thirds of one wall of the vault. They watched in amazement as the page became a cohesive document, with sections of text highlighted and neatly drawn illustrations set within the margins.

"It's like a star chart, but with text, almost like a giant datacache," Harry declared, moving through the manuscript, distorting the image. "But it's two-dimensional; there's no reverse or side angle. What could it be? It appears to be the only one here of this design."

Distracted by what she saw, Laurel took Harry's hand and drew him out of the document's field. The field stayed dim momentarily as it adapted from Harry's encroachment into its light, then the text once again formed a coherent pattern.

"It's probably a historical document and maybe only responds to whole souls," Laurel said, her voice becoming distant as the symbols leapt towards her, a few familiar, others vague.

"Whole souls aren't native to this universe." Harry liked the feeling of Laurel holding his hand, even though he realised she didn't realise she was still holding it. "Perhaps encrypted by a whole soul slave," he added helpfully. "Can you read it?"

Laurel turned to him, her eyes wide and her voice full of wonder. "As a matter of fact..."

Her response stunned Harry. Every day with Laurel brought surprises, but this day, in a vault on a planet in a universe not her own, she could understand an archaic document composed by a forgotten civilisation. His awe of the document paled beside his admiration for the woman standing before him, her brow creased in concentration. He couldn't stop looking at her.

She glanced up and caught him staring. "Harry, that writing here is like your written language."

He peered at the document. "Yes, but it's not modern era. Early era would make it five thousand or ten thousand years old, maybe more."

Laurel ran a finger down the holographic columns. "The body of text tells of a civilisation sold into servitude," she said slowly. "The language is very early Hebrew, I mean the earliest Hebrew, Paleo-Hebrew, I think, but I don't know enough to piece it together." She shook her head as she examined each column of text, feeling both privilege and reverence at the same time. She straightened and looked at Helen. "My God, whoever wrote this could have taken it from the Bible!"

Harry lifted his hands in confusion, seeking clarification from either of his female companions. "I'm lost. The Bible?"

"A book that forms the fundamental belief systems of Christian religions on Earth," Laurel told him, returning her attention to the document. "Even if we had the time, I can't translate the entire text. If I use the illustrations and the passages of language that survived into later Hebrew, it speaks of a race of people, delivered from their oppressor by a great leader; one who led them to a promised land."

Helen looked at the document, twisting her head to see if it read better on its side. "Does it say where this promised land is?"

"No. This part here looks like Seera, but I can't understand the words. Harry, can you translate?"

Harry patted his lips with the back of his fingers, deep in thought as he examined the file. Laurel fixed her thoughts on the text. Discovering this stone meant something.

Harry pointed out a single word. "That word is Canaa, and this five-petalled floral symbol here represents the Transcender."

"Canaa?" Laurel echoed. "There was a land called Canaan in the Middle East."

Harry looked blank. "I don't know about Earth, but here, it's a planet. Well, more a planetoid to be fair, in the Levent system. There are two lesser worlds, Canaa and Uruk; they come under the prefecture of Levent. They lie inside the League boundary and are both uninhabited. The Levent are friendly to the League and part of the treaty of planets but keep themselves to themselves. League researchers uncovered evidence of ancient civilisations and fragments of artefacts on both Canaa and Uruk, but also signs of destruction. They concluded the former inhabitants intended no-one would discover anything about them. That was a common assumption. If what you say is correct, I understand now."

"I could be wrong, Harry. Are we able to go to this system?"

"We can, but there's nothing to see by all accounts. It's impossible to establish a standard orbit; you must either land on Levent and shuttle across or park your ship and enter by axispod. I've never been there."

"And you say the flower symbol portrays the Transcender?"

"History depicts the Transcender as a flower that opens and closes."

"Ah," Laurel ran her finger over a series of markings. "These show the flower opening, and the text alongside speaks of enemies. It seems the Transcender allowed the oppressed people through, then closed on the people pursuing them."

"This must either be a legend," Harry said, "or someone witnessed these events."

"Does it say what transpired when they got through the Transcender?" Helen asked, without realising that someone would have to return to make a record to accomplish that.

Harry pointed that out to her, adding, "Not likely if they were fleeing."

The corners of Helen's mouth turned down; she hadn't thought of that, but Harry made good sense.

Lost in thought, Laurel wasn't listening. "The Bible has a similar story to this," she murmured after a moment.

Harry waited.

"The Bible account is of a sea parting to let the chosen people through," she told him, "And when their pursuers tried to follow, the sea closed in on them, leaving the chosen people to continue to freedom."

Harry had to agree; the two accounts were uncommonly similar.

"I think it's us!" Laurel whispered, feeling her breath catch in her throat.

"What do you mean?" Harry said.

Laurel jabbed a finger at the document. "I mean, I don't know for sure, but those chosen people might be us. Think about it: our abilities aren't evident on Earth, or only in a very mild form like in Xavier's case. What if whole souls aren't from Earth but here, and we didn't find freedom through the Transcender because the Soul Mongers found a way through and kept coming after us."

For Helen, what Laurel said was all too unbelievable. "But Darlen said only Soul Mongers could activate the Transcender."

Harry, who also found this unbelievable, still felt compelled to hear Laurel out.

"If you're right, Laurel, then the people from Canaa somehow discovered a way through." He ran his hand through his hair and sighed. "I can't believe your people originate from here. I'd hate to think this is another League secret."

"I doubt it." Laurel gave him a smug smile. "This piece of rock only opens to a whole soul. A whole soul wrote it for discovery by one of our kind."

Harry conceded she might have a point. "I'd like to know how it ended up here. I've never heard any stories about this, no myths, no legends. I'm sure the Levent Prefecture has no knowledge, either. Besides, they're quarter souls, and as far as I know, were never slaveholders."

Helen made a scoffing sound. "Quarter soul, half soul, that doesn't mean anything," she declared.

"What?" Harry grinned at her in bewilderment, but he caught Laurel's warning glance. Realising they knew something he didn't, he looked from one to the other. "Of course, it does," he said slowly.

"No, Harry," Laurel sighed at Helen for not picking a better time. "When we—" she indicated to Helen, "as whole souls' for want of a better description, look at someone, we perceive an aura. None of us can explain it, but the auras are either here—" she touched the area under her collarbone, "or near the heart. In the beginning, we believed the auras distinguished quarter souls from half souls because we were trying to match them up with your labels. I suppose it's reasonable to give each race a collective attribute, but individually, it's not the case."

Harry frowned and twisted his mouth one way as he digested Laurel's revelation, then the other as he registered his caution. "Why didn't you say something?" He would not accept any challenge to a long-held belief system without further information.

"We only had the Semevale couple and Corobetti out on the asteroid belt to compare at first," Laurel explained. "The aura misled us. As our skills increased, we saw other half souls at the bases on the asteroid and 100 moons. When we got to Semevale, we saw quarter souls among the enemy and half souls among the Semevalians, but of course, our understanding was skewed."

Harry kept a level gaze at Laurel. He needed more.

"I'll give you an example," she said. "The Gartryan prisoner on 100 moons, Collitt. Would you call him aggressive?"

Harry shook his head. Collitt was a decent man.

"He wasn't aggressive by nature," Laurel smiled, "he acted under orders, just like you did. There were many spiritual men among the enemy and a few aggressive people among the Semevalians."

Harry trusted Laurel, but quarter and half soul distinction was part of the Leagues and some of the independent systems core beliefs. He protested, but with perhaps less confidence than he would have a few moments before. "All Semevalians are quarter souls."

"Not so, Harry," Laurel said patiently. "I sensed the guard at the fortress. I gave him the handle of quarter soul because he was entirely at peace with himself. Let me tell you now; he didn't have an ounce of spirituality in him. When I look at you, I see the aura, but if I apply your criteria, you have both half and quarter soul attributes. And we only call ourselves 'whole souls' because you do. So, Helen is right; there's no real difference."

"I am a half soul," Harry said, pulling in a deep breath as he clung to his birthright, "born from a whole soul."

Laurel sighed. There wasn't time for this, but Harry wasn't going to let it drop. "I think the concept of quarter souls and half souls has its roots in the whole soul story," she said. "It led to that distinction. The aura is just energy we perceive. As far as we can tell, it means nothing, measures nothing, at least not that we know, and it certainly doesn't mean someone is necessarily aggressive or creative. You say spirituality defines the Semevalians, but I can assure you, it has nothing to do with their soul or the aura we perceive." She smiled slightly at his expression; he'd need further convincing. "I can see we just burst a bubble, but we won't tell, I promise."

Harry couldn't help his scepticism. He also knew no-one in the League would believe it either.

Laurel curled her fingers around the stone, and the document closed. "My world had a theory about left and right brain thinkers," she told him. "The left hemisphere of the brain contained logic, analytical skills, critical thinking and therefore gave rise to the notion of 'left-brain thinkers'. The right was for creativity, thoughtfulness, subjectivity. When the brain worked together, there came speech, emotion, but it was thought one side dominated. I'm not sure about the science, but it puts me in mind of your tradition."

"How do you sense other whole souls—each other?"

"Well, Harry, that's harder to explain." Laurel hadn't mentioned this even to the others. "You, and you too, Helen, might require a leap of faith."

Helen was mightily intrigued. "Meaning?"

"It's possible whole souls are a different species."

Harry didn't blink. What Laurel asked him to believe was almost as staggering as the revelation about half souls and quarter souls. "Are you suggesting you are more evolved?" he said.

Laurel hesitated; she just didn't know, so she gave a slight shrug. "I only know we don't have an aura, only non-whole souls have one, but we recognise each other nevertheless, just as I am certain we didn't originate on Earth. We are from this universe."

Harry found the only chair in the vault and plopped himself down with a breathy "Wow!". A veil of dust shrouded him as he pondered these last few minutes. He needed time to absorb all this new information, even though they still had work to do.

"We need to get on with what we came for," Laurel prompted. "Can you deal with your confusion later?"

Harry didn't move, although he did acknowledge her. "Yes, we should get on," he agreed as the cloud of dust settled on him like snow.

Laurel arched an eyebrow. "Harry, did you just say, 'wow'?"

Harry snorted. "I believe I did. It seemed relevant."

"You've been spending too much time with Helen;

now *move*."

Helen looked as if she had something to say but instead crossed her legs and sat on the ground. Without a word, she picked up a scroll and unwound it with unseeing eyes, her mind in a whirl of emotion as she considered which questions to ask, given this revelation. She didn't feel more evolved but wisely decided not to be the cause of any more diversions.

"I'd like to spend time with this rock," Laurel said, "maybe find out why we can go through the nebula, but not the Transcender, without being changed." She stuffed the rock inside her shirt.

Harry leapt out of the chair then, dust trailing behind him like a phantom in pursuit. "Laurel! What are you doing?"

"Stealing it," she replied. "It's no use to anyone else, and we're not here for this particular part of history, so I don't want to waste any more time." Laurel picked up on his uneasiness, casting her senses around again to see if anyone was likely to creep up on them and discover them not only guilty of treason but also theft of government records.

"Relax." She squeezed his arm. "I did some time with classical languages at university. I fancied myself as an archaeologist. I'd like to know what happened to this civilisation and why; this looks like a blend of several old languages. I need time to translate it, but even then, I can't be sure I'll be accurate enough to make complete sense of the manuscript. I'm just disappointed the Soul Mongers found a way to cross the Transcender and bring us back to slavery."

"I think the League has made amends by banning slavery," Harry offered.

Laurel sighed. "Maybe. Let's keep digging." She sat down beside Helen.

"Are you okay, Helen?"

"It's just what you said about us being different. I'm not different. I'm so ordinary; it's not true."

"How many humans do you know who can turn themselves invisible?"

Helen blinked slowly and nodded her head. "None, I guess."

"And does it feel strange to you?"

Helen tilted her head and frowned. "Not strange, exactly. I had to get used to it, like driving a new model of car, get a feel for the controls." Then she smiled, her blue eyes twinkling as she returned to the task at hand. "I guess it's part of who I am now."

Helen discovered the damning communique from the duke in a transcript on a modern datacache, complete with a reference from Canon Akkuh. It linked them to an old datacomp containing a sanitised version of the League acting as a saviour to the Inikamarans following a natural disaster. The data looked revised, but Harry assured Laurel the original data could never be entirely erased. Beside it, another datacomp claimed the League withdrew due to civil war, finally evacuating the inhabitants and annexing the planet. Both datacomps showed signs, to Harry's trained eye, not only of tampering but of having been opened within recent months.

"As I said, I've never heard of Inikamara," Harry said, his d-com highlighting the system in question, and sketching a pattern through the star chart. "The file gives these coordinates, but age can corrupt them. These are so old, and so much is missing."

"That's it!" Laurel exclaimed, pointing to a blue and green planet.

"No, that's Norik. It belongs to the Canonical family."

"How long have his people lived there?"

"Generations. A handful of them live in the Northern Hemisphere."

"And that's where Epo'negra is sourced," Laurel declared. "Does the Canon get compensated for supplying the mineral?"

"Well, yes…considerably." Harry blew out his breath as the pieces of the puzzle came together. "If the original data matches your claims, we can prove the Gartrya are the rightful owners of the mineral."

"More accurately, the Inikamarans. The Canonical family stole the planet and the mineral."

"This is unbelievable, Laurel." Harry's mind raced. This was huge. All along, he dreaded what might result if they proved Laurel's theory. What takes place next would have massive consequences for the League.

"To cut out a civilisation would have been a monumental undertaking and would have required a vast number of officials," he pointed out as his confidence in the League took a hammering.

"Yes, Harry," Laurel said, "but they were all

benefitting. On the learning program, our tutor told us the Canon nominates his or her successor."

"That's right, and then Congress agrees or disagrees."

"Do they often disagree?"

"Not that I know of," Harry shrugged, "but then, Canon Akkuh has been in power all my life, so I have no practical experience of the appointing process. I have heard it said that if a Canon has done a good job, then why question? This war was the only major incident in centuries."

"But he didn't choose to restore the Inikamaran's birthright. He ignored the duke's petition, and that action led to war and the deaths of thousands of Semevalians."

Harry's disappointment showed in his voice. "I didn't disbelieve you, Laurel, but to have this confirmation, see it with my own eyes, I almost can't believe it of him. The people of Gartrya—of Inikamara—must have restored to them what is rightfully theirs. Congress will have no choice."

CHAPTER NINE _

Through a trusted former associate in the Constabulary, Harry wasted no time recovering the original records from the datafiles, documenting the true fate of the Gartrya/Inikamarans. The Canonical family's ancient conspiracy, along with the communication from the Gartryan Duke, confirmed Canon Akkuh's deceit.

Not wishing to risk Harry and Helen further, Laurel insisted she present the evidence to Congressman Bela alone. Harry and Helen both took some convincing, feeling that as they were there from the start, it was only fair they see it through. Laurel was adamant. She had seen inside Congressman Bela's mind and knew she was free from guile or deception. She would listen, but if Laurel happened to be wrong about her, then only she would suffer the consequences. They all agreed Laurel shouldn't mention the stone that contained the history of the whole souls.

Congressman Bela welcomed Laurel to her chambers, delighted at the unexpected visit. She sat quietly, taking occasional deep breaths as Laurel recounted what she learned from Gabriel in the fortress about the history of the Gartrya/Inikamarans and the communication Canon

Akkuh hid from Congress. As she admitted her illegal entry to the archive, Laurel handed over the restored datafile containing the duke's communique, along with the doctored file. Congressman Bela not only listened but asked pointed questions Laurel knew were designed to assure the Congressman of the truth. Only when she satisfied herself that Laurel spoke in earnest did she examine the evidence.

As she read the damning datafile and the unaltered communication from the Duke, Congressman Bela's usual gentle features became grim, and Laurel felt the anger simmering below her composed exterior. Tempered with those emotions, Laurel also had a sense she would not like what Congressman Bela was about to say.

"What you've brought me," Congressman Bela said, closing the datacaches, "if revealed, represents the potential destabilisation of the League and the fall from grace of its most prestigious family—a family known for its fairness and leadership—and one who has governed the League for much of its existence." She took a seat at her desk and steepled her fingers as if in prayer. "Laurel, the Canonical family of Mentelci were instrumental in writing the League's laws and mandates since its foundation. Indeed, they were there at the very first word, the first whisper that this region of space needed unifying. Without their support, their honour, the League would not have flourished."

To enter the Congressman's mind to see what decision she would make screamed wrongness to Laurel, so she mustered the patience to wait. She felt Congressman Bela's eyes on her, and her empathic sense felt the waves of emotion and weight of these revelations wash to and fro in the Congressman's thoughts.

Congressman Bela didn't hurry and didn't move from her seat as she pondered her course of action. Laurel bowed her head, waiting. Minutes passed before she heard the swish of Congressman Bela's robe. She looked up to see the Congressman invite her to the window where the panoramic view of Mentelci's capital swept into the distance before them, the captivating Wind Field Sea, and from here, the majestic spectacle of the distant upper and lower Temples, with the Ponsecki river winding peacefully between them.

"Laurel," the Congressman placed her hand lightly on Laurel's shoulder. "When we, as leaders, are faced with a task such as this, we have to choose whether we should allow the loss of one person or destroy an empire that has stood for millennia."

"I've heard something similar before," Laurel said, remembering Gabriel's last words.

"And the choice was made?"

"Yes," Laurel said. "The choice was to lose the one person."

Congressman Bela nodded sagely. "Then you understand we must weigh up very carefully the damage this might do to the League."

"Canon Akkuh must answer for his crimes," Laurel said firmly, her hands clenching into fists.

Congressman Bela turned her gaze back to the view. "And he will," she answered calmly.

But her assurance was not enough for Laurel. "With respect, Congressman, I sense you will deal with him too gently. Not enough that he kept the secret of his family's genocide but was complicit in allowing a war that slaughtered thousands so that he could protect that secret. I was in that war," she said, fiercely. "I killed Gartryan men: men who had wives and children. I held—in my arms—" Laurel reached out her arms in supplication, "dying Semevalian men, women and children during battles! Congressman, you weren't there! I was!" Laurel fought the tears, but still, they came, made worse by the sorrow and understanding in the Congressman's eyes, but she didn't want to stop. She wanted the Congressman to know how it felt to be there, how *she* felt. "And the enemy bartered for weapons with a cannibal race, paying with the flesh of young girls," Laurel whispered, the horror of it all still so raw. "Canon Akkuh could have prevented it. He could have prevented it all." Laurel sniffed, drawing in a deep breath to compose herself.

"Yes." Congressman Bela gently wiped a tear from Laurel's cheek. "And that war is over, peace is restored, and the treaty planets no wiser as to the Canon's deceit."

"What about justice for the Semevalians? For the Inikamarans?" Laurel sat down, the fight fleeing from her bones.

Congressman Bela sat beside her. "Canon Akkuh must atone for his sins and the sins of his fathers," she said. "He will not implicate other family members, but I doubt his ancestors were ignorant of what went before. You speak of justice, but it's too late for the Semevalians. To tell them the Canon knew of their impending slaughter, what would that accomplish? Would it bring them peace, take away their sadness? Offer closure? They believe in the League; they uphold everything it stands for. Would you have me remove that faith now, when they are trying so hard to rebuild? Deal them yet another blow?" She squeezed Laurel's hand. "I have the authority to remove the President of the League from office if I can prove a crime."

"But you still won't tell the treaty planets why? Isn't that letting him get away with what he's done?"

"I know you want justice, my dear," Congressman Bela said, "but there is a wider view. If we stand down the Canon's family members in office, whether they knew of the Canon's crimes or not, we can appoint new council members in their stead. We can deal then with the Canonical family away from the scrutiny of League representatives. Of course, questions will be asked, but I am prepared to deal with that."

"And Congress won't hold him to account?"

"Not if we are to protect the integrity of the League. As to the separate matter of the Inikamara homeworld, we will honour the duchess's petition. She seeks a place in the League but has not made a specific appeal for her planet of origin. I will see to it that compensation for the mineral is removed from the favour of the Canonical family and restored directly to her people."

Laurel saw the wisdom in Congressman Bela's words. For herself, she would have screamed Canon Akkuh's crimes from the rooftops and, in doing so, would have added to the Semevalian's misery and undermined their faith in the League, perhaps the faith of many other systems as well. This approach meant Shumuyi'beh would be granted a new life here among the treaty planets with some of her ancient rights restored. It would be a positive outcome, provided Laurel never had to set eyes on Canon Akkuh again.

CHAPTER TEN _

As Congressman Bela predicted, any implied cooperation from the Canon's family could not be demonstrated. Privately disgraced, Canon Akkuh resigned his office on the pretext of ill-health and then entered self-imposed exile. His assets were confiscated, and Congressman Bela was elevated to High Chancellor. Due to the conspiracy's long-standing nature, a secret decree known only to the High Chancellor and her Congressmen was issued, denying any office to the Canon's immediate family while the League remained.

Following Canon Akkuh's dishonour, the Gartrya elected a leader, a man who fostered opposition to Shumuyi'beh's proposal to be admitted to the League, asserting that as the duke's daughter, she would lead them into further war. In the aftermath of the election and revelation of the Canon's crime, the League granted asylum to Shumuyi'beh and her followers. Numbering only around two hundred thousand, the League relocated the Gartrya to Danfos 4 at Shumuyi'beh's request. Congress offered Norik, but Shumuyi'beh felt it prudent to start anew, not try to pick up where her ancestors left off in a place where the ghosts of old bitterness rested. The Gartrya's new home became a treaty world, in a system that embraced them and one where the new duchess's people, with the League's help, would flourish. The League retained control of the valuable mineral on Norik, but compensation went to rebuilding a new society for Shumuyi'beh's people. And Laurel's illegal accessing of the archives went unrecorded.

After her visit to Congressman Bela and during the changes to the League hierarchy, Laurel finally found time to pick over the information on the stone file she took from the archive. She found the task painstakingly slow as she realised her enthusiasm for the project greatly outweighed her ability. Ancient languages, mainly Hebrew, had been more than a passing interest throughout her life. Still, a few semesters at university and night classes just didn't cut it for something like this. It called for an expert. And that wasn't her. She figured out parts of the symbolism and a few of the written entries; some made sense, but there was so much more she had to leave out. Days later, she'd only got a little further than she did on first viewing it in the archive. She knew the whole soul Canaanites possessed empathic and psychic skills, along with enhanced physical stamina and speed. Their world, Canaa, was accessible only to those with specialised awareness of a phenomenon called the "Tide of Gravity". The words "Soul Monger" leapt from the document, even though the entry that held those words contained no letters or symbols she recognised, and she was unable to gain any further knowledge about the Soul Monger's place in it all. She realized that in trying to decipher the meanings, her understanding came from empathy with the text, even though so much of its meaning mostly lay frustratingly beyond her grasp. With the sense she might be approaching the translation from a too-intellectual angle, Laurel tried to allow her empathic ability to make sense of the text but found English and Seeran language constructs cluttered her mind.

She made little headway. A few entries similar to Masoretic text raised her hopes, but again, she was no expert, and the phrases were fragmented and meaningless. She felt like a blind person trying to feel their way through a forest, needing someone to lead her, show her the way.

Pulling up an infochart, she looked for similar written languages, and although she went through thousands of different dialects, the infochart could not overlay similar constructs. In the end, Laurel resorted to recording each entry or symbol she believed she understood onto the infochart and copying the document into the database. In that way, she might find at least a rough translation sequence. As advanced as it was in this universe, it turned out that technology knew as little about the complexities of the stone's language as Laurel. She sat amongst the data floating around her head until she developed a massive headache. Irritated with the infocharts repeated requests for more specifics, she tried a datacache, less intrusive but similarly useless. Weariness and discouragement took over. She'd spent every spare moment poring over the document. How could she expect technology to translate a text that didn't even have an equivalent in the known universe simply by transferring a few symbols? She needed fresh air.

Laurel walked across the Galleria and took an auto

shuttle over the Wind Field Sea. The breeze blew the cobwebs and symbols from her brain, and she watched the little wiks in amongst the plants and trees below. She caught occasional glimpses of the small, long-beaked rodents that lived amongst the bushes; shy creatures who never left the sanctuary and lived on the abundant insect life in the Wind Field Sea. Laurel loved to do this; take time to enjoy the tranquillity of the sanctuary, and as her head filled with peace and silence, parts of the ancient texts became clear. Her mind snapped open. She requested a return journey and hurried back to her apartment. This time, she ignored the infochart and used only the stone, connecting her feelings directly with the texts. It wasn't much, but it was there. The superior abilities possessed by the Canaanites led to them becoming known as whole souls because they were considered "complete". In time, contrasts between societies brought about the terms "half soul" and "quarter soul". A brief entry added to the illustration of the five-petalled flower confirmed the Canaanites rose up and followed a leader into the Transcender. Again, Laurel tried to learn the fate of those left behind, and again, she found intellect got in the way. However, she did recognise a six-pointed star that assured her that somehow, this document had a definite link to the ancient Hebrew people.

Laurel concluded that if the League sent a civilisation from Inikamara into the nebula on several ships, then a good number would fit on a single vessel to enter the Transcender. Only one ship was mentioned in the Exodus document, reminding Laurel of yet another biblical story, Noah's Ark. She arranged a get-together so she could share what she had analysed with the others. The entire saga of the recovery of the information fascinated Eli, Marta, and Chloe, and they chided Laurel that she'd not let them be part of its discovery, but Helen found Laurel's interpretation as disturbing as she had in the archive.

"We escaped from slavery, and they brought us back," she said, making a face.

Laurel pointed to the spectacular, modern apartment she shared with Helen. "Look at this place, Helen. We're not slaves."

"No, we're war heroes!" Eli chuckled. "I've never felt so free!"

Harry was off-world, so Laurel invited Darlen to join them. Harry still hadn't warmed to the reformed Soul Monger despite his help during the war, but Laurel hoped Darlen might have some Soul Monger lore to add, seeing as the title was so clear to her from the document. She wondered if he may have some insight and perhaps fill in any gaps. Either way, Laurel doubted the picture would be accurate, but it was all she had. She sensed Darlen was unsure of his welcome, even when reassured Harry wouldn't be present. He was, after all, the one paid to steal the whole souls from Earth.

When he showed up, all eyes turned to him, and each jaw dropped in amazement. The matted hair gone, Darlen now sported a shiny bald head, and with his clean and tidy clothes, his droopy, sinister eyelid lifted surgically, and his chin free of stubble, Darlen cut a somewhat unexpectedly handsome and roguish figure. He still looked dangerous and reckless, but they all guessed that was a carefully cultivated persona. Or perhaps a barrier.

When she had their attention, Laurel recounted as far as she could the story carried in the stone. When she finished, their eyes shifted to Darlen as one, taking Laurel's thoughts as their own; that a Soul Monger was just as invested in the whole soul story and was more than just their value as slaves. He saw the shift. They didn't even need to ask.

"Ah," he said, nodding and looking down as if he would find his cue written in the carpet. "My turn."

They waited for him—five whole souls, able to interpret his every thought and intent, reaching out for an answer.

"There's not much, only myths, legends, all possibly changed through the centuries. Little more than stories."

No-one other than Soul Mongers knew the history, and Darlen felt a tug of disloyalty to his ancestors, but Laurel had unearthed that title in an ancient text. It was at least enough to form a suspicion, and she allowed the others to feel along with her. And here they were, Soul Monger and whole souls. The last of their kind, at least in this universe.

"Darlen?" Laurel encouraged him when he seemed reluctant to continue.

He looked up at her. "It would be quicker if you read my mind."

"It'd take her ages to sift through that brain of yours," Helen bellowed. "Spit it out!"

"Just tell us, Darlen," Eli said, settling himself in for a saga.

"Okay." Darlen slapped his hands on his knees. "I

don't know the origins of the people who put the whole soul society on Canaa, whether you are naturally occurring offspring or the result of experiments. They feared you; we know that much."

"Why?" Helen asked.

Darlen seemed to think the answer was obvious. "Because some of you can cast your spirit while remaining in the natural realm."

Laurel shook her head, puzzled. "I can't do that." She looked at the others as they shrugged a rumbling consensus of "me, either".

"One of you can." Darlen looked directly at Helen.

"The invisible thing?" Helen replied in disbelief.

Darlen nodded. "The Unseen. The Mantle. Call it what you will. It's spirit matter that forms this mantle, and it's how you preserved the children. The spirit of a whole soul is very powerful."

"I don't believe in spirits," Helen scoffed. "Only the ones in a bottle."

"Darlen," Laurel said. "Are you saying everyone has a spirit?"

"No. I'm saying that there's an essence that appears to dwell within whole souls. I have no idea if anyone else has it. I don't think so. Soul Mongers have a long-held belief that whole souls didn't begin as flesh and blood like the rest of us."

"That would be where the idea of souls came from on Earth." Eli sat forward, fascinated. "Christians believe we all have one."

"Laurel told us we might be a different form of human

to everyone else," Marta said. "And you are saying that whole souls are not just physical matter but some other kind of matter as well?"

Darlen pulled at his earlobe and frowned. "Look, I don't know the science behind it, but I'll tell you this for nothing, this spirit thing? It's natural, not supernatural."

None of what Darlen said persuaded Helen. "If the whole souls were so mighty, how come they let someone round them up?"

"I didn't create this history, Helen," Darlen said. "It was passed down through the Soul Mongers, possibly as a justification for our actions or maybe even as an explanation for them, I don't know which. Soul Monger lore tells us Canaa was home to a people of unique abilities."

"So, who feared them?" A mountain of questions formed in Helen's head. Even a glance from Chloe, who found Helen's rampant thoughts distracting, failed to settle her down.

"No idea," Darlen said. "Gods? Their parents? I don't know, but whoever put them there were referred to as the 'Masters'. When a child was born on Canaa, which wasn't often, the master's returned and took the child."

"Took it where?"

Darlen glared at Helen. "I'm trying to tell you, don't interrupt!" he growled. Helen fell to silence, but her anger at being shut down simmered. Darlen knew it but continued, "The masters were too afraid to kill the child, so they sold it as a slave on a far distant system, in the belief that if it was separated from other whole souls, its abilities wouldn't develop. In time, word reached the masters that some of the children they sold exhibited amazing talents as they grew, and the buyers wanted more of them."

"Did the people who bought the whole soul children eventually try to breed them?"

"Yes, Chloe, they did, and they failed. But they did learn that breeding a whole soul with half and quarter souls produced an ordinary child that could be used to manipulate the whole soul's obedience."

"And so, they developed a system of slavery." Laurel saw the pattern emerging.

"There was slavery before that," Darlen said, "but the practice of loyalty leverage using a child? That's only been since whole souls."

"You know this half soul, quarter soul thing is rubbish, don't you?" Helen cut in again, drawing an exasperated look from Darlen.

"What do you mean, rubbish?"

"Helen!" Laurel tried to shush Helen, but Harry knew; Darlen may as well know too.

"We realised after the first battle on Semevale," Laurel began, "that the distinction isn't as important as your societies believe. Individual cultures are labelled by birthright, even though you acknowledge that half souls are capable of spirituality and creativeness, and quarter souls capable of leadership, but the Semevalian's aren't exclusively quarter souls. And neither were the Gartryan exclusively half-souls. We don't yet understand why we can see a lucency below the throat on non-whole souls, but it's got nothing to do with how you compartmentalise the races."

Darlen chewed over the information for a few seconds. His planet, Caltobar, his people, bred only low life's, traders, and Soul Mongers. He waved away the information with a gesture. "I can't tell souls apart, anyway, other than by what society decrees."

"So, how did you know we were whole souls?" Laurel asked. "You said yourself, not everyone on Earth is a whole soul."

"Yes." Helen bounced in her seat, indignant, even though she'd long made her peace with living in a different universe. "How did you know? You could have taken someone who wasn't. How would that have worked out?"

"I'll leave that to the end of the story," Darlen answered with a grin. "When the masters' realised that mating between whole souls and non-whole souls produced an unexceptional child, they saw a way to breed the whole souls out of existence. A half soul male was secretly introduced into the whole soul society, possibly a master. He must have been a smooth-tongued bastard because somehow, he managed to talk a couple of whole soul women into bed. Each one produced a male child, which, in each case, was rejected by the mother. These children ended up sold too."

"Tell us more about the man they placed on the planet," Eli said. "The father of those children."

"The sole reason we suspect he wasn't like other humans is because of what his children became the forerunners of. His children didn't possess whole soul attributes, but the whole souls must have discerned something to reject them."

"How many of these children were born?" Eli asked.

"Not many. As far as I know, there was only one man given the task. He had a few women to persuade."

"Why didn't the whole souls' rebel?" Laurel said. "They were stronger, faster. Surely they could have easily overcome their oppressors?"

"Canaa is an odd planet, Laurel," Darlen said. "It's possible the masters selected it because of its specific gravity pull. Whole souls lose speed and physical strength there. On Canaa, you become more like us and less like yourselves."

"And the rejected children became Soul Mongers?" Marta so far had remained silent, but it seemed a reasonable observation and likewise, an appropriate place to comment.

Darlen nodded.

An unsavoury thought surfaced in Helen's mind, making Chloe, who caught the thought, giggle before she said it. "Does this mean you're possibly related to us?"

"Somewhere way back," Darlen said, smirking at Helen's sniffing disapproval. "But even if a Soul Monger impregnates a whole soul female, it's not guaranteed to produce one of my kind."

"We don't know what your kind is," Eli pointed out. "Not if your genes come from that unknown man?"

"That's about the size of it," Darlen inclined his head in agreement. "The only way of knowing if a child is a descendant is from the variance chamber or exposure to the Miran Forin nebula, or the Transcender."

Helen didn't put too fine a point on Darlen's origins. "So, you are the product of an act of rape by your father on a whole soul slave?"

And trust Darlen to be equally pragmatic in his response. "Yup."

"What happened to her?"

"You mean my mother? Helen, I have no idea, but it's why Soul Mongers impregnate whole soul females to continue the line. I've never produced a descendant child, so it stops with me."

"You have other children?"

"No."

"But you have taken whole souls from Earth before?"

"I did two runs with my father when I was very young, and another when I was in my late teens. That time, I collected a woman, but…" Darlen looked at Laurel, "she was already pregnant."

Marta cut in before Helen could say more. "A descendant of that unknown man led the Canaanites out of their slavery. How otherwise would the Transcender have opened? There must have been at least one mother who accepted her child. Or can whole souls open the Transcender?"

"No," Darlen shook his head, "only us, but we can't shield people from the nebula like you can, even though we can cross it."

"Who led them across the Transcender?" Eli asked. "And how did they know about it in the first place?"

"The story goes he was a youth," Darlen said, "and I know you're going to ask me how he managed to build a ship big enough to carry everyone. I don't know. I reckon they hijacked a master's ship. As to how the Transcender got discovered? I don't know that either."

"This story reminds me of Noah's Ark," Helen said.

"It does a bit," Darlen agreed. His dad brought back a Bible from Earth once, and Darlen read passages one time when he was dying of boredom. It didn't help.

"Someone tried to follow them into the Transcender as they fled," Laurel said, reminding them of the account in the Exodus document. "They were destroyed when the Transcender closed."

"Masters," Darlen said with absolute positivity. "The descendant would have survived the Transcender."

"I can't imagine an entire race of people disappearing without a trace."

"Laurel, I never said the masters were an entire race," Darlen said. "The story doesn't give specifics."

"So why can't we go back to Earth?" Helen looked at the others, but seeing their faces, mumbled, "Not that I want to."

"Soul Monger history tells us the first whole souls brought back didn't survive the return journey," Darlen told them. "An examination of the body revealed why; the whole soul's physiology had acclimated to life on their new planet. The Transcender rejected them."

"But you discovered a way to overcome that obstacle?"

"Yes, Laurel, an enzymatic process. We perfuse the whole soul's cellular structures with our own. As soon as the process—the Variance—is ended, the whole soul's Earth physiology reasserts itself, and they must purge the synthesised cells from their body."

"Is that what happened to the others you brought with us?" Laurel remembered Darlen telling the Canon the others didn't make it.

Darlen looked confused. "What others?" Then it dawned on him. "There were no others. I lied. I can only carry ten whole souls on my ship, and the League paid me for ten, but I could only pick up six. Earth's arrangement with time and space has become very unstable, and I didn't dare risk another visit. Plus, in all time periods from when I got you, Laurel, there's a lot of metalware in orbit. It's like a junkyard!"

Laurel was relieved to hear there weren't any deaths but wondered about the enzymatic perfusion process. "Where do you get the enzymes to place in whole souls?"

"Saliva, mostly," Darlen said, dragging a disgusted "ick" from Helen. "I can spit enough to service ten Variances."

Eli was unruffled by the revelation. He'd encountered all kinds of bodily fluids in prison. "Do you know how the youth who led them opened the Transcender?"

"Yes, Eli, because I can do it myself."

"Okay, I guess you're not going to tell us how. What was the youth's name?"

"Abram."

Like in the Old Testament, Laurel thought. Abram, from whom the Hebrew people descended. Darlen had no reason to lie; there'd be little point in a room full of telepaths, but although the account mirrored the Bible in so many ways, it was too mixed up.

Marta caught her views. "Maybe it's the Bible that's mixed up."

Laurel conceded that might be the case, but the

foundation of scriptural events appeared to have its roots in a distant universe.

"Darlen," Marta said suddenly. "I have never thanked you for bringing me here. I was contemplating suicide the day you took me." She leaned over and kissed him on the cheek. "You saved my life, and I will be eternally grateful."

Darlen's face became a portrait of surprise and embarrassment. "I've never been thanked for abducting someone," he said after shifting in his seat and taking a moment to find the right words. "I'm accustomed to being hated, abused, despised, but I've never earned anyone's gratitude."

At that, they each expressed their thanks, ignoring Darlen's awkwardness. Helen though, wasn't done with her questions.

"Now you're the blue-eyed boy," she declared, "tell us how you knew we were whole souls. Did you just take a chance?"

"No, Helen, it's like fishing. I chuck in a hook, and you take the bait. Only whole souls are drawn to me. In Xavier's case, he was waiting." Then Darlen grinned at Laurel, "And you? You'd been waiting a long time to come home."

Laurel was lost for words. Come home? Yes, home. Her experiences up to now, the war, for all its awfulness, the fortress, Gabriel. Somehow, she knew she was meant to be here. Not Earth. Never Earth. Her origins and ancestors lay elsewhere, and one day, she promised herself, she would find them.

CHAPTER ELEVEN _

A few years later, Laurel stepped from a medical transport into the cool just-before-dawn air, the sudden rush of cold igniting a memory of a similar morning in Chicago a long time ago and a whole universe away.

Following a nine-day journey from the Evegly system stuck in the medical frigate's cramped quarters, Laurel looked forward to a shower, a decent breakfast and kicking back for the rest of the day. Her apartment was far enough away from the med centre transport bay to give her reason to jog a little, to blow away the confinement of the ship and recycled air, and colleagues who talked too much about nothing in particular when she was too tired to listen. She'd arrived back a day earlier than expected and was due to begin several weeks of recreation, having been away from Mentelci for five months straight in Earth terms. Off-world assignments were a requirement for newly qualified physicians, and Laurel had gladly welcomed the opportunity to explore new worlds.

Laurel still had her old apartment that overlooked the Galleria and the Wind Field Sea, which ran through almost a third of the planet's inhabited territories, offering a sanctuary for wiks and the other diverse non-predatory wildlife native to Mentelci. The Protectorate forbade entering the sea without a conservation pass, but flying above it was a glorious experience. The colours, grasses, plants, and wildlife were so different from Earth and part of her heritage now.

Laurel's apartment building, raised from the ground by a central stand, gracefully swept skyward for one hundred and sixty storeys. Each apartment afforded unimpeded views and the most tasteful furnishings and modern technology, from ambient sensor lighting and window shades to visual communication from any planet in the League. Laurel lived on level twenty-six, perfect for a view across the sea and down to the vibrancy of the Galleria, with its markets and street performers, arched terraces housing funky cafes and saloons, and art galleries to rival anything on Earth. Marta lived on the floor below, in a West facing apartment, looking out over the bright lights and theatres of the Entertainment District, an area which at first reminded Laurel of Times Square, not in a melancholy, regretful way, but as something she might have once read about in a book.

The aroma of freshly baked delicacies wafted across the precinct as she jogged home. They smelled good, and her tummy rumbled. Often, when she was on her way home from the capital's medical facility so early in the morning, she diverted to that particular little patisserie for hot bread and Mentelci's equivalent of jammy preserves. But not today. Home beckoned. She'd been away so long, and there were decisions to be made. Now, finished with work for a while, she could give them the consideration they deserved.

She switched off her nostrils to the tantalising hot bread smell. That would have to wait.

Laurel didn't need keys or codes to access her apartment building. The concierge, a disembodied Artificial Intelligence, greeted her in an adolescent male voice.

"Good morning, Laurel. Long flight?"

Laurel sometimes slipped into English when her brain was soupy, and she answered,

"Long few months, Al."

Laurel had somewhat unoriginally named the Artificial Intelligence, Al, who allowed or disallowed entry according to security. It ensured each apartment floor had antigrav platform access and oversaw the delivery of residents and their guests safely to and from their apartments.

Al had elementary programming and did not need to measure time, but many residents here were medical people who made a habit of coming home very tired. Few spoke, but when they did, there was an occasional rambling, just like Laurel right now. Al swished an antigrav platform alongside his resident, and though he didn't need it, she thanked him as the platform conveyed her to her apartment.

Once inside, Laurel kicked off her shoes. A few lights came up to welcome her home, and the windows had switched from night mode. The luxurious carpet beneath her feet felt delicious, and the sense of being home was such, it was tempting to simply slip into her glorious high-tech bed and allow it to massage her to sleep.

Instead, she sensibly stripped out of her stale clothes and headed to the shower. In recent months, a couple of her postings were to places where water was too precious to use for washing, and she didn't feel clean using the oil pack substitutes, so running water over her body was heavenly. She closed her eyes. She'd make full use of the bed's massage function later, after breakfast.

Laurel took everything Mentelci offered for granted. Fresh water, fresh everything. Mentelci had no climate issues, no water or food shortages; simply, it was a utopia. She'd recently had ten weeks without respite on an outpost in the Rikonis system, where the citizens were quarantined after a spaceborne contagion hit and where water was recycled and foul-tasting. Unscrupulous dealers used the outpost, people "passing through," and others with good reason to go missing. No-one owned up to owning it, but it was inside League boundaries, and the nefarious goings-on largely got overlooked. The League appointed a rotating police presence, and Laurel bumped into Asde once or twice, but the outpost seemed to contain its activities.

From there, she worked on several other League planets. The diversity of ecosystems and climates were a wonder to Laurel. From sand-blown Krab with scattered cities and water rationing, to Macibib, green, lush, blue skies and the most annoying stinging insects, with tiny exoskeletons that defied any form of insect repellent and simply got up and flew away if you stepped on them.

It was from Macibib, Laurel's assignment schedule took her to Diriarden, a planet with vast volcanic regions and surprising, clear areas in deep valleys called Wellsprings, where humans lived in communities, farming small animals and vegetables for food. In the volcanic zones, they required breathing apparatus to protect against the toxic atmosphere, which seemed not to drift across the Wellsprings, allowing the air there always to remain sweet and fresh. League scientists had been allowed to study this phenomenon in the past but had never arrived at a conclusion.

Besides the Wellsprings, the planet was barely habitable, but it was near to the Miran Forin nebula, and that alone was enough to make Laurel smile. The sparse human communities of Diriarden made a pilgrimage every few years from the Wellsprings to pay homage to the mysterious wraiths who dwelt in the volcanic regions and who they believed were the spirits of their ancestors. Many pilgrims became weakened and damaged by the toxic atmosphere and appealed to the League to establish safe areas to offer respite from the poisonous gases. They rejected protective clothing, fearing it might form a barrier if a wraith wished to interact with their progeny. As far as Laurel could tell, no-one had ever encountered a wraith, even though many folk tales abounded within the communities. The League built several shelters for the Diriarden Valley Folk and provided a single resident physician at the shelters to offer care during the time of pilgrimage, with strict instructions not to interfere with the spiritual choices of the people.

The last of the pilgrims had descended back to their valleys, and Laurel's tour of duty on Diriarden neared its end. Each night, rather than gazing at the nebula through a shelter window, she donned a protective suit and went outside. The Valley Folk told her stories of the wraiths, how blessed they were that their ancestors' spirits watched over them from the mountains and that they too would join with them one day. None had ever seen a wraith, and several of Laurel's colleagues denied they existed, but the Valley Folk's earnestness appealed to Laurel, and she wondered if there was, at least on some level, some truth in what they told her.

The nebula was brilliant with light on that last night. Laurel knew that for others, the nebula was a still, ominous cloud that stood like a barrier at the edge of League space. To Laurel, it was a living thing, its movements gentle and calming, its rich, vibrant colours swaying and folding.

At first, she didn't register the whispering, even from inside her breathing suit. When the sound came again, she tore her gaze from the nebula. She looked about her; the mountain was dark with no natural light, just the faint glow from the shelter, and she was alone here, anyway. Perhaps a valley person had returned, but it didn't seem likely. She would have returned to the shelter to check, but on the black background of the mountain, a pale form uncurled before her, its wispy, floating filaments drifting into humanoid form, but small, no bigger than a child. It had no face nor definable features, and its lower limbs hovered a metre or so above the ground.

Laurel and the wraith gazed at each other for several moments. The wraith was the first sentient, non-human Laurel had physically encountered, and when it spoke, it spoke to Laurel's mind with no need for language or translation. The wraith had a message for the being known as a whole soul, visiting their homeworld, to be delivered on behalf of all Diri wraiths.

The wraith told her the story of The Children—the name they used for the Valley Folk. For what seemed like hours, it communicated with Laurel and not once did she feel fatigued or weary from standing. Other wraiths wafted in and out of her view, not speaking, not approaching her, and Laurel felt only curiosity from them. The wraith left her as the dusty volcanic dawn crept into the sky. For a long while, she didn't move. Since meeting Gabriel, she'd wondered at the origins of whole souls, but with her new life, her new responsibilities, she'd put the desire to learn more to the side. The encounter with the Diri wraith reignited that desire, and by the time she returned to Mentelci, she knew precisely her future path.

CHAPTER TWELVE _

The shower chased away some of Laurel's weariness, even though her mind wasn't quite stilled. The scent of the fresh bread stayed in her nostrils, making her stomach growl in anticipation of food. She didn't revise her plans for a day indoors, interspersed with lots of sleep, but first, she checked out a menu to order breakfast from one of the Providores in the art district. On Mentelci, food wasn't generally cooked in the home. If a dish purchased from a vendor or restaurant required heating, applying additive-specific mineral vapour warmed the food. Laurel had food preparation appliances, but she seldom used them. Takeaway food on Mentelci was healthy and well-prepared and way better than any of her own burnt offerings. When they shared this apartment, it dismayed Helen that food dispensers were solely starship commodities; she thought ordering a late-night snack for delivery lacked spontaneity.

Al buzzed up as Laurel dried her hair. "Laurel, two visitors. Security checked."

"Visitors?" Laurel wasn't expecting anyone. "Who are they, Al?"

A hologram of a man and woman flashed into view.

She didn't recognise the woman, but the man…

"Thank you, Al. Send them up."

Laurel closed her eyes, willing her heart to stop lurching about inside her chest. This visit was unexpected, although she knew it was a meeting she should have initiated years ago. Now, the universe had chosen the time and place. Laurel stood back from the door as the pair stepped from the platform. Taller than when she last saw him, with long, dark hair and grey eyes, Marcel was almost an exact likeness of Gabriel. She'd saved his life all those years ago, but they'd never even said one word to each other. But now, here he stood before her, that boy now a man.

"Marcel, what a surprise," Laurel smiled. "You are welcome to my home."

"Laurel, my lady." He performed a slight bow, then introduced the woman at his side. "May I present to you, my lady aunt, Duchess Shumuyi'beh of the Gartryan Nation."

Gabriel had never described Shumuyi'beh, only to say he always called her little sister because of her small stature, despite being two years older than he. The description was apt. The top of her head only reaching to Laurel's shoulder, Shumuyi'beh's wide brown eyes and broad, prominent nose were set in a perfect, pale complexion, her brow and nostrils pierced in the same manner as Gabriel's mother, with fine chains draping between each piercing. Soft, delicate, and lavishly embroidered and beaded sari-like drapes swathed her slight frame, and along with this picture of femininity, Laurel sensed an immense depth of character. And her smile was genuine.

"Duchess Shumuyi'beh. I am honoured."

Shumuyi'beh lifted Laurel's right hand and kissed the inside of her wrist. A respectful greeting, considering the duchess was the most senior figure of the Gartrya. Laurel invited them to be seated, requesting Al to order teas and refreshments. Marcel, so like Gabriel in his manner, assisted both women to their seats, bowing to his aunt when she permitted him also to be seated. Marcel turned to Laurel and smiled. Laurel had grieved for Gabriel, for the lost promise of what might have been, but it had taken longer for her to forgive herself for being part of his execution, a sorrow she hadn't shared, even with Helen.

"Please forgive our intrusion in your home," Shumuyi'beh said. "And also, if my speech falters. I am still unaccustomed to Seera. My lady mother taught me her forefathers' language, just as she taught my lord brother and my lord nephew. The only other language is that of my people, but I wish to become fluent in the League's culture. I know my lord brother was skilled in Seera and believed it a fine language."

"Yes, he was," Laurel said, remembering the first time she heard Gabriel speak. "I can converse in French, my lady, if you prefer, although I am a little out of practice."

Shumuyi'beh held up her hand. "Seera is acceptable. We come to pay our respects. If I may speak?"

Gabriel spoke so fondly of his sister. To meet her now, this diminutive woman who exuded strength and kindness brought Gabriel's memory closer. So often, Laurel regretted not contacting Marcel and Shumuyi'beh after the war, but she wasn't sure of her welcome as the one who supplied the instrument of Gabriel's death. She now regretted her hesitation.

"In a gesture of contrition towards Semevale," Shumuyi'beh began, "I offered agriculturalists and builders to restore the land ravaged by the war." She smiled and paused, dipping her head respectfully. "I realise the Semevalians have artisans, skilled at such restoration, but in a spirit of reconciliation, they accepted our offer. The Semevalian's most sacred citadel, violated by the duke, needed rebuilding. Gartryan workers cleared the lands in preparation, and deep within the ruins, they found a depository with the royal seal. I believe my lord brother intended it for transport, but perhaps the fortress was destroyed before he could make plans. We will never know his intentions. The depository contained four scrolls, cloth woven by our most gifted weavers—and inscribed—a skill taught to my lord brother and me by our lady mother. One scroll addressed the son of my brother—" the precious metals on her hand tinkled as she signalled to Marcel. "One, to myself and a third, to our lady mother."

Laurel held her breath. She knew for whom Gabriel intended the fourth.

"The final scroll, scripted in Seera." Shumuyi'beh took the small, ornate scroll from the pleats of her gown and offered it to Laurel. "My lord nephew informs me Laurel is the name of the woman who would have given her life to save him on Gartrya. He counsels me this manuscript is not for our eyes, that our purpose is to find you—she who is esteemed by my lord brother. The one who restored honour to our noble house."

For a moment, Laurel could only stare at the scroll in Shumuyi'beh's hand, then reaching out, she took it and tenderly turned the delicately embroidered fabric over several times in her hands, running a finger across the rich gold thread that wove an intricate pattern along each margin. Gabriel prepared this scroll for her, knowing they would never see each other again. Unlocking the clasp, the fabric gently unfurled at the touch of her fingers. Laurel had never seen Gabriel's handwriting, she didn't even know he could write, but his elegant, cursive script should not have surprised her. His voice came to her from the page, so near she imagined his soft breath against her cheek.

> *My beloved,*
> *The face of all the world is changed, I think*
> *since first I heard the footsteps of thy soul*
> *move still, oh, still, beside me.*
> *My love through eternity,*
> *Gabriel.*

She knew from where the lines came, one of the many sonnets by Elizabeth Browning he'd placed on the ancient VI panel for her to read. Instinctively, she held the fabric to her heart.

"When we met," Marcel said, his voice filled with gentleness and respect, "on the merchant's ship. I did not see then your importance to my lord father nor that you knew him. When the scroll was brought to us, I knew deep in my soul that the Laurel who saved me from Gartrya and the Laurel for whom my lord father prepared the scroll were the same." He tilted his head. "I desire to know what emotions are at play that you hold his words to your breast?"

"Umm," Laurel stumbled. "I was a prisoner at the fortress, Marcel. Your father and I became friends. Your father's actions and the efforts of your grandmother brought about the end of the war."

"And your actions, I think, mademoiselle." He gave her a broad smile, one without reproach of any kind. "You took the gems that destroyed the fortress." In his tone, she heard no accusation. He accepted that what needed to be done was done, and at the behest of his beloved lord father.

"It's strange to hear you speak Seera with a French accent," Laurel smiled back. "Your father did the same."

"He walks beside me, my lady Laurel."

Shumuyi'beh studied Laurel's face during the exchange with her nephew. Laurel sensed it and turned to her. "My lord brother," Shumuyi'beh lifted both bejewelled hands, "like you. A whole soul."

Shumuyi'beh may have known, guessed Gabriel's origins, but Marcel did not. His jaw dropped, and looking from Laurel to his aunt, confusion flushed his handsome face.

"My lord father was a prince!" He stood suddenly. His eyes bright with disbelief. "You are misled, my lady aunt. He was not a slave!"

Shumuyi'beh stayed calm while Marcel recovered himself. If he had any expectation to say more, to demand confirmation of such an allegation, Shumuyi'beh's face, set firm but gently determined, commanded him to silence.

"My lord nephew, be calm and sit." Shumuyi'beh waited while he complied, then reached out and placed her hand on Marcel's knee. "Your lord father could see and hear my thoughts and the thoughts of those who advised the duke. He saw things others could not; he understood where others struggled, and he remembered where other minds had long since clouded."

Marcel listened through his outrage at the revelation. He breathed deeply, occasionally glancing up at Laurel as if expecting her to interrupt, refute what his aunt said. But Laurel also sat quietly, allowing Shumuyi'beh to finally tell Marcel the truth.

"Your lord father uttered truths where many lied," she continued. "His skill in all these greater even than that of my lady mother. I prayed he would use this power to overthrow the duke—" she shifted an apologetic gaze to Laurel, "—who was not only the enemy of your people, my lady, but of his own."

Marcel struggled with this awful knowledge. If his father was a slave, then he was also born a slave. His thoughts were in turmoil. Did this mean his father and grandmother lied their way into acceptance into the royal household? How could such a thing come to pass? Whole soul slaves were a part of the past, practically a myth. His belief in his heritage blown apart, Laurel felt his bewilderment. He supposed himself of noble blood, and now, knowing this was not so, his faith in his family came crashing down like a landslide. He had not foreseen when he came here, to deliver this scroll to his saviour and father's most esteemed ally, he would hear such words. Had they been uttered by anyone other than his lady aunt, his duchess, he would have cried treason and executed the liar where he stood. Laurel saw it all and stepped softly into Marcel's mind, her presence there surprising him, but as she spoke, he became calm.

"Your father trusted me because I am a whole soul. He asked me to rescue you before the duke died, to save you. Your father was brave and noble; everything he did, he did for you and his people. Remember him that way."

At length, Marcel took a deep breath and closed his eyes. Then, gently blowing the air out through pursed lips in a gentle sigh, he said to Shumuyi'beh. "He was a prince. My father was a prince." Then to Laurel, "A prince to our people, and a prince to me."

Marcel's words hung in reverential silence before Shumuyi'beh spoke again. "I feared the duke. I feared the conviction of his beliefs, that he regarded his forefathers as weak. I learned our history, and I knew that his pride and arrogance would turn to vengeance one day. He planned to exploit the trader who arrived from across the nebula, but when our scientists exposed the lifeform's vulnerability, he believed the gods had smiled upon him."

"The Canon isn't without blame," Laurel pointed out.

Shumuyi'beh waved her hand in dismissal. "It is past. The League have now embraced those of us who wish to settle here, those who yearn to start anew. We have left behind the old ways and look now to the future. My lord brother was gentle and kind to all living things, and of men, the most good. Although I do not understand the forces that brought you and he together, his heart was full for the love of his family." She rose and again took Laurel's hand in hers and kissed the inside of Laurel's wrist. "That you found a place there honours our noble house."

Laurel was greatly moved by this great woman's gesture, her spirit one of grace and forgiveness and her voice trembled in response.

"I knew Gabriel for such a brief time, my lady," she said. "And he *was* good and kind; his thoughts always turned towards the safety of his family."

Shumuyi'beh's small smile showed her appreciation for Laurel's words. "Will you tell us something of my lord brother's last days? Those things of which you spoke together and how you were removed from the fortress?"

Laurel told Shumuyi'beh and Marcel of Gabriel's patience as he taught her his language, how she showed him the city of his mother's birth, led him along the streets she would have walked, all by telepathy. She had long since forgotten how she felt when she first was captured, her mistrust, her anger. All she remembered now was Gabriel's gentleness, love for his family, and desperate plan to save them, even if it meant sacrificing himself.

"He often spoke of you both and his mother," Laurel said, then paused. "I don't know your lady mother's name." She was sure Gabriel never mentioned it.

Shumuyi'beh curved her lips into a smile. "Ava. My lady mother's name was Ava."

Laurel stood in the doorway for a long while after she farewelled her visitors. She'd taken a moment to still herself after the shock of hearing Gabriel's mother's name. It was so unexpected. She still held the scroll in her hands, and running her fingers once more over the rich tapestry, she allowed the silk to fall open. She could almost believe she heard the softness of Gabriel's voice as she read the poem for the last time. After learning the truth about him, when he begged her for help to save his family and end the war, her fear and anger moved aside, their places taken by trust, understanding and purpose. Laurel would never deny the special place Gabriel held in her heart but knew many years would pass before there would be any reason to open the scroll again.

Laurel settled herself on the soft, comfortable, curved window couch, looking out over the Galleria towards the Wind Field Sea. Sleepy now and spent from the emotion of once more seeing Gabriel's son, she tucked her legs up under her and rested her head against the glass. She closed her eyes and allowed the early afternoon sun against her cheek to warm and comfort her while she slept.

CHAPTER THIRTEEN _

Laurel woke with a start. A rumble from her stomach reminded her she only nibbled at the refreshments served at Shumuyi'beh's and Marcel's visit. She pushed herself from her perch and massaged the base of her spine, numb from sitting in one position and stretched her stiff muscles. Rubbing her eyes, she reached absently for her civilian-issue d-com to message Al to send up sandwiches and fruit.

The day crossed into early evening, but Laurel barely noticed, caught up in memories and emotions. Usually, she loved to watch the pink and gold striated sky envelope the tops of the buildings as the sun dipped behind the mountains, the fog that stole across the Wind Field Sea and in the distance, the golden spires of the raised city of Cambor as they glinted in the evening sun. As each day drew to its close, a light mist surrounded the city's foundations, and it appeared as if floating. A sky-dwelling city—or as Helen, not given to romanticism once pointed out with characteristic dryness—an elaborate cake ornament.

"God, I love it here," Laurel said out loud as she gazed through the broad windows. And she did. To leave it now would prove to be a wrench because she loved Mentelci's evenings, its mornings, the times in between. She loved the sweet air, the breezes, loved to wonder at the splendid cities, and soak up the tranquillity of the Wind Field Seas.

Twilight turned quickly to night on Mentelci. As the pink and gold hues melted, the spectral curve of the near moon of Imbri morphed into translucent existence. In the far heavens, the second moon, Imbus, hung bathed in golden light. Watching the nightfall, Laurel recalled Darlen's words that she wanted to "come home". Increasingly now, she felt the need to know why.

More than four years had passed since the end of the war, and the others had found their happy endings. Eli, so passionate about his life in the guard, so determined this would be where his future lay, startled them all when he gave it up to marry Ru and become a fruit farmer on Leyis. Their second child was due any day. Marta gave away any idea of returning to the commercial world when High Chancellor Bela, with whom she had developed a deep friendship, recommended her for a seat on the Protectorate council. They rewarded Marta's dedication, integrity, and advocacy skills with rapid advancement through the ranks to become a junior congressman. Chloe grew into a beautiful, confident young woman, continuing with a career in the League Constabulary. She and Asde were as close as ever.

That only left Helen, who battled for so long with self-worth and depression, never finding her 'place' as the others had. Then two years ago, Laurel came home to their apartment and found a note:

"*Sorry, Laurel. Sorry, everyone,*
Gone with Darlen. He needs someone to look after him.

See you,
Love, Helen xx."

It was a shock. Darlen only visited infrequently, and usually, Helen erupted over some remark or other he'd made. There was no warning she would go off with him, or even that he'd ever invite her, but Helen had never fitted in on Mentelci, living her life vicariously through the ambition and accomplishments of her whole soul friends and later, immersing herself in supporting Laurel, who also struggled.

A year passed before Laurel saw her friend again. Helen had dyed her fringe white, and purple streaks punctuated her straight, shoulder-length black hair. She no longer sported her trademark fancy manicured fingernails, and she'd adopted the garb of a trader, messy and funky at the same time. Helen described herself as "shabby chic", and Laurel found the metaphor apt.

Yes, Helen, Marta, Eli, Chloe's lives were on track. Happy and fulfilled. That only left Laurel.

The window blind clicked into morning mode. Blinking, Laurel got to her feet, almost pushing her hand into her sandwich and fruit which lay untouched on the couch. Groggy from sleeping all night in a sitting position, she softened her body and sharpened her mind in the shower, then slipped into one of her few dresses, a simple, velvety gown that reached to the floor, in the fashion the green-tinged Mentelci women favoured. Laurel released her hair from its constraints and shook her head, allowing the profusion of curls to fall where they fancied. Slipping into outdoor shoes, she called for a platform.

Laurel stepped into the crisp morning air. This time she made her way to the far side of the Galleria, toward that tantalising scent of baking bread. It was a source of amusement to Laurel that on almost every settled world she'd visited since arriving here, and on practically every trading post or station, there was a local version of a café or restaurant. 'Foodery' was the best translation from Seera, with their creations of delicacies, drinks, cakes, and native foodstuffs. The creature comforts of mortals in any universe, Laurel happily and gratefully observed, were not so different.

She found a terrace table outside the foodery, with a view over the Wind Field Sea. There was still enough of the night left that the mist hadn't completely rolled away, creating a mysterious carpet in the well of the Wind Field Sea. Imbus and Imbri had slipped out of sight. The waiter served her usual bread and preserves and tea, as two tiny wiks, followed by an adult wik, flew overhead as they made their way into the city to look for plants and trees. One baby wik diverted and hovered above her; a phenomenon, even though wiks were inquisitive, they seldom ever made contact. But they always did with Laurel.

Laurel dipped the tip of her finger into the sticky preserve. The baby wik spun wildly in excitement, making tiny sucking noises as it savoured the jam's sweetness. The second baby came for its share while the adult wik hovered nearby. When both babies had tasted the jam, they skimmed past Laurel's face in a "thank you" gesture, then went spinning away to their mother. Or the father. There was no way of telling. Baby wiks were common here; the Wind

Field Sea had a nursery somewhere amongst the rocks and dense woodland.

Laurel pressed her comms and sent the five messages she'd composed while on the medical transport she left the day before. It seemed so much longer than just yesterday. Seconds later, her comms buzzed replies. One message made her smile, and within minutes, she spotted Harry across the Galleria, heading from the direction of his apartment block. Beside him, gripping his hand, a dark-haired child, a little over four years old, with violet eyes, who so favoured her father in looks. She squealed with delight when she saw Laurel, breaking free from Harry and dashing across the pavement at a speed known only to a whole soul child.

"Mommy," the little girl squealed as she ran. "Look, Howie, it's Mommy!"

CHAPTER FOURTEEN _

Gabriel and Laurel had spent those last few precious hours at the fortress in each other's arms. Even though mindful of the terrible fate that might befall them if the merchant did not hear the message, Laurel felt strangely at peace so close to the man who had been her jailer. She'd come to understand him, to understand his suffering and the awful life that had been his, a life that if the merchant came for her, and the plan successful, would be sacrificed for love of his family.

When at last Gabriel slept, his breathing soft against her hair, Laurel wondered at the bonds that drew one person to another. Making love with him went beyond physical pleasure, beyond empathy, and somehow Laurel knew their shared heritage, the origins of the whole souls, drew on something far more profound. She knew he felt it too and that it was as much a mystery to him as it was to her.

Wrapped in his arms and unwilling to move for fear of disturbing the beauty of the moment, Laurel watched a tiny point of purple light appear over Gabriel's right temple. The light trickled along his cheek and onto his shoulder, tracing a delicate trail along his arm before dipping down between them. For the briefest moment, it hovered in the well between their bodies, then rose onto Laurel's waist, making its way down to her thigh before vanishing.

"What are we seeing?" Gabriel had stirred as the light materialised and made its radiant other-worldly journey between them.

Laurel remembered smiling at him in bewilderment.

"Is this something from your world?" he'd asked, gently kissing her forehead. "When two people share their bodies?"

"I'm not sure Earth is my world, Gabriel," she'd murmured, not suspecting then how prophetic her words would become in time. She'd rested her cheek against his chest. "It's not yours either." She believed then if she survived the war, she would one day seek the truth about whole souls.

And then their final moments came. *Wake up, Laurel. You must leave!* Gabriel had startled her from sleep, his voice urgent. She remembered clearly how she responded that night, dazed from sleep, trying to follow his orders to dress, to hurry, and that there was no time.

She ran through the catacombs, her hand in his as he dragged her along, dread rising in her as the awful realisation this might be the last time she would see him dawned on her. Then she saw the woman who would martyr herself for her people, and Helen, pulling her onto Darlen's ship. It all happened so fast—no parting words, no broken kiss to imprint forever on her lips as Helen dragged her from him onto the ramp. She never even saw him walk away. Then to be confronted by the Soul Monger, to once again go into battle, only to fail to save Gabriel's mother. In quiet moments, she grieved, but only for a while. Gabriel wanted freedom for his mother and son, and he would not have chosen for her to become a slave to her sadness or failure. And he never got to know the legacy he left behind.

The little girl threw herself into Laurel's arms, giggling as she tried to dust her mother's hands from tousling the child's curly hair, one of the few things Ava inherited from her mother. In most other ways, she resembled Gabriel, including his eyes. Laurel kissed the little face repeatedly until the child begged her to sit down so she might climb onto her lap.

"We been to Granpa's," she said, her little face wreathed in happiness at seeing her mother. "Howie took me, and we went on Auntie Helen's spaceship, and I sat on Mer's lap. I drew on his face, and he let me drive. I drove all the way home!"

Laurel laughed, hugging her little girl close, breathing in her scent. She'd been away far too long. "What a big girl. Well done." There followed an animated discourse on the visit to Harry's father, a polishing spree on Mer, and an animal sanctuary on a planet called "Upry", which neither Harry nor Laurel had ever heard of, but their response mattered little in the grand scheme of getting the tale told.

"I going to get a stick," the little girl announced, her greeting and report on recent activities to her mother completed. She jumped from Laurel's lap and headed into the café, climbing up onto a high stool to repeat the entire narrative to the steward.

Ava was a favourite here, always scoring a treat when she visited, and she'd been away a few weeks, so she had a lot to tell the steward. Already, she showed signs of her whole soul origins, often speaking to Laurel without words. Laurel gently reminded her that not everyone communicated that way, but Harry's elderly father, now frighteningly frail but whose telepathic skills remained sharp, indulged the child he adored, and the two engaged in all kinds of secret conversations. But it served to remind Laurel that Ava was alone in her generation of whole souls, and as a mother, that knowledge worried and saddened her.

Harry waited until Ava finished greeting her mother before leaning down and kissing Laurel. He grinned at the sparkles in her hair.

"Looks like you had a close encounter with a wik."

"One stopped by for some jam," she laughed, brushing the glittery pollen from her hair. He reached out to help, lovingly twirling a fair curl in his fingers.

Laurel recalled the first time Harry kissed her while he was still recovering from his injuries and his desperate hurt when she told him she was pregnant, only weeks after taking the petition for Canon Akkuh's removal to the Protectorate. Her pregnancy was as much a surprise to her as it was to him, and she could only watch as his heart broke, at first unable to comprehend what she was saying. Trying to offer comfort, she stepped inside his mind, and in so doing, endured the pain of heartbreak with him. Laurel tried to explain about Gabriel while lamely trying to offer friendship, but Harry loved her and hoped that she would come to love him in time. It was too painful; he couldn't acknowledge her apologies, nor her explanations. Within days, Harry transferred to Semevale 8 to assist in the post-war restructuring of the medical facilities. He didn't even say goodbye.

Laurel missed him. She suspended her medical training for the last two months of the pregnancy, and Helen was her support when the baby came. Throughout the pregnancy, Laurel knew the baby would be a girl and that she would call her Ava, not knowing it was also Gabriel's mother's name. Chloe and Asde saw Harry when their duties took them near Semevale 8; they reported he didn't seem happy, but he never asked after Laurel, even when they told him the baby had arrived.

Harry returned to Mentelci when Ava was nine months old, to transition through to an independent system. Laurel resumed her medical training when she felt she could leave Ava, and a delighted Helen took over as a nanny to the baby. Helen met Harry unexpectedly at the medical facility, and in her no-nonsense way, encouraged, or rather insisted, he visited.

Harry hadn't lasted long on Semevale 8. His feelings for Laurel got in the way of everything he tried to do, despite trying to lose himself in all manner of amusements in some shady places in a few far-flung systems. Seeing Laurel again at Helen's insistence was agony to him, and then, Harry kicked himself mentally for caving into Helen's bossiness. He wasn't over Laurel—that much was clear—he always thought her beautiful, even when he first saw her with shorn hair, her amber eyes angry and defiant. Now, she was lovelier than ever. Motherhood had made those curves curvier, her skin glowed, and her hair now a mass of curls that reached almost to her waist. To him, she was the same vision she had always been. Harry could never hide his thoughts from Laurel, and after all the time that had passed, she still felt his pain. She'd looked at Helen reproachfully.

'This wasn't a good idea.'

But Helen either couldn't, or she pretended not to hear her.

Ava, though, was delighted to have a new person visit, to show off to. The grownups awkwardness was of no interest to a curious child, right at the stage of hoisting herself up on furniture and any available legs. The little mite shuffled over to Harry and climbed up the side of his seat, rocking herself for balance and flashing him an irresistibly toothy grin. Harry made casual conversation with Helen while still wondering what in heavens name possessed him to come, all the while paying no attention to the determined little girl clutching at his pants.

It was then Ava uttered her first word, after insisting Harry look at her, giving him several hard pats to the knee. "Howie," she said loudly, not able to get the "r" sound around her little tongue. Then she gnashed together her half a dozen teeth and wrinkled up her nose. "Howie," she repeated.

It stunned Helen and Laurel. And Harry? Well, Harry was lost.

Following Ava's claiming of Harry, he resumed his post at the medical facility on Mentelci a few months before Helen left with Darlen. Harry shared Ava's care with the medical centre creche so Laurel could complete her medical studies. In no time, Ava and Harry formed a mutual fan club. She adored him, and he adored her.

On one of the few evenings they were off duty together, Laurel told Harry as much of the story of her time in the fortress as she felt he needed to know. He stayed with her that night and many nights afterwards. She grew to love waking up to him sleeping beside her when work commitments allowed. When she was off-world or working long shifts, he would take Ava to his father's home or to see Helen and Darlen. Harry's dad became a surrogate grandfather, his home a perfect place for a tomboy. And through all of it, although Laurel hadn't expected to love Harry, she did, unreservedly.

"I didn't expect you till later," Harry grinned. "You should have called; we got back late last night."

"I was a day early, but there were a few things I needed to deal with. I didn't want to drag Ava back if you were out and about."

"What things did you need to deal with?" The steward arrived and arranged a few items she ordered earlier on the table in front of them. Harry eyed the spread, his attention diverted. Mentelcian's didn't use alcohol to celebrate. Their cuisine sported very particular delicacies, so Harry raised a quizzical, rather suspicious eyebrow.

"Hot SperelySour sticks with glaze? What are we celebrating?"

He looked over to the café interior where Ava had her

mouth wrapped around a SperelySour stick of her own, the syrup running unabated down her chin as she tried to chatter through the steam and sweetness.

Laurel smiled, following his gaze. "I just thought it would be nice. A welcome back treat."

"Nice? I feel truly special." Harry picked up a sweet dumpling and pulled it off the stick. It was too hot, and he tossed it from hand to hand with several exclamations of, "Ow, ow, ow." She'd learned that about him when the seriousness of war was behind them. He was a clown. He could also paint, play several musical instruments, sing beautifully and dance like a professional, much to Helen's delight. He pulled a face as he tossed the dumpling back into the syrup.

"Is this the sweetener before you say we aren't going to Khobe 27 tomorrow?" He gave her an accusing stare, believing he'd uncovered a conspiracy or bribe. "Helen and Darlen are coming back in the morning to pick up Ava for a couple of days."

Laurel leaned forward. Taking his hand, she laced her fingers through his, sticky from the syrup. Keeping her voice low, delivering what she knew would be unwelcome news.

"Would you mind if we don't go to Khobe 27?"

Harry looked down at their fingers, intertwined. He dabbed absently at a drip of syrup with his other hand. "You do know I mean the Khobe 27 where we get to swim—naked. Eat—naked, walk around naked and where I can lust after you all day? Where the sun is warm, the evenings balmy—" he didn't stop for breath but sighed before continuing, "No work, no emergencies and the only thing spying on us when we make love are a few wiks. Not forgetting I've only seen you, very briefly, twice in five months." He shrugged. "Why would I mind if we don't go?"

Laurel knew he was disappointed, but he would also understand her very good reasons not to go to Khobe 27, which was indeed the paradise he described, but she believed her plans would appeal more once she convinced him.

"That's just it, Harry. I don't want to leave Ava again." Laurel hesitated. That was the truth. Her plans meant she would never be separated from either Harry or Ava. Now she had to sell those plans to him, tell him about the encounter with the Diri wraith. "Besides, I have a better idea."

"No, you don't," he declared, disentangling his fingers from hers and prodding the syrup-soaked dumpling with a stick.

"Yes, I do. I just don't know how you'll take it."

Harry stuffed half a dumpling in his mouth. "Go on. Hit me."

Harry had no idea what was coming. He wasn't even taking it that seriously, assuming she'd chosen another destination for their recess, probably somewhere more suitable so Ava could come along. The syrup scorched his tongue, and Harry busily fanned his mouth while he waited for her answer.

"How would you feel about giving up your apartment?"

Harry swallowed, the rest of the half-eaten dumpling

staying in his fingers until he saw the syrup dripping down his arm. He abandoned the messy cake to the table.

"What?" His expression was pure disbelief.

"I said…"

"I know what you said. You want me to move in with you and Ava?"

"No, that's not it." Laurel shook her head, ignoring the hopeful images that arose in Harry's mind. "I'm giving up my apartment too." Laurel looked over to where Ava was bending the steward's ear with tales of her Granpa's cabin by the lake. "We can all be together, just not here, just not on Mentelci."

Harry sat back. His sense of fun now taking a back seat. A moment ago, he was joking about Khobe 27; now, he saw Laurel had something serious on her mind. Knowing Laurel, it would likely be something world changing. "You're not making sense, Laurel."

"Harry," Laurel drew a deep breath. "You've heard of the wraiths of Diriarden?"

Harry didn't answer. He didn't need to; everyone had heard of them. Their existence was well-documented, unverifiable, but he had no reason to dispute what the human population of Diriarden recorded.

"One visited me while I was there."

Harry remained impassive. "Why?"

"The wraiths are eternal but tied to their environment," Laurel told him, "And they have memories that go back for centuries. But they are also telepathic. The wraith told me a vessel came from the nebula and established an orbit around Diriarden, centuries ago, before the League. The wraiths were curious about the ship. They'd seen others pass through their system but none so close, nor had they ever encountered any other lifeform before, probably because so much of their planet is inhospitable. The ship's orbit was low, and the wraiths went to investigate."

Harry waited. If the wraiths existed and had a message to deliver, it would be to Laurel. But Laurel gave him no time to consider. "The wraith described a massive rectangular vessel, one-third of which contained 'sleeping people'. The wraith said these people were empaths. The next third contained children and human adults, and the final third contained a humanoid race. From what the wraith described; these humanoids observed strict adherence to worship. The wraith said the ship had a strange, 'elik', their word for spirit." Harry opened his mouth to ask a question, but there was too much still to tell him, and Laurel held up her hand.

"No, sshh. The ship stayed in orbit for several days; then a pod dropped towards the planet before leaving orbit. The pod contained six children—two boys and four girls. The boys communicated telepathically with the wraiths, who lead them to food, water, and shelter in the Wellspring areas of Diriarden. Those two boys and the girls are the ancestors of what the wraiths call the 'Children'."

"I see, and who we call 'Valley Folk'. Are you saying this incident was the advent of the whole souls?"

Laurel nodded. "Partly. The ship came from the nebula. According to the wraith, the children stated they were born on the ship. The wraith struggled with the concept of time, but from what it has learned since Diriarden's involvement with the League, the boys would have been about ten. Wherever these beings came from, their journey took them more than ten years. Another thing, the wraith referred to the humanoids as Farisee. When they looked into their minds, they saw compassion for the 'sleeping people', but they feared them as well."

"How did they round up whole souls? Couldn't have been easy."

"Same as your people did, I guess," Laurel said. "Leverage. Or they have some other kind of control. According to the wraith, the Farisee kept the little ones separate."

"Did the wraith offer any clues as to where the whole souls originate?"

"Ah, that's the interesting part—" Laurel's amber eyes lit up, "—the Farisee aren't telepathic. You know, I suspect the whole souls are naturally occurring, a rapid evolutionary development, either that, or they're from another planet. But that's just my theory. The wraiths were unable to read the Farisees' minds with any great degree of accuracy."

"So, the Farisee took the whole souls to Canaa, and from there began the entire whole soul slave era?" Harry said.

"Yes. I suppose. The Farisee must be the masters."

"Were you able to extrapolate from which part of the nebula the ship emerged?"

"Harry, this is an ancient story related to me by a phantom that can't tell the time. I know only that it came from beyond the nebula. If that boy was born on the ship, it might take us a lifetime to find out where."

"Us?" Harry should have known. "This is your better idea?"

Harry didn't know what to feel. His plans for being with Laurel didn't involve hiking around the galaxy, searching for a nebulous race that may not welcome them with open arms. He'd planned a cosy life, the three of them once Laurel agreed to move in together, taking vacations on the more hospitable planets. And there was his dad to consider. He would be gone soon.

Laurel saw it all and understood. She offered an uncertain future, and if he refused to come with her, it would be a lonely one, but she had to do this. The time was now. When Harry didn't respond and just continued to gaze down at his hand, she resisted the temptation to look at what was going on in his mind.

"Harry?" she coaxed him for a reply.

"We'll need a ship," he sighed. He would grant anything Laurel asked of him.

"We've got one," Laurel said brightly. "Helen and Darlen are coming with us. She messaged me just before you arrived here. I told the others, but they elected not to come."

Harry didn't look happy. "Darlen and me shipmates?

"You'll be fine."

"It'll be cramped, five of us on that freighter."

Laurel patted his arm. "It's a tried and tested ship, and the wars been over a long time, Harry. If you've got a problem with Darlen, you'll be the only one fighting." She smiled. "You'll make it work. Ava is the last whole soul. You know that ever since I arrived here, I've been drawn to the nebula. Some of the answers lie there, and I need to know why. I owe it to Ava to find out what whole souls are, and..." she trailed off.

"And?" Harry prompted.

"If there are any more like her, like us."

Harry looked out to the Wind Field Sea, and Laurel tried not to see his second thoughts, his weakness in resisting her when she made up her mind. She knew that loving her and loving her child was one thing, but asking him to give up his home, maybe a little too much. Indecision and questioning finally gave way to acceptance and resolve. He had to do this willingly, not just to appease her. Gently, he picked up her hand and kissed her fingers. He smiled. "You seem to have all your ducks in a row."

"You sound like Helen," Laurel smiled back.

"Well, she has a saying for almost every occasion." He laughed a little. "Laurel, do you genuinely believe you can stand the thought of bringing up Ava on a trader's ship and living with Helen and Darlen? To never see Mentelci again? I know you love it here."

Laurel had thought of nothing else since her encounter with the wraith.

"It's not the future I planned with you, Laurel, I'll be honest," Harry said, pursing his lips together for a moment, "but it is a future I can accept."

Laurel jumped up and planted noisy kisses over his cheek over and over in gratitude. "We need one detour before we go," she declared. "Shumuyi'beh and Marcel came to visit me yesterday, and I told them about Ava. She should meet her half-brother."

Harry twisted around in his seat. "Wait! What? The duchess came to see you?"

Laurel sat down, bringing her excitement under control. "I should have contacted Marcel to tell him he had a half-sister."

"But you felt you'd let too much time pass. And I said it's never too late," he reminded her.

Laurel smiled, her heart melting at the gentleness in his voice. "You were right, of course. They had a scroll they needed to deliver. It was from Gabriel and addressed to me."

"What was in it?"

"A poem." Laurel would have said more, but Harry stopped her by kissing her gently.

"Precious memories to keep close to your heart," he said softly, his eyes meeting hers, then she ended the tender moment by resuming her noisy kisses all over his face.

The steward cleaned the sticky syrup from Ava's face and fingers before returning her to Laurel's lap. "What are you talking about, Mommy?" she said, patting Laurel's face.

"We thought we'd go on a trip with Auntie Helen and Darlen. A long, long trip."

"Are you coming, Howie?" Ava asked, wriggling around to face Harry.

"We're all going, sweetheart. We're going to find out why you and your mommy are so special."

"Is that right, Mommy?" Ava wriggled back to look at Laurel. "Are we going 'sploring?"

"Yes, Ava," Laurel said. "We're going exploring."

CHAPTER FIFTEEN _

"Auntie Helen, we're going 'sploring on your ship. We're going today!" Ava, barely able to contain her excitement, danced around Helen, who responded by lifting the small child into her arms.

"I know, right? How lucky are we? We're gonna go through the nebula and look at all the colours!" Ava wriggled to get free, so Helen plonked her down, and the little girl ran to Darlen to give him the lowdown.

"Are you ready for this?" Helen asked Laurel, catching a stray, telepathic hint of hesitation.

"Ready as I'll ever be." Laurel lowered her voice. She had felt a stirring of last-minute doubts. "Helen, we're not making a mistake, are we?"

"It's a bit late to be having second thoughts."

"Not second thoughts, but after the initial shock of Harry agreeing, I thought about, you know—," Laurel dipped a glance towards Darlen and pulled a face, "—their relationship. It's not exactly close."

"And that's down to Harry," Helen grinned. "Darlen's changed, and Harry needs to see it. Jeez, you'd have thought him helping the League win the war would have made a difference." She patted Laurel's arm. "Don't worry, living so close to each other; they'll have to get along."

"It's a big step, isn't it?"

Helen grabbed Laurel's bag. "It sure is, but I took a big step—" she jerked her head towards Darlen. "It worked for me. Come on, say your goodbyes to this place. Marta's meeting us at the landing ports."

Marta wasn't alone. Laurel informed High Chancellor Bela of her plans, and she wanted to accompany Marta to farewell the group.

"I wish you well, Laurel," the High Chancellor said, kissing Laurel on both cheeks. "I'm excited for you to be going on such a quest. And you, Harry." She embraced Harry in the same manner. "We hope you will keep in touch for as long as you are able and perhaps, one day, you will return."

The High Chancellor turned to Helen and Darlen, leaving Laurel alone with Marta.

"Laurel," Marta said, her eyes brimming with tears, "I can't bear to think I'll never see you again."

Laurel felt the same. "I don't know how far this is going to take us, Marta. Perhaps too far for us ever to find our way back."

Marta hugged Laurel close. "The masters brought our ancestors here from somewhere," she said, her voice shaking. "We can only hope that 'somewhere' has a road home."

"It may have." Laurel stepped back to look into her friend's eyes. "Or the road there may be so long, only Ava will make it back."

Marta shook her head. "I still don't understand what you hope to gain from this."

"Knowledge, Marta. We spoke of Earth as home. Now we speak of Mentelci as home, but we don't originate from either place. I'm not sure now where we come from. I need to discover the truth about whole souls."

Marta nodded miserably, and Laurel could tell she was unconvinced this mission would bear the fruit Laurel hoped. "I'll miss you. Chloe's picking up Eli; they'll see you on Danfos 4 when you go to see the duchess." Tears slid down her cheeks. "I'll be the only one left here."

Laurel squeezed her hand. "You've made so many friends, and Congress values you. Please understand, I have to do this."

Marta sniffed. "I'm glad Harry's going."

"Me too," Laurel smiled. Even at this late stage, there were moments when she feared he'd pull out, then what would she do? She took care not to let him see she had doubts.

In the short while between deciding to undertake the journey and meeting at the landing stage, Darlen cleaned and equipped his ship to cater for the extra people on board. Since Helen had been crewing, Mer and the bulkhead were far cleaner than the first time Laurel saw the ship, but it took a long time and a lot of effort to slough off the years of greasy patination. Mer, scrubbed to within an inch of his metallic life, was commandeered to help Helen and the result was nothing short of spectacular. The exterior had repair work carried out on the hull, even though Darlen's request for a League cloak had been denied, with the engineers pointing out the danger of "just anybody" cruising around with classified League technology. The ship was well-stocked and made as comfortable as possible, but the engineers who tested the engines observed that although it was in good condition, the ship was two hundred years old, and the accessories that made up the domestic systems might prove unreliable. Darlen was unconcerned. He'd flown just about everywhere in known space—and unknown space for that matter—and the ship had never let him down. He didn't doubt its capacity to go on for many years yet.

Leaving Marta was far tougher than Laurel imagined. The telepathic bond they shared was always stronger than with the others, and Marta's layers of sadness peeled back as they hugged each other again and again until Darlen called Laurel to the ship. And she knew she still had to face the same sadness with Eli and Chloe.

Danfos 4 was a minor planet, colonised by mainly self-sustaining communities, with possibly a dozen provinces turned over to shipyards that built League scouts and smaller trading vessels. A few provinces also manufactured domestic appliances and personal vehicles for use on planets that permitted individual ownership of planet-based transport. Many unskilled Gartryans integrated into the small societies and found labouring work on farms while extending their skills as builders and tradespersons. Others set up farming communities with the focus on establishing a co-op between the other communities. Those with a technological background settled near the shipyards and manufacturing plants. The population on Danfos welcomed the Gartryan people, and already, intermarriage and intercultural activities had become commonplace. Many Gartryan scientists followed Shumuyi'beh, but with their skills not gaining full utilisation on Danfos 4, they appealed to the League for positions elsewhere more suited to their abilities.

With her people dispersed across Danfos 4 and the League, Shumuyi'beh's sovereignty over her people was greatly diminished. Laurel was surprised to see that the transformation caused Shumuyi-beh little concern.

"I am but a figurehead now, Laurel," she smiled, watching as Marcel discovered the wonder of having a sibling, carrying Ava on his shoulders, the little girl helpless with laughter. "My sons will succeed me in the Charter, and respected as sovereigns, but in name only." She laughed. "Dukes and Duchesses, pleasing to behold but with no true authority."

"Why do I sense relief?"

"We are safe, Laurel. At peace. I rule alongside my people, not over them. What need have I of power?" Shumuyi'beh cast her eyes down, her father's sins still weighing on her heart. "My father desired it. I do not."

"You are very wise, your grace."

"I had a vision, Laurel," Shumuyi'beh said as they looked out over the simple gardens of Shumuyi'beh's modest home. "I hated slavery right through to my soul, and Gartrya was becoming empty as the duke tore out its heart. I learned of the League first through my father, but his words were filled with hatred. Later, when my lord brother spoke of the League, I learned of its fairness and freedom. Then I prayed they would defeat my father." A tiny laugh escaped her lips. "You could say the duke and I wished for the same thing, a return to the League, but on vastly different terms."

"Others have elected to stay behind."

"They have," Shumuyi'beh conceded with a nod, "even knowing the day would come, as the whole souls and Soul Mongers pass away, migration through the nebula would end." She sighed. "I mourn them, even as I value their decisions. And at times, we can embrace those few who change their minds, thanks to the whole souls."

The two women fell to silence, observing the antics of the newly united brother and sister. "Marcel is certainly taken with Ava," Laurel said; then to her surprise, Shumuyi'beh raised Laurel's hand and held it to her heart. She looked deeply into Laurel's eyes. "Laurel, I cherish my lord nephew as my own sons and daughters, who look up to him as they would a father, as they would if their father had survived the war. But he is still a child."

Shumuyi'beh's thoughts closed the distance between them. Laurel shook her head slowly, even though Shumuyi'beh's feelings were unmistakable.

"I don't believe he would ever leave you. He loves you. You are his aunt."

Shumuyi'beh squeezed Laurel's hand tight. "You are wrong, Laurel." Her words spilled out in an urgent whisper, as if she had only a short time to convince her friend. "Ava is his half-sister, and for all my love for him, we do not share blood. It is Ava who is my lord nephew's family. It is right and proper that they be together. It would have been his father's wish."

Shumuyi'beh loosened her grip on Laurel's hand. Laurel still felt dazed by the duchess's suggestion. It wasn't something she'd considered. Gabriel's son go with them? Harry might have strong feelings about it, but given Shumuyi'beh's compelling plea, she had no choice but to ask him.

"I need to speak with the others first," Laurel said.

"Of course, you must," Shumuyi'beh agreed, "and I will not speak of it until you advise me of their response. They will see the wisdom." And Laurel knew that for Shumuyi'beh at least, the matter was settled.

"Marcel?" Harry's face moved from surprise to puzzlement and back to surprise.

"Yes, Harry. He is Ava's half-brother."

"I realise, but…"

"I don't see what the 'but' is Harry," Helen interrupted. "He's family."

Harry didn't want to say that as much as he'd come to like the lad in the brief time they'd been on Danfos 4, the fact of the matter was, Marcel was Gabriel's son, and Harry had never expected to be near a person who might remind Laurel every day of what she lost. But then, Ava was also Gabriel's child and never once had Laurel made him feel he was anything less than a father to her. It might work, he thought, but he couldn't answer straight away.

Laurel watched as Harry's face worked through those few emotions. Maybe she should have come to Harry with this first, but Helen cottoned on something was going on. Harry's generosity of spirit would win out; all he needed was a little while to take it in. Meanwhile, they still had to say goodbye to Chloe and Eli.

Of course, Eli brought his family. Ru, radiant in the final month of her pregnancy and their toddler Jacob, only a little over a year old. The farming life suited Eli. His previously lean frame now sported muscles to spare, and Laurel swore he'd sprouted a couple of inches. With no demand for words between them, Eli's thoughts communicated his peace and happiness, but most of all, his pride in his beautiful family.

Just into her early twenties, Chloe took time from her law enforcement duties to visit Danfos 4 to say goodbye. With her fair hair drawn back in a tight bun and her demeanour strong and positive, Chloe's eyes still held the softness of the girl the whole souls first met all those years ago. It seemed a contradiction to the uniform she wore, that of a second officer in the Constabulary. To achieve such a status, Chloe would have shown Congress and the Protectorate there was little "softness" in the execution of her duties. Chloe was every inch the officer, and her whole soul friends were immensely proud. As always, Asde accompanied Chloe. Asde was the more emotional of the two, finding the prospect of never seeing his friends again affecting him deeply, even though he envied their adventure. He'd developed a fondness for all the whole souls and found friendship with his former Commander plus an unlikely acquaintance in Darlen. Although Chloe shed a few tears, she firmly believed she would see them again, and in years to come, they would return with news of their adventure and exciting discoveries.

They planned only a short visit, Canaa was a journey of many weeks, and they were eager to be on their way, but the visit grew into several days. Strangely for Laurel, when she said goodbye to Marta, she doubted she would ever see her again, but in saying goodbye to Chloe and Eli, she felt as Chloe did, that it seemed more of a "see you later" rather than a final farewell.

They spent the last evening with Shumuyi'beh, Marcel, and Shumuyi'beh's children, five of them ranging from around eighteen to eight years old. Shumuyi'beh didn't bring up the notion of Marcel accompanying them, and Harry had still yet to give Laurel a response. She saw what was in his heart and the dying embers of his uncertainty about the appeal. She knew he wasn't even sure why he felt any uncertainty. As it turned out, Laurel didn't need to ask him again. The situation was settled by Ava.

Ava climbed onto Harry's lap and angled his face so she could look at him. "Howie, Marcel said his daddy is my daddy."

Harry blinked. "Um," he didn't quite know how to answer. The truth, maybe? "Yes, sweetheart. That's right."

Ava's emotions crossed to Laurel, and she glanced over, tuning in to the exchange.

"Well, I like you being my daddy," Ava declared fiercely. "I don't want anybody else in the galaxy to be my daddy; you're my Howie."

A delighted Harry hugged the little girl. "I love being your Howie!"

Ava latched her arms around Harry's neck, and he beamed across at Laurel, who at once felt his mind free of any doubts about asking Marcel to join them.

Shumuyi'beh had likewise seen and understood what took place. She grinned as Laurel came to sit beside her.

"He may choose to stay," Laurel cautioned. Shumuyi'beh shook her head. She knew the choice her lord nephew would make.

And it was as his aunt predicted. Marcel had contributed to establishing his people on their new homeworld. He no longer considered himself a noble. He was now one with the people, seeking to make a home, working alongside them wherever he could, farming or building homes and towns. But Marcel shared the same pull to family as his father. He loved Shumuyi'beh and her children, but brief as the time was that he'd spent with Ava, his bond, his blood ties to her, found their place in his heart.

CHAPTER SIXTEEN _

Harry was right. Darlen's ship was cramped. The variance chambers were part of the ship's framework, and separating them would prove impossible, but it was the cabin most suitable for Harry and Laurel, with a small bed for Ava. Helen erected a curtained compartment in the cargo bay to give Marcel privacy, and Helen shared Darlen's quarters anyway. Despite his excitement at the venture, Marcel was awkward with the relaxed style of communicating on the ship, finding it challenging to not prefix their names with "lord" or "lady". It made Harry uncomfortable.

"I don't like being called 'Lord Harry'," he confided in Laurel and Helen.

"I love being Lady Helen!" Helen said. "I feel like royalty!"

"I've told him it's just 'Laurel' and just 'Harry', but he forgets," Laurel smiled. "He's spoken that way all his life."

"He doesn't call Darlen 'Lord'," Harry pointed out.

"That's because Darlen's a trader," Laurel said, then dropped her voice. "He's beneath being called a lord."

Helen smirked. "He'd love that."

"Perhaps we should just remind Marcel from time to

time," Laurel said. "But I doubt he'd stop calling Ava 'my lady sister'. I think that would go right against his upbringing."

Notwithstanding his deferential habit of prefixing their names, Marcel quickly proved himself an enthusiastic member of the crew, but the skills he'd brought from Danfos 4 hardly equipped him as crew on a space-going vessel. He couldn't pilot a ship, and his knowledge of technology was dated and irrelevant. He had some experience in robotics and holographic datacaches, but it was only where such things would be used in farming.

This discovery of Marcel's lack of knowledge was the single unifying thing Darlen and Harry agreed upon. As soon as they were properly underway, Marcel needed an education.

The plan for the journey was to retrace the original whole souls' route back to their origin, hopefully finding clues along the way to point them in the right direction. Laurel believed she and Helen might have a sense of the course they took, and Canaa, as the furthermost planet from the Miran Forin nebula, seemed the sensible place to start. After Canaa, they would cross to Diriarden, in the expectation the wraiths may communicate with Laurel once more. Then, if the wraiths had any more knowledge to convey, they would hypothesise where the supposed ancestors exited the nebula.

"Landing will be an issue," Harry stated, taking the opportunity while they weren't at widespeed to co-pilot, improve his relationship with Darlen and drive away the old relics of prejudice against Soul Mongers.

"No, it won't, Harry." Darlen pointed to the star chart. Canaa's exosphere was obscured by flowing eddies and tiny 'gravity' blisters, which opened and closed at random. "This ship will weather the Tide of Gravity phenomenon; I can set it down."

Harry had only ever seen the Tide of Gravity displayed on League ship sensors. It was generally accepted only small ships could navigate through the exosphere, assuming you didn't encounter the gravity wells as you descended. It was a good reason not to trouble yourself to visit this place, but Darlen's orbital sensors highlighted every nuance of the field. Clearly, this ship's equipment had something League sensors did not.

"Why didn't you share this technology with the League?"

Darlen didn't miss the edge in Harry's voice, just as he knew he referred more to the sensors rather the ship's ability to negotiate the phenomenon. Harry's old views of him would have to change in the cause of harmony on the ship, and he'd do his bit, but some details are just sacred.

"It wouldn't do them any good. Navigating the tide isn't technology, no more than Laurel and Helen's telepathy is technology. You can't put everything down to machines, Harry." Darlen tapped the side of his nose and raised his eyebrows. "There are things operated by forces outside what you see with your eyes, my friend."

Laurel watched them from the modest common room where, in the past, Darlen and his father had secured their whole soul slaves' recovery. It was the only place to sit together in reasonable comfort on the entire ship, and the control room was little more than a cubicle. She saw the two men were trying to get along. At least there were no raised voices. That happened only once, and Helen had immediately slapped them both down.

Helen distracted her by jabbing her in the arm and indicating to where Marcel sat on the floor. He seemed to prefer the floor to the chairs and used the bulkhead to prop his back while observing the experienced members of the crew going about their business, his lanky frame often needing stepping over. He was eager for his education to begin, but while he waited, he used the time he had on his hands to reflect upon and consider the personalities he was getting to know on the ship. Like his father before him, Marcel loved philosophical conversation.

"I am thinking...Laurel," Marcel said as he lifted his handsome face, his grey eyes bright, and pointed to his temple when he saw Laurel and Helen were watching him. With a note of triumph, he declared, "I now understand telepathy. I have seen that you and my lady Helen understand each other so well, and my lady sister, Ava, speaks to me often in my mind."

Helen made noises that he was probably mistaken in her case, but Marcel's triumph also had a tiny trace of bewilderment. He frowned and tilted his head to one side. "I do not understand how Darlen has skills that arise from the spiritual as well." He glanced towards the control room, "I struggle to see how one is light and strives only for good—" he took in Laurel and Helen with a single nod, "while another—" he pointed discreetly towards Darlen, "has been used for ill." He gave Helen an apologetic flick of his eyelids. "I mean no disrespect."

"None taken, son," Darlen grinned as he left Harry in control and stepped into the common room. He had been listening. "Spirituality doesn't govern us. It's a tool, like an engine or technology. These good ladies use it in a positive way to influence their own lives and those around them." Darlen waggled his head comically from side to side before admitting. "I have in the past used it to positively influence only my own life." Darlen crossed his legs and sank to the floor to sit beside Marcel. "The energy source we tap into is the same. It's not good or evil. It doesn't have that discernment. Your father was a good man?"

Marcel nodded as Darlen continued.

"Yes, Marcel, he was, and a spiritual man who at times used his abilities to further his own agenda."

Marcel understood. "It would seem spirituality abides within the conscience; however one uses it." He brightened. "I have much to learn of the nature of good and evil. Of many things. Thank you, trader...Darlen."

They encountered fewer problems navigating the gravity well on Canaa than they did with coaxing Ava from the ship. A bout of violent nausea and vomiting erupted the moment the landing ramp was released. Even though neither of her physician parents could ascribe a physical cause, it became clear that any attempt to leave the ship caused considerable grief and anguish, to the point where Laurel had to stay on board to comfort her child while the others explored. As her weeping settled, Laurel tried to draw Ava out on what had unnerved her. It rarely happened, but Ava locked her mother out of her thoughts.

"Did you see something, honey? Something the rest of us can't see?"

"There are horrid things here, Mommy," the little girl sniffed. "I want to go."

"What horrid things? Can you see them?"

"No, they're in my head, and they've got bad faces."

"Are they talking to you?"

Ava nodded, wiping her eyes on Laurel's sleeve. "They say, 'Get out of my house'."

It didn't make sense to Laurel, but this level of distress made it impossible to believe this was just imaginings, even the imaginings of a child such as Ava.

"We're not in anyone's house, Ava." Laurel made shushing noises and cuddled her daughter close. "We're in our ship. We're safe here. Auntie Helen and I will be able to sense anything that might harm us."

Neither Helen nor Laurel sensed anything apart from the already known locations of artefacts from the ancient civilisation, and the others brought nothing back of any value.

"You need to go out there and fossick, Laurel," Helen said. "You know I'm just not certain about anything I'd find. I'll look after Ava." But Ava's distress returned at the prospect of her mother leaving the ship.

"We could sit together right at the top of the ramp," Laurel suggested as she held Ava tight. "Mer will come, won't you, Mer?" Mer made his seesawing answer to affirm. "It's a very pretty planet." Laurel appealed to Ava's little girlishness. "Lots of little moths and wiks, and the sky is blue."

Ava stilled her crying. She was very fond of wiks. She nodded.

Mer headed out first to add his measure of security, and Laurel kept Ava in her lap as they sat right at the top of the ramp.

"See, it's lovely here, isn't it?"

Ava lifted her head. She didn't panic, just turned questioning eyes on her mother. Her mind was still closed to Laurel.

"Can you hear something?"

"I hear people."

"What are they saying?" Laurel tried to attune her senses, but she heard nothing outside the usual noises of nature.

"There's no-one here, Mommy. They've all run away."

"Who did they run away from?"

"People like Uncle Darlen."

"Were there other people? People who weren't running."

"Yes, men with mean faces."

"And where are they now?"

Ava shook her head. "I don't know. Can we go back inside?"

Ava didn't wait for Laurel's agreement. She jumped up and ran back into the ship, leaving Laurel trying to work out what all this meant.

"Well?" Harry said when Laurel returned.

"She doesn't like it here."

"She can probably sense the history."

"Very likely. She heard voices at first, telling her we had to leave. Then she said people were running away from people like Darlen."

"That makes sense," Darlen cut in. "According to legend, the Soul Mongers abducted many whole souls from here."

"How can she sense something that happened so long ago?" Marcel's lap had become a refuge for Ava while Laurel remained out on the ramp. Laurel had no answer. Ava had shown herself to be sensitive to surroundings and atmosphere, but never so specific.

As the ship pulled away, Ava's little face relaxed, and her usual exuberance returned, but Laurel felt a nagging disquiet, not because of Ava's reactions but because of what it might portend when they reached the end of their journey. She had a few, very natural, very human doubts about this quest, and she knew that at one word from her, the others would abandon the mission and return to their old lives. It was then Ava's mind opened to her, and Laurel heard the unspoken words.

"We are the deliverance."

CHAPTER SEVENTEEN _

"We aren't going back to that place, are we, Mommy, promise?" Ava said as Laurel tucked her into bed.

"No, honey. There's no need." Laurel was disappointed the visit to Canaa yielded nothing of value, only serving to upset Ava.

"Good. It made Uncle Darlen cry."

Laurel knelt beside Ava's bed. "What?"

Ava turned over to look at her mother. "In his head, he cried, and in here," she touched her hand to her chest, "it went all wobbly and sad, but no tears came out 'cause he was shy."

Laurel planted a kiss on Ava's forehead. "I've told you before about looking inside people's minds."

"I know, but he loves me, so I can. He thinks Auntie Helen's bottom looks nice too. He's funny."

Laurel opened her mouth to tell Ava it was still impolite to read minds uninvited, but then it occurred to her that Ava's abilities might exceed her own, and to curtail them might not be in the child's best interests. A word to Darlen might be in order, and Harry, for that matter, who occasionally sent Laurel one or two thoughts not suitable for a small child to overhear. And despite prompting, Ava did not mention those few profound words she communicated to her mother earlier.

Harry and Darlen were plotting the most direct route to Diriarden when Laurel returned to the common room.

"It's do-able in one hit," Darlen was saying. "There's the Masiennes Cluster dead ahead; we can't use widespeed, but it's still quicker than going around it."

"Except it's usually full of people escaping justice," Harry declared.

"You know this part of the galaxy, Harry?" Laurel asked.

"All newly qualified officers from the constabulary end up here at some stage in their first year, Laurel. I think it's to measure their tolerance to tedium. A few petty criminals hide out up here too."

"I've always travelled it alone." Darlen glanced up, "Boredom's never been a feature."

"You should try covering the Masiennes in an axispod and environmental suit."

Darlen nodded, understanding how such an endeavour would indeed be decidedly dull, not to mention uncomfortable, but he had an idea. "I think it's an excellent place for young Marcel to try his hand at piloting."

Marcel's eyes widened; he hadn't expected such a launch to his education. "Me?" He held up his hands. "No, no, no, I could not. I have never flown a ship in space."

"We've got a couple of weeks then for you to learn." Darlen stepped away from the controls and invited Marcel to join him. Helen gave Marcel a push. He resisted at first, but a single stomp from Mer sent him scuttling to the control panel.

Then they couldn't tear him away from it. He took guidance from Darlen easily and tirelessly. When Darlen suggested placing the ship on autopilot after a couple of hours so they could all sleep, Marcel only reluctantly complied. Mer always remained disengaged from his alcove when the ship was on autopilot to safeguard if problems occurred. Still, the next morning, when Laurel rose before anyone else, Mer was supervising Marcel at the controls. When he saw her, Marcel relinquished control of the ship to Mer.

"I remember my first attempt at flying," Laurel told him as she brought coffee for them both. "It was in an axispod. I loved it."

"I lived in such confinement in the palace, my la...Laurel," Marcel said with a sigh, pressing the L of her name to stop himself from saying "my lady". "The duke forbade me to leave the palace grounds. I spent much of my time with my lord father before he went away. He was so wise and so kind. He made me laugh and told stories to fill our lonely days. When the duke sent him to war, Grandmere distracted me with reading and learning." He glanced around and grinned. "Possibly not the right kind of learning for here."

"I loved to learn about ancient cultures and ancient languages back on Earth," Laurel said. "It was more than just something to pass the time, but I never for a moment thought I would use the knowledge, so you never can tell." She laughed. "And here, in another universe, I came across a document, a chronicle of my people written in one of those languages!"

"And you deciphered it?" Marcel's face lit with undisguised admiration.

"I didn't realise you didn't know! Marcel, this is the reason we're here. One day, I'll tell you the story of how Harry, Helen and I broke into the archives beneath Canon Akkuh's residence." Marcel's eyes grew wide. He wanted to know right now, and his eagerness reminded Laurel of the time at the fortress when she allowed Gabriel into her mind to walk the streets of Paris. He too had turned to her with that same wide-eyed wonderment she now saw in his son.

"Do I remind you of him, I mean, my lord father?" Marcel decided not to press her for the story when he saw her expression change.

"Oh! Well," Laurel stumbled on her words, "I, yes— you do. His eyes were a different colour, but yes, you do remind me of him."

"My lady sister is like him. I see it," Marcel laughed. "But she has your curly hair. See, mine hangs like unwoven thread!!" His face became suddenly serious. "The Scroll. My lord father made it for you. To show his love. It is the way of my people."

Any reply Laurel may have given got lost in the sounds of the others waking and making noises about breakfast. Ava squealed as she ran along the deck to where Laurel and Marcel were sitting, jumping first onto Laurel's lap for a good morning kiss and then onto Marcel for the same, before using the ever-patient Mer's leg as a post to climb up to the viewport. Laurel joined Harry in the doorway. Placing his arm around her, he rested his lips against her forehead.

"I wondered where you were," he murmured.

"I still had Ava's experience on Canaa on my mind. I was so hoping we would find something that would help us; it kept me awake. I got up and found Marcel out here with Mer."

"I think that young man has a few untapped abilities," Harry said. "Not just piloting. He's a quick learner."

Helen shoved between them with a few dishes balanced on her hands and arms. "I'd like him to learn how to cook. Either that or I take on the job, Darlen's concoctions are gross."

"Cook it yourself then," Darlen yelled from the galley.

"I just said I would," Helen yelled back.

The food was very ordinary. Vesanec food dispensers were a high-maintenance piece of equipment found only on consular ships, which probably accounted for the very minimal choice Gabriel fed Laurel in the fortress. The so-called nuvpaks, which Darlen called "space rations", were just squares of protein but looked suspiciously as though someone had ground a stick of celery with the heel of their shoe and sloshed the whole mess into a vacuum pack. The taste was a trivial factor and relied on embellishments that the consumer had available; these embellishments were the concoctions to which Helen alluded. The insipid celery-coloured slop was presented as the first meal of the day, pink cardboard look and taste-alike for the second meal and a tube of yellow jelly for the last meal, all of which, when showered with a mineral-based liquid, provided a balanced meal. Helen refused to consume the rations directly from the packaging and delivered the contents to the crew on plates to be "civilised". Oddly, Ava loved the variety of nuvpak served at the first meal but needed considerable coaxing to eat the others. Darlen and Helen had a variety of teas onboard, plus the coffee that required considerable getting used to and several drinks secured from the places they visited as traders. They also had a preservation processor for fruits, which provided a welcome relief for their tastebuds.

Darlen set up the control room for the several week journey through the cluster. It seemed as if Darlen knew the region well but evidently had not brought Helen here during their travels. She sat beside him, her legs bent and feet up on the panel, watching as they drifted through the cluster, the hull "wiped" from widespeed until they re-entered normal space.

"We hardly ever go anywhere this slow," she said to Darlen.

"That's because the galaxy is a big place, and we always have someplace to be. We don't get the chance to go cruising."

"But this is beautiful." She sensed Laurel and Ava enter the room. "Laurel? Isn't this beautiful?"

Laurel joined them, and Ava climbed onto Darlen's knee for a better look. All knees were now available for her use, including Mer's.

"I like the planet with the sparkly rings and the little planets inside," Ava said, her face lighting up as she pointed through the viewport.

The said planet lay angled against the starry backdrop,

too distant from any sun substantial enough to give it full light but sufficient to provide the rings with a shimmer, highlighting the tiny moons spinning within. It was pretty, as Ava said. A space trinket.

The viewports display of the cluster provided a continuous panorama of celestial riches, bright planets, shining clouds and occasional moving objects, which might have been a ship fleeing from the Constabulary. No-one asked or checked the sensors. Marcel, Helen, and Laurel spoke about the universe's harmony and choreography as Harry and Darlen's eyebrows raised in disdain at their poetic descriptions. They'd both seen the cluster before and saw nothing that made them wax lyrical. But to the others, it was a wonder and a marvel. As they usually travelled at widespeed, Laurel and Helen never had the opportunity to simply watch the galaxy go by, and with little else to stimulate their senses, planet-watching became a happy occupation for them over the next few days.

Harry and Darlen both took Marcel under their wing. Darlen taught him to fly the ship and interpret the sensors. Harry instructed him in the use of star charts, star fields, infocharts, and datacaches with a holographic interface (which opened simply by drawing one's hands apart, but despite repeated hand waving, didn't seem to respond to Marcel). Harry also gave him a few lessons in weapons and combat. Harry had petitioned the Constabulary for Triconomic interfaces, but as he was planning on leaving League space, they gave the same reasons for denying the cloaking device; that the technology may fall into the wrong hands.

On the third evening in the cluster, Laurel and Helen chatted about their old life on Earth. The discussion included a fascinated Marcel, who kept the conversation very lively with questions. He didn't allow the two women to finish answering before deducing the endings, giving a more colourful, if rather fanciful viewpoint. Harry listened in for a while but excused himself to put Ava to bed. He'd fallen asleep, but later, when Laurel slipped in beside him, trying not to wake him, he turned over and propped on his elbow.

"I tried to tell myself it was pity, fear or some other emotion, you know," he said.

Laurel peered at him in the dim light that reflected from the metal bulkhead. "Concerning what?"

Harry teased her hair down onto her cheek. He'd learned to recognise if she was inside his mind, and Laurel had learned to take care not to go there, to always allow him to speak his mind himself, but she knew to what he referred.

"Gabriel. When I heard Marcel say his father loved you, I realised you never said at any time, at least not to me, that you loved him back."

"We were close, Harry. As close as two people could get if you look at our circumstances. I did feel sorry for him, but love? Perhaps briefly, for a few hours, a few days maybe."

"Do you still mourn him?"

"Mourn?" Harry's use of the word surprised her. "Harry, I have you, and I have Ava. Gabriel knew what awaited him. It held no fear for him if his family could be saved. He would be overjoyed to know his son and daughter

192

are together and that I found you."

"He was a brave man."

Laurel reached up and squeezed Harry's nose. "Are you jealous?"

He sniffed. "Yes, I want to be the love of your life."

"Does it help if I say you are?"

"I just wanted to hear you say it."

His arms enveloped her, and she curled up against his chest. Laurel felt safe tucked up tightly in Harry's arms. Ava stirred, and they both held their breath in case they disturbed her, but she settled, and Harry bent down and kissed Laurel's mouth.

"I love you, Laurel. I would say to the moon and back as you say to Ava, but it seems like it might have to be to the ends of the universe and back."

"No regrets?"

"Not a single one."

CHAPTER EIGHTEEN _

Ava sat up, her confusion flooding Laurel's mind and reaching as far as Helen in her quarters. Harry went on snoring softly as Laurel lifted Ava from her bed.

"What is it, honey?" she whispered.

"I don't know, Mommy. Can we go and look at the planets?"

Helen was in the control room. "Ava woke me and told me to come out here."

Mer was at the panel.

"Have we encountered something, Mer?" Laurel checked the sensors. It all looked fine, and the starchart reported nothing untoward.

Mer made the odd seesawing harmonica sound no-one understood, but now, Laurel guessed the robot was assuring her all was well.

Ava pointed out the viewport. "The men with the mean faces were here."

"What men?" Helen asked.

"The men from that other planet, Auntie Helen."

"Do you mean Canaa?" Laurel crouched down and held Ava's hands. "There was no-one there."

"I heard them," Ava said, looking back towards the viewport, "from when they were there in olden days."

Laurel had no other explanation. Ava must have heard a telepathic echo, if such a thing existed.

"And you can hear them now?"

Ava's finger wiggled, then pointed to a planetoid. "They went there. I don't like their voices in my head."

"Helen?" Laurel looked to Helen for any input.

"Beats me." Helen also crouched beside Ava. "What do the voices say, sweetie?"

"They say, 'get out of my house'."

"Wow." Helen stared at Laurel, "That doesn't make much sense."

"No, it doesn't. C'mon Ava," Laurel stood and held out her hand. "Let's go back to bed. Helen, do you mind waiting here?"

Helen sat down with a shrug to wait while Laurel settled her child.

"What do you make of it?" Laurel asked when she returned, accepting the herbal tea Helen made when the wait got too long.

"Apart from it being creepy, you mean? That voice she hears doesn't sound very friendly."

"No, Helen, think. She said that entire phrase in English. Ava's first language is Seera."

Helen thought about it and concluded the language wasn't that important. "Yes, but she can speak some English. I've heard her talking to Harry's dad."

"Accepted," Laurel agreed, "but the whole phrase doesn't translate to Seeran. There's certainly nothing familiar enough to Ava for her to drop it in this context."

Helen considered for a moment. "Do you think she genuinely hears voices?"

"I reckon it's some sort of echo from a time long gone. I just can't figure out why it keeps coming back to Ava, though."

"Well, she's the kid of two whole souls," Helen pointed out logically. "She might be stronger than both of us. If so, it might pay to listen to her."

But Laurel didn't want that kind of burden on Ava just yet, and closed her eyes, rejecting the evidence of her own ears. "She's four, Helen. I hope it's just childish over-imagination."

"Have it your way." Helen looked over at Mer. "She's pretty creative." Mer wore a homemade earth-style pirate hat perched on his head and a black patch drawn on one side of his square face, Ava's artistic rendition of Long John Silver as she saw him from Laurel's improvised recounting of Treasure Island.

"Harry seems to have taken to Marcel," Helen said, switching the subject. "I wondered how he'd go."

"Yes, he's never asked me any actual questions about Gabriel, but he did last night. He asked if I loved him."

Helen threw her a cheeky grin. "Did he now? And did you? Love him, I mean? You seemed pretty upset when you found out the fortress got bombed."

Laurel turned her face to the side, reliving that moment. "I never had the chance to get to know him. I spent the first few weeks despising him. It took me a while to recognise he was a prisoner as well."

"Well, you must have liked him at least once," Helen grinned, gleefully referencing the fact that together, Gabriel and Laurel produced a child.

Laurel laughed softly. "Yes, in those last couple of days, something passed between him and me that was…I hesitate to say 'special' because that doesn't go far enough, but love? Nothing like I feel for Harry. And I have Ava. Someone wonderful to come from a sad situation."

"And you're Marcel's surrogate mother. Gabriel would have liked that."

"He's nearly twenty, Helen. Hardly in need of a mother."

"He's still got to find his feet out in the…I was going to say the world, but I should say galaxy or universe."

Laurel turned her gaze to the viewport. "I feel like I was born here."

Helen raised her eyebrows. "I get that. I made it through the war because I had no choice. To have refused may have meant being separated from you and the others, and I couldn't have handled it. When you all found your place, and I didn't, and Darlen gave me the chance to go with him, I wondered what I had to lose." She pivoted a little on her seat. "I knew you and Ava and the others could cope, but this life, the freedom? I don't think I've ever been so happy."

"You and Darlen argue all the time."

"I used to hate him—" Helen just caught Darlen's shadow as he appeared in the doorway, so she added for effect, "Sometimes when he's a pain, I think I still do."

"You don't hate me, Helen. You'd be lost without me."

Darlen dragged a chair closer and joined them. "Girl talk?"

"We started off discussing Ava. The voice she heard on Canaa? She heard it again during the night." Laurel pointed out the viewport. "She said that planetoid called to her."

Darlen pulled up the star chart. "It's just a number in a star cluster, low gravity, atmosphere...you'd need a suit. League Classification Code 3. Hostile to human life. But that's for ordinary humans, not necessarily you."

"Have you ever been there?"

Darlen shook his head. "There's nothing there, no point."

"Why would Ava point it out?"

"Can you sense anything?"

"Nothing."

"Did the voice give her anything specific?"

"Not really, but she repeated the phrase, 'get out of my house', both times in English."

Darlen's surprise was genuine. "That is odd. I can't think of a Seeran equivalent. I could work it into a few other League languages, but Ava hasn't had that kind of exposure. Perhaps she's mishearing and giving you what she thinks she hears."

"That's a possibility, Laurel," Helen said, backing up that theory.

"Yes, it is. We'll keep an eye on it. We'll see if she mentions the planetoid when she wakes up."

The next day, Ava did mention the planetoid but shook her head when the suggestion was made that they establish an orbit. "But they came this way."

"Who did?"

"Mommy," the little girl frowned. "I told you, the men with the mean faces."

Laurel beckoned Harry out into the corridor. Marcel followed them, and the three stood in conference. Laurel told them about the possibility of Ava picking up on telepathic echoes, although she admitted it was just a theory.

"I have a strong sense from Ava," she said, "that she knows the path these beings—I suspect the masters—followed."

"Are we ultimately heading into trouble, then?"

"I don't think so, Harry. If we find the masters, it's reasonable we'll find the whole souls, our ancestors."

The mention of "ancestors" stopped Harry in his tracks. Laurel was invested in this journey, but his father was a whole soul, Marcel's father a whole soul, every person on this ship was the progeny of whole souls. That made it their journey, too.

Marcel paid close attention to what Laurel said. Theory or no, he respected her instincts.

"When I was a child," he said, "my lord father told me a tale of a prince who was so powerful, he held power to hear words spoken across great distances and could steer a starship using only his thoughts. Perhaps there was some truth in the story. Perhaps he spoke of himself. Could it be my lady sister has inherited this power?"

Harry didn't instantly make the connection. "She's never shown signs of being able to control technology with her mind," he said, but Laurel understood.

"No, Harry, but if she's sensing an echo, she might be

picking up a telepathic trail over unlimited distances."

Harry looked over at Ava, chatting with Helen through her breakfast. "She might lead us straight to them, but I would prefer to find the whole souls first. The masters may still be hostile."

They passed the planetoid without another word from Ava. The days continued, Mer got a different hat and face courtesy of Ava's imagination, Marcel continued his education and Helen and Darlen continued to bicker. As normal space appeared on the starfield, before they could see it with the naked eye, Ava made another surprising announcement.

Standing with Harry in front of the starfield, she was busy joining the points of light.

"Where are we going now, Howie?"

"We're on our way to Diriarden, for Mommy to talk to the wraiths."

"When we've been there, we have to go here." Ava pointed to a distant star, its coordinates placing it partly inside the Miran Forin nebula.

"Why do we have to go there?"

Both Helen and Laurel stopped what they were doing as they caught the child's thoughts.

"It's on our way, Howie," Ava said before returning to her play.

"What do you make of that?" Harry said to Laurel.

"I think we should do as she says."

"Agreed." Harry opened out a smaller virtual stellar chart for info on the planet. "I've been there a couple of times. It's hot; the soil contains minute crystalline fossils that absorb heat. The only cool place is the Western hemisphere, but the planet's rotation keeps that region close to the nebula during this phase of its orbit. The atmosphere is breathable, but after a while, it feels like your lungs are burning. It's devoid of categorised life now, apart from a few small reptiles. Even wiks are rare and tend towards the nebula side. They used it as a penal colony; prisoners just left there to survive as they could. No women. Males only so they couldn't build a civilisation."

"Does it have a name?"

"Planets this far out are usually just designated as numbers. This one is OL3321. The indigenous populations usually name planets."

"Well, we planned on heading into the nebula even before Ava's intuition kicked in. We're going in the right direction."

Darlen looked over Harry's shoulder. "That whole system is a tip."

Harry twisted his head around to look at him. "One of your stomping grounds?"

"A place to rest." Darlen dismissed the comment with a flick of his hand. "Hell is as good a place as any," he said before turning away.

"More likely hide," Harry whispered to Laurel.

"Hell?" Marcel mouthed the word a couple of times before saying it aloud.

"It's an Earth concept," Laurel said. "A place of punishment after death for people who are evil."

"Is it on your planet?" The picture Laurel painted made Marcel glad Earth was a place he wasn't ever likely to visit.

Laurel bit back a grin. "Marcel, it doesn't exist; it's just something religious people believe in."

Harry was just as fascinated. Even after all these years with Laurel and listening to the things she told him about her world, it seemed extraordinary to him that a single small planet could be so divisive, have so many factions that believed in various divine beings and supported so many political systems and languages. Part of him would have been intrigued to see it, but he wasn't sure he would have appreciated the chaos. He shrugged.

"Well, we'll see if this hell matches yours."

CHAPTER NINETEEN _

Their trip to hell via Diriarden got postponed when Laurel and Helen pointed out a heavily armoured Constabulary cruiser barring their course. The ship's sensors registered an anomaly in space dead ahead, but a cloaked ship was an unexpected hurdle. As Darlen brought the ship to all stop, the cruiser dropped its cloak. A scaled-down version of the consular ships, Constabulary cruisers carried a crew of two hundred and seventy highly trained officers. Harry told the others it was out of the ordinary for such a nominally patrolled and desolate region of League space. The cruiser held a position directly forward.

"I don't understand," Harry said. "Why would they deploy something as large as this out here? We just used to scuttle around in scouts and axispods using a squad carrier as a base. What do they expect to find?"

"Well, they found us," Darlen replied. "Maybe we're who they're looking for."

Harry's face was serious. "Do you sense anything, Laurel?"

Laurel shook her head. "I'm not sure. I see your point about overkill, though. Let's see what happens when they make contact."

The cruiser kept them speculating a few minutes more before hailing them.

"Trader. Constable Minet of the League Constabulary. You are in an unsanctioned region of League space. State your business."

Darlen turned from the comms. "Unsanctioned? There are no unsanctioned regions. What's he talking about?"

Harry paid no attention. He was beaming. "Minet? It's Harry!"

At once, a visual of Constable Minet appeared, a look of surprise on his face and with a greeting considerably more restrained than Harry's. "What are you doing here, Harry? And with Darlen of all people?"

"We can axispod across and tell you."

A few seconds of silence followed, heavily underlined by Minet's communicated sense of not wanting to be delayed. Even so, he responded, "Very well, just you."

"Can I bring someone else?"

Minet hesitated. "Just one other and not Darlen. Minet out."

"Minet and I were at the Constabulary on Mentelci," Harry explained, rather pleased at this unexpected diversion. "We did several tours around the League, but we've had no contact since before the war. Come with me, Laurel?"

"He's not keen on either of us going, Harry."

"Of course, he is. That's ridiculous. Besides, I'd like to know what a ship that size is doing here."

Helen folded her arms. "He's hiding something. Even

I can tell that."

Harry turned to her. "What nonsense, Helen. Minet's a good man."

"He might be," Laurel said, "but he doesn't want us here."

Harry backed off his enthusiasm. "What do you sense?"

"Subterfuge," Laurel said after a moment's consideration. "At this distance, I'm not sure. His intent is confused, as if he's conflicted."

"We'll be careful. He may be on a classified exercise."

"Whatever you say," Helen said as she sat Ava up on her lap. "See if they'll give you some proper food to bring back."

Minet was a slim man around the same height as Harry with woolly brown hair that receded on both sides of a pronounced widow's peak, giving his naturally thin face an added sense of length. He smiled too much, and although he invited them to sit for a while, Laurel saw his smile of welcome was not sincere, as if refusing Harry's offer of a visit might raise suspicion. Already, he was considering ways to cut the visit short. He kept curling and uncurling his fingers in his nervousness, but Harry was utterly blind, not seeing that Minet's responses to his attempts at communication were met with terse and dutiful replies. Laurel and Harry had been away from Mentelci for many weeks now with only basic communication, owing to Darlen's antiquated comms system, but the Constabulary ships had the most advanced communications technology in the League. So Harry was eager for news. Minet explained the cruiser was on exercises and contact with the League had been severed for several weeks. He brushed aside Harry's questioning about this new tactic, one Harry had never encountered. He also changed the subject when Harry asked about a cruiser being assigned to one of the least active regions of League space, saying only the cruiser was enroute to OL3321, the same planet Darlen's ship would head to after Diriarden. Laurel was content to observe. Minet's mind was reachable, but his body language gave much away, and there was plenty he wished to keep hidden.

"So, Laurel," Minet leaned forward, trying to deflect Harry's puzzled enquiries by bringing Laurel into the conversation. "I always imagined Harry as married to his work. Do you have children?"

Harry jumped in. "Yes, Ava, she's four."

Minet smiled slightly and nodded. "Laurel? That's a curious name. Are you originally from a treaty planet?"

"No!" Harry cut in again, grinning with pride, and Laurel knew he was abandoning caution in the wake of what he believed about his old friend. "Laurel is one of the whole souls employed in the war. She came across some documents that gave us a clue as to the origins of the whole souls. One of the Diri wraiths spoke to her while she was on Diriarden, about a ship that orbited the planet. The wraiths are telepathic."

Minet swallowed hard. It was easy for Laurel to see the news she was a whole soul caused him considerable concern. He battled to keep his voice conversational.

"I've never met anyone who's seen a wraith."

"Me either," Harry said, "before Laurel anyway. We're heading up the Miran Forin, northwards if what the wraith said is correct, to see if we can locate the origins of the whole souls."

In a rush to clear his mind, Minet drew Laurel in. To peel away the layers of secrecy would take her more time than she had, but the unwelcome fact they were all heading in the same direction was firmly in his thoughts. He didn't want them going near the planet. Minet stood abruptly, glancing at Laurel as his brain scrambled to cover up both thought and intention.

"Well, all that sounds amazing! Look, sorry to cut this short, but I am on a schedule. It was great running into you, Harry." He patted Harry on the shoulder and turned his non-genuine smile to Laurel. "Nice to meet you, Laurel."

"We just got dismissed," Laurel said over Harry's shoulder in the axispod.

"Did we?"

"He didn't want to be in the company of a telepath."

"What makes you say that?"

Laurel gave an "as if" face to the back of his head, then let the impression seep into his mind.

"He's straight up, Laurel," Harry said. "He's never set a foot wrong."

Laurel kept the face and the expression boring into his mind.

"Okay," he sighed. "What did you sense?"

"Only that he doesn't want us to go to that planet."

"Why would he not?"

But Harry got no reply. Just the mind probe.

"Okay, then that's probably a good reason to go there."

Back on Darlen's ship, Helen was only interested in the fresh fruit they'd brought back, taking Ava into the galley to cut it up. She'd moved on from her earlier remarks about Minet and didn't pick up on Laurel's suspicions. But Marcel did the instant he saw her.

"You're troubled?"

"Yes, Marcel. Minet isn't what he appears to be."

Marcel gestured to the viewport. "Well, they are leaving. Look." The cruiser passed silently overhead. Marcel turned back to her. "You do not believe that is the last we will see of him?"

Laurel didn't even need to answer.

They reached Diriarden with no more constabulary encounters. Marcel, now a confident and capable pilot after several weeks in the control seat, set a synchronous orbit over the volcanic area where Laurel met the wraith.

"What do we do now?" he asked as the engine turned to low power.

"We wait," Laurel answered, knowing that the wraiths would know she was here. Harry, Darlen and Helen waited with them.

Ava stood, smiling as two wraiths drifted through the bulkhead. She reached out, and they copied the form of her hand, then joined with her, making her squeal. "It likes me,

Mommy! See everybody; the ghost likes me!"

To the men, the wraiths were visible but appeared as moving smudges. To Laurel, Helen, and Ava, they appeared as pure, luminous beings of light.

"Thank you for coming," Laurel spoke telepathically, making sure that Helen and Ava heard. She knew it would be a silent exchange for the men, but that couldn't be helped. The wraiths were expecting them, probably sensing them through widespeed.

"You seek your ancestors?"

"My daughter has a sense of the direction they came."

The wraiths moved closer together as if in a discourse of their own.

"The child's spirit is as the male Children from the past."

"We need to learn more about the Farisee. If we encounter them before we reach our destination, we could be in danger."

A vision came to Laurel's mind. The wraith moved towards Laurel, and as it joined with her, she felt the breath leave her body. The second wraith approached Helen and joined with her in the same way. As the wraiths' lifeforce surged, it provided them entry to its memory. Ava watched the proceedings, then took her mother's hand, and the wraith extended its reach to the child.

"It's okay, Mommy, I'm with you," she whispered.

Together, in the minds of the wraiths, Laurel, Helen, and Ava moved unseen among the eerie echoes of the Farisee ship. They wandered the cathedral-like chambers of the interior and gazed upon the sleeping whole souls, recumbent, statue-like and evocative of the religious icons that adorned every bulkhead. The whole souls and several sleeping children were in the care of a lone guard whose face was covered, and his or her body swathed from neck to floor in grey fabric. The wraiths' energy propelled them to a central area where whole souls performed tasks at tables. As before, a similarly clad and lone guard stood watch. In the forward area, they encountered the Farisee. The ghostly, ancient figures were humanoid, slightly less than average height but undoubtedly mammalian. Unlike the guards, their garments sported a tighter fit, their generous breasts protected by a breastplate moulded to fit. These beings had brown skin, large eyes, long limbs, normal-looking hands, and long hair, twisted and tied in knots. Their eyes were wide apart with a small, upturned nose. The guards in the children's area were slighter in build, but to Laurel, they had a masculine form. Laurel knew she could have this backward; she was walking like a ghost through a memory, but the impression was strong that before her, she viewed a matriarchal society. The wraiths' memory held them in the forward section; at the moment it collected these visions, it had gone no further, so had nothing more to offer Laurel save what she could observe.

They seemed to be on the bridge of a massive ship. Laurel could not make any estimate of the size, more interested in what she saw before her. The vessel ran on ritualistic behaviour. Any being carrying out a task requiring movement from one location to another gestured at one of the icons depicted on the bulkhead. Every action where their mouths moved now in silent and long-forgotten speech involved a precise bow, preceded by a movement of the arm. So many centuries intervened, and still, Laurel strained every sense to hear their voices but heard only the silence of the ages.

They stood still as the figures moved around them. Laurel knew she was watching events from the wraiths viewpoint and that the wraiths had different expectations when they visited here in ancient times. They were only mildly curious as to what this strange craft might be. What motivated or directed this unknown species was of little interest. The worrying factor was the pervading sense of fear. Laurel was uncertain if Ava should see this, but the little girl appeared only to be watching with interest, accepting the scene as part of the past.

The wraith moved aside, and Laurel, Helen and Ava were back on Darlen's ship.

"I believe I can remember many of the things I've seen. We appreciate your kindness."

The wraiths acknowledged Laurel and drifted back through the bulkhead. Marcel was incredulous. "The only other species I have seen are the Ferle." He held out his hand to Laurel, "You seemed as if in a trance."

"It felt like that to me," she smiled. "I know now what the Farisee look like. I believe they're a matriarchal society; I got the impression those in command were females. The others guarding the children who weren't in stasis appeared to be male."

"I got that too," Helen said. "That armour they had on their chest looked uncomfortable." She flattened her already small breasts. "I'd hate it. I wonder if we'll encounter any other sexes as we go along? Seems male and female work whatever universe you're in."

Laurel ignored the remark. "Did you notice the icons, the gods or deities that form part of their rituals or prelude to whatever task they undertake? Some had human form."

Helen shrugged, and Laurel wondered if the wraith that inhabited Helen had paid any attention at all.

"I suppose the Farisee, if they are the masters, may have evolved since they passed through this system."

"It's unlikely the physical form has changed, though the rituals might have," Harry said.

"Why didn't the wraiths show you this before?" Darlen asked.

"I hadn't planned on this trip. I'd pushed the idea of finding our origins out of my mind until Ava was older, although it was always something I resolved to do."

Darlen suggested visiting the Valley Folk to see if they had any historical perspectives to offer, but Laurel shook her head.

"They believe the wraiths are the ancestors. They would likely reject any suggestion they came from space."

Darlen handed her a datacache. "Are you able to draw your impressions of the aliens? I've seen several renderings of beings that might be the masters. It would be interesting to see if they look similar."

Laurel wasn't much of an artist. She did her best, and Darlen matched Laurel's version to an ancient Soul Monger's impression. There were enough similarities between the two renditions to agree the Farisee featured in Soul Monger lore.

"Ava?" Laurel spoke to the child, now occupying herself with decorating Mer. "Were those people the ones with mean faces? The ones who frightened you?"

"No, Mommy," she said without looking over. "I didn't see any of those on that ship. Everyone was nice."

Laurel huffed out her breath and turned to the others, "I must be wrong in thinking the Farisee were the masters."

"Perhaps there's more than one ship?" Marcel suggested.

Laurel tapped her head. "Ah! Yes. More than one ship. So, there's an even bigger picture. One the wraiths didn't see."

Marcel smiled. It was a rare thing for him to offer advice to the wise lady Laurel.

CHAPTER TWENTY _

"What about language? The further we go from League space, the more likely we are to run into species who speak a language we don't understand." Darlen and Harry were discussing or, rather, bickering about the possibilities of encountering alien civilisations on either side of the nebula. In the months since they left on this mission, Harry had recognised the barrier to him and Darlen being at least colleagues stemmed from his own prejudices about slavery. He tried hard to change his attitude, which worked most of the time, but Darlen was too mellow for Harry.

"Don't worry," Darlen said. "I've always managed."

Harry considered Darlen overly smug about his abilities to overcome any problems they may face, not just in communications but about the whole journey. He hated feeling that Darlen was pacifying him with his answers. Darlen simply wouldn't accept there might be situations they couldn't handle, and it made sense to set up at least a basic contingency plan to deal with any eventuality. He met every one of Harry's suggestions with his usual carefree "it'll work out" attitude. As a former member of the League Constabulary and the military, and despite his own penchant for bending the rules, Harry preferred a little more structure. He was getting nowhere with Darlen, and the nearest person to pick up this most recent discussion was Helen, who sensed his exasperation.

"I don't know why you're bothering to argue with him," Helen said. "He's not going to change. You're a military leader. Why don't you give us a few ideas so we can work out something in the event something does happen. Anyway, I agree with Darlen; you're gloomy."

"I'm practical," Harry retorted. "Embarking on this mission without any strategies to deal with problems was reckless."

"Did you say so to Laurel?"

Harry hesitated. He hadn't said so to Laurel. It was only now, after encountering the Constabulary cruiser and hearing Laurel's concerns and Ava's intuitions, that he thought developing a plan might be overdue.

Helen laughed and poked her finger at him. "I knew you didn't. You got swept up in the adventure. Just like I did!"

"Not exactly swept up—" Harry lowered his voice, and Helen leaned closer, "but I did have concerns about working so close to…" he glanced up at Darlen, who wasn't listening anyway, "to other individuals."

Helen pointed at Darlen, declaring in her usual loud voice, "Him? He's not the problem, Harry. Get over what he was, and get over what you were. We're none of us the same now. We're a crew on a small ship on a different quest, and it's peacetime. Don't look for obstacles."

"You think I'm making a fuss for no reason?" Harry

knew it would have been impossible for Darlen not to have heard.

"No, we need to be prepared, but you need to stop picking fights with the captain because you think you know better. You don't."

Harry thought he heard Darlen snort a laugh as he went to find Laurel and Marcel to enlist their support.

Since the war, the League had warned the whole souls of the dangers of travelling beyond League space boundaries. Many of the independent systems were home to crime cartels and traffickers. The existence of the five whole souls was common knowledge and a grand prize for any overlord prepared to risk entanglement with the League. There was no way into League space for any ship that didn't carry a League tagging device. A trader, like Darlen, would have to allow the League to connect the identifier to their ship, the League's technicians ensuring the whereabouts of the technology would be impossible to determine. Even with his tenacity, Darlen had never discovered where they'd attached his tag. The only people ever to get through the perimeter were the Gartrya, and so far, even the League hadn't discovered how they accomplished it.

Their next destination would take them as close to that boundary as Harry would go unless they were inside the nebula. It was one thing where he and Darlen found common ground.

"There are a few systems just outside League boundaries, but I'm not aware of any Gale or cartel activity. There are no inhabited planets," Darlen told Helen and

Laurel, "but Harry's right, once we've finished on this planet, we need to head into the nebula."

"Will we be safe?" Helen looked around to see if anyone else had concerns. "Maybe we shouldn't leave the ship this close to the edge."

"It's inside League space, Helen," Darlen said. "The League will track any ship it can't identify at the perimeter. It would be powered down remotely until the constables come to board it and take the crew into custody."

Laurel was studying at the starchart. "It's a shame. It looks fascinating outside."

"Well, if you're not in a hurry, we'll slow down for you to take a look. But it's mainly asteroids."

It seemed to Laurel, there were few directions to look in space that weren't spectacular. Darlen was right, there were a few asteroids, stellar dust, and nothing that a seasoned traveller would find compelling, but to Laurel, this was all fresh, only a few years old. Even those regions she'd seen that were empty were the stirrings of an adventure, each distant point of starlight promising something new, something unexpected. Helen tuned in to her thoughts.

"And heaps of nasty surprises, as well."

Laurel looked at her and grinned. *"You need to see Harry's all-events contingency strategies. I hope we never get to use any of them."*

Helen allowed herself a smirk. Harry had got his way with plan-making after all.

The journey between Diriarden and the prison planet gave Helen and Laurel time to teach the others a few Earth games, modified somewhat to suit four-year-old Ava. These few weeks were a time of personal growth for Marcel, who was fascinated by the games. He believed himself educated, but he realised now he knew very little. Each day, Darlen spent time with Marcel to help him improve his physical strength; not easy with the restricted space on the ship, but Darlen's use of the term "soft" spurred Marcel to work hard. Over the course of only one or two weeks, the benefits to Marcel's body were showing. His slender frame bulked out, and he gleefully displayed his abdominal muscles with no hint of self-consciousness, loving the term "six-pack" without even asking Helen for an explanation. Laurel and Harry organised lessons for Ava, and Marcel used every spare moment when he wasn't piloting or working out to sit in on those lessons, eagerly soaking up every piece of knowledge available. And when the classes were over, he would take pieces of Mer apart and put him back together under the robot's instruction. Marcel read specifications on datacaches then revised them with Darlen. He studied medical references and practices with Harry and Laurel, absorbing enough practical knowledge to become a field medic. And he also found time to teach Ava to speak French, knowing it was of little value out here, but like Earth history, was part of their shared heritage. Ava loved having Marcel to herself; as a result, her ability to converse with him in the language of his father increased rapidly.

"Marcel is a different person," Harry said as he and Laurel cuddled up one night. "I don't think I've ever seen anyone so motivated outside an accelerated learning program. Even then, he leaves those students standing."

"I think his education was geared towards Gartrya

being victorious. His father also had this ability to absorb information and once he was on Semevale 7, became quite the expert on League politics and history."

"Marcel's an outstanding pilot. And teaching Ava his language…" Harry laughed, then with sudden seriousness. "Are we redundant? Ava has a brother, and an aunt in Helen, and also has Darlen. Do you ever think of the days when it was just the three of us?"

Of all the group, Harry was the most out of place. Laurel had earlier resolved to speak to him, but now he'd asked that question; she knew his situation bothered him.

"You seem unsettled, Harry?" She tightened her arms around him, wanting him to know she was on his side. "You seem resentful every time Darlen asks anything of you."

She heard him sigh as she rested her face against his chest. "I don't know, Laurel," he said. "I've never been just a crew member before. I'm not finding it easy to adjust. I feel underutilised. Here, I have no use as a physician nor as a law enforcer. I don't even have a use as a pilot; that falls to Marcel and Darlen. The best I can do is make up games to amuse everyone. We're heading into unexplored territories, and we have no idea what's out there. I've tried to speak to Darlen—he is the captain after all—but he brushes me off."

"He's spent his life out here, Harry. It's fair to assume he has some sense of what we might encounter."

"We're going beyond League space, beyond anywhere they've charted. He doesn't know, Laurel, any more than you or I, and it's foolhardy to leave what we may encounter to chance."

"As you say, it's beyond charted space. It's possible your contingency plans may not work out there."

"I know, but I made the plan based on what I do know, not what I don't, and we're not in uncharted space yet."

Laurel hated that he felt so useless, but he was the only one who felt that way. She knew Darlen liked Harry, but Harry wouldn't believe her if she said so, not yet anyhow.

"You need to stop letting Darlen ruffle your feathers. Accept him for what he is. He's not so bad."

Harry chuckled. "Helen said something similar. Only louder."

Laurel reached up to kiss him goodnight. "I'm in the same boat as you, but I was only a physician for five minutes. Now I'm...just a telepath, I suppose." She wriggled around so Harry's body spooned hers. "We just have to be Mom and Dad to Ava, whatever that means to her."

CHAPTER TWENTY-ONE _

They arrived safely at the abandoned penal colony planet, but Darlen made sure that there was no prospect of unwelcome encounters on the surface with several sensor sweeps. There was no sign of the Constabulary cruiser. Laurel, Marcel and Helen had listened to Harry's concerns and encouraged Darlen to take the question of security more seriously, the most basic of which was to investigate any destination closely with whatever means available before any question of leaving in an axispod or landing the ship.

"The most immediate danger here is the weather," Darlen said. "A storm will whip up in seconds, and if you're out in it, you'll find yourself deposited somewhere else on the planet, most likely dead. And don't touch the plant life; most of it's toxic."

"What did the prisoners eat?" Helen asked.

"A few provisions were left with each prisoner," Harry explained. "At one time, this place had large native lizards, but the convicts hunted them to extinction. There are a couple of lesser species, though. Water would have been a big issue; most of it is subterranean." Harry felt no sympathy for criminals, but his natural respect for life caused him to add, "It must have been pretty harsh, never knowing if you were going to die of thirst or hunger, surviving from one minute to the next."

"None of us knows when we're going to die, Harry," Darlen said. "I've been waiting for it to catch up with me for years."

"What about the storms?" Helen needed more information before she would step out onto that planet. "Will the ship give us any protection?"

Darlen held up a palm-sized sensor. "None of the prisoners had technology, so they couldn't predict the storms. Mer will be tracking any storm activity, so we should be safe. There are a few predators here; he'll track those too."

"Predators?" That was it. Helen plonked herself in a seat and crossed her arms and legs. There was no way she was getting off the ship.

"They're small, Helen!" Darlen laughed, pulling her out of the seat. "Don't be a baby! Look, Ava's excited about going."

Ava did seem completely unbothered about any dangers the planet held. She sat up on the control panel, pointing to low red and black mountains and vast tundra, all the while chatting with Mer about getting off the ship. Laurel took Harry aside.

"I'm worried. Her feelings that we should come here were strong when she communicated them to me, I had no doubt, but now, with Minet's obvious secrecy…"

"You're worried about safety?"

"Ava's safety."

"Darlen and I have put every precaution possible in place. You can stay on the ship with Ava if you like. Marcel, Darlen, and I can check out the locale."

But Ava was unhappy about being excluded. "We're here to find things, Mommy," she said. "Howie and Darlen won't know what to look for." As they had followed Ava's instincts this far, Laurel had no choice but to relent.

Despite the bleakness of the planet, the air was breathable, and the nebula hung like a colourful frieze behind the western hemisphere—the entire system comprising only four of these minor planets, with many tiny moons spinning in orbit.

The sun stung them as soon as they left the ship.

"What an odd place," Laurel said. Despite the heat, a shiver ran the length of her spine.

"I'm not sure why Ava wanted to come here," Helen said, looking around. "It's just scrub and wasteland."

Marcel was listening in. "My lady sister believes we should be here," he said, his voice firmly showing his trust in his little sister's intuition.

"Marcel's right," Darlen said, picking up a handful of gritty, red soil and wrinkling up his face as he examined it. "Ava seemed convinced."

"Those rock formations to the south—" Harry moved away, allowing his retinal optimiser to guide him, "show signs of abandoned habitation. Perhaps there's something there that might answer that question."

Ava ran about unperturbed, squeaking disapproval at Darlen when he picked her up and brought her back to the group. "There aren't any human life signs on this planet, but it doesn't mean there aren't non-humans. I think it pays to play safe."

"Shall I stay at the ship with her?" Helen offered. "I don't mind missing out on an archaeological find." But Ava and Laurel had had this discussion, and although Laurel could dig in her heels with her headstrong daughter, she sensed Ava's instincts to guide them were true. Her telepathic senses moved to high alert. She felt uneasy, not just from what she knew of the planet, but something else she couldn't quite identify. On the face of it, with Mer guarding the ship and sensors, there seemed no immediate reason to worry. So, they all went, even Helen.

The rock formations were over fifty metres high and overgrown with woody vines and large, dry, lichen blemishes. Lower down and dotted over the cliff face, they found small hollows that opened into larger caves. The caves were uniform and most likely man-made, the recessed entrances possibly created during natural erosion and then further hollowed out by the convicts. It was in these they found evidence of previous occupation, undisturbed for many years.

Laurel peered around the gloomy interior. "Do you know when this stopped being a penal colony?"

Harry shrugged. "Two hundred years, maybe."

"This is a sad place," Marcel observed, standing at the cave entrance, looking towards the desolation outside. "I imagine death was a welcome visitor."

Darlen held a torch aloft, illuminating a gallery of rough paintings and etchings lining the walls. "I've never seen these before," he said, holding the torch higher to get a better look. "I normally stay on the ship."

The graphic depiction of the desperate fight for survival of the former inhabitants instantly drew Laurel's attention. The storms featured across all the paintings and engravings, with scenes of bodies piled one on top of another. "Is this world any more hostile than, say, Campil or Diriarden?" she asked. "Humans manage to survive in those places."

"Not any more hostile," Harry replied, turning full circle to view the depictions, "but Diriarden has the Wellsprings and the Campil live underground when the sun is up; they've got a system for survival. But it's not the hostility that keeps this planet unclaimed; it's too close to the nebula. People don't want to live where the nebula infiltrates. They're frightened of it."

Laurel shook her head, "That's crazy. The nebula margin barely brushes the western hemisphere. Safe enough for humans."

"Yes, but folk are superstitious." Harry looked around the cave, wrinkling his nose at the smell of age and dust, the very things that stirred Laurel's imagination. "I suppose it has a sun, several moons, sister planets," he added grudgingly. "With the right tech to keep them safe, who knows?"

Darlen was listening in and raised an eyebrow. "I know. The humans on Diriarden are the only humans who don't fear the nebula. This is one planet that will never see pioneers."

Helen and Ava, busy poking through remains of

ancient pots and wall coverings hidden by an overgrowth of plant life, distracted them.

"What's this?" Helen held up a remnant of a textile Ava had found. "It's handwoven, whatever it is."

"If there's no animal life here," Marcel took the cloth from her, "what materials would they use to weave?"

"They left animals here at each intake," Harry said, "but again, only males, so when the meat ran out, they had to turn to vegetation to survive, and much of it's toxic. They might have used plant fibres for weaving."

Helen rubbed the fine weave between her fingers. "This looks like wool or fur of some sort. It's got a definite pattern as well." She peered at the fabric, indicating to Darlen to bring his torch closer. She raised it to her nose and sniffed, then, her face contorting with disgust, tossed it away. "It's human hair, ugh!"

Laurel picked up the remnant and took it to the cave mouth to examine in daylight, but dirt and age made it difficult for her to make out the patterns.

"It's text, I think."

"Do you understand it? Is it the same as the text from the archives?" Helen spat on her hands to clean them and rubbed them over her slacks.

The others were all watching Laurel as she puzzled over the fragment. She looked up.

"It has elements of Hebrew, but—it's so old. Harry, how long was this planet used as a penal colony?"

"History says it was a dumping ground for several systems until the League came into being, but we're talking centuries, Laurel. Old era records aren't that reliable. You know that."

Helen hooked the artefact from Laurel's hand on the end of a stick and tucked it into a bag. "We'll take it back to the ship to give you a chance to nut it out."

"Wait, Helen!" Laurel was horrified and attempted to snatch the fragment back. "We can't disturb this place; it's like taking flowers from someone's grave."

Harry shook his head. Earth humans had odd practices. "We can image it if you like," he offered, but on second thought, Laurel preferred to examine the real thing. She stepped back from Helen and allowed her to remove the cloth.

"I don't see any dead bodies, anyway," Helen declared, making a reasonable point.

"She's right." Darlen made his way outside. "This might be what Ava wanted us to find. Marcel and I will check the other caves."

Laurel and Helen moved deeper into the hollow, trying to leave everything else they found undisturbed. They left Harry and Ava to examine the wall paintings. Ava pointed to an area roughly corresponding to her height. The same symbols they saw on the weave were also painted there. Harry called out just as Laurel and Helen emerged from the deeper end of the cave.

"Look at these, Laurel. They're identical to the weave. They must be significant. Ava?" Harry crouched down to Ava's level. "Do these pictures have anything to do with why you wanted to come here?"

But before Ava could answer, an explosion had them ducking dust and a minor rockfall. Harry grabbed Ava into his arms, and they ran to the mouth of the cave. Darlen and Marcel, heads down and arms up to defend themselves, skidded into the cave to join them.

"Is it a storm?" Helen positioned herself a little further back inside the cave.

Darlen was trying to see through the dust. "No, someone fired on the ship." He d-commed Mer. "Mer, who's attacking?" He tried again, but Mer didn't answer. "Whoever it is blocked the signal."

"We're sitting ducks," Helen wailed. "We need to get back!"

"If they wanted to destroy the ship, they probably would have. Harry, you're a munitions specialist. Are those gamil mines?"

"I'd say so; they smell like it." Harry nodded at Laurel and Helen. "Gamil mines have a distinctive smell but minimal burst. Someone's trying to warn us."

"To leave or just draw us out of the caves?"

"I don't know, Laurel. But they haven't hit the ship."

Helen stepped forward, confidence replacing the fear from a moment ago. "If we stay close together, I think I can cover us for that distance." A second's hesitation to register a great plan, then they quickly formed a tight group around Helen and took off towards the ship.

CHAPTER TWENTY-TWO _

Laurel sensed the attacker the moment Helen's mantle faded. "The cruiser!" she shouted to Darlen as he raced to the control room ahead of her. "It's in orbit. They've cloaked."

Darlen checked the sensors. "Nothing, but if you say they're there, that's good enough for me." He looked up and raised his hands. "Do you have any idea where?"

"Directly above, take off towards the West. They might not follow us into the nebula."

"They're faster than this old ship," Harry said. "Once they see the direction, they'll intercept. I think we should find out what they want."

Darlen agreed. "We won't outrun them. Let's get off the ground and face them. At least in space, we have manoeuvrability."

Laurel guided them to a position between the cruiser and the nebula. Darlen swung the ship around. "I can't see a thing," he said.

"They're there," Laurel pointed to the viewscreen, "dead ahead. They've got forward cannons primed. Are they likely to fire?"

"I don't think so," Harry said, "they'd need to drop the cloak, and I'm willing to bet that right now, they're wondering how we got back to the ship without being seen and how we know where they are now."

"Gamil charges are contraband," Darlen said. "How come a Constabulary cruiser is deploying them? A couple of the big Cartels use them, but I've never seen one in League space."

"None of the Constabulary ships would have these in their possession," Harry agreed. "Not legally, anyway." He paused, his mouth set in a grim line, realising there was more to Laurel's mistrust of Minet than he'd given her credit. "And we're a logged vessel. Minet was a good colleague. His behaviour is mystifying. What would he expect to gain by firing on us?"

"He was pretty keen to get rid of us when you told him I was a whole soul," Laurel reminded him.

Harry gave her a sheepish nod. He should have listened to her.

"I sensed he was cagey from the start," Laurel said. "He had a whole load of layers to his dishonesty once I got inside his head. It would have taken longer than we had to sort through; he really wanted to keep us away from the planet."

"He might have been relying on the fact no-one ever goes there. Our plans must have come as a surprise."

"It doesn't explain the explosives," Darlen said.

The cruiser decloaked and hailed them. Harry demanded an explanation without granting his former colleague the opportunity to speak.

"Why did you fire on us? We didn't provoke you in any way."

Minet's expression was impassive. "Harry, you weren't there for a picnic. Now move on. There's nothing for you here."

Darlen held up his hand to stop Harry from responding.

"There's something for you though, Constable, isn't there?" he said.

Minet merely flicked his eyes across to Darlen. "I have nothing to say to you, Soul Monger."

Darlen ignored his disdain. "So, what is it? Not human contraband, that would have shown up on our scans. Precious metals? Gemstones? Fire ore?"

"Fire ore?" Harry said sharply. "Darlen, that's not possible. This place would be crawling with…wait," he turned back to Minet. "Are you guarding Fire ore? For a cartel? For the *Gale?*"

Minet didn't miss a beat. "Precisely, Harry, we believe the Gale got wind of a Fire ore seam, and we need to defend the planet until Congress supports the League's claim."

"The League?" Harry shook his head in disbelief. "Do you take us for idiots? The League doesn't require Fire ore. It has no value among treaty planets."

"The planet is in League space, and the Gale has been sniffing around outside the boundary." Minet's hologram shimmered; Laurel's presence unnerved him.

"It's only just inside League space, Minet." Harry noted the cruiser cannons remained primed, but turning tail and running might not be safer than staying here and getting answers. "It has seven days before its orbit takes it over the boundary. How do you plan to protect it then? Illegal gamil charges?"

"None of this is any of your concern, Harry. I suggest you leave."

But Harry would not be deterred. He continued to press his old friend for an explanation.

"How would you fare against the Gale? They don't travel singly,"

"The Gale knows the League is protecting its interests," Minet replied, "and they won't venture into League space while we're patrolling."

"The League is protecting its interests? Or the canonical family?" Laurel cut in. Something was reaching her. It was even reaching Helen, and she glanced across at Laurel.

"Just move on and let me do my job," were Minet's final words as transmission cut. The cruiser turned a graceful circle and moved away at normal speed, leaving Darlen's ship still at all stop, with Darlen making no attempt to leave.

"Do you believe him, Harry?" Darlen said as the cruiser retreated.

"About Fire ore? You must be joking! He's here for some other reason. That's why he's so jumpy." Harry turned to Laurel with a questioning look. She shook her head.

"I know he's lying, but I do think the League is involved somehow."

Helen clapped her hands together. "Stop! We came to this planet for no other reason than something drew Ava here. Now we've found the tapestry. It may mean something that will help us with our journey and probably what we came to find. We left the League behind; if they've got problems, we don't need to be part of it. Can't we just get out of here?"

But Darlen had a thought. "Fire ore is valuable on some worlds. It might be valuable where we're going. We may need currency or something to trade on the way."

"It won't be just sitting around on the surface waiting to be picked up, though," Harry said. "Isn't it normally a single seam?"

Helen looked up the details on a datacache. "I wonder how they discovered it?"

"Routine survey probably," Harry said. "The planet spends almost its entire orbit within the League boundary. I doubt anyone would bother surveying during the time it's orbiting outside the boundary."

"Well, it says here that Fire ore, in its raw state, can be found away from the original seam." Helen held up the datacache for Harry to see. "Seismic activity, weather conditions and the like can move small pieces." She looked at Laurel. "It's probably like alluvial gold."

"Is it worth going back?" Marcel asked.

"Not us," Darlen said. "Mer could get in even without an axispod, but we'd have to hang around here to identify any deposits."

"Is this Gale a criminal organisation?" Marcel had never heard of them.

Darlen turned away from the controls. "The Arransiak Gale is the most powerful and ruthless of the syndicates, but mostly, it stays out of League space and affairs. At the moment, that planet is transiting through League space, which means the Gale will keep its distance. They can't enter League space, and they don't need to. They have plenty of star systems to keep them busy." He glanced at Laurel. "But it still doesn't explain the presence of the cruiser."

"Minet is lying."

"Of course," Darlen saw it, "but if the Gale found out we had three whole souls on board…well, you would be a valuable acquisition, possibly worth taking on the League perimeter defence and a Constabulary cruiser."

Laurel felt a moment of panic. "Harry, you told Minet I was a whole soul. If he's somehow involved with the Gale…" She held up her hand as Harry made to speak. "I think we should just move on." They had to consider Ava. "We should forget sending Mer to pick up ore."

They all agreed, so Darlen brought the ship around but immediately powered down, turning the ship dark in space—a trick he used when he didn't want to be seen. A vessel was crossing the League boundary.

"So much for immobilising trespassers," Helen said as they watched the ship move unimpeded towards the surface of the planet. It was directly in their path.

"That ship is Arransiak Gale," Darlen said. "And it's in League space."

"It must have a tag," Harry shifted his attention to the sensors. "The perimeter isn't on alert. Darlen, have they seen us?"

"No, they don't appear to be looking. But the Gale travel in twos."

The second Gale ship dropped into their sensors just as the first ship landed on the planet. The second ship, which Darlen described as a Gale raider, was about the size of the Constabulary cruiser, sleek and elegant, with four fin-like structures around its middle and a v-shaped compartment at the rear end. Heavily armed, it looked like it meant business, although it didn't appear to have spotted Darlen's ship.

"Have you ever encountered the Gale before, Harry?" Laurel gathered Ava close.

"Not in League space; they operate in the independent systems, and they're a murderous bunch. I think we need to hide you and Ava."

"What about Helen?"

"I've met them before," Helen said. "They have no idea I'm a whole soul. They think I'm just some bimbo Darlen picked up on his travels."

"So, you've had actual dealings with them, Helen?"

"A few times, Laurel. Blokes run it, I mean misogynistic blokey blokes, and they don't talk to me. The women who hang around them are like trophy wives, dripping jewellery and fancy clothes. I look like something the cat dragged in by comparison."

"They sound like the Mafia."

"They're the equivalent. If you want it and can pay, the Gale can get it."

"And I'm a sitting duck whole soul?"

"You might be, but they don't know about Ava and me. Darlen has a few tricks up his sleeve, let me tell you, and he knows these people."

"Please tell me you have never been involved in slavery, Helen."

"No, but…" Helen shrugged, and Laurel caught the admission in her thoughts. She could forgive Helen a few shady deals provided they hurt no one or involved human trafficking.

"We wouldn't be able to stop them boarding," Darlen said, "but the raider will stay in orbit. The best we can do is stall them and look for a split-second escape avenue. Mer, tap into the controls and put up the shield. If they fire on us, they'll cop some of the flak themselves, not enough to do much damage at this distance, unfortunately."

"Why doesn't Auntie Helen hide us?" Ava patted Helen's arm. "They won't find us even if they count to a hundred!"

All eyes turned to Helen. Even Mer's head swivelled around.

"I'm not sure I can hide a whole ship."

"It's our best shot, Helen," Laurel said, taking in the nods of agreement from the others. "And don't forget, Marcel's father hid me from an entire army. He also hid his ship from League troops on more than a few occasions."

"But if that ship on the ground has seen us…you said we couldn't hide if we've been seen."

"They've not shown any signs of having seen us," Darlen said. "Maybe they aren't scanning because it's so isolated, and using sensors might draw attention to their presence."

"Or maybe because they have League support." Harry pointed out the Constabulary cruiser heading towards the planet. "They might alert the Gale ships. Helen, I suggest you get a move on."

For the first time, Laurel was in a position to watch Helen wrap them in the mantle. In an instant, her blue eyes glowed bright, her gaze became distant, and from her fingertips, a tendril of smoky ectoplasm-like substance coiled and threaded its way around the group. Undistracted by chaos and urgency as they had been on other times Helen performed this feat, Laurel alone saw the disconnection, the thing the masters' feared most of all, the separation of body and spirit. It was subtle, visible to Laurel and perhaps to Ava, but the three men saw no change in Helen.

They were just in time. The Gale raider sent out a sensor sweep as the Constabulary cruiser alerted them of their presence. Darlen hit widespeed before the cruiser issued coordinates to the other ships. They entered the nebula as the raider abandoned its search for the invisible vessel.

Helen flopped in a chair. "I hid a bloody ship!"

Ava climbed onto her lap. "I liked your smoke, Auntie Helen, and your eyes; they had sparkles!"

"Did they, sweetie?" Helen appreciated the dose of reality. "I've never seen what I look like when I do that."

"You looked like a fairy."

Helen smiled. "A fairy? I looked like a fairy? How special!"

Marcel breathed a sigh as if he'd been holding his breath this whole time. "We didn't see that which my lady sister sees, but I am sure that ship couldn't see us."

Darlen and Harry weren't so confident. "The one on

the surface did," Darlen said, checking sensor logs. "We debated too long and gave Minet the chance to identify us. I doubt they'll let us go."

"Do you think they'll follow?" Marcel checked that they were alone in the nebula.

"They'll see if they can trace us, at least for a while. I expect they know about Laurel now." Darlen turned to Harry. "Looks like your constable friend is doing a little lining of his own pockets."

"He's a decent man…or at least he was."

"Well, if he's helping the Gale and told them about Laurel, we need to be where they can't find us."

Laurel felt the need to check the sensors herself. "Would they follow us for one whole soul?"

"Believe me, Laurel," Darlen said, "a single whole soul is of considerable value to the Gale, and they would take Ava as leverage. Not only that, they'll also guess we know they're not there on League business."

"If the Gale can cross into League space," Laurel said, "does that mean Marta and Eli and Chloe are in danger?"

Darlen quickly swept a finger across a starchart. "Leyis is the closest planet to here. We need to send Eli a message." Darlen immediately sent a priority warning directly to the Leyis homeworld. "Under the circumstances, I won't use League frequencies, particularly for Chloe. So, I'm sending to Marta to recall Chloe from duty."

"Should we go back?" Marcel asked.

"I suggest we continue on and travel through the heart of the nebula for a while."

"For how long?" Helen wailed. "It's so bloody

boring."

"The Gale ships can easily overtake this piece of junk. All we've got is the nebula for sanctuary. They can't enter the heart, but if they had you, Laurel, they could, and of course, they know there are other civilisations on the other side to corrupt or join in their corruption. We have to protect you and Ava." Then he added. "And Helen, unless you want to wait it out and fight off the Gale because you find the nebula dull?"

Helen was ready with her response, and while she and Darlen bickered, Laurel's head filled with worrying thoughts. She'd been prepared to meet a few dangers when she set out, but real threats to Ava? She hadn't considered it. The people of the League, the planets she spent time on, seemed so benevolent; it was simple and naïve to assume it would be the same everywhere. The course they plotted included no planets after Diriarden; they were to head for the nebula after that, but Ava's senses had directed them differently.

"Shouldn't we just abandon this and go back to Mentelci," she announced, suddenly losing all her courage.

Harry shook his head. "The Gale will anticipate that. If Minet is involved, he'll be able to screen all the perimeter alerts for our signature. We're safer out here."

"They never tried to get us before," Helen said.

"Right now, I'd say they're getting some unsanctioned League help," Harry said. "You three are fair game. I'm sorry—" he made a gesture of helplessness with his hands, "this is my fault. I thought Minet was straightforward."

"I've been all over League space and out of it a couple

of times," Helen said. "I felt perfectly safe, but…" she made a pointed comment towards Harry. "Loose lips, sink ships."

"What the hell does that mean?"

"That you dropped Laurel in it with the Gale. They'll only bother with us because they know she's a whole soul."

Harry went to say he'd already taken responsibility, but Laurel shushed him. "Why would you leave League space, Helen?"

"I never let on I was a whole soul and never drew attention to myself. That's why Darlen stopped going back to Caltobar, just in case. That's where the Arransiak Gale has its headquarters." She gave Harry another accusing look. "Now, they know for sure Laurel's on board and that she has a child."

"Minet has access to League personnel records," Harry said. "He may investigate now and find Helen on their database as well. And he's going to be worried we'll rat him out to the League. He may regret not using real charges."

"Oh, well, shit," Helen shrugged. "The nebula it is then."

CHAPTER TWENTY-THREE _

Laurel stood in the narrow control room squeezed between Ava, Mer, and the console as they entered the nebula. To her, it was the most wondrous place in this universe and bringing Ava here for the first time and seeing her wonderment only added to Laurel's satisfaction. They reached what Darlen called the heart in less than a day, where the nebula's dense colour and clouds spiralled into an infinite corridor. To Laurel, it was more than a heart; it was a conduit for the lifeblood of the nebula. A living entity, filled with glowing colours and stars and exquisitely fine filaments that reached in through the bulkhead to entwine gently through her fingers, just as she imagined doing the first time she saw it from the consular ship. Ava also felt the same enchantment when the colours flowed across her bed and lit her dark curls in all the colours of the rainbow. Marcel and Harry only ever saw one or two blue or red flashes and were mystified by Laurel and Ava's fascination. The nebula held no such wonder for them other than a hiding place.

While widespeed took away the viewport visual of the nebula for Ava and Laurel, an occasional tendril still drifted through. They could hear Ava giggling as she chased them through the ship's passageways and gangways. But for Marcel, with the ship needing little piloting, the nebula's heart meant boredom. He perked up when Darlen complained loudly that priole precipitation—the spontaneously occurring phenomenon that facilitated widespeed—was less dense at the nebula's core and would slow them down if they had to stay within it for any length of time. There followed several days study of widespeed, which benefitted not only Marcel but also Laurel, who had never completely understood how it worked, despite Harry's best attempts. Darlen's teaching style assumed Laurel and Marcel were fools who lacked any modicum of intelligence, an approach Laurel would have ordinarily found condescending, but in this, it was much appreciated.

A month went by, and everyone on board, except Darlen, who was accustomed to spending time in the nebula, and Ava, who was a welcome diversion with her demand for attention and games, felt the effects of lack of daylight, too many space rations and each other's short tempers. Darlen called them all together.

"Going by Ava's sense of direction," Darlen smiled at the little girl on his knee, "we're heading toward the northern catchments. There are a few inhabited planets along the catchment corridor, but we'd have to leave the nebula, and unfortunately, we won't be out of the Gale's reach even this far out."

"Why would we need to leave," Helen said, "if we're okay for fuel and supplies?"

"We've enough fuel to take us to eternity," Darlen

agreed. "It'll outlast the ship. Food, yes, but nothing fresh."

"No Macca's burgers," Helen winked at Laurel, drawing a puzzled frown from Marcel.

Darlen ignored her. "Water is the reason I need to speak to you all. I didn't think the gamil charge damaged the ship, and structurally, it didn't, but the evaporator is growing mould spores. We can't use it."

"I thought the League mechanics overhauled the ship's systems?" Harry said.

"They did, but they also warned me age was against the accessories. This evaporator is the same age as the ship, and while they call it an accessory, it's built into the hull, same as the slot. They work off the same system. It's never let me down, and as far as I know, it didn't let the previous owner down either or his father before him, and two hundred years ago, its systems could easily withstand a gamil charge, but now? Well, this is the first time since I've had it that it's been that close to a detonation."

"So, we can't replace the evaporator because it's built into the hull?" Marcel asked.

"That's right," Darlen replied, lifting his hands in a hopeless gesture. "We need an independent unit."

"We have the reservoir," Helen said hopefully.

"Yes, but we might need to put a water ration in place until we can leave the nebula and source something more sustaining. The reservoir won't last us on the journey we're taking. I didn't anticipate us becoming prisoners in the nebula."

Mer left the ship daily to track for signs of the Gale, and

each day came back with the same results. The tagged raider was moving at the same speed just outside the nebula margin. Harry explained how sensors could be modified to identify other tagged ships. It was illegal, but that likely was of no interest to the Gale.

Darlen proposed a course on the other side of the nebula, where they could travel outside the heart and where full widespeed precipitation was available, but Mer's scans detected several fleets of Ferle ships. They all agreed that for now, they had to stay in the nebula.

This turn of events gave Laurel time to consider the writing on the tapestry and the cave walls. She felt the same connection she had with the history stone from the archives, but the language had a greater sense of age. The more she examined the weave and held it in her hands, the stronger the feeling the words came not from the weaver or wall artist but were dictated by someone or something else. Her senses told her that this language was not the native language of the men who produced these works, which would definitely explain the symbol's crude form. Finally, after hours of study and cross-referencing her notes from the archives, she pushed the images and cloth away in frustration and wandered out to the common room. Marcel was seated on the floor, telling Ava the stories his father and grandmother told him. Ava's eyes were closed, but Laurel could tell she wasn't sleeping; she was simply enjoying having Marcel as a big brother. Laurel knew a child couldn't have too many people who loved and cherished them.

"No luck?" Helen looked up.

"It's gobbledygook," Laurel sighed.

Harry raised an eyebrow, and Marcel laughed. "You and my lady Helen have such odd sayings."

"It means it doesn't make sense." Laurel flopped down beside Marcel and Ava. "I kind of see it, but each symbol is representative of something else. It may be a Hebrew dialect; it has similarities. I'm wondering if the language belongs to the whole souls or perhaps the masters."

"Could be both," Harry suggested. "One might have a distinctive inflexion, like on your world. You had a different accent from Helen when you first arrived, and you said your written language had differences. Perhaps this is the same."

"Maybe. I'll have another look." Laurel blew a raspberry on Ava's neck, making the child giggle. "Only not tonight."

Another month passed before they dared leave the nebula and even then, only moved the ship out to the inner margin. There was no sign this time of the Gale ship. An ageing space station nestled between two gas giants was a possible destination for water or evaporator parts and home to a society of humans, the descendants of the original crew complement. Darlen and Helen had been here before, and so it seemed, had Harry.

"An epidemic," he explained. "I was still studying. They sent out for help, but communication out here is pretty slow, and only a few passing ships were heading for League space—I mean legitimate ones. The inhabitants were sensible enough to quarantine the station, and they are largely self-sustaining. They have evaporative systems to supply water."

"Are we likely to bump into the Gale?"

"It's a dump, Laurel," Harry said, "definitely a place contacts of the Gale might use to filter contraband."

"Harry's right," Darlen agreed, "Marcel is the only one who wouldn't be recognised. There are vendors there who sell drinking water bags at a high price. He can tandem up one of the axispods in the hold and fill up. I can't risk sending a message to any contacts on the station, just in case the Gale is hanging around."

"Are you okay with that, Marcel?" Laurel said, suddenly feeling very protective of him, despite his being twice her size and possibly, since she hadn't had much exercise, also twice her strength.

"Of course, Laurel. And while I am there, I will keep my ears and eyes open."

"You're starting to sound like Darlen."

That brought a snort from Helen. "As long as he doesn't pick up all his bad habits."

The prospect of an away mission was exciting for Marcel. Flying an axispod had become second nature to him, and he was utterly laissez-faire at the prospect of making this trip alone. Laurel caught a glimmer of thought that at last, after all his education, he felt he had something useful to do, that he felt needed.

From within the nebula, they watched the axispod head towards the station.

"Won't they wonder why he's arriving in an axispod and not a ship?" Helen asked. "I should have gone with him and hid us."

"And appeared out of nowhere when you went to a

vendor? As if that wouldn't attract attention," Darlen grinned. "Or would you just steal the water bags? Do you remember that time when we…?"

Helen stopped him with a glare. Darlen bit his lip, but even though Helen silenced him, Laurel saw his resolve to one day relate that tale.

"Some ships that pass through here are too big to dock, so they use shuttles and axispods." Harry answered the question Helen asked before she got distracted. "The axispods don't have League markings."

"I hope he doesn't run into trouble."

"He shouldn't," Darlen said. "It's one of those places where people don't want to be identified; people like traders and slavers. They don't ask questions here. That's why we need to keep a lookout for the Gale." He checked the sensors. "I can't detect any Gale ships, but that doesn't mean there aren't agents, so I might be wrong."

Laurel wasn't comfortable, but this wasn't a telepathic sense. It occurred to her it was the unease a mother might feel when her eldest child ventured out alone for the first time. The others all seemed relaxed until Helen caught the seed of her thoughts and looked over. Ava sat quietly in a corner, sensing Laurel's concern. She refused even to draw on Mer's face, even though he expected it and even presented her with a colouring pen. Laurel's thoughts affected Ava, so she stopped dwelling on Marcel and instead mused upon the fact that Mer became a boy when Ava learned to talk. It didn't stop her from dressing the robot up in what she called princess and fairy clothes, and characters from fairy tales and stories told to her by Laurel. Harry's childhood stories didn't seem to inspire her imagination in the same way, even though she loved to listen to them. Mer alternated between Aurora from Sleeping Beauty, Long John Silver, Spiderman and various Disney characters, to pantomime hybrids. Before Laurel knew it, she was laughing at Mer's face, coloured with pink and green flowers; her concern for Marcel pushed to the back of her mind.

CHAPTER TWENTY-FOUR _

Marcel's first solo mission took more than a day longer than anticipated. Darlen scanned the area continually for Gale ships, and although no-one voiced it, they feared Marcel might have fallen foul of one of their contract agents. Ava, refusing to be alone until Marcel returned, was asleep on Harry's shoulder when a scan picked up the axispod.

"Something's wrong!" Laurel grabbed the portable pandroscope and ran for the landing bay as the axispod docked. An almost naked Marcel climbed down from the controls. He wore only the thin League-issue activewear pants Harry gave him for his exercises. His shoes were gone, and a wide gouge opened from his collarbone to his nipple. A huge swelling covered his left eye and cheek, and dried blood encrusted his nose and left ear. His knuckles were bruised and stained with blood. He attempted a smile, but most of his handsome face had suffered an impressive rearrangement.

"I got the water," he said, leaning against the axispod for support and wiping the blood from his eye.

Darlen supported Marcel while Laurel quickly checked him with the pandroscope, which showed mostly superficial injuries. "He's not in any danger. Let's get him to his bunk." Together, she and Darlen carried their battered and bruised colleague to his bed.

Harry was not impressed when he came to see the patient. "I bet he didn't walk into a door, Laurel. Someone attacked him."

"Just wait, Harry. We don't know what transpired. He'll tell us when he can."

Marcel groaned and tried to shift his position, placing his hands protectively over the area where two of his ribs were cracked. He opened his eyes. "I'm sorry," he croaked.

Laurel shushed him, leaning over to place healbot panels over his broken skin. She was going to say he could tell them all about it later, but the reason for the injuries suddenly became clear in her mind. She straightened.

"Marcel, did you pick a fight?"

With his one good eye, he looked from Laurel to Harry and attempted a shrug.

"I didn't start it," he said, the apology muffled by a large flap of swollen skin.

"Well, it looks like you finished it." Harry pointed to the wound on Marcel's chest, "This is a pretty deep laceration. It's nicked your pectoral muscle. What happened?"

Harry poured balm into the wound, and Marcel winced as it worked to sterilise the area. After a moment, when relief from pain set in, he told them what transpired on the station.

"I did as Darlen instructed," he said. "I purchased the water and directed the dealer to the axispod. I reviewed the shipment and noticed there was a bag less than I had paid the fellow for." Marcel attempted a defiant lift of his chin. "A crime had been levied," he declared, "and I wished it remedied."

"Marcel, you weren't supposed to attract attention." Laurel put her hand to her head. Earlier, she'd felt like a mother seeing her son off on his first venture alone. Now she felt like a mother exasperated by that same son's behaviour.

Harry raised an eyebrow in amusement. "You hit the dealer?"

"No," Marcel shook his head. "I hit the table in front of where he stood. I believed this sufficient to express my displeasure at his treachery. But he has a son, taller than me and around the same age. It was he who hit me."

"I would never have picked you for a brawler," Harry grinned, ignoring the danger Marcel had put himself in, perhaps all of them. Marcel made gestures of contrition, but Laurel wasn't buying it. "Marcel, you enjoyed it!"

Marcel inspected his knuckles, healing but still with signs of scuffing and bruising, and sighed. "In all my life, I have only been in the company of my lord father and lady grandmother. To be sent, to be entrusted with a mission is an adventure above all adventures for one who has lived such a sheltered existence." His bruised face broke into a satisfied, lop-sided grin. "An adversary, matched in both height and strength, deemed me a worthy opponent." His grin widened. "When he punched me in the face and, therefore, challenged me, it was glorious above imaginings."

Harry and Laurel could only look at each other. This

young man, who astonished them with his tenacity for serious study and learning, now waxed poetic on the virtues of a fistfight.

"Where did this deep scratch come from?" Harry scanned the rapidly healing wound.

"That was my adversary's good lady wife. With her bare hands," he said, pointing to the cut, a note of admiration creeping into his voice.

Harry straightened to look at Laurel, his expression bemused. "You said his father was a gentleman."

Laurel shook her head. "I'm just as surprised as you are."

Darlen, however, didn't mince his words. "You're an idiot, Marcel. I should have gone myself. Did you attract attention?"

It was a valid question. They'd instructed Marcel to get in and out without creating problems. Helen joined in with one of what she called statements of the "bleeding obvious".

"Of course, he attracted attention, Darlen. He was brawling. What else did he need to do?" Marcel hung his head at Helen's displeasure, disappointed he hadn't shown more maturity.

Laurel smiled. *"He's only a lad, Helen. Cut him some slack."*

"We're not safe yet!" Helen shot back, reminding Laurel the fight may have come to the attention of the Gale or its agents.

Darlen huffed a few times at Marcel, then turned his attention to the axispod logs. "You're lucky; it doesn't seem anyone tracked you back to the nebula. This water will last us for a few weeks—hopefully until we get the recycling system going."

"What's the farthest you've travelled into the Northern reaches?" Harry asked Darlen.

"Only another twenty or so incils, no further. The round trip took about three years from this station and back. There are a few more star systems on the way, but we still need to put some distance between the Gale and us."

"Are you sure they'll follow?"

"No, Laurel. If we find a likely planet or station to stop at, we could send Marcel again. The Gale doesn't know him."

"They might do now since the fight."

Darlen checked Marcel was dozing from the pain relief before answering. He lowered his voice. "The Gale won't pay any attention to youngsters having a brawl," Darlen said, "that sort of thing wouldn't even register." He paused. "Marcel was irresponsible, and now, I'm just wondering where that Gale raider is."

Several days later, Mer's axispod scan confirmed Marcel's maiden fistfight had not gone unnoticed. The Gale appeared to have resumed their tracking, making sure Darlen's ship couldn't leave the heart. Regular scans on the other side showed Ferle activity, so that wasn't an option.

"The vendor probably informed them we purchased a load of water," Harry said. "They may plan on keeping us here until we've got no choice but to leave."

"My guess is," Darlen said, "they'd given up following, assuming we'd stay in the safety of the nebula. The Gale hunt down their prey relentlessly, but even they know when to give up."

"And they were still in the vicinity when Marcel's little argument alerted them?"

Darlen looked thoughtful. "Possibly, probably. Chances are they questioned the water vendor."

"Is there anything we can do to make them think we've gone to the other side of the nebula?" Marcel asked, seated on the floor, remorseful and hunched over, his head in his hands.

"Two things are in their favour, Marcel. Firstly, they know we carry a whole soul, and secondly, Harry told the League soldiers where we're heading."

Harry gave Marcel a wry smile. "It seems we both got it wrong."

"We can't change the heading," Laurel said. "And it's common knowledge that whole souls can enter the nebula since the evacuation of Gartrya. We'll just have to face facts. We're staying here in the heart."

Helen shook her head. "The evaporator needs fixing before we go much further."

Ava was sitting in the co-pilot seats, listening to the conversation. "We can stay in the nebula for ages, Mommy. We don't have to go to any more planets."

"We need to fix the recycling, sweetheart." Laurel smiled indulgently at her daughter making grown-up contributions to the conversation. "The water Marcel brought back isn't enough."

"We'll all just have to go to sleep," Ava whispered to Mer as she smeared coloured pigments on his face.

CHAPTER TWENTY-FIVE _

"Any luck?" Harry gently kneaded the tension from Laurel's shoulders.

"Not yet." She closed her eyes, but the strange symbols from the tapestry still mocked her from behind her eyelids. She breathed a deep sigh as Harry's hands sent waves of relaxing tingles right down to her toes. He got to his knees beside her.

"Oh, god, don't stop," she groaned, pushing his hands back onto her shoulder, "that's gorgeous! My neck is killing me!"

"I'll do it again in a minute," he promised. "Have you made any headway at all?"

Laurel slumped forward and looked at him through bleary eyes. "I've seen the symbols someplace before, but I can't get them to make sense."

Harry picked up the woven fabric. Most of it was rather primitive, but the symbols themselves appeared to be well-worked, as if they carried importance. He knew Laurel was tired and, at times, regretted she'd asked them to come on this journey, which was becoming more dangerous than any of them initially expected. But they were here now, and

Laurel the only one capable of interpreting the symbols.

"The fabric might be bait, a lure for an enterprising whole soul," Harry said.

"I thought of that," Laurel rubbed her eyes, "but I think they're part of a trail, like tying a string to a tree, so you can retrace your path if you get lost."

"Or markers for someone else to find you?"

Laurel nodded slowly; she'd thought of that too. She leaned back in her chair.

"Can I have that massage now?"

After hours of serious concentration and the benefits of Harry's neck rub well and truly past, Laurel decided on a break from deciphering and wandered down to the cargo bay. Marcel was there working out, attempting push-ups with his little sister sitting on his back.

"Ava, why don't you give Marcel a little privacy?"

Ava slid off Marcel's back with a giggle, and he stood up with a grin. "It is well. My lady sister finds amusement in observing me as I try to strengthen my body."

"Not planning on any more brawls, I hope." Laurel pulled up a crate and sat down. "It's a small ship, Marcel; it's important we have time to ourselves with no distractions."

Marcel wiped his face with a towel and sat cross-legged in front of Laurel. "My lady sister is a joy, and I wish more of her company, not less."

As the joyful child turned her attention to bouncing on Marcel's bed, Marcel turned his gaze to Laurel.

"Something troubles you?" he smiled.

Laurel gave a frustrated sigh. "I've been trying to decipher the symbols we found on the tapestry and in the caves."

"Do you think it is necessary to decipher them? Perhaps they are of no consequence."

Laurel was about to say that she felt driven to find their meaning even if they turned out to be meaningless, but Ava spoke to her silently, causing her to look up sharply.

"I saw them in your head, Mommy. I know what they say."

"And what do they say?"

"Get out of my house."

"The same as the words you heard? Are those the words on the cloth?"

Ava shook her head as she continued bouncing on the bed. Ava wasn't talking about the tapestry; she was saying the words she heard on Canaa were inside Laurel's mind. Laurel suddenly saw the symbols laid out like a computer keyboard. Realisation dawned. Once, during a language lesson, someone had demonstrated an ordinary qwerty keyboard with phonetic Hebrew symbols added. It was something the student developed for his personal use. It had looked highly unreliable to her, and although Laurel had a passing interest, she knew little of Common Era languages. Somehow, though, it must have registered for Ava to have seen it. Leaving Marcel surprised at her sudden departure, Laurel ran back to her quarters. The symbols made more sense, but she still felt the frustration of not being certain. She studied the cave symbols first. Her memory of the Hebrew keyboard was fuzzy at best, and it didn't gel. She was missing something. Perhaps what Ava saw as a keyboard was figurative, a translation tool, like a crystal ball or seer's stone. Laurel had no belief in the occult, but here she was, a telepath, an empath, travelling through a nebula in another universe. Maybe the time had come to embrace more of the unimaginable.

Unconsciously, Laurel balled her hands into fists. Squeezing her eyes shut, she tensed her entire body and willed her mind to search for forgotten symbols or even fragments...

Laurel's eyes snapped open, but her body didn't relax.

Sitting and holding the weave up, Laurel felt like weeping with frustration. She thought of the time in the archives when she'd first seen the history of the whole souls. It took time for her to make sense of the language, and even then, a sixth sense had helped her unravel the mystery. It may happen now if, as she believed, she was destined to be following this path. She folded her arms on the table and, with a sigh, rested her head. No matter how hard she racked her brains, the tapestry and cave records yielded nothing. In the quiet, her mind drifted to the computer keyboard once again. Idly, as her thoughts applied Aramaic symbols to the keys, she felt herself smile. It wouldn't be accurate. There were no keyboards then...

Laurel sat up. Holding the image in her head, she grabbed a datacache and tried to transcribe what she saw in her mind's eye and set up a lexicon before the images faded. But as she watched, the symbols dissolved, and the keyboard reverted to a regular English keyboard. Laurel mentally touched each letter of Ava's phrase — "Get out of my house"— and waited. A line of symbols made their way into her vision. From somewhere deep inside her mind came the translation. The symbols didn't need to change to English or Seera for her to understand them. Hours later, after intense telepathic study of the tapestry and throwing logic and everything she knew out a symbolic airlock, Laurel believed she had a result.

"Arrival and departure.

The garden of Eden, fallen from grace.

The serpents are out of Sheerguhd.

The bringers of stars."

She took her results to the others.

"Are you sure it's accurate?" Helen asked, twisting her head from side to side as she tried to work out the symbols Laurel recorded on the datacache.

"Not entirely, but Ava mentioned a keyboard she'd seen in my head from my university days. I used the focus as a translator, but I had to use telepathy as well. 'Get out of my house,' in English translated to 'arrival of the Gods,' but it was such a mix of primitive languages. And this one," Laurel pushed the data out to surround them and stop them crowding around the device to get a closer look, "says, 'Fallen from Grace and Garden of Eden'. It fits with the other theological themes we came across, but you can't translate ancient Aramaic using a British English keyboard. I used telepathy—instinct—but I might be way off."

"And this?" Harry pointed out the other phrase, which prompted Laurel to see she had written her results in English rather than Seera. It suddenly seemed odd to her that was the case. She considered Seera her language now.

"That one says, 'The serpents from Sheerguhd',"

Laurel said. "I don't know what that means, but according to one of Earth's religions…"

"A pretty dominant one," Helen cut in.

Laurel nodded, "Yes, apparently God told two people not to eat an apple. A snake, a serpent, told them they would be ignorant if they didn't. Well, who wants to be ignorant? So they ate the apple, God cast them out, and they went on to populate the Earth."

"Sounds like the serpent did them a favour," Harry grinned.

Laurel pulled a face. "It's nonsense, Harry. The story is told in the book I mentioned, the Bible. It's riddled with plot holes, and scholars through the ages have pulled it to pieces, but it's still the cornerstone of Christianity."

"There are a few civilisations in the League that worship deities," Harry said. "Some people take comfort in rituals."

"Like the Farisee, you mean?"

"Maybe."

"Perhaps this Garden of Eden or Sheerguhd is where the whole souls originate," Darlen suggested. "Maybe one of the captive whole souls got a message out to the prisoners. Maybe that's why it's so fragmented. They wouldn't have understood it, so they engraved their thoughts onto the cave wall then later made tapestries, maybe realising its significance."

Harry's eyes narrowed in thought. "If the Eden thing is a metaphor and the whole souls fell from the grace of their gods or creators, and these masters represent the serpent, why were they captives on that ship?"

Laurel shook her head. "Like I said, I could be wrong."

"Does anyone on Earth believe these tales?" Marcel, who'd so far only listened in and who did not believe in any form of god, waved a dismissive hand at the notion.

"You'd be surprised," Helen said.

"Do you, Laurel?" Marcel asked. He loved Helen, but to him, Laurel was the whole soul with the greater intellect.

"I ceased being surprised by anything when Darlen's ship dropped out of widespeed, and I saw this universe for the first time. Asking me if I believe in a god is probably not a fair question under the circumstances."

"I understand," he smiled as he cast a glance at Darlen and Harry, silently conveying the same question he asked of Laurel.

"Not me," Darlen said, reading Marcel's expression. "Can't abide all that hypocrisy. Earth is the worst planet I ever visited for that."

"I thought you spent time on Stipe Prime?" Harry chuckled. "There's nowhere in the galaxy that matches that place for double standards."

Darlen gave a brief shrug, accepting Harry's observations but tactfully not pointing out that Stipe Prime and Earth were in different universes.

"Ava seems to have a sense of the route the masters took," Laurel said. "But going to the prison planet just to find this scrap of material was pretty risky. I'm not sure it's giving us enough to justify that risk. I'm going to tell her the story of Adam and Eve, just to see if any of it strikes a chord."

CHAPTER TWENTY-SIX _

"Did God let those people go back home, Mommy?" Ava enjoyed the story of Adam and Eve in the Garden of Eden, listening attentively as she did to all of Laurel's stories. Laurel's early education didn't involve religion, but her interest in ancient languages brought her into contact with many ancient texts, including the Bible. She wished she'd paid more attention. She believed evidence was evolving that the Bible's events had little to do with theology and more, much more, to do with space travel.

"No honey, their god banished them from the garden forever."

"Is their god ever nice to people?" Ava twirled her dark curls around her finger as she focused on the conversation with her mother.

"Umm," Laurel frowned. "I don't know. Lots of people think he's just a made-up person. Others believe he's the father of the universe."

"He's not a daddy like Howie, is he?" Ava said. "Howie's always nice. He'd let me stay in his garden even if I was very naughty."

"You're never naughty," Laurel laughed.

"Those men with the mean faces chased people out of their garden," Ava said suddenly. "They had to run away on a ship."

Laurel waited. When Ava offered no more, she asked, "Why would they do that?"

"It was a nice garden, but the mean people didn't look after it." Ava leaned against Laurel and yawned. "I tired, Mommy."

After Ava was asleep, Laurel told the others of the conversation. "Bit by bit, the Garden of Eden scenario is taking shape."

"Could it just be her imagination? Perhaps my lady sister is caught up in this…" he gestured about him, "this adventure."

Laurel disagreed. "She's a whole soul, born into this universe. I think there's more to it."

"Well, someone started the bible stories before they got to be bible stories," Helen said, stripping the ancient book down to its bare bones. "I doubt someone wrote the Old Testament as a novel then sat around dreaming up a sequel called the New Testament."

"That strange book of history could have been imaginings also," Marcel said, unconvinced.

"I'm not sure, Marcel." Laurel shook her head. "I don't believe it's divinely inspired, but more and more, I reckon at least some records came from either this or another universe."

"And what about the humans in this universe?" Marcel continued, "did this original male and female, this Adam espoused to Eve, also give life to us, or do we have some other common ancestor?"

"Good question," Harry replied, turning to Laurel, expecting if anyone had an answer, it would be her. She didn't.

"Maybe we'll find out," she said to several expectant faces, including Mer's. "According to science, which usually doesn't agree with religion, humans evolved from apes. But I know there are no apes of any kind in this universe."

"Apes?" Harry echoed. "Hmm, what do they look like?"

Helen was in like a shot. "Like Darlen, only hairy!"

Laurel bit back a smile, but Darlen merely flicked an eyebrow as he answered, "There's nothing like that species anywhere in the galaxy, Harry. We've nothing to compare. As you know, science indicates we came to this galaxy less than a billion years ago."

Harry nodded. "Darlen's right, and of course, it begs the question 'Where from?' and that in itself has spawned many fruitless expeditions."

There followed a lively but not too serious discussion on humankind's origins, each with different theories and ideas. Marcel hung onto every word spoken, hungry for knowledge, eager to understand, intrigued by the fact that two of his comrades came not only from a different universe but different times. He felt great pride and proud to count his lord father as one of their number. He finally found a place to offer a comment.

"It is the belief of the Gartrya, or perhaps I should say the Inikamaran, that life is eternal," he said, "that we are a creation of cosmic energy. The people refer to that energy as having a physical form, like the god of your Earth. They believe that we live and die within that energy; that we return with different attributes according to our deeds in whatever physical form our mortal bodies take. If we do good, our next life will be easier. If we do wrong unto others, then we suffer accordingly."

"I bet the duke is having a hard time of it then," Helen snorted.

Marcel shrugged. "I didn't really know the duke."

"What do you mean? You didn't really know him?"

"He rarely summoned me to his presence," Marcel explained. "It was his wish I remain within the palace with only the company of my lady grandmother and lord father. Since the war, he isolated me even from my lady grandmother."

Laurel and Helen looked at each other; they both sensed it. "You're angry," Helen declared. "That's why that punch-up was so much fun."

"Yes, my lady Helen," he grinned. "I'm angry. And the 'punch-up' *was* fun."

"I can rough you up a bit if you like, Marcel," Darlen said, wearied by philosophy and theology. "I've got a few holoenemy programs in the cargo hold that'll keep you dancing."

Marcel slapped his knees and beamed. "Thank you, Darlen. I would enjoy that."

Laurel rolled her eyes at Harry, sending him a thought. *"He's going to teach him to be a thug."*

But Harry just grinned.

They soon faced another test. Unable to separate the slot flushing and compaction function from the reservoir reserve, the water situation became dire. And without the water processor to break down residue, the slot smelled. Helen made jokes about sticking one's bum over the side like they do on boats, but the joke was lost, even on Darlen. There had been no signal from the trailing Gale raider in three days, so Darlen brought the ship to the edge of the nebula's heart.

"This is an old slot system; the caripic convertor needs water to work."

"Why didn't you get a recent model installed when they overhauled the ship?" Harry said.

"To be honest, I didn't think about it. It's only ever been me on this ship for so long, and it's worked well."

Helen looked at Laurel. "Couldn't have taken him camping. He'd be useless."

Darlen brought up a starfield to give them all a better view. "There's a system, Qaziri, a few incils outside the nebula; farming communities mainly, minimal space travel, no widespeed except for emergency transports. This part of the northern reaches is self-sufficient, and they've resisted the League for centuries, but they're the food bowl of this sector, and they have some manufacturing plants, export only. That's why there's so much shipping. The first and sixth planets of the system are inhabited, but the others are just rocks. The Gale has come up this far, but there's not much for them here."

"I'm suspicious as to why the Gale appears to have given up."

"Who knows, Laurel?" Darlen gave a dramatic shrug and flopped his arms back to his sides. "I have to go by the fact they're not showing up on sensors, I can't find a tag signature, and we're in a desperate situation. If the Ferle weren't on the other side, I'd go there. I can't offer an alternative."

"Marcel and I can go in on axispods, Darlen," Harry suggested. "My concern is that the Gale is lurking somewhere in the vicinity."

"I've followed your protocols, and there's no sign of their tag."

Harry raised a sceptical eyebrow. "Just because the raider's gone, it doesn't mean the Gale hasn't positioned other operatives and ships here."

"You're right," Darlen said. "But I say again, we have no choice, and there are no inhabited systems ahead. We're at the limit of known inhabited space and our last chance."

"Ferle space must be massive," Helen said.

Darlen nodded. "According to Mer, there are quite a few populated planets in that region, and we have no way of knowing if we could get across Ferle space and find someone sympathetic; at least with the Gale we know what we're dealing with."

"Do the Ferle eat the people on those planets?" Helen asked, wide-eyed.

Darlen shrugged. "I don't know. They're cannibals, and they like young girls and boys around fourteen. They know that if they keep raiding planets, that source will dry up."

"You mean they want free-range meat?"

"I know what that is, Helen, and I suppose, yes, they do. I've seen them bartering on Gartrya, but they're not meat farmers."

Harry was checking out Qaziri's first planet, Darlen's proposed destination. "The planet has a lot of shipping lanes," he said, "it might be better for us to take the ship. If we could get across open space, it would be easy to anonymously slip into one of those lanes; they don't appear to be directing or tracking traffic. It's a free for all."

Helen looked over his shoulder. "Anonymous if there are no Gale agents."

Harry huffed his agreement but saw little alternative.

"The trading posts on Qaziri know me and what I was," Darlen said, "and I won't be welcome. The capital gets a fair mix of people from this and the outlying systems, so you should be able to find an evaporator and get out, providing Marcel doesn't go looking for trouble." He threw Marcel a warning look. "Helen, we're going to test your mantle. How long do you reckon you can keep it going?"

"You said there weren't any Gale ships?" came Helen's dismayed reply.

"I said we couldn't detect Gale ships and that we were taking a chance," he reminded her. "Let's reduce the risk and get across to the planet without being seen. They didn't detect our tag when you hid us before."

Laurel felt Helen's anxiety about this responsibility. Holding the crew's safety in her hands frightened her, but that fear was precisely what she needed for the transformation to take place. The ship was invisible before it left the nebula's heart.

This time, instead of standing still during the transformation, Helen continued her duties alongside Darlen; keeping the mantle active appeared to require no particular effort. Once again, Laurel perceived the change in Helen's appearance. This time, she saw something more. A smoky shimmer lifted slightly upwards from Helen's body. It wasn't a spirit, not in the given sense of the word, anyway. The phantom had facial features, but it didn't look like Helen; the closest comparison Laurel could make in her limited experience was with the Diri wraiths. Ava came to stand beside her and looked up, her pretty lips curving into a knowing smile. "It's nice, Mommy, like us," she said. "It lives inside Auntie Helen and helps her keep us safe."

Laurel held her breath as she tried to process this startling information. She looked from her daughter back to Helen. At the same moment, Helen turned from her task to look straight at Laurel. She smiled, and as she did, a point of brilliant blue lit in the centre of the entity's forehead. And it too, lifted its solemn gaze.

CHAPTER TWENTY-SEVEN _

"I hate this," Laurel said to Helen as they watched the axispods speed away. "I feel like I should be helping." They'd shifted into a high orbital shipping lane undetected. If anyone saw their sudden appearance after Helen's mantle faded, no other ship even made any hint of evasive action. It was as though they were still invisible. She maintained the mantle for over two days before she became overcome by a rapid debilitation, only relieved when the mantle faded, but by then, they were safely in orbit.

"I suppose there's nothing we can do," Laurel said. "Just wait. And you need to rest in case we need you to hide us again." Laurel would have loved to have discussed Helen's transformations but felt an odd constraint, as though Helen might not be ready for any revelations. So, she sensitively stayed silent on the subject.

They expected to wait a couple of days, but on the morning of the third day, Laurel knew something was amiss.

"What's holding them up?" Laurel closed her eyes; between her, Darlen and Helen, a heavy sense of alarm filled the ship.

"They may not have been able to secure an evaporator

kit in the part of the city I directed them to," Darlen said in an effort to mollify her and trying ineffectively to bury his own concern. "There are a few dealers on the planet. I can try contacting them if you like, but according to sensors, the axispods haven't moved."

His reasonable explanation did nothing to ease Laurel's growing concern. "I think the Gale has them."

"There's been no sign of their ships, even on long-range scans…" Darlen would have said more, but Helen silenced him with a fierce glare.

"Are you doubting Laurel's senses?"

Darlen backed down. Helen was right. His knowledge of the Gale and this galaxy didn't match the ability and senses of a whole soul telepath. When Laurel insisted on going to the surface, he advised against it if she was sure the Gale were there.

"You heard her," Helen stepped up to him. "We're going."

Darlen turned to Mer. "Drop into the lower lanes."

Mer's flat-screen head swivelled, and he made his seesawing, munching noise. His eyes lit red.

"What did he say?" Laurel demanded.

"Buggered if I know," Darlen replied. "I've never understood him. I can read his data during an interface with the ship but not when he vocalises. He rarely has anything to say. I only know when he's pissed off, his eyes light up. I suppose he's pissed; maybe he likes conflict, and that's a sign he's happy."

"I think he should interface," Helen said. "Mer, plug yourself in."

Mer pushed one of his interface pointers into the console.

"What did you say just now?"

Mer repeated the sounds.

"He says they impounded the axispods," Darlen read from the interface. "The forcefield has a local signature, short-range, designed not to show on normal scans."

Ava joined in the conversation. "Mer says Howie and Marcel aren't in the axispods."

The three adults looked at each other. "You understand him?"

Ava nodded. "Yes, Mer's my friend." She smiled up at Mer, whose eyes once again lit red. Darlen was wrong. Red eyes on Mer didn't necessarily mean he was pissed off.

Darlen turned to the women. "Laurel, you and Helen stay here with Ava. Helen, can you shield the ship?"

Helen shook her head. "Not right this minute. Maybe I need to rejuvenate or something."

"Get the ship back to the nebula if you have any signs of trouble. I'll go to the surface and find out what's going on."

"What if it *is* the Gale?"

"It's more likely Harry and Marcel violated some rule or other, Helen. Perhaps sending Marcel wasn't a good move. He may have let his fighting spirit get the better of him."

"That's not it, Darlen."

"Okay, Laurel." Darlen headed off towards the cargo bay. "Let's not second guess. I'll call in as soon as I find out anything."

"Is Uncle Darlen going to rescue my lord brother?" Ava asked as the axispod detached.

"You don't need to say, 'lord brother', Ava," Laurel said as she picked up the little girl. "Marcel speaks like that because that's how he was brought up."

"I like calling him lord brother," Ava smiled. "I want to call you Lady Mommy and Auntie Helen, Lady Auntie Helen."

Laurel tried desperately to push away her concerns for Harry and Marcel, but Ava was too sensitive. She patted Laurel's face and looked into her eyes.

"Don't worry, Mommy, Howie will be okay. But we need to hide."

"Hide? What…"

The ship angled as the first blast hit, the shot shearing off and catching another ship in orbit, sending it hurtling towards the planet. Mer made urgent warning sounds. The attacking ship had used the busy traffic lane, concealing its approach behind other signatures.

"Mer's warning us," Helen said urgently. "It must be the Gale. Get us out of here, Mer."

Helen leapt to help as Mer configured and reconfigured failing controls.

"Damn," Helen shouted. "Helm isn't responding. Mer, configure the hull for widespeed, we'll…." But another shot knocked them below the shipping lane, perilously close to the atmosphere. Mer locked himself into the interface to stop the ship's orbit from decaying, but in doing so, he would be powerless to help when the Gale boarded.

Laurel held Ava close. "Helen, does Darlen have any

secret compartments on this ship? If we hide Ava, you and I might be able to take them down."

"There are compartments," Helen said as the ship stabilised, "but it's likely the Gale knows where they are. They've raided this ship before."

"It's me they want." Laurel looked around helplessly for somewhere to hide Ava. "They don't know you're a whole soul, and if we can hide Ava…"

"No, I'll hide you both. They've never seen either of you."

"But…" Laurel's protestation that she thought Helen needed time to recover got lost as Helen pushed her and Ava into Mer's alcove. In a second, Helen had shrouded them in a cloak.

The ominous sound of a docking clamp attaching to the ship sent shivers through Laurel. Mer attempted to remove his interface, but he was locked out of the controls, helpless with his interface probe stuck firmly into the console.

Six Gale retainers stepped coolly into the common room. Ordinary looking, powerfully built men dressed in grey shirts and dark slacks. Each man was heavily armed but wore bored expressions as if boarding ships were an everyday occurrence. One man approached the control room where he encountered the small-framed woman who stepped promptly into his path, barring his way.

"Helen," he said with a sneer, "what a pleasant surprise." He sniffed the air as the slot odour reached his nostrils. "And what a delightful smell. A new perfume? Or perhaps the deodoriser in the slot has failed?"

"You brought that smell on board with you, Sicler." Helen stood, her legs planted firmly apart, her hands on her hips, too short to be nose to nose with the man, but fierce as dammit.

Sicler inclined his head. "Is that right? I overheard you and Darlen left League space. Headed somewhere nice?"

Helen's voice and expression dripped sarcasm as she crossed her arms and gazed up at him, a picture of defiance. "I couldn't leave without saying goodbye."

Sicler pushed past her and circled the room. "Did Darlen leave the whole soul female on board?"

"There's only me. She went to the surface."

Sicler turned slightly but kept his gaze on Helen and his sidearm at the ready. Laurel wondered at the circumstances in which these two had crossed paths before. Certainly enough for him to respect that Helen was perfectly capable of holding her own. Sicler snorted and turned to his men, barking, "Search the ship."

Laurel knew the men couldn't see them through Helen's cloak, but fear for her daughter threatened to squeeze the breath from her lungs. She tried to cover it for Ava's sake, but all Laurel felt from the child was a sense of bemusement and curiosity and an inordinately mature understanding of the need to allow Helen to deal with the situation. There were no axispods on board to effect an escape, even if Helen could hide the pair from the men if they made a dash for it, so there was no choice but to remain where they were, huddled in Mer's alcove.

The men reported back the rest of the ship was clear.

"So," Sicler stepped forward and thrust his face into

Helens, making him bend quite substantially, comically even. "Where is she?"

"I told you." Helen stood her ground. "She went to the surface with the others."

One man interrupted. "Not possible, sir, we seized two axispods on the surface, and there's only docking for three on this ship. She couldn't have left if Darlen took the last one."

"Helen," Sicler thrust his face threateningly close, "let's not waste time. You know we have the two men. Now, I want you to play nice. I'll ask you again." Sicler took Helen's hand and rubbed her fingers, suddenly tightening his grip. "Where is the woman?"

Helen didn't flinch. "I told you, she's..."

"Yeah, yeah, she went to the surface. It makes sense for Darlen to take his most prized cargo with him, but in this case..."

"She's not cargo. She's a passenger."

Sicler laughed heartily. "A passenger? C'mon Helen, Darlen's a slave trader born and bred. He might tell you she's a passenger, but that'll only be until he finds a buyer. Your old man's a rogue, always has been, always will be. The Gale is keen to secure the whole soul, and we already have a buyer, for the young man too. Our buyer likes strong, pretty boys."

"Darlen isn't dealing anymore."

Sicler snorted. "He won't pass up on a whole soul, although I must say he took a chance taking her out of League space. That makes her fair game.

"I suppose that treacherous League constable told you

about Laurel."

Sicler raised an eyebrow. "Treacherous? Who is he betraying? Canon Akkuh owns his arse. He's useful."

"Rubbish. The League wouldn't stop looking for him."

Sicler shrugged. "They'll leave him be unless he strays back into League space."

Helen was about to say that was where they first saw him, and in League uniform but hesitated. It could be the League constable was a double agent, but struggled with her emotions, and Laurel's as well, when they heard Sicler's next words.

"Nah, it wasn't the constable. We learned about the whole soul from Akkuh," he grinned. "Payback."

Helen felt Laurel's anger. *"Akkuh!"*

"Now Helen, as pleasant as it is chatting with you, I have a whole soul to locate. We have the two men, and it's only a matter of time before we recover Darlen. That whole soul isn't on the surface." Sicler raised his firearm and pointed it at Helen. Laurel had to act; Helen's mantle would give her cover and perhaps provide some protection. She may be able to disable a few. Mer still could not disengage, so he couldn't help.

But in the moment it took for Ava to catch Laurel's instructions to stay in the alcove, Sicler fired, and Helen collapsed to the floor. In the shock to her body and her subsequent loss of consciousness, her link severed, and Laurel and Ava became visible.

"Well, well," Sicler smiled. "What have we here? How come we didn't see you hiding in there?" He glanced around at his men with a scowl. "I assume you're the whole soul, and this little lady is…?" he squatted down to Ava's level. Ava just stared at him. "No matter, loyalty leverage anyway. Take her."

"What about Darlen's woman?" one man said as he shoved Helen's prone body with his foot.

"Leave her. We don't need her now. She's only stunned. She can be a message to Darlen when he gets back not to mess with the Gale."

"You only want me. Please leave the child," Laurel pleaded, pushing Ava behind her.

"Can't do that, but they'll let Darlen and the physician go. They plan on selling the younger man to King Obtinias on Farek. He's made an offer on you as well. You'll love it there," Sicler laughed.

Laurel knew of the Farek homeworld, in the furthermost reaches of the galaxy and well out of the League's reach, but little of the wealthy King Obtinias besides his involvement in brutality and slavery. Laurel doubted she'd love it there and began to formulate plans to escape. Only the knowledge the Gale had not yet captured Darlen gave her hope.

One of the men reached out, and surprisingly, Ava allowed him to pick her up. Laurel glanced back to see if Helen was okay, but she was still out cold. Sicler grabbed Laurel's arm to lead her to the Gale ship, and she caught Ava's thoughts. Ava was staring at the man who carried her. Laurel heard her talking to him.

"My name's Ava. What's yours?"

The man smiled and answered pleasantly, as if being a ruffian was just his day job, and it was okay to be nice to a kid.

"My name's Jiffe. I've got a son about the same age as you."

"Do you?" Ava smiled back. "Does your little boy like fire?"

"Er, no," the man looked taken aback, "not especially."

"Do *you* like fire?"

"Sometimes. When the weather's cold."

Ava, slightly higher than him as he held her, looked down at him, her smile fading and her next words chilling Laurel in their warning.

"You won't like the fire Howie's making for you."

The man shook his head, puzzling over who or what a 'Howie' could be. Sicler saw and heard but shrugged in response. And he didn't care. He'd attained the prize, and the Gale would compensate him. And somehow, Laurel realised, Ava already knew the outcome of all this.

CHAPTER TWENTY-EIGHT _

The Gale thugs led Laurel, her anger simmering, onto their ship, binding her wrists and feet with anchors. Jiffe sat opposite, Ava on his knee. She looked relaxed and, for the moment, curious about her surroundings, asking Jiffe questions about the Mer-type robot they had on board, where the control room might be, and if he liked being in space, but she stayed telepathically close to her mother.

"It's alright, Mommy. They don't know about me," Ava sent to her, and nothing in her expression gave away that the clever little girl and her mother were communicating.

"And they mustn't know, honey. Howie will come for us soon, I promise."

"Darlen found him and Marcel." Ava flashed a vision of a cell built into red earth, bars, level with the ground crisscrossed above. Laurel felt a clear impression of Harry and Marcel imprisoned, but Darlen scurried in shadows, his intent strong. Relief flooded her. They hadn't caught Darlen. Laurel smiled inwardly and sent a thought to Ava.

"Marcel? Not my lord brother?"

"He's my lord brother at home and Marcel when we are having an adventure."

"Is this an adventure?"

Ava looked up at Jiffe—who gave her a big grin—then back to her mother. *"You have an adventure when you all go home safe at the end. It's not an adventure if someone gets lost. That would be sad. Jiffe's little boy will be sad."*

What an extraordinary thing for a small child to say! How wise and prophetic? Ava not only read minds but seemed to know of the future. And a sense of the ancient journey of the whole souls. Would she be like her father, Gabriel? Or like Helen? But for all her wisdom, Ava was not yet five years old, and she needed her mother's protection.

The ship landed in a quadrangle surrounded by terraces and worn, aged furnishings and tapestries. The smell of manure hung in the air, only slightly better than the stink on the ship, and elderly men and women, who paid them no mind, worked in the gardens. Laurel opened her other senses to her surroundings. At least six more guards besides those who brought them here were coming to meet them; a further forty or so, all with intent, were positioned around. She sensed their confidence that she would not attempt to escape nor attack while her child was close. Although most had heard of a whole soul's abilities, they also knew that assurance of their child's welfare would preside over any opposition.

Sicler indicated to the man carrying Ava, who nodded and moved away, ignoring Laurel's cries of protestation. Laurel moved to hurl herself at Sicler, but Ava's thoughts came through quickly, calming her.

"It's alright, Mommy. I'll see you soon."

Laurel stepped back, and Sicler laughed, glancing at his men. "See? They won't take a chance with their children."

Minutes later, Laurel found herself tossed into a dug-out cell several feet below ground level. Despite her whole soul agility, she still landed with a thump on the hard ground. The bars above her caged her in, and unless any prisoner could jump incredibly high, coupled with enhanced strength to bend the bars, it was an effective prison, even with no wrist or ankle restraints. Fortunately, Laurel could leap high enough, but on further examining the bars, decided that she may not get far with them. She sat on the ground and searched for Ava, finding her nearby, quite relaxed.

"Hello honey, what are you doing?"

"I'm playing a game with Jiffe. He's letting me win."

"Are they looking after you?"

"They gave me some food. It was nice, and a drink."

"Was the drink nice?"

"Yes, Mommy, but I don't like where you are."

"It's only for now. Uncle Darlen will come soon."

But Darlen didn't come, no-one came. Laurel sat on the stone floor as day turned to freezing night, causing her to spend a shivering few hours until the scorching sun rose again. She tried to meditate to relieve her thirst, but since the war, she'd let such practices slide. She reached out to Ava, but she couldn't find her—she often couldn't if she was sleeping—and she felt nothing had happened. She reached out to Helen, but again, nothing, and Laurel hoped she hadn't suffered serious injury. She sensed Harry and Marcel close; they didn't seem in distress, but nothing of

Darlen. There was nothing to do other than wait and trust Ava's instincts.

That wait took many hours. When they finally came for her, they hoisted her none-too-gently up to the surface with an old-fashioned rope. Applying anchors once more to her wrists, Sicler led Laurel back to the quadrangle and into a hall where an oversized, ornate chair was set on a raised stand. Jiffe and Ava stood off to the side. Ava's just a little girl, Laurel thought. It seemed wrong to put so much faith in her instincts. Ava suddenly smiled and waved, and Laurel smiled back.

From all the men in the room, and there were many, she felt their curiosity about her. Eclipsing this exuded a mild fear and mild admiration projected towards something, someone approaching a few metres ahead. A portal door twisted open, and Laurel was thrust forward a few paces before being thrown to the floor. For a second, she felt Ava's concern but quickly reassured her telepathically that she was okay. Laurel was forced to remain on her knees, her head bowed. She sensed the ship in which she'd arrived behind her, but strangely, no local men and women as there had been the previous day. They were all gone. The quadrangle deserted save for herself, Ava and the Gale thugs.

Before her, the presence was strong in its intent, any semblance of humanity buried under avarice and hunger for power and control. So, it surprised her to see, when she raised her head, a thin, moribund-looking old man, seated on the chair. His face rested in his palm, his elbow on the arm of his seat, observing her. His clothing was little different to the men who kidnapped her the day before, besides an ornate chain around his neck. Laurel probed his mind briefly but found *nothing!* No memories, no compassion. He watched her for a long moment with his cold steel-blue eyes, then put his hand out to Ava, calling her forward.

Laurel tried to leap to her feet, but the guards restrained her. "Leave her alone; she's just a child. I'll do anything you want!" Laurel's desire to protect Ava surged. At this moment, she felt physically invincible, but rationality dictated that apart from being unarmed, she was also outnumbered. This was the leverage of which Gabriel spoke. Now she knew the awful powerlessness he felt and why he did the things he did to protect the people he loved. She would do whatever it took to protect Ava.

The almost dead-looking man dropped his hand but indicated Ava remain at his side.

"Of course, you'll do anything we want." He turned his head and smiled an empty smile at Ava. "It seems your mother will do anything to protect you."

Ava tilted her head. Mommy said she mustn't get into people's heads, but she couldn't always help it. This man didn't have a mind, so there was nothing to read. It felt strange, uncomfortable, unknown, and she didn't like it. So she began to cry.

The man ignored Ava's weeping, and after a moment, he spoke, addressing Laurel in fluent Seera.

"The Soul Monger left you exposed by removing you from League space. You are to be sold to King Obtinias along with the youth we captured. I suspect this child might be a whole soul, so I will keep her until I see evidence of those abilities. If so, the Gale will train her."

"She's a half soul," Laurel spat, her anger making no impression on the man.

"I know you were a captive in the fortress on Semevale 7 during the League war," he said, "and that the duke passed off a whole soul slave as his heir. This child might be a product of a...romantic union?" the man concluded, lifting a thin eyebrow in question.

"Whole souls don't reproduce together."

"No? What about a whole soul born into this universe? We know from history that whole souls reproduce together on your planet. If this child is born of a union between such a whole soul and you, perhaps it is possible."

"All supposition," Laurel sneered. "No whole soul children have ever been born into this universe."

"Hmm," the man scratched his chin, then turned to Ava. "You can stop crying, child. I'm not going to hurt you." Then he turned to Laurel, his eyes gleaming cruelly. "But I am going to hurt your mother."

In those moments, Laurel realised loyalty leverage went both ways. She heard Ava screaming as Laurel was pushed flat, her face ground into the floor as the guard above her fired a bolt into her thigh. Agony from the missile ripped through her body, but Ava's distress was far greater torment. The guard grabbed Laurel's hair and pulled up her head so he could sneer into her face. Laurel's eyes darted to the restraint control he held in his hands, and seeing her glance, he held it up and pressed. As her body convulsed, she heard Ava's screams and felt the pleasure this power over them gave the guards. As the convulsing ceased, Laurel lay on the cold floor, exhausted from the intense burst of pain and trying to send to Ava that soon Darlen and Howie would come to get them, and all this would be over. But the old man stopped Ava from going to her mother, patiently waiting until Ava's kicking and screaming came to a silent, weeping halt.

"We've inserted an anchor into your thigh," the Gale leader said, unconcerned with Laurel's pain and distress. "The child will remain with me until we can establish whether she is a whole soul. You will be removed to the Gale headquarters and then on for negotiations with King Obtinias. The presence of the anchor and the knowledge that we have your child will ensure your co-operation." The man waved his hand, and a guard stepped forward to remove Ava.

Laurel sensed Marcel's presence at the exact moment weapons fire rained down on the room. Unable at first to identify its source, the guards fired in all directions as Laurel leapt to her feet, detaching her wrist anchor courtesy of the sneering guard who was the first to fall, sprawling across her. A Gartryan knuckle weapon flew through the air. She caught it as the guards turned their fire on her.

Marcel had done a fair amount of damage from his concealed position on the terrace. The moribund leader vanished back through the portal, abandoning Ava when, with the speed of a whole soul, she dodged his grasp and jumped behind his chair. The leader was left defenceless with his personal guard felled and the others engaged in combat, so he retreated to save his own skin.

"Stay behind the chair. Make yourself really small," Laurel sent to Ava.

Many more Gale guards poured through the door, and Laurel positioned herself between them and the chair to protect her child. Her training from the war reasserted itself, joining with her inherent strength and speed. Laurel was still a capable fighter, taking men much larger than her down in pairs, shooting one and disabling another, finishing one off before the other had even lifted their head from the ground. Marcel, his experience with weapons use only coming from holoenemy games in the cargo hold, took a couple of scrapes, but he shadowed Laurel from his vantage point, mopping up the stragglers she kicked to the ground.

The fight was brief, the end punctuated by a sudden silence. All around, Gale men lay motionless. Laurel estimated fifty or more, who moments before believed a single whole soul with a child for leverage would be no match for them. The smell of scorched flesh and the blue air reminded Laurel of the war. Never for a moment did she dream she would be in a combat situation again, and this time fighting to save her child. Ava ran from her hiding place into her mother's arms, just as Marcel appeared at the door, urging them to hurry.

"The axispods are this way."

After taking only a few steps, excruciating, intractable pain from the bolt burned into Laurel's leg. Ava wouldn't run fast with her mother incapacitated, and Laurel struggled to keep up with Marcel. After the adrenaline-filled fight, her body was reminding her it was, in fact, mortal. Marcel saw it and slowed his pace, but Laurel urged him on as she stumbled towards the axispods. Willing herself to keep going, she suddenly felt herself swept up into strong arms. It was Darlen.

"I got the guard," Marcel called to him as they ran. "But they'd already used the restraint; it's probably done damage. Did you disable the communications?"

Darlen waited to answer until they got to the axispods. "Communications are down. Get her on board and tandem the 'pods, full armour. Sorry, Laurel," he quickly checked the bruised, swollen area behind her thigh, "this is going to hurt."

"Where's Harry?" she asked, steeling herself against the pain as her thigh contacted the axispod seat.

"Being a hero. Don't worry; he can take care of himself. Ava, you need to squish yourself into a small ball and sit in front with Marcel," he instructed. "Can you do that?"

Ava nodded.

Darlen somehow fitted Ava in the footwell of the axispod in front of Marcel's feet. As they took off towards the ship, Darlen thanked the gods he'd recently learned about for saving at least those three. Now it was just him and Harry.

———

"I saw it, Laurel," Marcel said as the axispod soared towards the atmosphere, "but I hardly believed it. How can you leap so high into the air?"

Laurel tried to smile through her pain.

"And to fight so many men at one time, to defeat an armed destroyer," he continued over his shoulder. "I am impressed."

"The League brought me here for the sole purpose of fighting a war," Laurel reminded him, her entire body tensing against the pain. "We were trained well. All whole souls have speed and agility."

Marcel glanced over his shoulder. "I am proud to have fought alongside you today."

CHAPTER TWENTY-NINE _

With the Gale ship's disengagement and no longer locked out of the controls, Mer stabilised their orbit. For now, they weren't in danger of crashing into the planet, but he kept the ship low to minimise the time it took for the axispods to return. Helen had recovered from the stun, and she and Mer had restored widespeed configuration for a quick getaway once they cleared the planet's atmosphere. It shocked Helen to see Laurel hurt, but she couldn't leave Mer to repair all the damage on his own, and instead coaxed a somewhat overwhelmed Ava from Marcel's arms so he could help Laurel to her bed. Laurel knew the bolt had lodged through her muscle, and movement from the subsequent battle had caused further deterioration to the ligaments at the back of her thigh.

Shaken by the mess the bolt made of her leg, Marcel pushed his hands up through his hair and held his head. "I don't know how to treat this injury, Laurel," he said helplessly.

"It's okay, Marcel." It took a supreme effort to keep her voice steady, but the position of the bolt meant Laurel couldn't remove it herself. She needed him to focus. "I'll talk you through it. Get the pandroscope; it'll be able to identify the bolt and advise us the best method of dealing with it."

Marcel nodded and headed for the door, grateful for Laurel's presence of mind. Moments later, he was back with the medical equipment. Harry and Laurel supervised him often in operating the pandroscope, and he knew how to set it up to examine Laurel's leg. As it scanned, it flashed a warning about the prohibition of Darkadian bolts in League space.

"At least we know it's a Darkadian bolt," Laurel said as Marcel poked at the pandroscope to make the warning disappear. The best he could do was minimise it.

"Is that good?" he said.

"It's harder to remove. I've never seen one before. As the pandroscope says…"

"Yes, it's prohibited in League space. Look, Laurel, it's built the image. Can you see?"

Laurel was flat on her stomach, so she craned her neck around to see the pandroscopes imaging. "It's embedded in the muscle, but it hasn't hit the femur. It looks as though the central nail has a bio permeate to anchor it to the muscle structure. Can you see where it's already beginning to integrate?"

Marcel nodded, his head clearer now, but still unable to see how he could deal with this emergency. "It needs to be removed before it does further damage. We must wait till Harry returns."

"We can't wait," Laurel's voice was level, calm. "If we do, I'll lose part of that muscle and possibly compromise the bone. You have to take it out."

"I can't!" Marcel stepped back. "Let me get Mer or Helen."

"Mer's keeping this ship flying, and Helen would become the patient. Marcel, you just wiped out a room full of men almost single-handedly." Laurel made no attribution for the success of their fight to her. She rolled herself painfully on her side to look at his stricken face. "You can do this."

"I will hurt you," he said, even as he arranged the equipment beside the bed.

"That can't be avoided." Laurel rolled back on her tummy. "Transfer the pandroscope reading to a datacache and open it here." She pointed to the head of her bed. "I'll direct you. Once you divide the muscle from the bio permeate, it'll be easy."

It wasn't easy; it was excruciating, even with a surgical painbot patch placed at the exit site. The painbots detected pain elsewhere in Laurel's leg and kept migrating back and forth to where the sensation of pain was most felt. As Marcel drew out the bolt, he placed a painbot patch over the wound while the other bots cleaned up and cauterised.

Marcel knelt beside the bed and peered at Laurel's tear-stained face. "Are you alright? I think I pulled out some muscle at the same time. It was really thick."

Laurel didn't care; muscles heal, and right now, her body felt weary. She blinked slowly and, mustering the smallest of grins to reassure him, fell to blessed unconsciousness.

Several hours later, Laurel woke to find Harry sitting beside her. Immediately, she reached for him, and he gathered her into his arms, holding her tight and kissing the top of her head. She cried against his chest, her tears soaking his shirt.

"Harry, I was so worried. We didn't have time for Darlen to tell us where you were." She tilted her head back to look at him. His face was filthy, his eyebrows and the front of his hair looked scorched. He'd lost a tooth, and his arm was strapped from shoulder to elbow.

"What happened to you?" Laurel asked, her own wound momentarily forgotten.

"I immobilised the Gale agents." Harry's green eyes flickered, "I mean really immobilised."

"How?" Laurel tried to sit up, but the heal-bots running around inside her wound protested. Finally, grimacing with pain, she puffed out her breath and obeyed their commands.

"I'll tell you later," Harry said. "Right now, you're the one with injuries."

"Ava saw it all, Harry." A fresh tear rolled down Laurel's cheek. "Until then, she was so brave and fearless. It was only when we couldn't read that Gale leader's mind that she became scared."

"She's resilient," Harry soothed, although he couldn't imagine what it could have been like for a small child to witness her mother being shot. "When she sees you're okay, she'll be okay too."

"Harry," Laurel said. "Ava knew what the outcome would be. She told one of the Gale officers about some sort of fire you'd bring down on them." Laurel expected him to explain. Instead, he just continued to smooth her hair.

"When the heal-bots have done their work," he said, "I'll fix up the skin on your leg with a dermotrim. It'll take a few days, but at least you'll get the feeling back. Then, you'll be good as new."

He flicked on the pandroscope and located the image of Laurel's wound. It showed the busy healbots inside the wound; one of them had returned to the skin patch, its work done—a good sign of healing.

"How could the Gale do this," he whispered to himself.

As Marcel said, a small section of muscle had detached when he removed the bolt. Such side effects were unavoidable. Harry had removed these bolts before, but fortunately, he had the equipment to repair Laurel's muscle. These barbaric devices were developed for permanent integration into a troublesome slave's musculature, with pain delivered at their master's whim or pleasure. Banned for centuries within the League, some Independent and far edge systems still used them.

Laurel had no such experience, but she heard his thoughts. "That's what I was to them, a troublesome slave so whatever they did was okay. And that strange man, the Gale leader, was convinced Ava was a whole soul."

"How would he know that?"

"He knew about Gabriel."

Harry tutted. "Canon Akkuh knew about Gabriel; his story was in the debriefing. He must have told them."

"The League didn't know then what they know now. How did you get away, Harry?"

"Darlen." Harry took a deep breath, and Laurel could hear his heart beating as she leaned against him. It seemed a cosy place to be discussing what was essentially a fight for their lives. "Helen commed him to tell him they got you, so he made sure the Gale guards knew where to find him; they only have the one prison pit zone, and once you're in, they only come back if they need to, so they thought Darlen would be where they left him. When the residents of the quadrangle started packing up and leaving, the Gale had no idea why, but they didn't suspect Darlen, thinking he was safely ensconced in a cell."

"And, of course, he wasn't."

Harry grinned. "It seems there's not a prison that can hold him. They turned their backs, and he walked in and out as he needed to throw them off the scent." He chuckled. "Don't ask me how, and he's not saying. All the prisons are dug into the ground with bars above."

"I know. I was in one for a day. And Marcel? He knew where to find us."

Harry nodded. "Darlen told him, and he told him how many guards. Darlen has a fair inside knowledge of the Gale, but getting to you was our priority, and at that time, we didn't know you were injured. We had to disable the Gale ships; there were two of them, a Gale raider with no markings and interestingly, a civilian signature, a new trick for them; that was the one that brought you to the surface. The other was a Supero Class scout, used solely for the Krows, the Gale leaders. There's no sign of the raider that's been following us. Darlen disabled communication, Marcel went to find you, and I sabotaged the ships."

Laurel listened with both fascination and admiration. She leaned back her head to look into his dirty face. "Wait, Harry?" Harry looked down at her. "Ava asked one of the Gale men if he liked fire, then told him he wouldn't like the fire you were going to give him."

Harry frowned. "How could she know what I planned to do even before I planned it?"

"Something from your past, maybe? Her idea of the computer keyboard came from my memory."

"It's not the first time I've blown up a ship," Harry conceded.

"I'm starting to think Ava may not just be a telepath or an empath. Was she right, Harry? Was there a fire?"

"Well, yes, she was right," Harry said. "While you and Marcel were otherwise occupied, some locals drew the guard's attention, and I rigged explosives underneath the two Gale ships. I would have hardwired detonators in other circumstances, but there was little point in blowing up the ship without the Krow and his guards on board. I had a great view of the ships, again courtesy of the locals, so as soon as the guards were back on board, 'Boom!' " The sound reverberated through Harry's chest, and she felt his arm lift to add drama. "Both ships went up together."

"Where did you get the explosives?"

"From Darlen, he slipped the components into the cell before he let the Gale capture him. He also dropped in an old wrist lick, and so I was able to magnetise the devices." He grinned down at her. "You just need a bit of know-how."

"And we got the Gale leader?"

"He's just a cog in a much bigger wheel, Laurel. The true leader has clones, so you never know if you are dealing with him or one of them. The fact you couldn't get into this Krow's head confirms he was a clone."

"How did you get off the planet? There was only a single axispod left; there wouldn't have been room for both of you."

"Two others in our prison pit. In exchange for releasing them, they agreed to bring me back to the ship. They actually kept their word. I have no idea what their crime was, so I hope I haven't unleashed devastation on the galaxy. Darlen brought back the other pod."

"The League shouldn't have dismantled the cloak on this ship after the war," Laurel said. "We could have stayed hidden and undetected in high orbit. The axispods might have slipped in without the Gale noticing. It's too much for Helen to keep hiding us."

"The League didn't sanction the cloak in the first place," Harry admitted. "Remember Hamer? Who developed Helen's gas? He installed it on Darlen's ship when Darlen came to 100 moons with the information about you in the fortress. He removed it when he returned with the minerals. Hamer took a risk. If Darlen went anywhere outside the war zone during that time, the fact he had League technology might have been detected, and he, and me, would have been in a lot of trouble."

Even after all these years, this was news to Laurel. She knew Harry initially kept the word of her rescue and subsequent mission to Gartrya from the League, but for a while, he had run the real risk of losing both his career and his freedom. All because he put his trust in her and Darlen, a man he had once despised.

"Helen's okay, isn't she?" Laurel asked.

"She's fine. She sat in here for a while when you were sleeping. Do you know she helped Mer with the hull alignment for widespeed? It got knocked out when the Gale blasted the ship." Harry chuckled. "She's easy to underestimate."

Laurel agreed. "That underestimation worked in her favour. The Gale has no idea she's a whole soul or of her ability to cloak us."

"Well, we've all come through this intact, save for your wound, but we'll have to land somewhere to organise repairs or get water supplies. Marcel had a couple of grazes."

"I am truly grateful for him rescuing us."

"He's great in a fight. So is Darlen, for that matter."

Harry's opinion of Darlen was finally reforming. Progress, Laurel thought, wishing it hadn't come at such a cost. She smiled and held him closer.

Laurel's rehabilitation took only a couple of weeks, and, unable to walk while the ligaments healed and skin regenerated, she continued with Ava's education, even allowing Darlen to speak about Soul Mongering, provided he kept out the parts about impregnating whole soul females. When Ava read it in his mind, she projected it to Laurel, who diverted the thought.

Water rationing continued, and washing oil was substituted in the slot as a temporary measure to keep it working. That meant no showers, but body odour was less of a problem than slot odour circulating in the air.

"Why don't we send Mer to check the other side of the nebula?" Marcel said, his voice muffled after jokingly seeking refuge from the smelly slot inside a hull maintenance helmet.

"We can," Darlen agreed, "but I don't know what's out there. The Ferle might still be active in that region; they were pretty far-reaching." Darlen looked around at the others; they were running out of options. The ship had a failing waste facility and little water. A decision had to be made, and it couldn't be his alone. "It might be safer to take our chances with the Gale."

"When will we be beyond their reach?"

"They'll follow us for now, Marcel. We took their prize, pri-*zes* if you include Ava. Any meeting with a Krow is transmitted live to Caltobar, to Gale headquarters, so the Gale knows. Add to that we killed dozens of their men and one of their Krows, not to mention destroying two ships."

"They might suppose we're on the other side of the nebula and inaccessible," Helen suggested.

"Hopefully. It's been weeks since Qaziri."

"It makes sense to go out the other side." Marcel took off the helmet and opened a star chart. It showed vast empty spaces with an occasional point of light.

"And right onto the Ferle's dinner plates?" Helen folded her arms. "Not bloomin' likely!"

"We have to resolve the water problem," Harry said. "Short-term by fixing the recycler, and long-term, something more durable and modern. Of course, beyond Qaziri, there aren't any charted systems." He turned to

Darlen. "I doubt the Gale will follow us for too long; they rely on League information to assess inhabited systems. They'll give up."

"If you say so, Harry. This is about the limit I've travelled." Darlen grunted, "I must admit, even I'm getting fed up with space rations. I've never liked them." He grinned at Helen. "What I wouldn't give for a couple of Big Macs!"

"Oh, God, me too!" Helen patted her stomach. "Those space rations are making me fat. Too many carbs and not enough exercise."

"We could shove you out an airlock and let you run after us," Darlen grinned.

But Marcel had a more practical suggestion. "Perhaps you need to join me in the cargo bay Helen, when the water is restored. I think it would be good for you."

Helen rolled her eyes. Lifting weights with Marcel would be the last resort.

Darlen's expression changed as he remembered an echo of a conversation from weeks before. He hadn't paid attention, but now it made complete sense. He made shushing noises to get their attention.

"Ava said we could all go to sleep," he said. "I remember her whispering it to Mer. That might work. I could put us all in stasis. Mer can interface and run the ship's systems and scan for suitable planets to get water or a replacement or undertake repairs. We'd have to give him a time limit, but in the meantime, he could do an axispod sweep at intervals to see what may or may not be lurking either side."

Harry checked their position on the star chart. "By the chart's calculation, we're parallel with the roof of Qaziri space and entering the Nyzan system. We won't find anything there. We can't know about the other side, obviously, but a few months in stasis may be just what we need to bypass species like the Ferle."

"I prefer that option to leaving the nebula to face cannibals on one side and the Gale on the other," Laurel said, seeing the complete sense in this plan and wishing she'd paid more attention to her child's suggestion.

"What if Mer doesn't wake us?" Helen looked up at the black robot, who she was never sure had forgiven her for making him clean the ship. "He might leave us asleep forever."

Darlen turned to Mer. "You wouldn't do that, would you?"

Mer made a noise like blowing through a comb and paper. They'd not heard it before, but his eyes lit red.

"You know he's joking, right?" Darlen looked at Helen.

"Very comforting." Helen crossed her arms and pulled a face at the black robot, his head swivelling as he returned to his duties, his expression, as always, unfathomable.

"It's strange how you view the nebula as a place of sanctuary now," Laurel said to Harry later. "You told me Miran Forin meant hostile in Seera. It's not hostile, and it's keeping away the bad guys."

"That irony isn't lost on me, Laurel," Harry agreed. "Though one day, I'd like to find out what stops it affecting you and why your presence here protects Marcel and me."

"That will be one of the questions we'll ask when we get to wherever they have answers."

Laurel had concerns about the stasis proposal, but it seemed a logical solution. Her wound was now healed and required no further treatment, and apart from the water system, the ship appeared to run well with no significant after-effects from the attack at Qaziri.

When their plans were explained to Ava, she had no memory of ever suggesting such a thing as "stasis" and responded as any child would at being placed in a closed tube and put to sleep for a long time. During the preparation of the chambers, Ava's mind stayed alert with anxiety throughout each night-time, reaching through to the other whole souls and not allowing either of them any sleep.

"I'm starting to look forward to this stasis," Helen yawned. She crashed onto Laurel's bed, where Laurel was attempting to get a few hours extra sleep one morning while Harry and Marcel diverted Ava from her worries.

"Yes, I know," Laurel said, making some extra room for her friend. "Ava is just getting worked up about the stasis."

"You should stick her in the same chamber as you; she's only little." Helen yawned again and curled herself up.

Laurel thought for a moment. That might just work! She turned to Helen to tell her she was a genius, but Helen was already snoring.

CHAPTER THIRTY _

Darlen adapted the variance chamber to accommodate both Laurel and Ava. Marcel suggested Ava watch him as he entered stasis to see how easy it would be, just like falling asleep in a bed. Laurel was glad Marcel took a relaxed approach; it gave Ava confidence. She kissed him "goodnight" as Harry administered the sedation and set the chamber. Ava placed her hand on the panel as Marcel's body settled into its long sleep.

"I miss him already," she said, her violet eyes bright with tears.

Laurel swung her into her arms. "You won't miss him for long. In a moment, you and I are going to get real cosy…" she rubbed noses with Ava, "and then we're going to sleep too."

Ava put her arms out to Harry. "Howie, can I have a goodnight kiss and cuddle?"

Harry left the chamber he was preparing for Laurel and Ava and took Ava from Laurel's arms. "Sure you can, sweetheart."

Ava had lots of kisses for Harry, Helen and Darlen, all designed to delay the stasis process, and as she kissed Mer goodbye for what seemed like the tenth time, he lifted her into the chamber alongside Laurel. Ava at once turned to her mother to snuggle close as Harry placed the sedation strip over the child's neck.

Helen slipped into the stasis chamber with a cheery "bye", but she squeezed Darlen's hand as he adjusted the environment. Harry saw him bend and lightly touch her face with the back of his finger, then stood as Harry approached to deliver her sedation. Harry didn't recall ever witnessing any tenderness between them. The truth was, they constantly bickered.

With the others asleep, that just left Harry and Darlen. The variance room was so quiet. Harry tenderly laid his hand on the chamber containing Laurel and Ava. They looked so peaceful, these two people he loved most in the world. He would give anything to keep them from harm. So far, he didn't feel he had done such a good job with that, not keeping his own counsel about Laurel being a whole soul, discounting her instincts. His arrogance led them into danger. When they woke, it would be different. He would partner his experience of interaction with other cultures with her telepathy and Ava's burgeoning abilities. He hated to be parted from them, even if they wouldn't be aware of the passage of time, but already the possibility of years apart stretched before him. It might be months before he saw them again. Laurel had tied up her hair, but there was a stray ringlet he longed to tidy. His heart leapt as he gazed on her now. He felt as though he'd loved her forever.

Darlen made the final adjustments to the variance chamber that was to be Harry's.

"Darlen?" Harry said, not taking his eyes from Laurel's sleeping face. "Do you remember what you said to me that day on the consular ship? That I think myself better than you?"

Darlen didn't look up, just continued with his task, his voice soft in the quiet, darkened room. "I sure do, Harry."

"You were right. I did."

Darlen allowed himself a small internal smile. He'd judged Harry too, but Darlen seldom apologised, so if there was a spare apology floating about, well, hey, he'd accept it.

"So has that changed?" he said.

Harry spotted Darlen's amusement, and he turned to face him. Darlen looked up for a moment from his task and grinned.

Harry might have reformed his opinion, but... "You're still a smug bastard, Darlen. You know I didn't fully trust you when you came to 100 moons with that story about rescuing Laurel." He considered telling Darlen this over the years, but their relationship had been brittle, to say the least. Harry accepted most of the blame must rest on his shoulders, so he pushed the thoughts to the back of his mind; now, he felt they needed an airing. Darlen continued with his preparations, listening but only responding with half a glance. He knew what Harry thought, and he knew he'd beaten himself up about it, but Harry hadn't finished.

"If the other whole souls hadn't read your mind, I might have rejected your plan as reckless." The prospect he might have done just that tortured Harry. He might have lost Laurel because of his own prejudice. It had weighed heavily after the war, but he never permitted himself to speak of it to Darlen. Or even thank him. Instead, he avoided him on the few social occasions when Helen and Darlen returned to Mentelci.

Darlen flicked up his eyebrows and stood back.

"You're good to go, Harry."

"I misjudged you."

Darlen held Harry's gaze, then opened his arms wide. "What about a goodnight hug?"

Harry's shocked expression brought a broad smile to Darlen's face as Harry sidestepped him and slid into the variance chamber.

Darlen commenced sedation, setting the variance chambers sequencers to close and begin. He waited until all controls settled into hibernation setting, then stood for a moment, thoughtful.

"I'm not sure you did misjudge me, my friend," he said aloud to the gloom. "Not then."

Mer finished the routine of settling his master into the chamber then plugged himself into the interface. Darlen set the robot to wake him in an emergency or if sensors detected a suitable planet close enough to the nebula, failing that, he would wake him in six years. All ship's systems, including the chambers, ran through Mer. His eyes lit red as a piece of fabric fluttered from the console where Ava had been playing dress-ups with him only that morning, and she called him her best friend.

CHAPTER THIRTY-ONE _

Fourteen-year-old Ava sat in the co-pilot's seat, knees bent, bare feet on the console and dressed in a jumpsuit that once belonged to Auntie Helen. Today was an exciting day for her; she could speak to Mom and Howie for the first time in years. Mer was speculating about the new inhabited planetary system they'd observed, mainly to occupy his young friend while she waited. In the years since she woke, as the only individual on board who understood Mer, she had become an authority in translating his sounds to the only other person also awake for those same number of years, Darlen, who was right now busily deactivating the stasis chambers that held her family. Ava refused to meet them in the variance room, even though she scarcely curbed her excitement, but she knew they would all be naked, the mineral-based gowns in which they were placed when they went into stasis long since dissipated. She decided it might be icky for her and embarrassing for them without their clothes. Besides, Uncle Darlen could manage without her.

Darlen poked his head around the common room entrance. "I've initiated the process. Helen will wake first, then your mom." He wavered. "Tidy up a bit in here, will you? Helen won't like it messy."

Ava slid from her seat and pushed the chairs around to neaten them up. "I can't wait, Uncle Darlen." Cleaning hadn't been a priority all this time, but the ship had never returned to the state it was in when Helen first took over. "Do I look alright? Do you think Mom will be proud?"

Darlen would have said her mom would be proud, but there was little point. Ava had asked this repeatedly these last few hours, and each time he confirmed what the girl already knew.

"And I'm looking forward to getting off the ship for a while," Ava added.

"Yes, well, don't let on to your mother I showed you how to gamble. She'll have a fit." Darlen headed off back towards the variance chambers, calling out, "It's going to be enough she missed you growing up."

Darlen had the privilege of watching Ava grow into a lively, bright teenager, ever since Mer alerted him after five years in stasis that Laurel and Ava's chamber was compromised due to the fact Ava had grown. Darlen extracted her without waking Laurel, but it puzzled him why Ava wasn't still the five-year-old he'd seen entering the chamber. Even now, four years later, he couldn't explain it. And every day of those four years had been a delight. Ava was intelligent, eager to learn, and an excellent opponent in any card game, even when she didn't cheat by reading his mind. Mer was more evenly matched, but even he often failed miserably. Between them, Darlen often reflected, Gabriel and Laurel had produced a remarkable creation, reminding him of the beauty of the woman he took from

Earth so many years before, Gabriel's mother, Ava's grandmother. It felt strange to Darlen that he was now part of Ava's family, and her presence in his life was a gift. But still, he missed Helen, her skinny little body beside him at night, her biting wit and quick temper, but also her fierce loyalty, her fighting spirit. He'd indulged himself by making her extraction the first.

For the second time in her life, Helen rose from a variance chamber. This time, there was no tube dragged from her throat, no milky fluid slurping its way down her body. She sat up, her memory quickly returning. Darlen lifted her into his arms and carried her carefully out to the common room, where years before, he intimidated her into eating bapth and variance antidote. This time, she slid her arms around his neck, blinking as her eyes adjusted to the light.

"Did I miss you?" she murmured groggily, planting a soft kiss on his cheek.

"Every single day," he smiled.

Helen rested her face against his shoulder, not even bothering to greet Mer. Someone else was in the room too, but her brain was foggy, so she turned her head, pushing away from Darlen.

"My god! Ava? *Ava?*" Helen's eyes widened as Darlen set her down. Surprise at meeting a five-year-old who'd aged several years overcame any grogginess from the stasis. "Darlen, did you forget to wake me up?"

"Hello, Auntie Helen," Ava said, moving forward to hug the bewildered Helen. "I had to be woken up four years ago."

"Four years?"

"You and the others have been in stasis for nine years," Darlen explained. "Mer woke me when the variance chamber logged a change in mass. By then, she'd been growing for quite a while."

"A change in mass?" Helen echoed as she carried out a closer inspection of Ava's face. "I thought we didn't age."

Darlen shook his head. "Someone forgot to tell Ava's molecules. We've found a planet, or rather Ava found a planet. I'll debrief you when the others are awake."

Laurel wept when she saw Ava, holding her daughter tight and burying her face in her neck. "I've missed you growing up," she cried. "You're so beautiful. Oh, Ava!" She held Ava away from her to take in every detail. Ava's eyes were as vivid violet as she remembered. Her hair was a tumble of waist-length, thick, shining black waves. Her mouth, curved in a beaming grin, showed perfect teeth and soft, deep red lips. She was the image of her father, and the family resemblance to Marcel was unmissable. Her daughter had grown into a beautiful young woman. Laurel felt so proud. And she'd missed it all. She hugged her daughter close again and closed her eyes. Ava laughed.

"It's okay, Mom; Darlen looked after me. He taught me heaps." Ava caught Darlen's eye. "And we've found a planet. The whole souls have been there."

Laurel sat down, not letting go of Ava's hand. "How do you know?"

Ava's face lit up with the same cheeky grin she had as a small child. "Same as I always did," she said. "Not everything's changed, Mom."

Harry and Marcel joined them shortly after. Harry became fixed to the spot when he saw Ava, his disbelief and confusion mirrored by Marcel, who, overcome, leaned against the bulkhead, supporting himself as he sank to the floor.

Darlen urged them to stay calm while they recovered from stasis. The filling-in of Ava's missing years could wait. There was still a situation that called for their attention.

"We still don't have enough water?" Harry asked.

"Not for all of us," Darlen confirmed. "I did consider leaving you in stasis, but…" he looked at Ava.

"It was the right thing to do," she said simply.

Marcel sniffed the air. "The odour is gone, Darlen. Did you fix the slot?"

"It's not fixed," Darlen said. "We emptied the compactor over an uninhabited planet and flushed the convertor. A year ago, we detected a deserted system with a distant star. I didn't want to venture too far out, but a sensor sweep of the system showed a gas giant with several moons; one of the moons had polar ice caps. We had no way of transporting ice in the quantities we'd need, and we'd have to run extensive and time-consuming toxin scans on the ice to ensure the resulting water was safe to drink. Mer took an axispod for an initial closer look and brought back a sizeable block he'd carved. It turns out there was no way we could remove the pollutants, so we used it to flush the convertor, but we couldn't repair the slot. The ice was just a temporary fix."

"You said there's a planet." Laurel and Ava still held each other's hands, Laurel only letting her go to greet Harry and Marcel. Ava nodded.

"Breathable atmosphere, water, industry."

"It's on the Ferle side of the nebula." Darlen showed them the sensor log. "As you know, the widespeed prioles are less dense in the heart of the nebula. They constructed this hull to convert the priole signatures trillions of times every second. If there are fewer prioles, the ship is slower. The bottom line is, you might have been in stasis for nine years, but in fact, we have probably only travelled distance-wise, the equivalent of six."

"Your point, Darlen?" Harry prompted, ignoring his feeling that part of his life had just been disposed of.

"I don't know how far Ferle activity covers. It takes three years to travel from one end of League space to its furthermost point. It's possible we might still be within reach of the Ferle."

Laurel shuddered. "And there might be other, unknown hostile species."

"There's definitely traffic in that system, but I don't have configurations of all ships, Laurel. It's going to have to be our best guess. Even Ava can't tell if it's in hostile space."

"We won't know unless we land."

"Well, we can't turn up out of nowhere," Harry said. "That could be regarded as a hostile act. It makes sense to contact the planet from high orbit and hope they don't have guns bigger than…" he stopped mid-sentence as Laurel and Ava leapt towards Helen, grabbing her as she slumped forward. They laid her gently on the floor.

"Her blood pressure might be low from the stasis," Laurel said as she and Harry knelt beside their friend. Marcel rushed to retrieve the medical instrumentation at a nod from Laurel.

The technological capacity on a ship the size of Darlen's could not support a full diagnostic array, but in this instance, however, the limited portable pandroscope was effective enough to pinpoint the cause of Helen's light-headedness quickly.

"She's pregnant." Laurel sat back on her heels.

All eyes swung to Darlen. He knew what they were assuming; that he'd taken advantage of the unconscious Helen during stasis, in the tradition of Soul Mongers with their captives during variance.

"I swear." He held up his hands, protesting innocence. "I did nothing. I don't understand how this happened."

Marcel looked at him in disbelief. "I cannot comprehend how a man of your age does not have this knowledge."

"He knows how it happens, Marcel," Harry said. "We're just wondering when?" Harry turned his attention back to the now gently moaning Helen. "How far along, Laurel?"

"The foetus looks about four months; give or take a few days."

Harry nodded thoughtfully. "She must have been pregnant before the stasis?"

"That would mean she's carrying a nine-year-old foetus with a strong heartbeat." Laurel looked up at Darlen. "The baby is fine. It seems unaffected by the stasis."

Darlen sat down heavily and ran his hand over his bald head, his expression confirming to everyone in the common room he was just as stunned by this revelation. Laurel discreetly pointed the pandroscope towards him. "Elevated heart rate, elevated cortisol," she whispered slyly to Harry. "He is in shock!"

"He's not the only one," Harry whispered back.

"Variance doesn't hurt the foetus, and it's far more invasive than stasis," Darlen said when he got his breath back. He looked at Laurel hopefully. "I doubt this child will suffer damage either."

"The baby looks normal, Darlen," Laurel reassured him.

Helen tried to sit up, leaning against Laurel and feeling the floor around her for support. "What happened?" Helen blinked a few times. "Did I faint? God, I feel sick. I fainted last time as well, do you remember?"

"So, you did," Laurel said as she and Harry helped Helen onto a chair. "This time, though, it's different. Helen, you're pregnant."

Helen raised her eyes to Laurel, shaking her head in disbelief. Then, as her face changed to a furious red, she turned to Darlen.

"You didn't! You dirty bastard!"

"Helen, calm down. No, he didn't." Laurel's voice reached in as Helen's words finished spewing forth. Then she spoke aloud. "You were pregnant before stasis. Remember you said you were getting fat?"

"But I'm too old. I'm…" Helen tried to calculate her age in her muddled head.

"It doesn't matter." Laurel squeezed her hand. "The baby is fine, and you're fine. That's all that matters." Laurel leaned closer. "I'm not sure about Darlen, though. He's still in shock!"

Helen drew in a deep breath, blowing it out in an unvoiced, "wow." She caught Darlen's eye and smiled. He shook his head as he smiled back.

"I suppose I'm still thirty-nine," Helen said to Laurel. "We can't count the time I was in stasis."

"I thought you had an automatic test for pregnancy when women came from variance," Harry asked Darlen.

"From variance we do," Darlen agreed, "but not stasis. Variance fluid itself detects the hormones. I had no way of knowing."

"Your baby might be a Soul Monger," Ava suggested. "You might not be the last of your kind, after all."

"I don't think the universe has any need for Soul Mongers anymore, Ava. I'm glad to be the last."

"Will stasis have hurt the baby?" Helen asked.

"It doesn't appear to have," Harry reassured her, "but we didn't count on this, so we didn't bring obstetric diagnostic equipment with us. We'll have to do this the old-fashioned way."

"The pandroscope will monitor the health of you and the baby," Laurel assured her, "And I've worked in labour wards in hospitals on Earth. There's nothing to worry about."

"I'm not worried, exactly," Helen said. "Just stunned."

But Marcel was delighted and far less subdued with his excitement. "A new member of the family. It is cause for celebration!" He lifted his arms to express his happiness, quickly dropping them as he realised the effects of stasis left a residual weakness that required sensible overcoming.

"Right this second, Marcel," Helen attempted a laugh, "I'm wondering how a baby will fit onboard this ship. We might have to trade it in and get a new one."

"We'll manage." Laurel gave Helen's shoulder a gentle shake. "We'll go to the planet and check things out. They may sell cribs and strollers."

"Strollers?" the others echoed.

"I'm joking," Laurel laughed. "Helen knows what they are."

Alone later, with Helen resting and Ava and Marcel catching up, Laurel and Harry took the opportunity to thank Darlen for his care of Ava over the last four years. He embarrassedly brushed their thanks aside and described the circumstances of Ava's awakening.

"I don't know if she continued growing or if it was a sudden spurt. Mer brought me out of stasis as soon as the chamber alerted him there was a problem. She missed you both and cried a lot at first. I suggested she go back into stasis in the chamber I was in, and I'd set up one of the others, but I had already decided I may as well stay awake. In the end, I gave in to her not going into stasis and hoped to just work it out with you when you woke up."

"I bet you told her about all the stuff you did before you became respectable," Laurel smiled. Much as she liked and respected Darlen, he'd been a reprobate most of his life and possibly not who she would have chosen as a mentor to her young daughter.

He feigned a look of hurt but grinned. "I'm still not respectable! I did tell her about the Gale and the danger they presented. But I suspect they're long gone. She remembered what they did to you and spoke of it a few times. Knowing you were safe helped. And yes," Darlen tried to push the thought out of his head, but it was only a matter of time before Laurel sprung him, "she can gamble like a pro." He sat up straight, immediately diverting Laurel onto more practical subjects, "But she can also run routine diagnostics on the ship's systems, fly an axispod as well as any of us, plus pilot this ship. I taught her a few dialects, though I don't know if we'll run into anyone who speaks them out here."

Laurel's shoulders sagged, just a little, but she didn't mention the gambling. "I feel like I missed out."

"She understands Mer," Darlen said, "I don't know how, but she does. She input the dialects I taught her, plus the command I have of Earth languages, into his database to get a store of syntax, inflexion, phonemes; anything we might need to construct a vocabulary. Ava would have to translate but," he shrugged, "I thought it was very clever."

Laurel smiled at Harry; his face flushed with pride at Ava's innovation. "That is clever."

"What about her telepathy? Or cloaking like Helen?" Laurel asked.

Darlen shook his head. "She's telepathic, and she has a strong sense of technology. We haven't tested much else; there's been nothing to test those abilities on."

Laurel listened and hung on to every word, trying to catch at least some of the years she'd missed. She read much of it in Darlen's mind as he spoke, and he accepted it, but he continued with the story for Harry's sake, who, to all intents and purposes, was Ava's father.

Darlen felt bad for them; there was no way they would get those years back, and he worried that even waking them may prove catastrophic. Both he and Ava suffered water restrictions, relying on the little moisture a rigged-up condenser provided and for three years, until the system got flushed, they had to endure the stench of the failed slot.

"Maybe when Helen's baby arrives, he or she will fill in the gaps between five and fourteen," he said, trying to understand what Laurel must be feeling.

Laurel couldn't help but envy Darlen that he got to see her little girl grow up. He hadn't done a bad job at being a surrogate parent, and she said as much to Harry that night when neither of them was able to sleep.

"It seems like yesterday when we went into stasis," she said, her voice soft and sad as she cuddled up to Harry for the first time in nine years. "And now I'm the mother of a teenager."

Harry kissed her head, silently declaring his understanding of how bewildering it must be for her.

She tilted back her head, trying to see his face in the dark, but only seeing a gleam of his teeth when he smiled, "It's nice to cuddle up to you again."

"We were only apart for a day," he whispered, mindful of Ava sleeping so close to them. Now she was so grown up; they would need to be very cautious with intimacy.

Laurel sighed. "It doesn't feel like it. The evidence that so much time has passed is right over there in her bed. And now Helen's pregnant. Probably good Darlen got in some parenting practise before we woke up."

Laurel laid her head on Harry's chest and felt his subdued throaty reply.

"It was a bit unexpected; he's going to take a while to recover."

"He'll do okay. It's knocked Helen for six too. Who would have thought it?" She yawned. "Are you getting sleepy?" Harry murmured.

"You'd think after a whole nine years, I'd have had enough, but you know, I think a nap would be nice.

CHAPTER THIRTY-TWO _

"Helen should remain on the ship while we check it out. Just in case," Laurel warned. "Her blood pressure's unpredictable."

"The system appears to have several habitable worlds," Harry said, believing the fresh air might be a tonic for their pregnant crewmate. "Provided they're friendly, we should be fine."

In the last few days, they'd held their position in the nebula, scanning the planet and nearby systems for any unwanted possibilities. Marcel wasted no time returning to his fitness regime in the hold, this time accompanied by his sister, who surpassed him in physical strength and stamina. They could hear the two, now physiologically even closer in age, laughing all over the ship as they went through their routines.

Scans of the closest planet showed cities, road networks and substantial industry, but only one accessible spaceport in the centre of what appeared to be the most major city in the southern hemisphere. All other spaceports were inaccessible, probably, as Darlen pointed out; they were for citizens and industrial cargo only. A few planets in the independent systems outside the League had only one clearing port, which wasn't so unusual.

Darlen sent a hail, but in reply, the ship got scanned as it entered the shipping lane. An automated landing clearance guided them via a positioning beam to a docking bay on the planet below. A mechanical "clunk" accompanied their arrival as their engines powered down.

"That sounded suspiciously like a lock turning," Laurel said, looking out of the viewport.

"I think you might be right," Darlen also glanced outside. "We'll check it out."

Marcel pointed toward Helen's quarters. "One of us should stay here and look after Helen."

Darlen raised his eyebrows. "Look after Helen? Marcel, no-one looks after Helen the way Helen does. Don't worry. She'll be fine. We have to take Mer; he'll be able to translate. I hope."

They stepped off the ship, and sure enough, found a docking claw connected to the side. Every ship on the landing strips appeared to have the same device. Two females approached, smiling and friendly, but their language was unfamiliar. Mer took a moment, then turned to Ava to translate.

"They greeted us and asked if we were 'outsystem'."

"Tell them 'yes'," Darlen said, "and ask why the docking clamp?"

Ava responded through Mer. The two women seemed surprised but answered that the ship was larger than most ships that docked here and would be released upon the conclusion of their visit or business and when they received the requisite payment. They applied the clamp to stop crews from leaving without paying.

"They'll detain us if we don't pay?" Harry was incredulous.

"It's like a car park on Earth," Laurel said. "You had to pay to park your vehicle. If you didn't, you had to pay a penalty."

The notion stunned Harry. "Could you remove your vehicle and not pay?"

"Yes," Laurel nodded, "but it's against the law. A traffic violation."

"I've never heard anything like it."

"We will not violate traffic," Marcel said to the women, who only smiled, not understanding what he was saying.

Laurel was going to correct him, but instead, she pointed out a rather belated fact.

"Well, we don't have money, anyway. How will we get them to let us go?"

"Ava?" Darlen pointed to the two women. "Tell them we're traders."

Mer gave Ava a translation, and she repeated it to the women. One responded, gesturing towards the city, bemused that their tongue needed explanation.

"She said merchants have to register with the Reliance," Ava said. "See that building over there?" She pointed to a tall building towering above the spaceport. "They'll issue a licence and give us currency."

They proceeded on an antigrav platform through the vast spaceport, passing lanes of merchant ships half the size of Darlen's and small shuttles of all configurations. As the platform deposited them at the entrance, they found themselves caught up in the frantic hustle and bustle of a large city; bodies jostled, vendors bellowed out their wares, and the irresistible smell of street food wafted to their nostrils and made their bellies beg.

"This looks no different to any market town on any planet." Laurel watched as a woman led a team of camel-like spikits along the street. "Where would they get spikits?"

"Well, everyone needs food and supplies; humans have the same needs pretty much wherever you go." Darlen shrugged, "I don't know how spikits ended up here. They got wiks as well." He pointed to a man with several tiny wiks held in cages, a cruel practice that always led to the death of the baby wiks. Several distressed adult wiks hovered nearby, only moving when the man swung a heavy stick at them. Laurel knew not to draw too much attention to themselves. It grieved her to see it, but she wouldn't interfere.

Darlen looked around. "It looks like they set the spaceport near the business district. I wonder what their main export or import is?"

Harry studied the throngs of people. "No-one's paying us any attention," he said. "They all seem to be human. I think this might be a trading centre like on Albery or Simica."

Darlen nodded, he knew both planets well, and Laurel briefly visited Simica during her medical training. But there was something here that wasn't on Simica, and as that thought came to Laurel, Ava spoke up.

"I don't like it here," Ava said. "I don't know why I felt so drawn."

"I feel a bit…I don't know, uncomfortable," Laurel agreed. "I wonder if the ancient whole souls felt this way."

"You've been in stasis a long time," Harry tried to reassure her, neglecting his pre-stasis vow to listen to her instincts. "We're not staying long."

Laurel looked to the distance. She had no idea what she might be searching for. The far-off hills looked peaceful in the afternoon sun; she was breathing unrecycled air; the sky above was an incredibly deep blue with not even one cloud. Her sharp instinct that this place wasn't all it appeared arrived suddenly, strengthened by Ava's comment at precisely the same time, but there was no real evidence of danger, at least not yet.

"Mom," Ava's voice came into Laurel's mind. *"Someone is searching for us."*

"Here? Can you pinpoint who? No-one here knows us."

Ava shook her head; she'd had little opportunity to develop her telepathy in a crowd of people, even so…

"Harry," Laurel caught his arm, "perhaps we need to go back to the ship."

Before Harry answered, Darlen turned his attention back to them. "Let's go to this Reliance. We might as well obey the laws. We need to get money anyway."

Harry shrugged in resignation and followed Darlen. Laurel and Ava looked at each other, and in the absence of any apparent or nearby threat, they followed them into the building.

The man who met them at the Reliance was pleasant enough but didn't take his eyes off Ava during the entire transaction, and he didn't speak, just listened to Ava as she translated. He handed over a tube of tokens.

"Did you see the way that man looked at Ava?" Laurel glanced back at the man as they left the building. He was still watching them. "And why would they just hand over money?"

"I couldn't read his mind. Could you, Mom?"

"No, I couldn't. It was empty. And he wasn't listening to your translation. It was like he knew the reason we were here. Could he be a clone?"

"Perhaps," Darlen said. "There are a few cultures where the currency is spent only in the community. It comes from a central treasury, but I do agree it's odd they offered it up to us so freely, as complete strangers." He sniffed. "That food smells good. Why don't we see if we can pick up an evaporator unit, get supplies, then go back and get Helen? We can get some real food before we go?"

Only Ava and Laurel hesitated. On the face of it, even taking into account the spooky clerk they'd just met, it seemed okay here. Laurel wondered if meeting the Gale clone had affected her, and now she thought all clones were bad. But Ava was less forgiving with her feelings, and despite the patience and pleasantness of every person they asked for directions via Mer's translation, Laurel felt Ava bristling.

"Ava, are you sure the whole souls came here?"

"Yes, but now I think only in orbit, the same as the prison planet and only passing through. I think I just sensed their path. We shouldn't have landed."

"Perhaps telepaths aren't welcome here."

"I'm not sure the whole souls went to every planet they passed,

Mom. Maybe their communication only comes from telepathy."

"I thought one or two might have gone to the prison planet and got to know the prisoners, hence the tapestry."

"No, I'm sure, they never went to that planet, nor this. Orbit only."

"So why do we feel uneasy?"

"I don't know," Ava said aloud as she looked around. Despite her physical strength and speed, Ava was still only slightly built, possibly due to the ship's food or perhaps she took after her grandmother in stature. Either way, Laurel worried about her if it came to a physical clash with an unfamiliar enemy. They decided to hurry the men along and return to the ship as soon as possible.

They found the machinery shops housed in a single zone. Even though the city was vast, no building rose taller than seven storeys, and each machine shop was stocked floor to ceiling with equipment. Spare parts were unheard of, and the man who assisted them had a mind as blank as the clerk. In each case, the men's gazes lingered on Ava.

"They must produce clones here," Laurel said. "The people tending the markets and fooderies all have blank minds."

"Going by the availability of machines," Darlen pointed to the long avenues of machinery storage, "I'd say they're androids. That might be their market."

"They look so real. There are humans here, but I don't get the impression this is their homeworld."

"Well, only you and Ava can tell who's human or not. Realism is what most android manufacturers aim for." Darlen watched as a few people strolled past. "I must say though, I have never seen any like these; I'm damned if I can tell them apart. What about you, Harry?"

Harry observed the same group Darlen used as an example. "Never. They could be either. There was a factory on Everbi outpost dedicated to developing androids. I couldn't believe my eyes when I saw them, but these, they're almost indistinguishable."

"Almost, Howie?" Ava tilted her head.

"They're not indistinguishable to you."

"They're creepy."

"Mer doesn't creep you out."

"Mer's not an android."

Darlen and Mer deliberated about compatible free-standing replacements for the recycler and eventually found one Mer and Marcel could modify, as Darlen lamented the days of integrated systems. Mer, Darlen and Marcel returned to the ship with their supplies and to collect Helen to get some food. Harry, Ava and Laurel found a foodery close to the port while Laurel stressed to Harry that neither she nor Ava felt comfortable. He asked them to be more specific, but they could only offer their feelings. The others found them quickly, though minus Helen.

"She still feels sick," Darlen said. "She can't face food, so I left Mer with her. I think we can manage without him while we eat."

"Okay, perhaps they do takeaway. I'd rather go back to the ship," Laurel said, still trying to put the finger on her unease.

"They might." Darlen perused the various unidentifiable creatures hanging over a roasting pit.

"Takeaway?" Harry raised an eyebrow.

"Like the delivery on Mentelci."

The spicy meal turned out to be a sharing plate, prepared in the firepit and not one they could remove without considerable effort. And it made a welcome change with its colour and aroma. After the flat, tasteless rations they'd been eating for almost as long as they could remember, it was a heavenly treat. A fascinating and valuable discovery was fluid delivered via a small ball-bearing-like object. A single unit, placed on the tongue, provided the body with complete hydration. Harry checked this by measuring Laurel's hydration rate before and after, and it seemed to work. Naturally, they purchased a quantity to lessen the pressure on the soon-to-be repaired recycling system. It meant they might be able to use water for washing. Laurel never got over her craving for a bath, and the thought brought forth a sigh. Slot oil showers just didn't cut it.

Twilight descended as they finished their meal, and the planet's twin moons rose in the sky. Seeing them reminded Laurel of Mentelci, and she felt a pang of homesickness. As she waited for the others to finish the hydration ball transaction, Laurel's uneasiness returned with greater power, and a sudden oppressiveness threatened to dislodge her meal.

"Can we go now, Mom?" Ava was at her side in a flash.

They had to drag Marcel away, who was drawn to the lights and busyness of the place, a busyness that didn't quiet even though daylight was almost gone. He kept turning to look with longing at the city as they made their way back to the spaceport through the crowds of traders and buyers. Darlen walked slightly ahead, Marcel and Harry behind Laurel and Ava. The two women only sensed their immediate danger the instant spiralling blinding lights flashed down and twisted them from the ground. Marcel tried to grab Ava, who was closest to him, but his arms went straight through her as though she were vapour. Harry turned to Marcel as the last of the light faded, but their shock was short-lived as the spiralling light blazed again, and they too were snatched from where they stood.

CHAPTER THIRTY-THREE _

Laurel woke in a bath. Her last thought as they headed towards the spaceport was of a bath. It seemed almost as if she'd manifested her last thought, except for the mindless, human-looking android hovering close to her.

"Ah, you are awake," it said in a soft, even voice.

"You speak Seera?"

"Yes, human. We listened to your conversation at the foodery. It is a primitive language, easy enough to extrapolate into a cohesive form."

"Where's my daughter?" The android stood back as Laurel hauled herself from the deep bath and looked around first for Ava, then feeling her near, she looked for her clothes.

"You must dry your body, and then you can join her. The bidding has begun."

Bidding? The Ferle! She threw a thought out to Ava but got no reply. Panicked, she made to disable the android, but anticipating her reaction, it held her arm in a vice-like grip, subduing her. "You must dry yourself before I present you."

Judging by the grip on her arm, Laurel knew this android would match her in strength, so she adopted a submissive tone and accepted the towel the android offered.

"May I enquire, presented to whom?"

"To the lord," the android said, taken aback as if Laurel were a fool not to know. "We are on his ship, and the lord himself oversees the bidding. The young woman is luscious and tempting. Her skin will be soft. All the overlords wish for her. They also bid on you," the android added as if Laurel should be grateful. "Your master was generously rewarded for the four units we purchased."

And it fell into place. The android at the Reliance building was giving payment for Ava. His interest in her was him sending visuals to the Ferle. Darlen had unknowingly sold Ava to the Ferle. That's why they'd received the tokens. She knew Darlen's suggestion of a treasury wasn't accurate.

The android didn't offer clothing and met Laurel's attempt to drape the thin towel over herself by snatching it away. It seemed that she was to remain naked.

The android led the way, politely inviting her into an antechamber. Ava was there, standing silently, her long hair tied up, so the skin on her body was on full show. The android did nothing to Laurel's equally long and even thicker hair, leaving it to fall, still damp, down her back. She knew instinctively she was to be a minor player in this bidding. Their lack of attention to her would allow her to devise a means of escape for her and Ava. As the android put Laurel in a position slightly behind and to the side of Ava, Laurel glimpsed Harry and Marcel standing beside a lone Ferle guard, anchors over their wrists and feet. They glanced up as Laurel entered, and she sensed Harry's distress and concern. He wanted to reassure her, but he had nothing to offer. Marcel quickly dropped his gaze, and in his mind, manifested scenarios of possible escape. Darlen was nowhere to be seen.

The room was chilly, cooled to accommodate the hairy Ferle's low body temperature. Goosebumps crawled over Laurel's skin, not just from the coolness but at the sight of the Ferle lord. She'd only ever seen an impression of the Ferle back on 100 moons, a mock-up made by Asde and taken from the Gartryan prisoner's descriptions. But the mock-up didn't prepare her. The real thing was much worse. Covered in a fine brush-like hair, besides the back of the hands and feet which sprouted long profuse tufts, the Ferle lord's face was leathery, grey-skinned, and lipless. Two rows of teeth protruded from both the upper and lower jaw, and saliva drooled unheeded from the side of its mouth, pooling and drenching the thin tunic it wore. It stood before them, with a device similar to a holographic datacache opened out in symbols around. It uttered guttural, unnatural sounds as it communicated with the bidding lords.

Ava glanced at Laurel and smiled as she entered the room, then returned her gaze to the Ferle lord, but inside, she continued smiling at her mother.

"Did they hurt you?" Laurel asked.

"No, they gave me a bath, although those hairy creatures could use one. They smell pretty bad."

"They're the Ferle, Ava. Cannibals."

"I know, just standing here and looking inside their heads, I've learned they only focus on a few things at any one time. And right now, they're focused on me. They'd be easy to distract, given the right circumstances. We have to watch for our opportunity."

"It seems Darlen inadvertently sold us all to them, but you were the prize."

"Darlen escaped. I saw him step aside from the light that got us. He'll figure it out, and Harry and Marcel are here. Don't worry, Mom. We won't end up as lunch."

Laurel fixed her gaze on the Ferle lord. She hated to see her daughter paraded like cattle in front of this beast, but she kept her fury in check. Ava had shown future insight before. She would know if there was more to Darlen's evading the light than immediately evident, and any attempt to disrupt proceedings may get Ava removed from Laurel's sight. Instead, she took comfort from her fourteen-year-old daughter's calm composure as pinpoint lights popped and flashed around the Ferle lord. He—the android called it a male—acknowledged each bid, but one didn't need to be a telepath to see he intended to keep Ava for himself. The Ferle lord glanced at Laurel as bids also came in on her. Impatient to conclude the bidding and finding bids on Laurel a distraction from the main prize, he caught up one offer in his leathery hand in a gesture of acceptance. Laurel had been sold!

The android propelled Laurel forward, bringing her before the Ferle lord, his tongue rolling, guttural barks making little sense. Reaching down, the Ferle lord thrust a slender, pointed clip through the skin on Laurel's upper arm, causing her to cry out in pain. Two lighted anchors were attached as a loop to each protruding end of the barb. As the anchors pulsated, so a shock coursed through Laurel's body, bringing her to her knees. Her restraints dropped from her wrists, but her arm dangled uselessly at her side, the barb rendering her nerves unresponsive. She heard Harry's intake of breath and Ava's silent protest, but the pain made her powerless. Silence descended as the Ferle lord stood to approach Ava. It seemed he had won the bidding war for her. Laurel learned during the evacuation of Gartrya that the Ferle celebrated young human womanhood in a ceremony that climaxed in the girl's consumption. The celebration would take as long as the Ferle owning the human female chose. The longer he took, the higher the frenzy of excitement. He could choose to share his prize with others or not. Only fair-skinned, dark-haired females were prized. Older females were not celebrated, nor young men who were skinned and eaten immediately unless the Ferle had other uses for them.

As the pain in her arm settled to a dull ache, Laurel watched as the Ferle Lord stood in front of Ava. He did not touch her. Laurel closed her eyes and focused her attention on her useless arm until she felt the strength returning. The barb was not designed for someone with strong mental powers. She caught Harry's eye, shooting him a thought.

"Something is about to happen; I can sense Helen. There's only one guard and the android in here. Get ready."

A dark shape moved through the bulkhead, spinning around the Ferle lord and spiriting him away in a smoky haze. Simultaneously, an explosion rocked the ship. Laurel yanked the barb from her arm and fought her way through smoke and debris to deactivate the anchors on Ava, Harry and Marcel and kick down the Ferle guard. The android was flittering in confusion; it being the simplest of the androids, programmed only for attendant and restraint duties.

Combat situations were not expected during an auction. A punch from Marcel to its human-looking face sent it spinning into the bulkhead. It tried to stand, but Ava had collected the Ferle guard's weapon. The android collapsed from a single blast. This time, it didn't get up.

"Helen's taken out the ship's cannons," Ava shouted as several more Ferle guards squeezed their way through the bulkhead door. But Ava and Laurel were too agile and too strong. It turned out the Ferle were little more than insects to the two women, despite their hairy and sturdy appearance. Ava and Laurel found them easy to subdue even without weapons, but the Ferle were accurate shots and, while mindful of killing purchased merchandise, aimed in a way designed to disable. Marcel was injured, but not before making a flying leap to crush his attacker. Harry used the android as a shield but was hit by ricocheting weapons fire. Laurel rammed the bulkhead door shut, and Ava disabled the commands. She picked up a Ferle weapon to examine.

"They're good shots."

"They shot me in the leg!" Marcel groaned from the floor.

Harry limped over. "It's self-cauterizing; they must have been worried about damaging us."

Laurel examined a slain Ferle's body. "Their physiology seems quite fragile. This one has multiple broken bones. It must be a side effect of living in space."

Marcel hoisted himself upright. "They'll send reinforcements."

But Laurel, like her daughter who grinned knowingly,

now knew the outcome. "They won't before Darlen gets here."

They didn't wait long. The Ferle ship was a private yacht, no bigger than Darlen's ship, but Helen had taken out their propulsion, power and weapons. The vessel listed in space. Outside the room, they could hear the level tones of engineer-class androids attempting to restore ship operations.

Mer burst through first, an android held before him, its torso caved in, its mouth gibbering in its programmed language.

Darlen was right behind him. "The androids have signalled for help, so we need to get away. Helen's got the ship up against the entry port. They haven't got a cargo airlock." Darlen hoisted Marcel's arm over his shoulder to prop him as he walked. Mer went ahead, shoving any confronting android aside. Dead Ferle lay all around, courtesy of Darlen and Mer.

"Helen cloaked the ship so they can't see who's firing on them. The Ferle are very superstitious; this will frighten them, and it seems no-one from the surface is coming to their aid."

They heard Helen yelling as they got back on board. Darlen dropped Marcel in the corridor and ran for the control room.

"Ferle ships, four of them. They're headed our way." Helen looked up. "They're not yachts, Darlen. They're armed. I think they may have got a lock, at least on our general position."

"Mer, interface now!" But Mer anticipated his master's

order. Darlen would engage widespeed without hull configuration. A human couldn't do it, but Mer robots could. His eyes lit red as they retreated over the heads of the Ferle and into the safety of the Miran Forin nebula.

Laurel looked down at her nakedness, forgotten in the melee. Harry pulled off his shirt, gave it to Ava, and then ushered Laurel from the room, stepping over the injured Marcel, who lay forgotten in the gangway. Moments later, after Laurel had pulled on a shirt, she and Harry lifted him and helped him to a chair.

"You'll live," Harry said after cutting away the fabric from Marcel's wound. "It's clean, designed to disable temporarily but not to inflict permanent injury."

Marcel winced as Harry inserted a single heal-bot into the wound. "It is excruciating," he declared.

"It's a painful location. There's a dent in the bone."

Laurel left Harry to fix the groaning Marcel's leg. Laurel glanced at the wound on Harry's foot, but it was just a scratch and didn't need urgent care.

"You knew we were in trouble?" she said to Helen.

"I couldn't miss it!" Helen would have laughed had the situation not been as dire. "Your thoughts, the surprise, or maybe shock. I felt your uneasiness earlier, but as you didn't return and I didn't sense distress, I thought I'd wait it out. Just in case, I got Mer to check out the strength of the docking device. He deactivated it but left it looking like it was still in place. And suddenly, everything changed. I knew you weren't on the planet anymore, and I didn't want to get tracked, so I thought I'd cloak the ship, but those two girls were still at the entrance to the port, so I just had to hope they didn't see me when they were talking to you earlier. I saw Darlen running for the port and commed him, then picked him up just outside the city. Those girls didn't see me leave. So much for not hiding that which has not been seen or whatever it is you say."

"The Ferle had no idea what hit them."

"They didn't see the approach, and as no-one saw me leave, no-one followed. God, they're creepy, those Ferle. I dread to think about what they planned for Ava. And you as well, Laurel, even if you are a bit past it."

Laurel was thankfully "past it" as far as the Ferle were concerned, but Ava wasn't, and the horror of what could have happened to Ava sickened and terrified her. Laurel broke down, weeping. Ava tried to reassure her they were safe now, but it wasn't enough. Laurel had missed many years of Ava's growing up, and only a few days after their reunion, she came so close to losing her to a terrifying fate. She took Ava into her arms and held her. Harry watched. He hadn't listened to their concerns and, once again, felt weighted with the responsibility for placing them in danger.

CHAPTER THIRTY-FOUR _

"It's not your fault, Harry," Laurel wiped away a few tears of relief. "We could have just returned to the ship and left you to it."

"I feel responsible," Harry said hopelessly. "I'd rather die a horrible death than let you fall into the hands of the Ferle."

"It was my idea to go to the planet, Howie," Ava said. "I think the whole souls must have visited heaps of planets on their journey. I'm just sensing their path, and there's no way we can be warned if those worlds are hostile or not. I was fine on the approach."

Laurel nodded. It was only after they left the port that she felt uneasy. "Perhaps the Ferle weren't alerted until the locals saw Ava."

Harry thought for a moment. "It may be the Ferle have an arrangement with the locals. It could explain the measures they take to stop ships from leaving. I've never seen a docking clamp like that one."

Laurel felt Harry's pain and reassured him by drawing him into hers and Ava's embrace. "In future," he said, kissing the tops of their heads, grateful they were here, safe and in his arms, "your instincts will be our default. Any uneasiness, and we don't leave the ship."

Laurel agreed, but these events made her fear her telepathic ability might let her down again, and she wouldn't be able to protect the people she loved.

"How did you avoid being captured, Darlen?" Marcel asked, shifting his gaze from a scene that, under the circumstances, had the power to move him to tears.

"I've seen their technology before," Darlen replied, "on Gartrya. One of the methods they use for transportation is a short-range transference beam. An aura precedes it; I recognised it but not in time to warn you."

Darlen's explanation reminded Laurel of the beam that moved her and Gabriel between floors in the fortress. "They had something similar in the fortress. A transporting beam. It was the same colour."

"Probably acquired from the Ferle and modified," Harry speculated, joining in the conversation. "How did you take the Ferle lord? All I saw was smoke."

Darlen hesitated. No Soul Monger discussed the Magen with non-Soul Mongers, but then, Soul Mongers seldom had friends. "It's what I use to gather whole souls. I can only take one at a time, so it seemed logical to take the Ferle lord out of the equation seeing that Helen had her battle plan in place."

Harry looked around. "Where is he now?"

"Floating back to his ship, I expect," Darlen replied, unconcerned about the welfare of the Ferle lord.

"You killed him?" Laurel said.

Darlen feigned surprise. "Were you planning on

signing him up as crew?"

"No, but won't it bring the wrath of the Ferle down on our heads?"

"Too late for that," Darlen snorted. "The Ferle have flagged us. They were keen on Ava. I've seen the bidding on Gartrya; they're ferociously competitive with each other. They can't follow us into the nebula, but once again, it means we're trapped." He glanced at the sensors. "The Ferle are tailing us, but we'll reach the inner margin before they catch up."

Helen pulled a face. "Gale on one side and Ferle on the other."

"Think of it this way,' Darlen said, "they can't get to us in the nebula's heart, and no species' space goes on forever. Besides, the Gale wouldn't waste resources for this length of time. They might be determined, but they know when to cut their losses."

Helen sat down, disheartened. "One bunch of problems leaves off where another load of nasty surprises lurk."

"I didn't foresee any of this," Laurel said quietly, her shoulders sagging. "All of this is my fault."

Helen reached up and caught Laurel's hand, pulling her down beside her. "Sweetie, I didn't mean anything. We all agreed to this. I'm just venting. I don't mind the nebula, but…"

"Auntie Helen, you get bored."

"I do, Ava," Helen admitted, "but I'm not sure I like the excitement of species like the Ferle either."

"We're okay for supplies now, though?" Harry felt it

might be better not to give Laurel's doubts too much of an airing. They couldn't easily turn back, anyway. They were committed to this venture regardless of what lay ahead.

Darlen nodded. "We'll use the hydration beads as drinking water, and the evaporator doesn't need any special installation. We have enough food, but as Ava says, we'll have an ample supply of boredom. As far as we can tell, there's nothing but empty space on the other side of the nebula."

Harry tried to remind Laurel of her initial excitement about the venture. "You said it would likely take a lifetime, remember?" he said, willing her to recall the conversation where she asked him to give up his apartment. She saw his recollection as the images went through his mind.

"I didn't factor in the hostile elements we seem to spend our waking moments trying to outrun," she said glumly.

"Laurel," Darlen said. "If you feel so strongly and want to terminate the mission…"

Ava suddenly fell to her knees in front of her mother, pulling at her hands, startling them all with a fierce, "No! We can't go back!" Her crewmates astonishment at her swift reaction reached into her mind, and she closed her eyes to centre herself. "Mom," Ava brought her breathing under control. "We can't go back." She looked up at her mother, her violet eyes appealing. "We're…we're on a *pilgrimage*." She shook her head and begged her mother from her thoughts. *"Mom, we can't go back!"* It was then Laurel heard a distant echo. *"We are the deliverance."*

This time, the words came from somewhere other than

the defiant and beautiful Ava, who held her mother's gaze before lifting her eyes to Darlen, Helen, Harry, and Marcel.

"I'm with the kid," Helen said at length.

"Me too," Darlen replied, his voice a little gruff. It had been an emotional day. "None of this is any worse than the life of a trader."

Once inside the nebula's heart, they all breathed a sigh of relief. The Ferle ships broke off pursuit when they reached the inner margins, and the group settled on the prospect of boredom until the opportunity to take a detour—this time hopefully to a friendlier planet—arose. As the Gale were no longer tracking them, it seemed sensible to travel directly through the heart to the other side, where widespeed precipitation was normal, and they could make up some time. Also, there were no signs of inhabited worlds that might harbour curious and hostile species, and it was a relief to be as far away from the Ferle as possible.

As they exited the heart of the nebula, Ava and Laurel stood side by side, watching the spirals of minimal widespeed precipitation reflect in the viewport. Ava struggled to understand what was in her mother's mind. Something from before…

As she turned to question, Darlen pulled the ship from widespeed and into all stop.

"There's a beacon, a buoy or something ahead."

"A warning beacon?" Marcel checked the sensors.

Darlen shook his head. "I don't think so, an alert maybe, but not…" He straightened up. "Harry, it's League."

Harry studied the sensor, requesting a schematic for

the object. "It's just a proximity beacon from a League scout." He frowned and looked at the others. "The question is, what is it doing out here? The League is years behind us."

"Stolen from a scout?" Marcel suggested.

"Unlikely, Marcel. These beacons are built-in. You'd have to dismantle the entire ship to pry it loose. Even then, you'd have part of the hull attached. Can you decipher the code, Darlen?"

"Mer's onto it, but there's no cohesive pattern; just random beeps."

"These beacons have specific protocols," Harry said. "They record catastrophic events, but only as they relate to the ship, then transmit coordinates. They're virtually indestructible, and their algorithms are encoded and embedded by nanotics. Once set, the algorithms are there for the life of the beacon. It's not possible to destroy them. They simply decay."

"This unit seems to be in good condition," Marcel said.

"As I say," Harry repeated, "it would be part of a ship's structure. It can't be altered once encoded, and the signature is embedded into the designated ship until it decays. It's impossible to change the encryption sequences."

"Eli could," Laurel said as she gazed through the viewport, her voice distant.

"Eli?" Harry looked up.

Laurel cleared her throat and turned. "Yes, Eli. He had a strong sense of technology."

"Why would Eli leave a beacon out here?"

"More like, *how* did Eli leave a beacon out here?" Darlen said. "Mer, grapple it into the cargo bay."

The cylindrical, unimpressive League-issue beacon lay on the floor of the cargo hold surrounded by six bewildered crew. Laurel squatted down and placed her hand on the surface, somehow hoping she could sense something of Eli in the object, perhaps an echo. But there was nothing. Helen answered Laurel's unspoken request that she try too.

"Not much point, chick," she said. "It won't give me anything either."

Ava pushed between them and knelt beside the beacon. "Mom, you said Eli wasn't much good with telepathy. You're hoping for psychometry, but I think he may have just sent us an old-fashioned message."

"Like a message in a bottle, Laurel," Helen said. Laurel saw the sense in that; even if Eli had been able to leave a telepathic signature, it would have contained no detail as to why he would send a beacon out here for them to find.

Mer lifted the beacon and found a suitable port to plug in an interface. They waited until Mer hummed out a few noises to Ava.

"He says the message is encrypted." She nodded at the robot. "It's from Eli, but Mer has to decipher it."

Mer took the unit back to the common room, where they all sat about, mystified. Darlen and Marcel went to finish installing the evaporator, more as a distraction than anything else, and Laurel did an obstetric check on Helen to pass the time. Ava stayed with Mer, idly folding cloth hats to put on him as he worked.

The encryption was cleverly sequenced and took hours to decode. Eli had clearly modified the beacon to appear as a malfunctioning piece of junk to anyone attempting to salvage it. Unless, of course, Eli's intended target found it. Mer stepped back with a snap and relayed to Ava the message was too extensive for her to relate; that it needed viewing. Mer interfaced with the starchart, it being the largest of the onboard visuals and downloaded the message. An image of Eli headed the text. He looked serious.

"If you're reading this, then I suspect you've got over your initial shock at finding the beacon, and Mer has been able to decode the message. I know you're asking how I got the beacon out this far, but that's not important. What is important is that you don't return to League space and don't ever believe that your journey isn't worth the risks you are taking or the perils you've faced and will face in the future. I'm here to say it is worth the risk.

"I say again; you must not return to League space. Canon Akkuh didn't go as quietly as we believed; he has raised a force against the League, and the Gale is backing him. The Gale discovered the wreck of a Gartryan cruiser adrift near the nebula; it had been there since the war. When they dismantled it, they found several devices with technology unknown to both League and Gale, but these devices allowed the Gartryan ships to breach the perimeter without a tag. They've duplicated the technology, it's not fully effective, but it's enough to cause chaos.

"As soon as the Leyis government received your message, Darlen, they recalled Chloe and me to Mentelci, but Chloe was with her squad in the Southern regions. The Gale intercepted and detained her, but her imprisonment was short-lived. An escort of cloaked League ships

346

confronted the Gale. Chloe is fine, but she, and my family and I have left the League and are in exile on a planet where the Gale nor the League will find us. Marta refused to come; she has remained on Mentelci to continue her work but is under heavy guard. Now, it is impossible to know who to trust. Asde is here with Chloe, as is Ru and the children. We are safe. The planet is unknown to both the League and the Gale. Its inhabitants are a highly advanced species in technology but otherwise live very simple lives. The Gale and Canon Akkuh believed us still on Mentelci, and no-one trailed us as they did with you. We spent several years in space, all of us on a League scout until we found this place, a cloaked planet only Chloe and I could see. The government allowed us to land and explain. They gave us asylum, and we have found peace here. Harry, we have one of your colleagues to thank for getting us safely off Mentelci. His name is Minet. He told us how he met with you and urged you to leave the area near the abandoned prison planet. Canon Akkuh had a hold over him for past issues and called in a favour; he had no choice but to comply, and when he saw you near the Masiennes cluster, knowing that one of the Gale's prizes would be the whole souls, he urged you to leave.

"The League is in chaos right now. A war between the most ruthless cartel in the galaxy and the League is being waged. I can't tell how it will play out, but apart from Marta, the Gale are robbed of at least some of their prize.

"Laurel, Harry, I wish I had time to tell you about our lives here, but I would need more than a single beacon, and I only had a single ship from which to remove the technology. I knew the Gale no longer tailed you, but I am not familiar with this region of space and what species or potential enemies of the League may come through here and try to salvage the technology. I mean the message only for you.

"Please don't try to find us. Instead, continue on your way. You are the deliverance."

Laurel's heart thudded in her chest. *You are the deliverance*. This was the third time she'd heard similar words. What did they mean? Ava's mind held nothing, no recognition of the phrase, only natural curiosity regarding the beacon and the message.

"At least we know they're safe. Eli and Chloe, anyway," Helen said. "I wonder where this hidden planet is? And how did they get this beacon here before we got here?" She shook her head, bewildered.

Harry reread the message. "He said not to go looking. I don't know what he means by 'deliverance'. It's pretty cryptic."

"Perhaps a message for the whole souls?" Marcel looked at Ava, who shook her head.

"It might be," Laurel spoke slowly; to hear this phrase, spoken by Eli, couldn't be a coincidence. "I've heard something very similar before."

"Where?" Harry asked.

"Ava." Laurel looked at her daughter, who gave a slight shrug to indicate she didn't know what her mother was talking about. "Then once more, when Ava said we're on a pilgrimage. She didn't speak the words aloud or communicate telepathically, but I still heard those words, and now, Eli's saying them."

"It must mean something," Darlen said.

"I came out here to find answers," Laurel sighed. "Instead, I'm finding more questions."

CHAPTER THIRTY-FIVE _

"Minet probably stole the scout to get away from Mentelci," Harry said later as they examined the message. "He'd have access."

"Were we wrong about him?" Helen said. "He came across as lying through his teeth."

"Eli alluded to him being held to ransom by Canon Akkuh," Laurel replied, "but the fact that he rescued Eli suggests he knew what the Canon and the Gale were planning for us whole souls. If so, he lied to stop us from getting too close."

"I told you he was straight up, but either way," Harry pointed out, waving a finger in the air, "that act of heroism won't save him from League justice, and he stole a ship."

"Says he who never returns equipment to the League," Laurel smirked, referring to the several datacaches, weapons and codes still in Harry's possession from his days in the League constabulary. "Not to mention treason."

Harry waggled his shoulders. There were exceptions in the name of righteous research. "I wish I'd smuggled triconomic interfaces; we could have used wrist licks then. I hate sidearms."

Darlen smiled thinly. "Let's hope we don't have many more opportunities to use any weapons at all."

As anticipated, after the excitement of the beacon and endless speculation as to how it got this far out from League space, life took on its regular routine. Ava rejected any deviation from course, besides them continuing in normal space, with occasional relief from the hypnotic and mind-numbing swirls of widespeed outside the viewport, coming in the form of investigating a nearby moon or planetoid. Ava spent her days in the study of robotics, a pleasure in which Marcel also indulged. Mer only allowed his most non-critical systems to be disassembled and rebuilt, often wearing one of the hats Ava still made to amuse herself in quiet moments, her mind too lively to acquiesce to stillness, except in sleep. Helen's pregnancy progressed, but sleeplessness and high blood pressure tested her. Laurel and Harry kept her under close surveillance, but they agreed not to wait any longer when her condition deteriorated, and she slipped into delirium.

"It'll have to be a caesarean," Laurel said as she checked and rechecked the pandroscope, the readings causing more concern by the minute. "Better get Darlen in here; it's only right he should be in on this."

At Harry's request, Darlen swiftly transformed the quarters to a makeshift operating room, seating himself beside Helen as Harry and Laurel worked. Marcel and Ava waited anxiously in the common room, leaving Mer to pilot the ship while they were both so preoccupied.

The baby was born bellowing at the top of her lungs.

With Helen still sedated, Laurel handed the howling little girl with the mop of dark hair to her father. Darlen took his baby's fingers in his big, rough hand and smiled fondly as the tiny fingers wrapped around his own. Slowly, the crying ceased, and the little mite settled against him.

"She's perfect," Laurel smiled, caressing the child's pink face and loving the reminder of the surge of emotion she felt at Ava's birth.

Darlen gazed down at the child in his arms. For the moment, he could not speak, content to hold and cherish the new baby while Laurel and Harry treated Helen. Harry expressed concern at the time it was taking for her to wake, but the pandroscope, not having the capacity for a whole-body scan in a single session, continued to record nothing of concern.

"I'm cursing myself that I didn't bring obstetric instrumentation, Laurel," Harry lamented. "I should have had more foresight. What if you'd got pregnant?" Ignoring Laurel's surprised expression, he manually pushed the equipment to its limits. "This portable pandroscope only gives us a fraction of the picture."

"It's enough, and it's served us well. Anyway, how could you know this was going to happen?" Laurel laid an encouraging hand on his arm. "And I don't recall us making plans for me ever becoming pregnant." She looked down at Helen's sleeping face. "We'll watch her closely for the next couple of days."

Ava was erupting with excitement to see the baby, so while Helen was still asleep, Darlen introduced the new member of the crew to her and Marcel. Ava scored a long cuddle, but Marcel was far too overwhelmed, stepping back when Ava offered him a turn.

"She's too little. I'll break her."

"I didn't," Darlen laughed. "And I am far clumsier than you!"

But Marcel refused, sitting down to observe the baby from a distance.

"How is Auntie Helen?" Ava asked as soon as Laurel emerged from the makeshift theatre.

"Sleeping," Laurel said, peeping at the cherub in her daughter's arms. "I've just come out for coffee. Harry's sitting with her."

Ava looked beyond where Laurel stood, frowning slightly, *"Will she be alright?"*

Laurel looked behind her, listening in on Ava's anxious thoughts.

"As far as we can tell, she's fine. We'll stay with her until she recovers."

Ava nodded and smiled at the bundle she held. "The baby is lovely. Auntie Helen will be thrilled."

A few hours later, Laurel settled the hungry infant into her mother's arms. "A baby girl?" Helen looked up in wonder at Laurel. "But I wasn't even in labour. I was having a nap."

"You were unwell, Helen," Laurel explained. "There were unforeseen difficulties, and we had to deliver the baby."

"Where's Darlen?" Helen looked around. "Has he seen her?"

"He has, and as expected, he's overwhelmed."

Helen smiled down at her child. "I'm naming her Scarlett. I always wanted to have a baby girl called Scarlett."

Darlen appeared in the doorway, a proud grin on his face. "I hoped we'd call her Darlen Junior." Laurel excused herself; she knew when she was extra.

Harry, Ava, and Marcel were all gathered in the control room, discussing widespeed with Mer, having returned their attention to matters at hand.

"How's Helen?"

"She's fine, Harry, but…"

Harry shifted his attention from the widespeed conversation. "But what…?"

"I want to tell her not to risk having any more children, but it's a conversation for another day." Laurel looked around Harry at the star charts displayed across the cockpit. "What are you doing?"

"Ava keeps getting glimpses of what looks like gigantic widespeed prioles within the nebula's heart," Harry said. "Mer managed to locate the phenomenon and probed them. I've never seen them before, but the preliminary test suggests they *are* prioles, but unlike the single spiral, these have a secondary structure, a kind of core. If we can harness them, it's possible we can improve on speed inside the nebula's heart, even if only in short bursts. Judging by their size, we'd expand on widespeed in the heart by a factor of seven, maybe eight, faster than normal space widespeed."

"That sounds good. What does Mer think?"

Mer munched around a few sounds.

"He thinks reconfiguring the hull would do it."

Ava glanced up from the sensors. "It's a risk, they may

jolt us, and that may lead to damage. We'd have to factor in STO variables." She flicked a hand in her mother's direction as she returned her attention to the sensor, not expecting a reply.

"Sure you do, honey," Laurel replied anyway, clueless. She understood little of the technology utilised in deep space. She remembered from Darlen's explanations that prioles were the harnessed agents for widespeed. She once saw a mind-boggling schematic of how these little individual spirals appeared joined together as one. They were present all over the known universe, even though not discernible to the naked eye.

Harry saw Laurel's vacant expression. "Remember how Darlen explained that widespeed precipitation is less dense the deeper we pass into the nebula, slowing us down?" Harry showed Laurel the results of Mer's closer inspection of the larger prioles. Laurel nodded. She knew that was why they moved less swiftly than on the outside margins or in normal space. "It turns out that now," Harry said, "there are larger spirals, with normal space in between."

"How much space?" Laurel attempted a sensible question, expecting a scholarly response, an equation, an algorithm, one she would have trouble understanding with her limited knowledge of widespeed. Harry was capable of such an answer, but instead, he scrunched up his face and held up his finger and thumb in a gesture, not at all representative of the infinitesimal distance between one spiral and the next. But she got the idea. It was weeny.

"Even so, the gap is bigger. Wouldn't we go even

slower?"

"No," Harry grinned. "If they're compatible with the ship's current widespeed progressions, a single priole cluster will connect to the hull each time they contact."

"And speed up the time it takes to cover the distance between prioles?"

"Exactly," Harry said, a delighted grin on his face, thoroughly at home with this type of puzzle. "It's fascinating. And we wouldn't have to take the chance of reconfiguring the hull to an algorithm that might have catastrophic consequences if we can't undo the reconfiguration."

"Is that likely?"

Harry shrugged, but his enthusiasm didn't dim. "This ship has run these calculations for more than two hundred years. It might resist change. Darlen might not think it's worth the risk to speed us up, but if the larger prioles increase our speed, then we think we should try."

———

Drawing the prioles to the hull was easier said than done. Darlen would only allow the most basic reconfiguration, echoing Harry's observation that the ship had been doing things one way for centuries and was possibly too old to adjust. Consequently, their widespeed remained the same.

"Does it matter?" Helen asked, up and about now two weeks after Scarlett's birth and settling effortlessly into motherhood. Baby Scarlett was up against her mother's shoulder, lulled by Helen's gentle patting, her new blue eyes seeking to focus on her surroundings.

"Not really." Darlen pulled himself out from under the

command console. "This journey doesn't have a predicted time of arrival. If we detour here and there, we might find a few friendly faces and get to explore some systems on the way. If we meet any hostiles, we can still travel in the nebula's heart. I'm just worried that if we make too many changes, normal widespeed might not happen for us when we leave the heart, and we'll be stuck on impulse engines. Ava?" Darlen pushed himself back under the console.

"Yes, Uncle Darlen?"

"Do you have any sense of how long this journey will take or whether moving away from the nebula affects our progress?"

Ava made a helpless gesture with her hands. "I only know that when we deviate from the course the ancients made, I feel displaced, uncomfortable, even when it places us in the Ferle's path. And I only really know which planets they visited when we get near." She turned to Laurel, "You feel it too, don't you, Mom?"

"Not to the degree you feel it, Ava," Laurel replied, only half agreeing with her daughter. "But my senses tell me the nebula is significant. I don't know why. I wonder if we need to find the place where the nebula ends."

"Well," Darlen's voice reached out at them again from under the console, "if we're searching for the end of a rainbow and we don't all want to die of old age before we get there, this reconfiguration needs to work. We might require longer bursts inside the nebula's heart and just come out when we identify a possible place to stock up: a change of clothes and stuff."

"But we're not altering the primary algorithm?" Harry

crouched down beside the console. "We're just giving it a push?"

"That's the plan."

Mer made a see-sawing sound. "Mer's right," Ava said. "The original hull programming will still be present."

"Okay, Mer," Darlen called out, "Try temporary isolation of the conventional widespeed algorithm. We can overlay it with the new one and see what happens. We may just be able to slide one out of the way as we need it. I doubt it'll be very stable at first; we can trim it when we see how it responds."

Darlen continued issuing orders, and Harry and Marcel turned their attention back to the widespeed configuration. Ava joined the team, learning on the job from Mer.

Helen and Laurel sat in companionable silence as the others worked. Laurel still had the word "deliverance" floating around her mind. Now, with Scarlett's birth out of the way, she had time to consider the meaning once more, but it was like the fragment of cloth from the prison planet, simply a puzzle.

"What were you doing ten years ago?"

Laurel saw the question forming as Helen thought it. The odd part was that Helen spoke aloud in English, her Australian accent surfacing for the first time in years. Despite the telepathic forewarning, the language change caught Laurel off guard.

"I...well, ten years ago? Ignoring the fact we spent nine years in stasis?" She had to give it a moment's thought. Ten years ago, she hadn't been born, at least not to this universe. Helen understood Laurel's feelings. She too had almost forgotten she ever had a former life.

Laurel frowned. "I was working part-time, studying part-time and living in New York, considering transferring to Chicago, which of course, I eventually did."

"You were rich, weren't you?"

"I…" again, Laurel saw the question coming, but still, she had to think about her answer. Rich, in her old life meant something different to what rich meant now. Their conversation reached Ava, who glanced across as Laurel's own accent surfaced. Ava had never heard it before—she loved it—to listen to her mother speaking as she did before she came to this universe. Laurel's occasional lessons in English now carried a Seeran accent.

"Yes," Laurel answered, unaware of the change in her speech, "rich enough to do the things I loved, which was studying old things."

"Why did you work then?"

Laurel had to consider that one. She liked to help, to feel useful. To have a purpose.

Helen watched her friend's changing expressions and nodded. She twisted her head for a moment to study the goings-on around the command console. Ava and Mer responded to Darlen as the ship took a diagnostic to prepare for the temporary reconfiguration.

"Do you ever miss it? Your old life?" Helen rearranged her sleepy baby so she could look at her face. Helen's expression was tender, a faint smile on her lips.

"You asked me that on Leyis," Laurel said. "I remember saying then I didn't miss it, but now—" she paused, "I don't even remember it as something I participated in. I certainly wasn't telepathic. Or empathic, for that matter. Discovering I had those abilities, for me, was almost like starting life over."

"Me too, although I was never up to your standard." Helen gave a short laugh. "Do you remember the first time I held Ava, and you said, 'Meet your Auntie Helen?'."

Laurel did remember. She had been so grateful for Helen's presence then, for her genuine love and support.

"I was so proud," Helen went on, "when you singled me out as Auntie to your little daughter. I didn't think anything would top it. It was the best, most meaningful thing that ever happened to me."

"Ava loves you, Helen. You are very special to her."

Helen didn't smile, just nodded. "She's special too. In time, her abilities will exceed ours; wait and see."

Laurel watched as Helen curled Scarlett's fingers around her own. "Everything wonderful that takes place is followed by something else more wonderful." Helen looked up. "To hold my own little girl, I never thought it would happen to me."

"And she is beautiful, Helen. She's very lucky to have you as her mother."

Helen smiled then, seeming as though she had more to say when Scarlett let out one of her ear-shattering howls. Helen stood, making a beeline for her quarters. "I'll feed this little one before she really starts squawking."

Laurel grinned. "That baby has a loud voice."

Darlen's voice drifted out from under the console. "Check out the mother!"

"I heard that!" Helen called out above Scarlett's yells

as she disappeared along the corridor.

Laurel allowed her mind to drift back to her pre-Helen distraction contemplations. Harry and Darlen were busy under the console, Marcel and Ava hunched down beside them, following directions. There was little Laurel could do to help them on this one. It all seemed so routine and harmonious. And Laurel had no sense of the heartbreak to come.

CHAPTER THIRTY-SIX _

Ava's head jerked up, her eyes widening with horror and confusion as she leapt to her feet, the datacache falling to the floor. Laurel sensed it, shivering as a shadow passed, whispering as it went, but she couldn't catch the message. Ava raced for Helen's quarters, but Laurel's legs moved so slowly, even her voice as she called for Harry seemed to hang in the air. Willing herself forward, she skidded to a halt at the doorway of Helen and Darlen's quarters. Ava was already there, her hand to her mouth, unable to take another step. Laurel pushed past her to where Helen lay curled up on her side on the bed. Scarlett, sated with milk, her little mouth still making tiny sucking movements against Helen's breast, slept peacefully in the crook of her mother's arm.

Harry was hot on their heels, assessing the situation before he reached the bed, shouting for Marcel to bring the pandroscope and resus kit. Laurel watched trancelike as Harry leaned over Helen; his mouth moved, but Laurel couldn't hear him. There would be nothing he could do. Nothing. Helen was gone. Laurel had heard her whispered farewell.

None-too-gently, Harry lifted Scarlett from Helen's

arms and handed her to Ava, who could only look down at the little bundle.

"Ava!" Harry hissed. "Take the baby! Laurel?"

Laurel turned her gaze slowly towards him.

"Some help here?" Harry ordered; his face grim. Laurel pushed herself forward. Between them, they gently turned Helen onto her back. Laurel dimly became aware of Marcel returning with the equipment and Darlen standing in the doorway with Ava. Anguish, pain, and the fear of each member of the group came at Laurel, but she could not reassure them, could not turn to them and say it was all a mistake. And in amongst that pain was Darlen, angrily and silently challenging the awful scene unfolding before his eyes.

Laurel moved like an automaton, positioning Helen's body for resuscitation. Helen was still warm, on her skin a hint of the life that coursed through her only moments before. Her face was relaxed and peaceful, as though she slept. As Laurel bent over her, a tear dropped onto Helen's cheek, catching the light as it rolled away.

The first resus delivery brought no result. The pandroscope glowed red, a sign that life was extinct. Harry and Laurel watched as the pandroscope delivered another stimulus, but again it glowed red, this time with a warning that death had been present for too long. Harry sat back on his heels, his shoulders slumping. He looked at Laurel and put his hands to his head. The pandroscope continued glowing but gave no indication as to what had happened. Harry's own grief now started to quietly claim his emotions with the realisation that Helen was beyond his help.

Laurel leaned over onto Helen's chest. She thought instinctively to try CPR, but Harry took her hands away.

"The resus is far more effective than any manual methods, Laurel. She's gone."

"But she's only been in here for twenty minutes," Ava said, her arms cocooning Scarlett protectively. "Scarlett had just finished feeding. I don't understand why you can't revive her."

"It depends on what happened and when," Laurel said dully as she looked into Darlen's stricken face. Slowly, she rose and moved aside. Marcel stayed in the doorway, his arms around Ava and the still sleeping baby. Darlen sat on the bed. Tenderly and reverently, he stroked Helen's face, then, squeezing his eyes tightly shut, lifted her lifeless body into his arms.

Darlen allowed Harry to conduct a pandroscopic autopsy on Helen, but with the pandroscopes limited post-mortem programming, it was a discouraging exercise. Laurel agreed with Harry's instincts that Helen had suffered a catastrophic cerebral episode, given her prenatal history. But Harry couldn't be sure. Without proper scanning equipment, he would have to conduct a manual autopsy, but Darlen declined. Instead, not being able to bear the thought of leaving Helen's body behind in the nebula, he permitted Laurel to see his thoughts that he never wanted to be parted from her.

He and Laurel lovingly wrapped Helen's body and placed her in one of the heavy fireproof containers in the cargo hold, then enlisted Harry's help in rigging up a remote mechanism to fire an old wrist lick placed within the container. Containing a wrist lick without a triconomic interface in that fashion would reduce anything in the immediate area to ash. They carried out Helen's cremation in silence, and at its conclusion, Darlen went to his quarters without saying a word. He closed the door, and they heard the locking mechanism strike. Marcel excused himself and headed for the galley. For now, he also needed to be alone with his grief.

"Darlen asked me to remove her heart," Harry said when they returned to the common room. "He placed it in a separate box and cremated it along with the rest of her remains. He plans on compressing it into a gem." He gazed sadly out of the viewport. Laurel sat beside him and wrapped her arms around his waist, leaning her head against his chest. She felt the comforting warmth of his hand as he stroked her hair.

"It's his way of keeping her with him always," she murmured.

"He says he'll bury the rest of her ashes," Harry's voice trembled. "Maybe on the next planet."

Ava put her arm around her mother. Harry reached down and kissed Laurel's head, and the three remained there, wondering how they would ever get through this unbearable loss.

Darlen remained in his quarters. He didn't venture out to check on the ship's operations or, more importantly, to enquire after his baby. Laurel and Harry allowed him to grieve as he saw fit, at least for the time being, and shifted their immediate attention to a dilemma of a different sort. Scarlett. At only a few weeks, she was still reliant on milk. In the days since Helen's death, Laurel had come up with a supplement from the supplies onboard that fulfilled the baby's nutritional needs but wasn't compatible with a baby's digestive system. Scarlett regularly screamed with colic until she fell asleep, exhausted. In the absence of paediatric painbots, they once resorted to a single small-stature adult painbot occlusion, but it overwhelmed the little mite's immature nervous system and made the matter worse. When Scarlett did feed, she whimpered as she sucked the preparation through one of Mer's uncomfortable-and-not-designed-to-be-sucked insertional ports. That she missed the satisfaction of suckling from her mother was undeniable. Ava, Harry, and Laurel all took turns in cuddling the baby as she fed. Even Marcel helped, who had no choice but to get over his fear of holding her. But they all suffered from lack of sleep. And still, Darlen didn't put in an appearance.

"This isn't good for her," Laurel said a few nights later as she listened to Marcel singing to Scarlett, seeking to soothe the miserable baby. "In days, she's gone from breast milk to a modified supplement. She's not even getting the satisfaction of sucking properly."

"Marcel's singing voice isn't good for anyone," Harry murmured in the darkness. "It's a good thing this ship can fly itself; everyone's too busy with that little scrap of humanity to do anything but see to her."

"You know what I mean." Laurel left it at that. Baby Scarlett had also worn him out. And that night, despite

Laurel's exhaustion, sleep wouldn't come.

"What are you doing?" Harry, sleepy and dishevelled, appeared in the galley doorway. Laurel was in her nightclothes, the ship placed on auto, and Mer was with her, the baby's milky preparation splattered all over his chest, a result of the fight each feed brought. His eyes glowed as he rotated his head towards the door.

"Shhh," Laurel warned, pointing to the corner and whispering, "Mer and I are experimenting."

Harry looked over to where Marcel, on the floor and half propped against the wall, slept in desperately needed, uncomfortable sleep. He'd bent up his legs to support the baby so he could relax without dropping her but had dozed off. Scarlett was safe but turned almost upside down when Marcel's knees flopped against the bulkhead as he reposed, her awkward position not affecting her exhausted slumber.

"Experimenting on what?" Harry lowered his voice and wiped the sleep from his eyes, peering at the array of medical equipment laid out over the galley bench. The pandroscope was in operation, busy scanning Laurel's endocrine system.

"Me. I rerouted the pandroscopes diagnostic subroutine through Mer to distract it. Then I uploaded Helen's last antenatal scan and superimposed her endocrine system with my own. Next, I'm going to gradually filter the subroutine back into the pandroscope, starting with a simple hormone test."

"Aren't you worried the subroutine might get assimilated into Mer?" Harry said. "He's two hundred years old. He's probably picked up a few rogue subroutines on the way."

Mer hummed in acknowledgement.

"I am a bit worried," Laurel admitted, "but we can't go on the way we're going." She glanced at Marcel and Scarlett. "Mer was able to isolate most of his pathways that would likely integrate with the diagnostic program, and he'll alert me of any bleedthrough."

"And the result will be the pandroscope thinks you're Helen?"

"Briefly, it will," Laurel said with more optimism than she felt. "The fact that we moved the diagnostic program aside might confuse it long enough to think that. But once I start reloading it, it'll sort itself out pretty quick, and it'll pick up it has been fooled. I only need those few minutes, though."

"Long enough to trick a highly sophisticated piece of technology into stimulating lactation in a non-lactating female?" Harry allowed himself a small grin. He got what she was attempting to do. "Very clever."

"It might not work, Harry," Laurel said, making a face. "I had to delete Helen's death from the system so it can look at my pituitary and think it's hers, not to mention adjusting all the other hormones, but it's a start. Look at Marcel," Laurel pointed to the corner of the galley, "at all of us. This way, I can give Scarlett what she needs: milk."

"You could stimulate breast milk just by letting her suckle."

"I know that Harry, but it could take days or weeks. We need a solution now."

Harry checked out the pandroscope as it searched for its diagnostic subroutine to advise Laurel—or according to its latest information—Helen, that she was in the post-partum period and that her prolactin production was deficient for milk production and required remediating. Harry attached a remedial interface to Laurel's neck, ensuring the diagnostic component only received limited information. The pandroscope built up a picture of what it thought was Helen's endocrine system, a stream of information appeared advising urgent treatment, and Harry allowed the subroutine to trickle through enough to correlate diagnosis and management. For a moment, the pandroscope hesitated, and Harry and Laurel held their breath while it found the interface and delivered the required stimuli to Laurel's pituitary gland. Immediately after it delivered the beam, the pandroscope withdrew for a self-diagnostic.

"It's realised," Laurel made a victory fist. "But we got what we needed."

"This means you're the only one who'll be feeding Scarlett from now on," Harry warned, secretly feeling relieved. The system would probably have worked on him as well, with a few more adjustments. He was glad Laurel hadn't suggested it.

***

In those first few days, Laurel got a sharp reminder of how uncomfortable she initially found breastfeeding Ava all those years before. She winced her way through the first week of feeding Scarlett, but the difference in the little girl was nothing short of a miracle. In no time at all, she became a textbook baby, happy and content and, thankfully, sleeping most of the night. Marcel, Ava, and Harry got some much-needed sleep and ship's operations returned to normal. Except for Darlen. They only knew he was still alive by the apparent use of the galley some nights. Besides that, he kept the door to his quarters closed, seemingly blind to the proceedings outside, his child's well-being or the ship's function.

"Do you think Darlen blames us?" Marcel asked.

"How could he?" Harry said. "We did everything we could."

Laurel recalled that moment she heard Helen's farewell. "I heard a whisper," she said, smiling sadly, "but not until it was too late. Perhaps she knew."

Ava shook her head, her lovely face still showing her grief.

"I don't think she knew until it happened, Mom. It's not given to us to know when we'll die. We simply make the necessary preparations to be where we need when it happens."

At only just fifteen, Ava had made many brief, meaningful comments over the years, not just startling Laurel with her wisdom but giving her a sense that Ava's insightfulness had a deeper origin. It brought her comfort, but with a sense of sadness that Ava seemed so much older than her years.

"Helen had no idea?" Harry asked. Ava's youthfulness seemed to have no bearing on her wisdom. Whatever she had to say, he was prepared to listen. He'd learned the hard way about not listening to the telepathic women in his life.

"She just didn't know it until it was happening, but Mom," Ava looked at Laurel, recognising her next words would stir interest, "You've seen it. You know Auntie Helen wasn't alone. Her spirit may have known."

Laurel felt unwilling to answer questions about what exactly it was she knew, she saw something once, but she couldn't explain it. Harry opened his mouth to speak, then closed it when Laurel folded her arms, creating a barrier to any questioning on the subject. Marcel likewise filed this snippet away to be resurrected at a later date. He slapped his knee.

"My lady sister is right!" he declared. "Helen brought joy to us, and now she sleeps. Let us move beyond our grief. Laurel has lost people dear to her, and I have lost a beloved father and grandmother. They live on in us." He gave Ava a playful shove to show his belief they lived on in her too. "Life moves forward, and we are bound up in its course. Helen's life force is within her child. We will survive this battle."

And as if prompted, at that moment, Darlen stepped into the room. He looked tidy, but his face was haggard. Without a word, he walked to the control room and took over the controls from Mer. As he passed, he glanced at Laurel.

"Not today," she heard. *"Don't speak to me today."*

Laurel woke the following day to find Scarlett gone from her makeshift crib. She wandered out into the common room where Darlen stood facing the viewport, swaying gently from side to side, Scarlett on his shoulder, her blue eyes peering at Laurel as she entered. Darlen turned, a little less haggard than the day before, but the darkened circles around his eyes remained.

"She was awake," he said. "I bathed her, but of course, I couldn't feed her. I know none of you has had much sleep, so I thought to keep her amused until you woke." He handed the child to Laurel. "I hope that's okay. I haven't been about to know the new routines."

Laurel took the baby from him. Scarlett's black hair was sticking up like a brush, evidently not washed by anyone with any expertise in bathing babies. She grinned as she settled the baby into her arms. "Of course, it's okay, Darlen. Scarlett is your child."

"I found the clothes Ava made for her. I hope they're okay."

"Darlen, stop apologising!"

He reached out and stroked the baby's face. "I know you found a way to feed her, Laurel. I'm grateful."

"We wanted to do the best we could for her," Laurel said, then hesitated. "And we knew you needed time to yourself."

Darlen nodded slowly. "Soul Mongers are taught never to become emotionally involved, not with anyone. I did before—" he took a deep breath, "but what I felt for the duchess paled beside what I came to feel for…" The sentence went unfinished, the precious name unspoken. Darlen raised empty eyes to Laurel. For now, perhaps for always, Darlen's heart was shattered. Even his love for his baby daughter would never completely dull the pain of losing Helen.

CHAPTER THIRTY-SEVEN _

Scarlett inherited all her mother's impishness and proved every bit as endearing, and with so many adults around, it was unavoidable that she would be a little spoiled and indulged. The only world she knew was her father's ship, and Laurel worried about her, even though she had plenty of attention. Ava, at seventeen, doted on the almost-three-year-old girl, but since the encounter with the Ferle, they had no contact with any civilisations, human or otherwise and came upon only a few barely habitable planets on their course. The widespeed conversion tested their technological skills to the maximum, and they devoted considerable time and energy to its development, but each time they tested it, they faced a frustrating fail, so for now, they made better headway in normal space, close to the nebula.

Laurel put her concerns to Darlen. "Scarlett's never seen a real sun, nor ever played in decent fresh air, and she's showing signs of needing to be let out."

Darlen rubbed his eyes. "*I* need to be let out," he said. "Those couple of planets we stopped by didn't have much in the way of nightlife."

"Uninhabited planets have a habit of that, Darlen,"

Harry said, joining in. He'd already brought up with Laurel they needed another stop. "There's nothing out here, though. I vote we re-enter the nebula's heart, have another go at the widespeed, see if we can make some headway and exit the nebula on the other side. According to sensors, this region of space is deserted for incils to come, not even any planets with breathable atmospheres."

"What if we run into the Ferle again on the other side?" Marcel said. "Aren't they the reason we've continued here all this time?"

Darlen nodded. "Yes, but even the Ferle would have limits. Harry, I've been bouncing an idea off Mer. We might get a few incils out of it. Let's concentrate more on getting away from uninhabitable systems and hostiles rather than reaching an indeterminate goal. At least for now."

Harry and Darlen turned to discuss Darlen's new plan while Mer turned the ship back into the nebula. Marcel sat opposite Laurel and smiled. Already tall when he first joined them, his body was now firm and muscular thanks to his daily workouts in the cargo hold, his raven hair was shoulder length and his deep grey eyes wide and expressive. Like his father, Marcel was beautiful rather than ruggedly handsome, but unlike his father, Marcel suffered vanity. He knew he was attractive, consistently choosing from his small wardrobe attire that accentuated his muscles or smooth chest. Laurel thought it was unfortunate that there was no-one here on the ship to appreciate it, although that fact didn't bother him.

"We rarely get the chance to talk, you and I," Laurel said, returning his smile.

"Not alone," Marcel agreed. "There's always someone," he pointed at Scarlett, perched on Mer's thigh, drawing on his face while Ava instructed her, "who demands attention."

"It would be good to let her play in the open."

"This is her life, Laurel. Her father is here, and we are here. She is content. I led a life like this, too, remember?" Marcel hadn't spoken of his isolated life recently.

"Are you ever sorry you came?" Laurel asked.

His eyes grew wide in surprise at the question. "Sorry? Not for a moment. All my life, I lived behind a wall. Now I am free."

"I worry that you might still feel cloistered, stuck in a ship with no-one of your own age."

"I spent much time without company after my father went to the war. Now, I value the presence of others and times such as these when we are explorers, pioneers. It gladdens me."

"Is there anything else that gladdens you?"

"Yes, Laurel," he grinned wickedly. "I am gladdened to lay an evil man flat with a well-aimed blow to the face."

"They're just cargo bay holoenemies, Marcel," Laurel laughed.

But Marcel's wicked grin became even more wicked. He liked to make people laugh.

"Marcel, you're very aggressive!"

"Indeed, in the protection of those I hold dear, I gain great satisfaction from breaking an opponent's nose."

"Is this what you think about when we head for a new planet? A fight?"

"I'm teasing you, Laurel. That is but one way to express energy; another is in exploration." He turned to look at Harry and Darlen as they pondered the widespeed conundrum for the hundredth time. "And there is still much that needs exploring."

Laurel nodded. She might have been putting her own feelings onto Scarlett. Perhaps she needed a little respite from endless weeks in space herself.

Ava looked up. "We are on the right track."

"I know, but it's nice to detour now and then."

"Just don't have regrets."

"I don't. I wasn't thinking it."

"Not right then, but you sometimes do."

Laurel met her daughter's gaze. Yes, she did wonder why she'd led them all out here. And she felt responsible for Helen's death. On Mentelci, Helen would have given birth in the medical facility with a fully equipped pandroscope instead of the limited field version they had on board. This would have immediately alerted medical staff to a variation in her condition. But as Harry pointed out, it happened days later when she wouldn't have been monitored. Even that very sensible reasoning didn't stop Laurel's heart from aching for the loss of her friend, and even now, not even encouraging thoughts from her daughter assuaged her guilt. She closed her eyes for a moment and allowed herself to miss Helen with all her heart.

While the others scratched their heads to promote more promising-looking enhancements to the hull, Ava and Laurel reorganised the ship to meet the residents' growing needs. Marcel's quarters remained in the cargo bay anteroom, and Ava rigged up a shared room for her and Scarlett on the other side of the cargo bay, a situation that delighted Harry now that he could have Laurel all to himself at night without a teenager sleeping close by. Laurel hoped they would find somewhere to put the ship down before the confinement caused tempers to fray. She marvelled at how they'd avoided it all these years, but that was before a demanding toddler came on the scene. Marcel and Ava enjoyed taking the axispods out every chance they could; Laurel had done the same once or twice just to be alone. Darlen often retreated to his quarters, occasionally picking up a protesting Scarlett to take with him and at others, turning pleading eyes on Laurel to let him have a break. Ava's patience with the inquisitive and demanding little girl with a comment about everything was never-ending. And then there was Mer, the black robot, now Scarlett's devoted friend, just as he had been Ava's before. Laurel fondly remembered a comment Helen made that Mer had missed his calling and should have been in childcare. She'd said it in fun, but without him, Laurel suspected they would have all gone quietly mad.

Several more weeks passed before Darlen felt confident to test his widespeed theory. The ship so far had thwarted all other attempts and shut out overrides. This time, the proposal, theoretical at best, would see the current widespeed configuration once again rerouted through Mer, so his child-minding had to take a back seat. Each time they applied the new configuration, they didn't fool the ship, and it looked for ways to upturn it. The project wasn't without risks either. The hull was untested at greater-than-normal widespeed, but Darlen believed a short burst would have little effect, reasoning that the hull withstood the pressure exerted on it during its course through the Transcender, a journey this ship had made often without ill effect. Even though enhanced widespeed could not be measured with time portal and multi-universal travel, they theorised the worst that could happen was the hull would reassert its preferred widespeed algorithm and lock Mer out. At the third attempt, the configuration didn't reassert, and while it wasn't practical to have Mer so disabled while the ship hurtled at seven times more than normal widespeed, it was a promising result.

Darlen and Harry were at the infochart, analysing the widespeed data, Mer stood motionless at the flight console, and Marcel was extrapolating their position on a starchart. Laurel had a sleepy Scarlett napping in her lap, and Ava was gazing out the viewport.

A familiar sense came to Laurel, the source from outside the ship, and she shifted her gaze to Ava. Although she could see the others, they appeared suspended in time. Ava was in her line of sight, and she turned in response to her mother's thoughts. As she did, a tendril of vapour emanated from Ava's fingertips, and she raised her hands, turning them over to examine them as the mist coiled and followed her movements. It started, and it was over. Laurel pitched forward onto the floor, bracing herself with her arms to not crush the startled Scarlett. Ava and the others were flung against the bulkhead.

Darlen leapt for the controls. "Did something hit us?"

"No," Laurel said as Harry helped her up. "An object, a lifeform, was heading towards us, but Ava moved the ship out of the way."

"We've registered a momentary ten-degree alteration to pitch," Darlen said, checking the sensors. "Why didn't we see it, whatever it was?"

"It was one of the creatures the Gartrya used to cross the nebula." Laurel picked up the still startled Scarlett from the floor to verify that she was unharmed. "That's the first we've seen in all these years. Its thought patterns were like the one released after the war."

"The same one?" Harry asked.

"I don't know." Laurel had no way of knowing if it was the same one. Perhaps they had a collective consciousness, and their thought patterns largely the same.

"So, how did Ava move the ship?" Marcel mapped the creature's trajectory, headed directly towards them on a collision course.

All eyes swung to Ava. "I didn't sense the creature, Mom did, and I got it from her that it was heading directly towards us. My instinct was to cry out and brace for impact, but something took over. You all just stopped—I mean—stopped, like in not moving and then vapour appeared from my fingertips." She held up her hands to show them. There were no signs anything unusual had taken place. "It's like when Auntie Helen hid the ship. Mom, did anything else happen?"

Laurel knew to what Ava referred. She was speaking of the spiritual entity harnessed to Helen. Now, she was asking if a similar manifestation had transpired with her.

Laurel shook her head slowly. "I saw nothing, honey, but then, I didn't the first time with Helen either."

"Look, I don't profess to know what you're talking about, vapour and the mystical 'anything elses'," Darlen said, "but we have another problem." His tone drew them back; this 'anything else' couldn't wait.

Marcel could not disengage the new widespeed configuration from Mer's sub programming. Harry and Darlen maintained the algorithms long enough for Mer to regain partial control, but he informed them the hull refused to re-establish the original algorithms back to the hull sequencer.

"Is this ship sentient?" Marcel asked, scarcely able to believe what Mer had just reported.

"Not sentient," Darlen scratched his bald head, "but it's been around long enough to get temperamental. These ships get assembled with the Mer interface. They have a unique relationship, one that allows familiarity between the subsystems. It does have a certain amount of autonomy if it considers it can improve on function, but it reverts if it can't confirm that improvement."

"It's decided it likes the new widespeed configuration better than the old one?" Harry said in amazement. "It's taking a *vacation?*"

Darlen shrugged. He hadn't anticipated this. The ship had never before defied him, but on top of its programmed ability to make changes, it could also override commands if the Mer interface robot was compromised. Mer had been through quite a few changes since his close association with humans began, and it was possible the ship didn't recognise him. The programming of trust between the Mer interface and the ship was a necessary precaution added by the Soul Mongers to safeguard their ships as they passed through the Transcender. These modifications would have been made soon after its first owner took possession of it, and each Soul Monger family had their own codes. Unfortunately, because Darlen disobeyed his father and was sent away, his installation as a Soul Monger was by default. His father died before Darlen received the codes, and he'd inherited this ship from the Soul Monger who'd been running the Gartrya gig. In essence, the ship could hold them to ransom if it wanted.

"What if we run into another creature?" Harry said.

"They're telepathic," Laurel answered. "It may have been drawn to us because of Ava and me. I didn't sense any hostility."

"Not intentionally, maybe." Harry pulled out the sensor log for them all to see. The creature was easily as large as the ship. Had it hit them, they would likely have been severely damaged.

"It may have thought the ship was a lifeform and came to investigate," Marcel suggested. "We may encounter more. It seems Laurel and my lady sister are more accurate than sensors at this speed."

"We're millions of incils from League space," Harry pointed out. "Those creatures must inhabit the entire nebula."

"Let's see how fast it was travelling as it approached us?" Ava waved her finger at the sensor log floating around her head. "I don't believe it!" she exclaimed. "Nearly as fast as us! It must use priole precipitation in some way."

"I wonder why we haven't seen any others?"

"They might prefer the other side of the nebula, Harry," Laurel said. "We've spent most of our time either in the heart or on the League side."

"Well, we don't have time to consider it now. If we can talk the ship into changing course, we can move into normal space where we'll slow down naturally." Darlen indicated to Mer to talk to the ship and try to reason with it. "Then we can decide whether it's worth trying this again or just be satisfied with what we had."

There was a murmured consensus, and Darlen and Mer got to work on coaxing the ship out of its sulk.

CHAPTER THIRTY-EIGHT _

The ship was not concerned with altering course or turning over the widespeed configuration. It had discarded improvements but refused to accept changes to speed until it completed a thorough check on Mer's systems. There was little any of them could do but wait as the swirling mist of widespeed and the heart of the nebula hurtled past.

Laurel thought some Earth astronomy might divert them while the ship continued its diagnostic. She set up a reasonably accurate holographic image of her planet of birth, courtesy of Soul Monger and whole soul slave contributors to 'A Treatise on the Cyclical Dimensions. A study into Whole Souls, Their Doctrines, Beliefs and Perceptions of Time', an extensive document brought to Laurel's attention during the war, by Harry, who never supposed she would actually read it.

"On Earth, scientists consider it impossible to travel faster than light." Laurel included a working diagram of Earth's solar system.

"What's the pretty one, Auntie Laurel?" Scarlett poked a finger through Saturn.

"That's Saturn. From Earth, at speed of light, it would

take less than a couple of hours to get there."

"Do they go there?" Like Harry, Marcel found the concept of several races inhabiting only a single planet in an entire galaxy bewildering. To him, finding a way to distance himself from all that chaos would be a priority.

Laurel laughed. "They don't! They've got as far as manned missions to the moon, and it took them a few days to get there. Earth's old rockets have never travelled at light speed."

"They never will," Darlen said, adjusting the lightspeed calculations on a datacache, using Earth formulas. "This is what they need to do."

They all leaned forward to inspect the new data. Laurel sat back, shaking her head.

"You've used a time sequence, Darlen. One of our scientists had a theory..."

"I know," Darlen cut in, "They're immersed in their special relativities and conventional matter; they're playing it safe. They should have listened to the crazy-looking guy with the mad hair. They put a lid on him and crushed his further research because he also suspected the time-variant that plays out around Earth. That's one of the reasons why they'll never get beyond Mars."

"Was Einstein a whole soul?"

"Probably, Laurel. He knew a darn sight more than any scientist before or since, and they shut him down."

"Who shut him down?"

"Government, I suppose. Whoever didn't want the status quo upset."

"Did they ever prove the time-variant?"

Darlen gave a non-committal shrug. "I can't say. Maybe someone knew the folds existed, but several of your scientists researched the possibility of time travel."

The conversation turned into a fascinating discussion on the role of whole souls on Earth, their possible origins, Ava's ability to move the ship and Helen's ability to hide them. Darlen turned out to be a mine of information about Earth's future; even though he'd only travelled as far as the year 2050, but he'd used Earth's time variances to make those journeys.

"What happens to space travel?" Laurel asked. "Do they can the idea?"

"They do. By 2050, Earth is so plagued by societal issues; there isn't a government left on Earth who has the time to conduct a space programme." He gave a small chuckle. "I've seen the amount of junk that orbits Earth in 2050. You couldn't describe what surrounds your planet as 'space'. It's full up."

"What societal issues?" Laurel pressed him. She knew she'd never go back, and she didn't even want to go back, but still...

"I'm not an expert, Laurel," Darlen admitted, "but you can probably guess. Even though there is a time distortion, each fold meets up, so the timeline I took Eli from eventually folds into yours, so he's in your past, and you were in his future. If you think of the problems in society in Eli's time, wars, drugs, crime, would you predict it got better?"

Laurel shook her head. "No, worse if anything."

Darlen blinked a slow 'affirmative' response. "After

you left, the pattern would have continued. But at least with the governments so inward-looking, there were fewer wars."

"It sounds like a terrible place." Marcel cast an apologetic look at Laurel. "Sorry, Laurel, I don't wish to offend."

"It makes me glad for the League, even if they're facing difficulties at the moment," Harry said.

"Greed," Marcel glanced at him. "The problems on Laurel's Earth. The problem on Gartrya, the problems with the Gale invading the League, all caused because people want more; more power, more possessions."

Although they all accepted Marcel's observations, now was not the time to become maudlin, so Laurel returned their attention to Darlen's entertaining forays into future Earth. Even Scarlett, who usually tired quickly of such grown-up discussions, enjoyed her father's animated explanation of his experiences 'hopping', as he called it, through time.

They didn't learn a lot, suspecting Darlen embellished most of what he told them for entertainment value, but at the same time, it passed a few hours while the ship continued its deliberations. In the morning, nothing had changed. Mer, still interfaced, was a captive audience and model for Scarlett, who dressed him up and drew on his face. When he rotated his head away to respond to the ship, she tried to pull him back, and when he swivelled his head in refusal so she would allow him to continue with his work, she told him he was nodding his head the wrong way. Mer lit his eyes and made a few harmonica sounds, but Scarlett loved him; he knew it, and he gave in to the child and himself up to multitasking.

"Scarlett understands Mer," Harry said, observing them.

"I know," Laurel said. "Ava's been teaching her. I think he sounds like he's running his speech through a metal recycler. It's all meaningless to me."

Harry grinned. "Me too. I would have thought Darlen could make sense of him, though."

"What I think," Laurel kissed Harry's shoulder and linked her arm through his, "is that Darlen doesn't like to give away all his secrets."

Several times, it seemed as if the ship was set to free Mer, but each time, it found a new reason to retain the interface. It reminded Laurel of those boring computer updates or waiting for something to download, the mesmerising blue circle rotating endlessly or getting a cup of coffee while waiting for the little bar to reach one hundred per cent. Only this one seemed stuck at 1. It had to end soon.

It didn't, and besides a few close encounters with the giant, flat lifeforms that both Laurel and Ava sensed, with Ava moving the ship out of harm's way, they continued as before. Weeks turned into months, and try as she might, and despite a burgeoning empathy with technology, such as Eli and Chloe had, Ava could not sway the ship from its present course nor slow it down.

"It's punishing us," she said to Darlen when she found him in the galley making routine checks on the evaporator. With Mer otherwise occupied, such things fell to the crew.

Darlen was crouched at the base of the equipment, poking around with a lightwrench.

"Don't be silly," he said, glancing up. "It's stubborn. It'll release Mer when it's ready. Besides, you reckon we're heading in the right direction. This way, we might get there quicker if the ship doesn't fall apart."

Ava pulled herself up onto the galley counter. "I only half meant it, Uncle Darlen. I was just running a few problems and projections through the infochart. I cross-referenced the results on a datacache, merging Mom's light-speed information with our current widespeed data."

"And?" Darlen got to his feet, waiting for the response he knew would have him making calculations.

"Remember that cluster of galaxies from Mom's universe? The ones she showed us on the starchart?"

"Which one?"

"The one that would take, in Earth time and using light-years, around three hundred and thirty million years. Well, we'd have gone past it."

Darlen stopped what he was doing and took the conversation seriously. He knew the cluster she meant. The Coma cluster. Widespeed didn't translate to light years accurately, but if he factored in time…

He headed for the door. "Show me," he said, as a bemused Ava jumped down from the counter and followed him back to the control room.

"See?" Ava said as Laurel, Harry, Darlen, and Marcel examined Laurel's diagram of the milky way galaxy.

"What is it we're supposed to see?" Marcel looked from Ava to Darlen.

"Ava reckons at our current speed," Darlen changed the starchart to astronomical data, "we would have travelled the equivalent of 330 million Earth years. That's around…"

"100 million incils from when we started the test." Harry finished the math for him. "How? We'd all be dust."

"We're travelling at plus seven widespeed at this moment," Darlen said, "but we only have a starting point. There's no course laid in, no endpoint, even so, unless there is a time variable, we couldn't have travelled more…"

Again, he didn't get to finish the sentence. Laurel pushed by him to look out the viewport filled with distorted widespeed.

"What is it?" Darlen followed her gaze.

"You call this the heart of the nebula," Laurel glanced over her shoulder, "but I don't believe that's accurate. I feel more like it's a vein, an artery."

A barrage of unspoken questions clamoured into her brain, and she held up a hand. "I believe we are travelling through a part of the nebula where time doesn't exist, but speed registers."

"Well, that makes a heap of sense!" Harry grunted and folded his arms.

"I'm sorry." Laurel tilted back her head and closed her eyes. It didn't make sense; it didn't to her either. "Harry, I don't pretend to understand, and I don't know how to explain it. I can only say that if we were to move outside the nebula now, you're right; we'd be more than one hundred million incils from the moment we started this test. Inside the nebula, it could be yesterday or the day before or next week. It's meaningless in here; time has no place."

"It does make sense, Laurel," Darlen said. "I have never spent so much time this deep inside the nebula, and we calibrate the ship's instrumentation to measure normal time. Of course, it's not calibrated to measure no time at all, so I have never noticed this anomaly."

"What does it have to do with the ship holding Mer to the interface?" Marcel asked.

"Whenever I bring the ship into the nebula's heart," Darlen explained, "I give it two references: simply, a starting point and an endpoint." He looked at each person in the room. "You're all pilots." He raised his eyebrows, "So you know any ship configures its hull for widespeed and drops when it reaches its destination." A few eyes darted looks at each other, and a few eyelids flickered as they tried to take Darlen's meaning.

"Come on! Or I'll never let you near this cockpit again!"

"The configuration is for speed, but it bases that configuration on time?" Marcel offered, unsure that his answer went far enough. Darlen glared at Harry, who should have known.

"There, give the man a cigar!"

Laurel bit back a grin. There wasn't a cigar to be had anywhere in this universe.

Harry looked sheepish. He should have seen what Darlen was getting at. "And we have no time reference to give the ship. It can't register the passage of time because there is none; to the ship, we're standing still."

"What about when we've been at widespeed in here before?" Ava countered. "The ship has always responded to commands to drop from widespeed."

Darlen agreed. "Yes. Normal widespeed, but this," he gestured to the viewport, "is unknown to us and the ship. They designed this ship to deal only with natural priole precipitation in normal space. I inherited this ship from the Soul Monger, who gave me the gig to Gartrya. My dad's ship got blown up along with him. The original Soul Monger who owned this one added the…" Darlen paused, feeling a certain loyalty to safeguarding the Soul Monger legacy. Information always led to questions. "He added Soul Monger language to its programming."

"And the ship never learned the language of enhanced widespeed?"

"It seems so, Harry. Soul Monger's had one purpose, and that was to travel the Transcender and bring back whole souls. There was never any need to explore the length of the Miran Forin nebula. At a guess, I'm the first who has."

Mer swivelled his head and seesawed a response for Ava to translate. "He said he could try to input an end time."

Harry rubbed his chin, Marcel pondered the control panels, and Darlen sat down. Mer waited patiently for a decision. For once, Scarlett recognised the weight of the situation and remained quiet in the corner instead of using a hiatus in conversation to make demands. Ava looked across at her mother.

"How could we have made such a mistake?"

"It's possible this was the only occasion an end time wasn't input. It wouldn't have occurred to me either."

"The nebula has always attracted you, hasn't it, Mom?"

Laurel smiled. *"Always, it feels like…it sounds silly, but there's something so familiar, and I see it very differently than others see it, except perhaps for you.* "She looked across at the unusually quiet Scarlett. *"She's nearly the same age as you were when we started this journey. I thought I considered every eventuality, but not the presence of another child. It changes the face of what's important. This is no life for her."*

Ava laughed, causing Harry to look up from his considerations. He guessed Laurel and her daughter were having a private telepathic conversation. *"It was my life, Mom. I've been very happy. And there will be a happy ending to all this."* She paused before adding, *"I know there will."*

CHAPTER THIRTY-NINE _

"I have doubts about entering an end time when we haven't got any time to enter," Darlen said, scratching his bald head and realising he sounded like he was rambling. Even the knowledge that the combined efforts of the others wouldn't come up with anything more intelligent didn't make him feel any more in control. He looked up at Mer. "Find a point around the time we found Eli's beacon," he said, "then give it an endpoint of, say, a day. Let's see if it causes a variation."

Mer complied. The ship registered no change.

"What about applying the end time for after we reconfigured the hull?" Harry suggested, "that way, there'll be a time sequence it recognises, and when it measures the end time, it may just see the enhanced widespeed as a glitch."

"It's worth a shot," Darlen agreed.

They set to work, but seconds later, all their deliberations came to nothing when without warning, Mer's interface exploded, flinging him upwards. The impact was such that part of the control room ceiling dislodged and joined him as he landed on the floor in an untidy metallic heap, surrounded by wires. Laurel and Harry were hurled against the bulkhead as fire blasted from one of the panels. Marcel, who'd been closest to Scarlett at the time of the explosion, shielded her body from the flames. Ava was the first to her feet. She closed her eyes, willing the ship to stabilise and with the widespeed configurations now inoperative, the ship responded to her will. The fire fail-safes activated, suppressing the fire and smoke before the ship pitched once more, then groaned to a full stop. Slowly, it drifted out towards what was previously the Ferle side of the nebula.

"All systems are out. We're dead in the water," Darlen said as he assessed the darkened control panel. Scarlett's loud complaining assured him she was not seriously injured. "Are you okay, Marcel?" he asked.

Marcel checked that Scarlett was indeed uninjured and lifted her into Laurel's arms. His shirt was scorched, and he sported a large burn over the back of his hand. Darlen glanced at it, but other, more urgent matters needed their attention. "See what you can do with Mer."

Harry had been briefly knocked into unconsciousness as he hit the bulkhead. He assured Laurel he was fine, but he had a large cut to his forehead. She placed the trembling Scarlett next to him and went in search of the pandroscope.

The control and common room were in the centre of the ship, but the galley was an addition from the early days after the ship left the construction line. It hadn't fared well. Had they been in the galley, it was unlikely any of them would have survived the blast. Twisted metal covered the galley entrance, and a protective forcefield surrounded a sizable hole in the outer hull. She ran back to the common room.

"I can't get to any medical equipment, Harry." She bent down. "You may need to rest for a while. You're probably concussed. The emergency lighting isn't enough for me to check you out fully."

"I feel alright, Laurel," Harry said, "and someone needs to look after Scarlett. Under the circumstances, it might as well be me. Go and help the others."

Darlen glanced over his shoulder as Laurel offered her help. "Mer is capable of self-repair, but he can't stand." He nodded to where Ava and Marcel dragged the robot from the cockpit. "As far as I can tell, life support is only working here in the common room. I'll seal off the rest of the ship. Try to keep the pitch stable."

"I just went out to the galley," Laurel said, puzzled. "Gravity, life support, they were both working a moment ago."

Darlen gave her a guarded sideways look. "The blast took them out, Laurel. Either way, we've no time to discuss it. Ava got the ship upright and level, but we need Mer to fully stabilise it to see if we can coax any power from her. Then we need to land, and fast."

Working together, Laurel and Darlen brought the ship's backup systems online, but without helm control and only minimal artificial gravity, the task proved difficult. They watched as the last smoky clouds of the nebula heart drifted by, and they entered the colourful strands of the nebula's inner margin.

"That was one helluva shove to have sent us this far," Darlen said as Marcel pronounced Mer unsteady but able to stand. He helped Marcel and Ava to hoist Mer to his feet. "We're lucky to be in one piece."

"It must have been the widespeed enhancement," Laurel said. "The ship couldn't take it."

Darlen agreed. "It's the only explanation. Even so, Mer should have seen a disintegration, however slight."

Harry struggled to his feet, holding the heel of his hand over his head wound to stop the blood from running into his eye. Scarlett ran to her father, and he hoisted her into his arms to watch the scene unfolding outside.

"I don't understand," Darlen said. "It can take days to get from the heart to the outer layers, but there seems to be hardly any distance at all before normal space." Beyond the nebula boundary, they saw purple and red clouds, ringed planets, small moons and other less vibrant nebulas. As it was everywhere else, the canvas for this amazing scene was speckled with tiny points of light.

"I've never seen anything like this," Harry said softly as Laurel tried to take a closer look at his injury; for her, the view could wait until she was sure he was alright. "And I thought Mentelci was magnificent!"

"Helen said she thought she'd fallen into a painting when she first saw Mentelci," Laurel said, giving up on Harry as he pulled a "don't fuss" face at her.

Darlen smiled. "That sounds like Helen; she was keen on every place I took her, even the seedy ones."

Ava found a working datacache. "That one," she said, positioning a point of light above them, then looking towards the viewport. "They were there."

No-one needed to ask who "they" were, trusting Ava's

sense of the path of the ancient whole souls.

Darlen peered over her shoulder. "The sensors say it's desolate, a wasteland, though there are signs of past occupation. But of course, the explosion may have damaged the sensors."

"Perhaps the masters wiped it out?" Marcel said.

Ava shook her head. "No, it's okay. We can land there." She looked at Harry. "This time, I'm in no doubt. Mom?"

Laurel nodded.

They secured Mer to the console while Marcel worked on his damaged leg. The robot set up an unsteady interface with the ship. The planet would have been less than a day's journey from the nebula at widespeed, but unless Mer succeeded in coaxing a spark of power from the failing system, it was anyone's guess where they'd end up. Together, Darlen and Harry hot-wired the navigational instrumentation, but with the star chart offline, it was like telling the ship to go "over there" or "over here" without providing a point of reference. Darlen offered Mer his best guess at coordinates using a datacache. Mer got a series of 'coughs' out of the propulsion system, and there was a definite shift towards the "guessed at" coordinates. They took comfort from the fact Ava and Laurel seemed confident they were heading in the right direction.

Darlen slid down the bulkhead to sit on the floor next to Marcel. "I can't do any more," he said. "We just have to wait it out." He rubbed his hands over his face and puffed out a sigh. "If Mer can't make any course corrections, he calculates we could miss the planet by about a million kilometres."

"How long will it take at this speed?" Ava asked. "Assuming we are on course?"

"I don't know, Ava," Darlen groaned. "Weeks? Months? I wish burned out technology responded to you. It would make this easier."

"I'm sorry, Uncle Darlen," Ava attempted a smile. "I've tried, but I know that planet won't be hostile. If we get there, we'll be safe."

It was hard to accept Ava's assurance when they were limping in space towards an unknown world, but Laurel suddenly felt something approaching their position.

"Do you sense that, Ava? What is it?"

Ava lifted her head.

"I don't know. Something travelling towards us." Ava jumped to her feet, startling Harry as she clambered across him to access the control room. Mer hummed a sound at her.

"No, Mer, look!"

A distortion headed towards them from the direction of Darlen's projected coordinates. It wasn't a plainly visible phenomenon, but Ava was confident it had a technological origin. Laurel watched as the distortion came ever closer. She turned to the others.

"It's from the planet," she said.

Harry peered out the viewport, scouring the panorama of space. "Nothing visual. Darlen, can you see anything?"

Darlen and Marcel both shrugged. The space outside looked no different from before, but as the ship's angle corrected and Mer released from the interface, Darlen attempted a manual override of the minimal ship's systems left operational. In response, the ship lost all power.

"It's a traction beam," he yelled in alarm, "and coming from the planet. They've overridden all the remaining systems."

Harry knew of several League and Independent systems seeking to develop this technology; none of them had so far got any further than tractioning a hair or a piece of cloth. To pull a ship of this size through space, for this distance, demanded very advanced technology. He was both intrigued and concerned.

"Whoever is doing this is an advanced civilisation," he said. "Darlen, the sensors showed a barren planet. Could this be technology left by the ancient civilisation, and we've just got caught up? Unless they're deliberately pulling us in."

Laurel touched his shoulder. She didn't share his or Darlen's concerns. "Harry, it's here to help."

"Well, we have no option," Darlen said, slumping back down the bulkhead to sit on the floor, Scarlett arranging herself in his lap. "It's taking us. We have no power to pull away or resist. All we can do is wait and see."

The last few kilometres of the journey saw them ploughing through red dust as the traction beam disengaged. Darlen tried to get a reading of the exterior of the ship and the immediate surroundings.

"The ship is hot," he said, "but we shouldn't get too much radiated heat. We may have to climb over the top. The gangway won't fully extend because we're partially embedded in the dust. Mer?" Darlen jerked his head towards the gangway, which answered to Mer's interface but, as Darlen predicted, hardly extended enough to give them room to wriggle through and use the end of the gangway to climb onto the ship. The ship's surface was indeed hot, scorching hot, although the traction beam had provided some protection as it entered the planet's atmosphere. They quickly slid down into the dust. The surrounding air was thick with a dense, red haze, and it took a moment for their eyes to adjust. Harry used the datacache to determine the safety of the air.

"It's got low levels of toxicity," he said, turning to look in both directions, "and it'll clog up our lungs, but it's denser here because we've just sent the dust metres into the air. It's probably not been disturbed in centuries."

"Why would the beam put us down here?" Marcel squinted into the distance. "It's deserted."

Laurel shook her head. "It's not deserted. I can't see anyone at the moment, but it's not deserted."

Darlen lifted Scarlett onto his shoulders. "Let's get away from the ship; there's no point in breathing in concentrated dust." He indicated to Mer that he should walk ahead. "We might find shelter near those foothills to the north. I've brought some water beads; we can dig out the ship if we need to and use it as a shelter when the dust settles. I picked up the emergency medkit through the hole in the hull." He handed the case to Marcel. "Here, stick a healbot on that burn."

The red haze seemed to penetrate in all directions. "I wonder if this planet has had a pollution problem, and they've gone underground?" Harry suggested. "There's no evidence of biological life other than a few microbes here and there." He primed the datacache and looked up at Laurel. "No evidence of humans. No evidence of advanced technology."

Laurel didn't answer. They were here, somewhere, and they would come for them. She knew it, and Ava knew it.

As they walked, the air cleared sufficiently for them to get a good look at their surroundings. Behind them, a flattened plain, apart from the mound where their crippled ship lay partially buried. Ahead were foothills and what had possibly once been an inland sea, and beyond these features, in the distance, vast mountain ranges. From where they stood, a mantle of red dust lay over the scene as far as the horizon.

"Something cataclysmic," Darlen muttered as he looked in each direction. He pointed out several distant structures rising through the dust. "That looks like a city."

Harry tried to get a lock with the datacache; all it showed were ruins.

"Why would someone rescue us and leave us here?" Marcel picked up a handful of dust and let it run through his fingers.

"This is where we were heading, remember?" Harry said. Marcel made some non-committal twitches of his shoulders.

"We were heading here because Mom and I knew it was okay," Ava spoke for the first time since leaving the ship. "Right now? I think we have an invitation."

"An invitation?" Harry's eyebrows shot up.

"Ava's right, Harry," Laurel said. "We should just stay here and wait."

"Okay," Harry agreed. "There doesn't appear to be extreme fluctuations in weather; we should be fine for now." He squinted against the dust as he visually scanned the area. "I'm not sure what this planet has to offer long-term. I hope your friends turn up soon." He looked down at the datacache. "Something's approaching our position."

From the north, a folding movement that cut through the dusty haze didn't cause the dust to become disturbed, and from the south, that same folding movement. As each fold neared, the group saw they flowed like black ink. One fluidic wave eclipsed the other, then merged, flowing together before setting into a single line as it met its opposite self. For a moment, it hovered before them, then parted to reveal itself as a doorway, opening out a scene of magnificent beauty. A stooped, elderly man peered around the frame of the stunning picture. He beckoned urgently, his pale face, almond eyes and odd robes an unexpected addition to the backdrop.

"Come," the man said in Seera. *"Come now."*

Ava and Laurel instantly moved forward at the man's invitation. The others followed, but Harry took Laurel's hand protectively in his.

Darlen inclined his head in greeting. "You are communicating in Seera?" He mentally noted that the man's mouth didn't move.

The man returned Darlen's greeting the same way, a long ponytail tied atop his head swinging around his face. He laughed, as people laugh in any universe.

"I'm not speaking anything, but to you, it seems as if I am. If I use verbal communication, you will not understand what I say." He

held out his hand to Laurel. *"This is what you do on your home planet, I believe?"*

Laurel took his hand. His handshake was firm and honest.

"Well, yes, it is a conventional greeting."

The man held out his arms and bowed slightly. *"Welcome to Isilia, our world. The name of the province upon which you stand is Meas, of which I, Onoth—,"* he placed a hand on his chest, *"am proudly governor."* He beamed as if he'd delivered an important address and expected applause. *"Our sovereign detected your emergence from the nebula; she saw your plight was urgent and directed us to deliver you to the closest point in order your discomfort would not be prolonged. She has asked that I take you to her."* His smile was warm and open. *"Our Empress would willingly have come herself, but it would have taken more time, and well,"* he opened his arms again. *"I am already the governor here."*

"Our ship is damaged," Darlen said.

The man blinked slowly. *"We will remove your ship from the outside and effect repairs…"* then he paused. *"Do not concern yourself. We will not disturb the remains of your beloved."*

Laurel had almost forgotten that Helen's ashes were still on board the ship. This man had sensed Darlen's concern they may be disturbed. The man was telepathic, yet Laurel was unable to see anything in his mind. Her empathic senses told her he was without hostile intent, without guile.

A large, bell-like compartment descended from above, and the man signalled them to stand close together.

"The Sovereignty is at the furthermost point of Isilia," the man explained as the bell dropped low and covered them. The clarity of the view as they rose into the air was staggering.

They all looked down but could not fathom how a clear floor had appeared and how the bell moved with no visible signs of controls. *"Our planet is most splendid. Enjoy the scenery; we will stop for hospitality on the way."* The man smiled and bent down to Scarlett, who was at the limits of being overwhelmed. She let out a yell and hid behind Mer, whose eyes glowed red as his arm shot out to defend his little friend. The man was unperturbed. He pulled a toy from his robe, an old-fashioned pipe with a head on one end and a string that passed through the hollow centre; he showed Scarlett that pulling the string caused the head to fall off with a popping and whistling sound, a toy designed to amuse a small child for hours. Scarlett's eyes grew wide, and without a word, she took the toy and held it close.

CHAPTER FORTY _

The bell sprouted narrow, flexible stalks from the rim of the mysteriously appearing base, and Onoth showed them how to perch if they felt fatigued from standing. The stalks opened out and enveloped their rear ends, extending upwards to support their lower backs. The devices were responsive, supremely comfortable and made a fascinating diversion for a three-year-old.

It occurred to Laurel that the view of the glowing, haze-filled landscape they faced before Onoth arrived was the same view they saw as they stepped through the portal. It was, she supposed, as it would have looked before whatever it was that befell the planet. A sparkling inland sea, green foothills, majestic mountains, and blue sky. Other than feeling safe with Onoth, she could not gauge what event had transpired to leave the planet in such desolation. She wondered if Ava had more information and glanced across, but Ava simply gave a slight shake of her head. *"You must have noticed he doesn't have a lucency below his collarbone, and he's not a whole soul."* The man caught the thought. *"I'm not familiar with those terms. I can see from your memory they depict elements of your society. To us, we make no such discernment, although certain of us, such as I, the governor of this fair province, are telepathic."*

"You appear as human," Marcel said.

"Indeed, we live much as you do. For us telepaths, speech has its uses, but our spoken word is bland compared to yours, which has music and tone very pleasing to the ear. When we rest, you will meet the subjects who communicate in your manner." He made a palm-up gesture to Marcel. *"Young man, the cadence of your speech is unlike that of your friends."*

"I speak as my father spoke," Marcel said with pride.

Onoth clasped his hands together. *"It is as pleasant on the ear as you are on the eye."* Marcel pulled a face at Harry and widened his eyes, taken aback at such a compliment.

"And I hear in all of you, these accents," Onoth continued. *"And I also sense the questions about this land. The sovereign will answer them. She has a grand story to tell, one to help you on your quest."*

Darlen appeared to concentrate hard on the passing scene, the mountains, the lakes, the rivers that stretched into the distance, trees of gold and maroon that reached high and skimmed the floor of the bell.

"This is a picot?" he said suddenly.

The man smiled in delight. *"My friend. Yes. How marvellous that you recognise this most benevolent phenomenon. It saved this world, and its people are indebted to the Hebre—"* He bowed to Ava and Laurel *"—for their deliverance."*

The word *deliverance* sent a shock wave through Laurel, earning herself a questioning look from Ava.

"What's a picot?" Harry asked.

"It's a kind of antechamber to a Transcender," Darlen said. "Staying inside a picot for eternity is possible. I've never seen one this size." He frowned. "Onoth, how much of the planet's surface is within the picot?"

"More than two-thirds, friend," Onoth communicated, *"and each province as beautiful as the next. Naturally, I believe my own province of Meas,"* he bowed and again placed a hand on his chest, *"of which I am its most humble governor, is the most remarkable."*

Harry leaned forward. "Darlen, does this mean there's a Transcender nearby?"

Darlen nodded. "For a picot this size, I would have to assume there's a Transcender. I only know of one other, and it opens directly into the Transcender that leads from League space."

Harry was puzzled. "I didn't realise there was more than one Transcender."

Darlen didn't respond, just returned to his private thoughts because he didn't realise there were others like this either. Transcenderal picots littered the galaxy, minor hiccups in time, no-one other than a Soul Monger, or perhaps a whole soul would ever notice them. For one to encompass, even partially, a planet of this size, there must be a Transcender nearby. Although Darlen felt an affinity with the picot, his body did not indicate to him the presence of anything more significant.

The bell set down in the centre of a town, leaving them standing as it withdrew upward. People passed them by, humans, but not of the same race as Onoth, and dressed in plain, functional clothing. The people barely gave them a second glance, although one or two recognised Onoth and nodded politely. Laurel looked up for the bell, but it had disappeared. Harry also looked up; he caught her eye and grinned. "I'd like to know where the floor went," he said, inviting her to take his hand. Onoth ushered them along a laneway that led to the outskirts of the town. There, they viewed the surrounding countryside. Wide pathways wove up and across the foothill overlooking the town where terraced dwellings, constructed with narrow planks, lined the paths. People, Laurel couldn't tell if they were male or female, made their way along the paths that led to the town, others heading up the hill. At the topmost course, a single, grander dwelling sat in splendour above all the others. All around, animals of many unknown varieties roamed free in harmony with the people and without fear.

"It is magnificent, is it not?" Onoth closed his eyes and drew in a deep breath as if inhaling the view. It was a delightful, rustic scene; the sky was blue, the sun warm against their skin. Before them, a large meadow opened up, inviting Scarlett to run and play. She pulled at Marcel's hand with a child's instinct to run, a pleasure sorely limited in her young life.

"Let her run!" Onoth cried with delight at her eagerness. *"It is a child's right."*

Marcel glanced at Darlen for permission. All seemed well here, but Darlen was her father, and Marcel respected his decision.

"Stay with her, Marcel," he said. He also felt it would be safe, but he hadn't yet got his head around the idea of a picot that covered almost an entire planet; dangers the inhabitants didn't see could be lurking. Marcel nodded and ran after Scarlett. Ava glanced at Laurel and took off after them. Laurel smiled. Ava was almost an adult, but all her life, she'd had little opportunity to run and play, same as Scarlett.

Two men approached and spoke to Onoth. They glanced at the others but made no acknowledgement. Onoth communicated with them verbally, but Mer, who'd held back the entire time, practically making himself invisible, munched a couple of sounds.

"I think he made sense of what they said," Harry suggested.

Darlen looked up at Mer. "Did you?"

Mer munched a few more sounds and flashed his eyes. Onoth laughed.

"Your mechanical man has analysed the syntax of the Chaese. It is a simple language. They will provide refreshment, and I will tell you of their society."

The two men laid a blanket on the ground, stepping back until Onoth had seated himself while the others followed his lead.

"There's a good bit of toadying to the governor," Harry whispered to Laurel. "It's obviously not a classless society, even though going by the way they dress, I would have thought it was."

Laurel nudged him. "Onoth is a telepath, Harry. Mind what you say."

But Onoth seemed to bask in the 'toadying', at the same time allowing his evident pride in the townspeople and the neat accommodations to reach into each of his companions' minds.

"Is this part of your province, Onoth?" Laurel asked

as the two men tore up flat cakes to place in a pile in the middle of the blanket.

"This is the furthermost containment. I seldom come here." Onoth looked up at his server with a smile. *"They are wonderful people. But, as Hebre, I'm sure you sense this as well."*

Laurel was dying to ask about the reference to Hebre but felt the governor might not be the one to answer such questions.

"I do sense this, Governor Onoth." Laurel looked out toward the hillside and to where Marcel, Ava and Scarlett ran and played in the grass. Laurel dipped her head in respect. "Your province is a credit to you, Governor. You have every right to be proud."

Onoth swelled with pride, unable to speak. Laurel sensed he had been waiting for this recognition. Since childhood, Onoth heard the stories of the Hebre, that one day they would return. To endorse a simple governor was a unique gift. The two men, standing to the side, looked from one to the other. Despite Onoth making verbal contact with them, it would seem he also allowed stray telepathy to reach them. One man, slightly built, olive-skinned and grey-haired, stepped forward, hesitating as he came to stand beside Laurel, then he dropped on one knee and bowed his head. Onoth applauded, content to share the limelight now that he had received an accolade from the deliverer. Laurel wasn't comfortable with anyone bowing to her and encouraged the man to stand. Darlen covered his grin with a hand, but Harry did not hide his glee at her discomfiture.

"This is exactly how I feel around you, Laurel," he teased.

"No, you do not!" Then, she turned to the man. "There's no need, please get up."

The man looked to Onoth for a translation, and a moment later, the man stood.

"On behalf of all his people and his ancestors, he thanks you," Onoth said with a beaming smile, as he waved the man away. *"All this,"* his gesture took in the immediate surroundings, but Laurel knew it was meant for the entire planet, *"was made possible by those who visited us in ancient times."*

These little snippets were so tantalising. Puzzles about the existence of the picot cluttered Darlen's mind. Harry was in sync with Laurel and, like her, curious about the society that sprung from the "deliverance". Onoth promised to tell them about the culture, and when Marcel and Ava returned, with an out-of-breath, pink-cheeked Scarlett, he did just that.

"The house at the top, that is the pitch-house. It is the house of the Guardian. Whoever takes the role must remain there for their natural life. The Guardian, be it male or female, must produce children and conduct the affairs of the containment. This town is a depository where each member of the containment shares what they have made or grown with the community." He smiled at Laurel, *"You call it 'village', after the language of your fathers."* He gave a small sigh, *"Your language has such music. Also, the Guardian is schooled in the practice of medicine, has mastery in the knowledge of the ecosystem, pollutants, climatic and weather conditions, botany, biomechanics…"*

Harry shook his head. "One person is expected to know all this?"

Onoth laughed. *"Perhaps I am too impatient to tell our story. Do you see the level below the pitch-house? The row of six dwellings?"*

411

Harry nodded.

"That is the lower house. There dwell those who aspire to become the Guardian. Their responsibilities are the same, but they have not yet attained that status. Some never do, but their contribution is no less exalted."

"And you have to have all these attributes, Governor Onoth?" Laurel asked.

Onoth touched his chest. *"I am merely a governor with few of these skills. It behoves our beloved sovereign that all children are schooled in the care of the environment. No, the real work takes place here,"* Onoth said, for a moment happily sidestepping his importance to promote the Empress's and the Guardian's contribution.

Laurel looked at the man who bowed to her, now serving them an enormous lunch of leafy vegetables and floral concoctions and directing small hovering kettles to deliver fragrant fluid into delicate cups.

"You are the Guardian?" she said, once again sensing the man's humility. The man tried to take her meaning, then Onoth stepped in and translated her words.

"You are correct," Onoth said as the man smiled and stepped back.

"And you just spoke to us," Marcel pointed out, "out loud. Not in our heads."

"Correct again," Onoth grinned. "I said I had few of the skills required to be a Guardian. But telepathy is a skill required of a governor. In speaking into your minds, you formulate responses to my words which are not verbalised, but you still try to hear me with your ears." Onoth laughed. He did that often. "I believe I have made sense of your

412

tongue."

Harry preferred aloud, and he was glad that Onoth's voice was the same voice he'd heard in his head. For years, Harry's brain had been a depository for telepathic meanderings, but he'd never got used to it, and both Laurel and Ava stayed out as much as they could.

Ava looked around. "You don't have many children. I haven't seen any close to Scarlett's age."

"During the time of the Fall," Onoth said, his thin, sad smile embracing both Laurel and Ava, "many of the races living on Isilia lost the ability to procreate. A single species survived this calamity: the Chaese. In ancient times, the Hebre left my people, our sovereign race, the Riynea, here. The Chaese's foolishness, their greed—" he clenched his fists, not in anger but at the injustice and as if he remembered this Fall and took it personally, "took from many of their descendants, the ability to procreate."

"Yet they survived." Marcel took in the mixture of small-statured, olive-skinned men and women, all seemingly happy; there were one or two babies in arms.

"Each guardian must go into a woman at least eight times in a month. Each woman must take every opportunity to mate. It is their duty."

"Any woman? Any man?" Harry was already calculating the hygiene risks even though they all seemed to have things under control.

"Yes, whoever they choose," Onoth said in a matter-of-fact tone, "they do not have a pairing system. Citizens may choose to spend their time with a favourite but must mingle their seed to provide the most opportunities for conception."

Darlen fought down an instinct to cover Scarlett's ears. He might be a bit rough around the edges himself, but a conversation about sex? His little girl didn't need to overhear it. He thought what Helen would say and promptly distracted Scarlett's attention.

Marcel's face was a mask, but his thoughts weren't, and Laurel knew the prospect of spending time here was endearing itself to him. Already, his athletic body and good looks had attracted the attention of many of the womenfolk and, Laurel noticed, many of the men. Onoth's fond looks at the Guardian suggested this society, at least this race of humans, the Chaese, had no inhibitions regarding sexuality.

"How often are children born?" Harry asked.

"In this containment, twenty children were born in the last lunar cycle, double the births in past cycles. This provides a good gene pool for the future. The females bear children as their childhood ends, and some have gone on to bear multiple offspring in other cycles. In other containments, we have had thirty or more in a single cycle. It is exhilarating, there have been many times the Chaese's numbers have dwindled, and we have feared for them, but their growth is consistent now, not rapid, but consistent." Onoth beamed, wide-eyed. "For centuries, we feared the Hebre's help had been in vain. When they arrived, they could not reverse the effect on the Chaese's bodies nor repair the legacy handed down to future generations. They could only heal the environment to give them the best opportunity to recover."

Again, Laurel felt that itch for Onoth to elaborate on

all this, but she got the impression he somehow thought she knew the history. Odd that he saw the word "village" in her mind and her references to Earth handshakes but didn't see her ignorance of the Hebre.

CHAPTER FORTY-ONE _

Their leafy luncheon ended, and well-rested, they thanked their hosts before returning to the town centre. The bell descended and once again buoyed them up, the floor solidifying beneath their feet. The stalk seats emerged and poked their behinds, rearranging themselves until the bottoms and backs they served rested in an optimum position.

"We are heading now to the sovereignty," Onoth told them. "We are above another province, see?" In response, the bell took them low into canyons, soared over mountaintops, and skimmed the glorious maroon and gold canopies of the forests before plunging them deep into the dark wooded groves, their passage stirring up the leaves as they passed through.

"What powers this transport?" Harry asked.

"Our engineers are most capable. We use a power source that promotes and recycles its energy. If it interests you, our sovereign will arrange for you to view how it is induced. Alas, I can't explain it. I am but a humble governor," he smiled.

Harry looked at Darlen. "Some kind of widespeed

precipitation?"

Darlen lifted a shoulder. "I have no idea. A Transcenderal picot this size would generate vast amounts of energy; maybe they found a way to tap into it. What I don't understand is..." he trailed off and looked up at the sky. They waited, even Onoth, "There's the sky above." He looked down, "and there's Earth below."

"We can see that," Harry said, waiting for further explanation as to why that would invite comment.

But Darlen didn't continue with that train of thought. "Onoth," he said. "Do you measure time the same way you did centuries ago?"

Onoth shook his head. "My friend, many things changed when this society failed. The Chaese measured time by when one would again eat, drink, or find another for company or find shelter. Their industry lay idle, and they abandoned their consciences in a bid to survive. When Hebre delivered them..." he looked out at the brilliant sunshine, at the mountains, at the beauty of this place, "and restored Isilia, they counselled the ancestors that time was an illusion. There is no time. There is only now for us to protect."

"You seek to establish a future. You wish to secure posterity," Marcel said. "Do you mean you must live only for the moment?"

Onoth gave Marcel's question thought. "Always the Chaese believed that tomorrow, they would attend to the planet's ills, and when tomorrow came, again they repeated that pledge. One day, on one tomorrow, it was too late. The Chaese now live for today, so their children can live tomorrow."

Marcel was good at cryptic replies, and Onoth's words reminded him of his father, who knew tomorrow would never come if he didn't allow the saving of today to be his priority. He knew his father's actions saved him and the Gartryans, but it had never penetrated so profoundly before.

Onoth preferred happier discussion and ably steered them away from what was for him, maudlin thoughts of ancient times. His pride, knowledge, and delight in this planet made clear as he pointed out landmarks and topographical features of particular significance to the Chaese, the bell taking them in each time for a closer look.

A magnificent, flaming crimson twilight had begun its journey across the sky as they arrived in the sovereignty.

"I've never seen a sunset that colour," Harry exclaimed.

"Ah, yes," Onoth said. "The Chaese call it 'the foolish sunset'. The dust of the foolishness of their ancestors remains in the atmosphere and casts its shadow across their land."

"The red dust?" Darlen held up the datacache to the side of the bell. "After all these years?"

Onoth barely reacted. "Your instruments may measure the red dust, my friend," he said softly, "but it will not register foolishness and lack of foresight. The crimson sunset reminds all of us of our obligation to our planet and to ourselves."

———

"I've never met a sovereign," Ava said after a moment's

slightly awkward silence.

Onoth stood and pointed towards the horizon. "Then you have much to look forward to."

Stately spires reached towards the sky. They were still some distance away, but close enough to see the terraces of the palace formed part of a cliff face. The decorative spires and turrets appeared made of precious or other shining metal, their brilliance reflected in the beauty of the sunset as they spread glistening ripples into the failing light. As they approached, low over an ocean, lights twinkled within the palace halls, the whiteness of the terraces even in the fading light was striking, and as they drew closer, the immense size and beauty of the building took their breath away. Scarlett begged to be lifted so she wasn't looking through people's legs.

"It's a fairy castle, Auntie Laurel," she said, pointing to the unworldly structure. "Will there be princesses?"

Possibly, Laurel thought, and unicorns, and elves. The place looked magical, like a Disney creation. But, most of all, it looked like harmony.

No guards guarded the palace, no weaponed soldiers, only smiling men and women eager to escort them to their Empress. They greeted Mer with a few giggles and what sounded like uncomplimentary comments. Laurel raised an eyebrow at Onoth, who grinned apologetically.

"They mean no disrespect, but they have never seen such ancient technology."

Laurel glanced at Mer over her shoulder. His eyes glowed, and he munched a few sounds. Ava grinned at her mother. "He's insulted."

Their escorts led them through a monumental entrance, easily ten storeys in height and possibly two hundred meters across. Pillars adorned each side of the entrance, inlaid with fiercesome gold and red-scaled creatures, their mouths wide, their claws raised to strike, with some already subduing what looked like an alien enemy. The depictions reminded Laurel of Earth's mythical creatures, dragons, or gryphons, and to her eye, there were striking similarities.

The entrance led directly into a dramatic colonnade. Great columns rose on either side, creating rows of connected arches stretching into the distance. Between each arch, domed ceilings painted with lavish floral or pastoral scenes drew several comments of "wow" and "amazing" from the group. Above each column they passed, the entablature hosted a frieze depicting what appeared to be a significant event. Laurel felt it would be impolite to stop and examine the friezes or even ask Onoth what the subject was, not when the Empress awaited them. Despite it initially appearing to offer them a rather extended journey, the walk through the colonnade took very little time and opened out into a circular portico. Grand, high windows overlooked a beautiful valley behind the clifftop, and on the opposite side, sweeping views of the ocean, both scenes brushed with the crimson of the twilight, which lent a pinkish hue to the white marble walls. A pair of large-winged, long-tailed bird-like creatures, similar in size to a peacock, their feathers a striking mixture of white and red, strutted through the portico, uttering soft sing-song sounds in time with their flowing movements. A curved, raised dais took up a third of the area and here, the Empress awaited their arrival.

Kneeling rigidly upright on a cushion, the petite young woman's hands were positioned flat on her knees, her sumptuous white and blue embroidered gown and over jacket carefully arranged about her person; not a single layer nor hem out of place. The Empress was of the same species as Onoth. Her almond-shaped eyes were the softest brown, set deeply into creamy pale skin, her mouth was small and bow-shaped, and her nose straight and perfect. Her long black hair was lifted from her face, elaborately ornamented in gold. Jewels spread out from the elegant knot on top of her head to fall over her forehead. From her ears hung long tasselled earrings. The Empress was stately. Exquisite.

To the Empress's side stood a man, perhaps a year or two older, as formally dressed and as noble and commanding as the Empress. He wore a brown, wide-sleeved silken coat that tied across his body almost to the neck. The garment swept the floor in several layers, each layer alternating blue and gold. The man's hair was long and straight, the centre pulled back into a ponytail, and from above each ear, a single strand of hair fell over his shoulders, reaching to his waist. He bore a striking resemblance to the Empress, and Laurel guessed this might be her brother.

Onoth arranged his charges in a line. They did as he bid, even as they tore their gaze away from the eye-popping scene before them. Laurel became acutely aware of how they must look and probably, smell. They hadn't had access to water for washing since the explosion on the ship, nor changed their clothes, and she'd noticed that Darlen wasn't so nice to be near when they were in the bell transport. It wasn't a bother when they were outside, but now, in here and in the presence of royalty…

Satisfied he'd sorted out the group, Onoth bowed to the doll-like Empress, so still, she didn't even appear to be breathing. Laurel and the others stood quietly, awaiting whatever was to come. Laurel felt no fear, and she felt none from the others, just different layers of curiosity, plus a little extra from Marcel, who was struck by the Empress's beauty.

Suddenly, the Empress's arms snapped up into a circle, one slender hand covering the other, and she bowed so low, Laurel feared the weight of the hair ornaments might stop her from getting up again. Her neck was very slender, and she had only tiny shoulders, but she raised herself easily. Onoth caught Laurel's thought that perhaps now, they should bow? He raised his hand to signify "no".

The man at the Empress's side stepped forward and, in a single, fluid movement, tucked his garment under his knees and knelt beside the Empress. Together, they raised their arms to circles and bowed deeply towards the group. This time, they did not rise.

Onoth indicated to Laurel and the others that now, they could seat themselves on the cushions. Harry went to make a circle with his arms, but Onoth stopped him. This is unnecessary, he told them telepathically.

"The Empress honours her visitors. She is here to see them. She serves them. Not the other way around. You do not bow to the Empress."

Onoth made the circular armed bow and remained with his body bent to the ground. Harry would have liked some instruction on what to do next, but the Empress and her brother raised their bodies back to their kneeling positions. After a moment, the man stood, followed by the Empress, who pulled the adornments from her hair, leaving it to fall like silk about her shoulders. She made straight for Laurel, her silken robes making swishing sounds as she moved.

"I'm so glad that's out of the way," the Empress said in perfect Seera. She looked down at Onoth, still with his arms in a circle and still low to the ground. "You can get up now, Onoth. The formalities are over."

Onoth uncurled himself and smiled at the Empress. "Thank you, Empress. I trust my ancient bones have not disturbed you in their creaking?"

The Empress laughed and took Laurel and Harry's hands in her own. "Onoth is a special friend, and we see too little of him."

Laurel tried not to stare. If she thought the Empress an exquisite creature as she knelt like a living statue on the platform, then the sound of her voice, her gentleness of spirit and her laughter doubled that appraisal, even though it rendered Laurel speechless.

The Empress moved quickly to Ava and Marcel, taking their hands in her own in welcome, then reached out to Darlen, who happily let her take his hand. Scarlett, however, was having none of it. With a wail, she reached her arms up for her father to rescue her.

"She's not used to strangers," he said, talking over Scarlett's screeching.

The Empress's beautiful eyes darted from left to right as she considered the words. "Ah! I am a stranger. Little one, what would make you happy?" The Empress wisely kept her distance while Scarlett decided; she'd heard that question from the grown-ups in her life lots of times, and usually, it just involved stories or playtime. This time, she chose something that Laurel had spoken about often, "Kittens, I want kittens."

"Then, you shall have kittens." The young Empress made a tiny cupping movement with her hand, and on the ground beside her, several tiny balls of fluff frolicked and played. Scarlett struggled in Darlen's arms to be set free and plopped herself down beside the little cats, lifting them gently into her lap.

"Do kittens look like that?" Harry whispered. "I've heard you describe them, and that's not how I pictured them."

"Almost, not quite," Laurel whispered back. "How did she do it?"

The Empress beamed. "I can create illusions," she said, with a noble tilt of her chin. "The beasts are not here, of course, but the child will enjoy all the sensations of touching and playing with them as if they were." She stretched out her arm, and the man on the dais stepped forward to stand with her.

"I am Ilivi," she said, "Empress of Isilia, and this is my brother, Baii."

Baii inclined his head. His smile showed perfect teeth, not to mention the endearing dimples on either side of his mouth. "I do not know how a sovereign greets her guests on your worlds," he said, his voice rich, smooth and melodic, with just a hint of bemusement. "The Empress has barely contained her excitement since we learned of your arrival. However, our culture demands a formal welcome in honour of Hebre."

Hebre? Laurel glanced at Ava. Onoth had used that word repeatedly today but didn't tell them what it meant. Ava flicked up her eyebrows. *"I don't know either, Mom."*

"I've never heard of one conjuring up kittens to amuse a child, but Scarlett appears very happy with your customs," Laurel said, sensing the others had silently elected her as the spokesperson. "You speak our language? Do we call you Majesty? Or Empress?"

"We had time to study this language," Ilivi explained. "A Hebre mortal dwelt in our midst some years ago when I was but a child. And to you, I am Ilivi. You do not bow before me nor refer to me as your regent."

Many of the questions Laurel wanted to ask could possibly be answered here, and she would have loved to know about the person who spoke Seera, but Ilivi engaged Onoth in a discourse about their arrival and had they enjoyed the Chaese's excellent hospitality? Ilivi spoke with undisguised excitement, barely pausing for breath. Her face reflected every emotion, every nuance of humour. This tiny woman was enchantingly open, genuine, and easy to like.

Ilivi took Marcel's arm and made to steer him towards one of the terraces with a smiling, unspoken request for the others to follow, but she stopped suddenly and turned, ceasing her bright chatter. It was then Laurel saw the telepathic link between brother and sister; he'd spoken to her, and reminded her of a duty. The Empress's mouth fell open in an undignified, "Oh!" She let go of Marcel's arm and called over the party of men and women who had escorted them here.

"As my brother rightly points out," she said, "I am a little excitable and quite overcome by the honour of your presence. A single visit from an honoured Hebre in a lifetime is a miracle, a second is a…is a," she lifted a pretty shoulder and laughed, "a double miracle! Of course, you must refresh yourselves after your long journey."

As the Empress's servants led them away, Laurel felt Baii's gentle eyes upon her and Ava. Like his sister, this young man was exquisite, not just in his looks but in pureness of heart. Harry caught her staring back and made a face.

"Come on, Harry, he's gorgeous!" she sent across to tease him. Harry fixed a thought in his mind, knowing she'd pick it up. *"You're twice his age!"*

Laurel smirked. *"Not if you don't factor in those nine years we were in stasis."*

Harry grinned and took her hand, but still, Laurel felt Baii's appraising eyes on them as they left.

When they were out of sight, Ilivi turned to her brother and covered her mouth in excitement. "Brother, they honour us. Did you see the young man's eyes? As soft as the Idi lily blooming in spring." She shook her head as if disbelieving of Marcel's striking looks.

Baii smiled. He'd sensed his sister's attraction to the young man immediately.

Ilivi went to the window to watch the rising moons shining on the ocean, allowing her thoughts to dwell for a fleeting moment on the handsome man the Hebre brought with them. She glanced back, silently willing her brother to join her. "The woman," she said, her voice steadier, "has eyes the colour of the moons."

Baii stood at her side. Seldom did his sister speak aloud, always their communication was telepathic, but the appearance of the ship from the nebula had greatly moved her, and she was young and excited. He placed his arm over her shoulder.

"Little sister, the two women are Hebre clothed in mortal flesh. Our forefathers recorded the deliverers had such eyes."

"We see these colours within the nebula, but could not these men be true Hebre also?"

"Ilivi," Baii turned her gently to face him. "We are speaking of the saviours of this world. Perhaps they have the power to change the colour of their eyes at will."

Ilivi knew he only said it to tease her. "And I suppose their arrival here in a disabled ship was simply their 'will'?" Ilivi shook her head. "They asked about the manifestation; they have forgotten who they truly are; this too is recorded by our fathers."

Baii laughed. "If a Hebre is clothed in flesh to make them mortal, does this make them human? The men and the child have echoes of Hebre, but it is the women with the power."

"Strange," Ilivi said. "In the older man, the father of the child, I sense something else."

Baii nodded. "An echo—" He paused, "—and a shadow, but his heart is pure, and we will have time to learn from them and for them to learn from us."

Ilivi's enthusiasm bubbled again. *"Will they approve of our planet, brother?"* she sent to him as they watched the moonlight on the water.

"We have protected their legacy," her brother assured her, *"And honoured their work. We have done all that they asked. They will be proud, my Empress."*

CHAPTER FORTY-TWO _

At the far end of the colonnade, the attendants separated the group to show them their accommodations. Scarlett went with Darlen; it would have been impossible to have pried her from around his neck at her grief at being separated from the kittens, despite the Empress's assurances she would bring them back when Scarlett returned. The attendant showed Harry and Laurel to a terraced apartment overlooking the valley side of the palace, where a deep, fragrant hot pool had been prepared. The attendant opened her hands to receive their clothing.

"Uh, we'll manage," Harry said, making a clutching motion over his jacket, leaving the woman in no doubt they would prefer privacy to bathe. As soon as they were alone, they tore off their clothes and sank into the pool. Harry went right under and stayed there; only the copious gurgle of bubbles rising to the surface reassured Laurel he still had some breath left in his lungs. He jumped from the water with a splash, laughing and gasping all at once.

"Oh, wow! This is unbelievable!"

Laurel grinned and closed her eyes, allowing the warmth and fragrance to seep into her skin. She hadn't washed in several days, and she wondered if that was why Baii sent them off before getting into any serious discussions.

"How did they know we were together," Harry said, swishing his feet out of the water. "The way Baii looked at you, I thought he was hoping you weren't spoken for."

"They're telepaths, same as Onoth," Laurel said, "and his gaze spent more time on Ava than it did on me."

"I guessed so." He sat up. "I've been around telepaths long enough to know that look."

"What look? We don't have a 'look'."

Harry grinned, and Laurel shook her head. "Onoth, Ilivi and Baii aren't ordinary humans. The Chaese are, I'm sure."

"And you know this from one meeting?"

"You've travelled all over League space, Harry, and beyond. Have you ever seen a species as pale as Onoth or Ilivi and Baii, or the attendants for that matter?"

"Never, but I haven't met humans with skin the colour of the Chaese. Either they're white like us, or they have black skin like Eli and some in between."

Laurel swished through the bath to sit beside him. "On Earth, there are lots of variances in the colour of skin and their physical features. Ilivi and Baii's facial features are what we would describe on Earth as Oriental; their clothing is reminiscent of ancient China."

"How did they get from here to there?"

Laurel blew out her breath. "I don't know. I'm even more confused now."

"Well, we're here because our ship broke and now,

we're surrounded by splendour, relaxing in a bath which you tell me you love and which I've never experienced." He snuggled her into his arms. "And we're overlooking a beautiful valley bathed in moonlight."

"The last time I had a bath, the Ferle auctioned me off," she murmured, dropping her mouth into the water and gurgling a few words he didn't catch.

"Ava is happy; you are happy, and therefore, so am I."

Laurel dropped her head against Harry's chest and joined him in quietly drinking in the view. She felt nothing here to alarm her. If she had to describe her feelings, she would say she felt peaceful.

Laurel would have gloried longer in the bath if she had been allowed, but the attendant returned. Although the same species as Onoth, she was not a telepath and Laurel and Harry could not make sense of anything she said. Laurel felt she might have been able to get into the woman's mind, but after a second's hesitation, decided against it. Besides, a set of towels placed on the side of the bath was indication enough it was time to dry themselves and get dressed. Laurel's empathic sense told her they were to return to the presence of the Empress.

"I hope they left our clothes," Harry said, refusing to get out of the bath until the woman went back into the apartment. When she'd gone, he jumped from the water and hurriedly wrapped the wide cloth around his middle to protect his modesty. Laurel giggled.

"What?" Harry said.

"Harry, we live on a ship where very little is hidden.

Do you honestly think this woman is going to care about what you carry on the top of your legs?"

Harry grimaced. "She's a stranger," he said, a mischievous grin spreading over his face. "Once she sees it, she may want some…" and opening the towel, he danced a side-to-side jig, unaware the woman had re-entered the apartment. She glanced at Harry and then continued with her duties. Laurel rolled her eyes and bit back a grin while Harry recovered his pride with the towel.

"Men," Laurel muttered to herself, "different universe, same antics."

Their clothing had not been returned; instead, the attendant provided loose robes. Laurel tried to dissuade the woman from attending to her hair, only to find herself on the receiving end of a barrage of firm language. She didn't understand but got the gist; the hair brushing was not negotiable. Laurel had taken to tying her hair back to keep the tumble of curls off her face and for practicality on the ship; functionality was far more important than looks, but she'd been reluctant to cut it. The woman skilfully tamed the curls, a surprise to Laurel as she had yet to see an individual without straight hair. The woman looked up at Harry and bade him bend lower, then with her hand, she simply roughed up his ginger locks and turned away.

"That's all I'm getting it seems," he said but thanked the woman anyway. "How do I look?" Harry pulled out the full-skirted tunic and lifted his foot, clad in soft sandals.

"Great," Laurel appraised him. "Many of the outstanding leaders on the treaty planets wear robes like that."

"You know," he said, "I was intrigued meeting the Empress, and she was so natural and likeable, but now…"

Laurel gave him her full attention. "Now, what?"

"I don't know. Look inside my head. I haven't got a meaningful thought."

"Inside your head," Laurel said, stepping close and tapping his temple, "is that part of you that shares the whole soul ancestry." She looked into his eyes and smiled. "You are as much a part of this story as Ava and Marcel. I believe we have much to learn here, but it's not the end of our journey."

"So why do I suddenly feel apprehensive?" Harry used her nearness as an opportunity to pull her into his arms.

"Up to now," Laurel said, slipping her arms around his neck, "we've only had snippets, teasers. This planet's ancient people directly interacted with whole souls—the Hebre. This is where we get confirmation. What you feel isn't apprehension, Harry. It's anticipation."

Ava, her hair elaborately braided, looked like a fashion model in an identical plain silk tunic that the others wore, waited for them at the Colonnade. It occurred to Laurel she'd never seen Ava wear anything other than Helen's old trader suits. She knew her daughter was beautiful, but the sight of her now, in the beige silk drapes, made the breath catch in her throat.

"Mom," Ava drew her attention. "I was telling Marcel and Uncle Darlen that the Empress and her brother are telepaths."

"I know," Laurel answered, "but the Empress's ability

to manipulate matter suggests they're more advanced than us."

"Ava can move a ship out of the way of a marauding life form, Laurel," Darlen said. "I'd say you're just about equal. Besides, they see you as something greater than them. It's not about tricks."

Darlen had a point. She was comparing apples with apples.

"Where's Mer?" Harry looked around for the robot.

"He followed us," Darlen said, "then two of the attendants led him in that direction." He pointed towards a gateway. "Mer went them without comment. I figured it was okay."

Scarlett was eager to get back to the kittens. She looked scrubbed and pink, her dark hair lifted and tied on top of her head. Someone—probably an attendant—had placed a garland of flowers around her neck, which she proudly showed to everyone.

Baii was waiting for them. He touched each of their hands as the Empress had earlier. "You look refreshed," he said. "We have prepared a ceremony on the terrace." Baii gestured towards the imposing arch that led to the ocean side of the grand portico. "My Empress wishes to honour you as you honour us." He followed them as they stepped into the freshness of the night. The ocean reflected not one but three moons. Laurel looked over the balustrade. Far below, even at night, she could see the crystal clearness of the water. She looked above and recognised where she and Harry had taken a bath on the terrace earlier. That struck her as odd; the view from the terrace was of a valley. She looked up again and sure enough, the same terrace overlooked the ocean.

"May I ask a question?" Laurel asked as she selected a large cushion on the ground, expecting to simply sit down and certainly not anticipating the cushion would rise to support her as she lowered herself. Like a flying carpet, it settled her where she needed to be. Baii enjoyed her surprise. "You may ask as many questions as you wish, Laurel."

"None of us gave you a name," Marcel said, placing his hand underneath the cushion to search for technology or wires. "Did you read our minds?"

"Nothing so invasive, I assure you," Baii smiled again. "Onoth sent a message. Laurel, with eyes as brilliant as the moons, Ava, whose eyes would cause the purple sunbells to hang their heads if she were to kneel on the ground before them, and," he looked at Harry, Darlen and Marcel, "three males and a small female child. He informed us of your names."

"Barely a mention," Harry nudged Laurel.

"It wasn't necessary to ask, but Laurel," Baii treated her to his dazzling smile, "you have a different question. Ah!" Baii became distracted as Ilivi entered with an entourage of servants. Small flying teapots entered in procession behind them, and a servant silently stood behind each member of the group. Ilivi knelt and placed a squat, rather heavy-looking table in their midst. She bent low, her head almost touching the surface, and began a slow humming sound which grew into a chant. As her voice rose to a gentle climax, so a calmness, a stillness, distilled the air about them. Laurel looked across at Ava. A tiny thread of vapour trailed from the tips of her fingers, and from Laurel's own fingers, that same phenomenon. The mist curled for a moment, then disappeared.

The humming was the only solemn part of the ceremony; a ritual passed down through the sovereignty to honour the Hebre deliverers. Only once before, since they left on their journey through the stars, had it been performed in the presence of the Hebre, when another visitor came to their world. The rest of the evening was rather merry, and despite the attendants seeming deferential to the Empress, they were not excluded from the festivities. Harry disliked the flying tea jugs, which insisted on replenishing his cup. Darlen was engaged in deep conversation with a man who often gestured to the heavens, and Marcel was similarly engaged with the Empress. The kittens returned, and Scarlett had dozed off on her cushion with two little fluffy cats sleeping in her arms.

Baii and Ava were standing together, looking out across the ocean. Harry touched Laurel's arm to get her attention. "Isn't there some kind of knockdown we can direct towards those tea jugs?" he joked. "They're like those bugs on Macibib."

Laurel remembered those bugs. The tea jugs were nothing like them.

Baii pushed a cushion close and sat next to Laurel and Harry.

"It's a splendid night. You've arrived at the perfect time of the cycle. Laurel, I didn't let you ask your question."

"I've discovered a few more since then, Baii," she

laughed. "I'll ask it later, and right now, choose another. Who was the person who came to you when the Empress was a child?"

Baii thought for a moment as the Empress turned and touched Marcel on the arm, indicating that they should now join the others.

"A human," Ilivi began the story, "brought from the nebula by one of the beasts that sheds its skin in the west. I was but a child." She half-turned to her brother, who took up the story.

"The man came to us in the belly of Cipica, a creature who dwells in the heart of the nebula. Cipica is telepathic and told our father he was carrying the man to safety."

"When was this?" Laurel asked.

"During the second cycle of the moons." Baii leaned forward to gaze into Laurel's eyes. "I see how you measure time," he said softly, then turned to Scarlett. "This child was not yet conceived."

"Did he tell you his name?"

"He remembered little," Baii said. "Not his name, nor from where he came. He told us of war but never regained any other memories."

"Where is he now?"

"His ashes lie beside those of our father," Baii said, sensing an immediate weight of grief descending on Harry and Laurel. "From the moment the stranger arrived until he passed from life, he was a kind friend to the Emperor. The Emperor requested the man, whom we called Cipi after the creature who saved him, be buried here within the palace grounds."

Baii reached out and took Laurel's hands. "This news causes you pain. I'm sorry."

Laurel closed her eyes against tears and shook her head. "I grieved for him a long time ago." She glanced at Harry. "We both did, but he was a friend and mentor and to me, like a father."

Baii nodded slowly. "After sunrise, I will take you to him. He lived happily amongst us."

"He had no memories, Laurel," Ilivi said with gentle understanding, "but he gave us so many."

"When did you realise he was one of these Hebre?" Darlen asked.

"The body is mortal," Baii said, "but the light of Hebre is not dimmed."

Ilivi stood suddenly. "I fear this news has saddened you, Laurel. May we make tomorrow a new day, with fresh memories and new words to gladden us?"

Laurel also stood. "I guess it's just that one moment, Xavier was gone, buried in the past, and now, it seems he lived another life after we mourned him." She smiled a sad smile. "It's a lot to take in."

"Xavier?" Ilivi repeated. "This name will be honoured as long as life exists on this planet."

They each went to their separate apartments. Ava kept her mind open and available until she was sure her mother's sadness was easing, and Laurel sent to her she must rest, that this was a drop of grief in a sea of wonder and for her alone to deal with.

CHAPTER FORTY-THREE _

Like the seating arrangements, the bed was on the floor, but it was supremely comfortable, heated according to your thoughts and cooled if you thought it too hot. Harry held Laurel for a long time, experiencing with her his sadness once more at losing a man and colleague he admired. Harry had never shared Laurel's empathy or experience with Xavier, but he felt his loss keenly.

Sleep didn't come to Laurel. Careful not to disturb Harry, she rose and stepped out onto the terrace, the cool of the night air shrouding her shoulders. She had nothing on her feet and only a thin, silky gown provided by the attendant for sleeping. But she didn't want to be warm and cosy right now. She wanted to think, to miss Xavier, to miss Helen. She closed her eyes and breathed deeply. The air had a salty flavour, it blew through her mind, refreshing her but not quite banishing her thoughts.

A movement behind her caused her to turn. A woman with multicoloured hair stood on the terrace. She wore a shabby trader's flight suit, and Laurel's heart skipped a few beats.

"Helen?"

"Hello, chick," the woman smiled.

"How…?"

Helen tilted her head to the side. "Don't ask me. I'm not really here, sweetie,"

Laurel wanted to rush forward, embrace her friend, tell her how much she missed her, but her legs wouldn't move. "I don't understand. If you're not here, where are you?"

Helen thought for a moment. "I don't know. I only know I was there, and now I'm here." A typically cryptic, confusing Helen-type explanation.

"Are you a spirit?" Laurel made a questioning gesture with both hands. "I saw something when you were hiding the ship from the Gale, but it didn't look like you."

Again, Helen looked puzzled, but Laurel immediately discarded her question. "It doesn't matter; you're here now. Helen, have you seen Darlen and Scarlett? It devastated Darlen when you…when you," Laurel couldn't say the word, not with Helen standing so close to her.

"I don't need to," Helen grinned. "Darlen's good. He's happy with his memories and his future with Scarlett. We made a beautiful kid, didn't we?"

"You did," Laurel grinned back. "She's such a cutie. Helen, Darlen might be glad to see you."

"It would unsettle him, Laurel. Besides, he didn't call me; you did."

"Call you?" Laurel didn't follow. "How did I call you?"

"You believe it was your choices that led to my death." To the point as ever, Laurel shouldn't have been taken aback by Helen's bluntness, but she was.

"I… Don't you?"

Helen shook her head. "No, I fulfilled what I was meant to fulfil. My purpose. When Scarlett was born, my life was complete, and I was removed."

"Removed? By whom? God?"

"I don't believe in God, Laurel, you know that, and although where I was escapes me right this minute, there aren't angels or gods or harps or any stuff like that."

"I wish I understood."

"You will when you fulfil your purpose."

"Am I fulfilling my purpose, Helen, doing what I'm doing?" Laurel pleaded for Helen to set her on the right path. "I'm so uncertain, but now, Ava has such a strong focus."

"As she says, it's a pilgrimage, a crusade, but who knows?" Helen shrugged. "Ava has strengths not yet revealed. She's different to you, me, and any other soul transported to this universe. Even her father."

"How can you know this when you can't even say how you came to be here?"

"I dunno, the words just came out." Helen poked herself in the chest, towards her heart.

"Have you seen Xavier? He came to this planet. The lifeform brought him after the incident at the nebula. He must have passed through time like we did."

"Xavier? You're assuming because you can see me, there's life after death? I can't confirm or deny that, but you're stuck in all that religious stuff. Laurel, don't make those evaluations until you know the whole truth. Right now, you don't, even though you're having a midnight conversation with a ghost."

"Will I see you again? I can't tell you the comfort this has brought me."

"Delighted to have been of service, chick." Helen smiled her happy smile. "I can be here whenever you want, but you don't need me. It will all become clear, I promise."

Laurel had no memory of returning to bed and was surprised to find herself once again wrapped in Harry's arms, the first streaks of dawn sending trickles of light across their bed. She nudged him awake and headed out to the terrace. The morning was clear and pure, and there was nothing to indicate she'd had a night-time visitor. Harry wandered out after her and leaned against the balustrade, yawning.

The early morning mist lifted its blanket from the valley, and the sun spread delicate fingers across the sky, bringing the promise of a glorious day, rolling back the breathtaking beauty of the landscape, the purple and gold forests that slanted down the hillside and the meadows and rolling fields. Beyond, magnificent mountain ranges, their peaks still shrouded in mist.

"I used to think early mornings on Mentelci were the most beautiful in the galaxy," Harry said. "Semevale 8 a close second, at least before the war, but this…" he took in a deep breath to savour the crisp morning air. He glanced sideways at Laurel before turning to her. "And you have something to tell me; you're not even looking at the view."

"I saw Helen. Last night, here on the terrace. I couldn't sleep, so I came out here for some air."

"Are you sure? You were upset when we came to bed."

Harry's pragmatism needed to suggest an alternative explanation. He trusted Laurel's instincts, but an apparition? Laurel ran the events from the previous night through his thoughts, word for word, scene by scene.

"Laurel, you weren't responsible for Helen's death."

Harry knew that Laurel blamed herself for all these years, and no reassurance could convince her otherwise. He stopped trying, but it was always there, tucked away in some compartment or other that Laurel would deal with in her own time. Gabriel was there too, though his memory never came between them. Laurel's mixed-up childhood and the loss of her aunt and uncle completed this box of sad memories. All hidden away. If Helen truly appeared to her, Harry had a strong sense much of the guilt surrounding Helen's death had been washed away. He kissed the top of Laurel's head.

"Helen doesn't blame you. She wants you to let go," he said softly. He felt her nod against his shoulder.

"There's something about this place, Harry," she said. "It's intensely spiritual. When Ilivi gave her incantation yesterday, both Ava and I had a manifestation of vapour from our fingertips." She tilted her head back to look at him. "It's never happened to me before, but I've seen it in both Helen and Ava."

"I feel—I'm not sure—an atmosphere," Harry conceded, looking around, "but I'm not an empath. Seeing Ilivi conjure the kittens reminded me of the stories of wizards and magic from your world."

Laurel laughed. "There's more to magic than even I once thought."

"What do you think of our hosts?" Harry asked. "We spent several hours with them last night; did you sense anything?"

"I haven't looked inside their minds if that's what you mean," Laurel said, "and neither of them nor the attendants have auras, but they're not whole souls."

"Even as a non-empath," Harry said as he lovingly smoothed Laurel's hair, "I can tell these are good people. They have the welfare of the Chaese at the centre of their existence. I'm looking forward to learning the history of this planet, its technology and what cataclysmic event took place that set the Hebre—" he looked down at her with the raise of one eyebrow, "—of course I mean whole souls, front and centre of their history."

"First up, though, Harry, I want to see where they buried Xavier and pay my respects. Then I'll let go. I promise."

Harry held her tight; he'd loved her for so long, and even though he always scoffed at any empathy in himself, there was enough compassion to recognise suffering, even suppressed suffering. Today, Laurel's remorse over Helen's death had dimmed, and he knew she would now allow Xavier to rest. If nothing else came from their time here, it was good that Laurel would be relieved of those sorrows.

A new, more mature attendant came out onto the terrace. The old lady, with a kind face and almond-shaped eyes creased at each corner, grinned, bowed, and placed her hands together away from her body in a sign of respect. She uttered a phrase in her language, and even though neither Laurel nor Harry comprehended, Laurel sensed the woman's fascination at meeting them, coupled with caring and kindness. Like her sovereign, her nature was towards the wellbeing and comfort of others.

The woman's mind was wide open, and her thoughts available and unhidden. She readied the pool, arranged towels, and left clothing, more elaborate than the day before, before retreating with a smile.

"I could get used to this bathing." Harry floated on his back in the pool. "Beats oil showers."

Laurel luxuriated in the aromatic water. "I love it too. All these years, I've daydreamed about taking a bath."

Harry sat up. "You read our attendant's mind, didn't you?"

Laurel opened her eyes. "Yes, none of the attendants seem to close off their thoughts, it wasn't that way with the Chaese, but I think in this race, the brain is wired differently. I wonder if there are two levels, those who have achieved a telepathic/empathic state and those still evolving."

Harry was impressed. "That's an interesting observation,"

Laurel nodded. "That's not all; we've only met three telepaths, one of whom has a remarkable power to manifest objects from the mind into physical objects. In the case of the kittens, Ilivi took a recollection of a kitten from me and made it real. Baii might have that same power. I sense more to him than meets the eye than just the brother of the Empress."

Harry nodded his agreement. "But those kittens weren't an accurate facsimile, were they?"

"Near enough, Harry, kittens have four legs, not two.

Therefore, I believe this palace is also an illusion, a manifestation."

"How so?"

"Last night, we were on the ocean side of the palace. I looked down, and as expected, I saw water and rocks, just like any seascape. Then I looked up and saw this terrace."

Harry frowned. "So we moved between floors without an antigrav platform or any kind of elevator? So, while you say Ilivi and Baii are open, the word illusion suggests deception."

"No deception, Harry," Laurel was still trying to make sense of it herself. "These people are sincere. I guess the answers lie with the Hebre."

"Could the palace be an advanced hologram?"

"It reaches beyond that." Laurel had already considered and discarded the idea. "This event that befell the planet, that wiped out the other civilisations, I suspect the Hebre corrected it somehow, and the enduring effect has something to do with the picot which Darlen claims is the access point to a Transcender. And what is the purpose of a Transcender?"

"A conduit between universes and time?"

Harry watched as Laurel stepped from the bath and wrapped herself in a towel.

Laurel nodded. "We need to ask Baii and Ilivi a few questions."

CHAPTER FORTY-FOUR _

Baii, his formal attire of the day before replaced by slacks and a loose shirt similar in style to that favoured by Marcel, was on the terrace with Ava, his silky black hair knotted up on top of his head. In earnest conversation with Ava, he lay propped on his side, who knelt on a cushion, dressed in a silk shift of a colour that complemented her violet eyes. Baii leapt to his feet when he saw Harry and Laurel and remained standing until they seated themselves on the floor cushions. A hovering tea jug appeared at Laurel's shoulder, but in front of Harry, a servant placed a simple-looking, non-technological pot of tea and a cup.

"The flying tea jug corps must have taken my remarks to heart last night," he whispered to Laurel, making her grin.

"Were you comfortable?" Baii asked politely. "Your accommodation has spectacular views." He raised his eyebrows at Laurel, almost inviting comment.

"It's wonderful, thank you," Laurel said, accompanied by a nod of agreement from Harry. Laurel tried to suppress the appearance of Helen, but her thoughts drew a searching glance from Ava. Laurel was in no doubt Baii would notice their telepathic exchange, but if he did, he made no sign.

447

"My Empress departed for the East very early this morning," Baii said. "She is visiting the Eastern Chaese. The people enjoy the Empress's playfulness and vivacity. She is welcomed wherever she goes. She took Marcel with her." He smiled as Darlen and Scarlett arrived on the terrace. "Your robot accompanied the Empress and Marcel on a visit to the East."

Scarlett looked around for kittens. When she saw none, she clambered into her father's lap, disappointed.

Baii smiled. "The Empress has the kittens, Scarlett. When I was your age, these were my favourite pets—" and with a smooth cupping motion of his hand, several frog-sized, soft, bandy-legged, toothless lizards appeared. They were adorable. One headed straight for Laurel and one for Scarlett, who squealed with delight as the little creature ran up her leg and made grunting noises at her, puffing out its cheeks and opening its eyes wide. Laurel picked up the lizard. It felt like a living creature. She stroked her finger down its back, and it trilled its pleasure at her touch.

Baii responded to her puzzled frown. "Certain of my species have the gift of manifestation. While we are present, our manifestations have the appearance of being fully authentic." He glanced at Scarlett and dropped his voice. "It is why there are no kittens." He winked and grinned. "Let us hope my efforts suffice."

Laurel peered around him at Scarlett. "I would say they definitely do."

"Where did they take Mer?" Darlen asked, glad that Scarlett was entertained but not happy to have his property removed from the palace without his express agreement.

Baii addressed the group. "May I respond to Darlen's query as I offer a little knowledge of the geography and industry of our world?"

Darlen shrugged. The attendants set out leaves and flowers and a mixture of seeds on the low table. They weren't provided with plates or cutlery, and Baii led the process by taking a leaf and adding several ingredients before folding it and popping it into his mouth. They all did the same even though Ava ended up feeding Scarlett, who mistakenly bit one of the lizards instead of her leaf sandwich. Baii assured them the lizard would suffer no ill effects.

Lizard crisis over, Baii made the same scooping action with his hand that summoned the lizards, this time a globe turned above the table. As he spoke, he drew their eyes to the areas he described, scenes of industry, farming and community.

"We tractioned your ship to the western lands as it had reached the point of breaking up. It was the closest point to the nebula," he said. "The western continent is a wasteland, but formerly, it was covered by lakes and rivers, by pastureland and farms. The people there were plain folk who worked the land and studied healing herbs and medicines. The food they produced provided one-third of the food for the entire planet."

"Isn't that where the lifeform brought Xavier?"

Baii nodded. "Yes, Laurel. And where Cipica moults. The western tribes loved Cipica. The life bringer. The shed skin has many healing properties, and they welcomed its presence."

"I heard it caused toxicity in plants," Laurel said, recalling what Gabriel told her about the lifeform.

"You heard correctly," Baii answered, a little startled at her knowledge. "Cipica releases a vapour that touches any vegetation in its surroundings. In the hands of the Western people, those plants are transformed to benefit the people. They continued in harmony with Cipica."

"On my homeworld," Laurel told them, "Many of our medicines can kill if too much is taken at once."

"That's interesting," Harry said. Then, he turned to Baii. "My culture has progressed beyond ingested cures for relief of symptoms. We use technology now."

"I know," Baii grinned, impressed. "Our engineers have come upon the little beetles you call healbots and painbots. In them, we have observed an unfamiliar world." He tilted his head. "We can learn from each other."

"And Mer?" Darlen prompted.

"The Chaese of the east are engineers, mechanics, masters of technology," Baii continued. "It is to the Chaese the Empress has taken Mer. He did not fare as well in the damage to your ship as it first seemed."

"He ran a diagnostic." Darlen looked around at the others for support. "He reported all okay."

Baii agreed. "If 'okay' is enough. The engineers in the eastern continents have gathered to study your ship and the robot. If we can return them to you, they will be significantly enhanced."

Lauren felt Darlen bristling. Scarlett looked up; this was about her friend Mer. Baii might be an accomplished telepath, but he should have chosen his words more wisely.

"If?" Darlen set his mouth in a grim line.

Baii, picking up his breach of manners from Laurel, hastily made the scooping gesture, and a facsimile of Darlen's ship appeared, intact, but in no better condition than when they left it in the sand.

"Every drive sequencer, what you call widespeed configurations," Baii explained, "every Transcenderal matrix, every internal and external sensor, every internal accessory and every ancillary system is irreparable. We cannot reverse the damage."

"Are you suggesting it's scrap?"

Baii thought about it. They scrapped nothing on this world, but he got the idea and nodded. Anxious not to repeat his earlier mistake, he added, "Mer requires repair. His long history with the ship will identify which systems are salvageable. He went willingly with the Empress."

"I have a lengthy history with the ship, as well," Darlen pointed out.

Baii nodded. "Yes, but it will never fly again."

Scarlett patted her father's arm. "Is Mer coming back, Darlen?"

"Yes, he is. He needs some work; then he's coming back." Darlen threw Baii a fierce look.

Baii realised Darlen's attachment to his ship was beyond his understanding and hastened to reassure him. "The ship won't fly, but you aren't stranded here. We will equip you with a new vessel, and you will proceed with your quest."

Darlen's ears pricked up. A new ship? That changed the face of it. Perhaps he wasn't so attached to the old one that he wouldn't consider a more modern replacement.

"Yes, our engineers have already formulated the designs." Baii sighed inwardly at having averted a further breach of manners. He gestured, and the plans morphed into view above the table.

"Impressive," Darlen nodded as he perused the schematics.

"The Chaese haven't left this planet in centuries," Harry pointed out. "And they've never travelled the inner part of the nebula. How can you be so sure they'll be able to build a ship equal to Darlen's?"

"They will base the design on Darlen's ship, and I promise you, improved upon. Please do not be concerned; you will not find the Chaese engineers wanting."

"I want to oversee the construction," Darlen said. Harry made valid points, and Baii was left in no doubt this wasn't a request. He inclined his head. "Of course, I will make arrangements. You may leave at sunrise tomorrow."

"Scarlett can stay with us," Laurel suggested. Scarlett went into a contrary mode, but the assurance of more kittens and lizards and even other children stopped her.

"Before Darlen leaves," Laurel said, "we would like to learn more about the planet, the events that led to the global catastrophe, and perhaps how the Hebre restored at least most of it to its former state."

"And how you can look up at a gallery situated over the ocean with a view of a valley?" Baii asked with a grin.

Laurel laughed. "That too!"

"We will walk in the garden, I will take you to your friend's resting place, and we will talk."

The gardens, a botanical park spread over an extensive area, were fragrant, beautiful and fascinating. Baii knew every individual species of plant, from giant vines dripping with multicoloured trumpet-shaped blooms to green trailing ivy, which reacted to touch by curling its leaves and sighing. Baii also understood each plant's property, its growing season, and whether it was for food, healing, or merely cultivated for its beauty. They walked through groves of towering, dense-canopied trees, inhaled the perfume of loams and mosses, and listened as Baii explained the role of the fungi that grew on the forest floor and its place in the ecosystem. The two magnificent white birds they saw when they first arrived turned out to have less clean cousins that resided in the forests, with tail feathers that coiled like lyres over their backs. They glanced up from their scratching at the ground to watch the strangers pass by but displayed no fear or concern. Other birds darted and hovered, and Baii told them these precious and colourful creatures almost suffered the same fate as the other civilisations on Isilia, that of extinction. The plants and birds owed their survival to the foresight of Chaese scientists, who accurately forecasted the collapse of life on their planet and preserved as many seeds and cells as they were able. It hadn't saved every human inhabitant, but it had allowed for the propagation of plants, insects and wildlife.

The palace was bare of any plants or cut flowers, and they learned from Baii that the Chaese respected the rights of all living things, and that neither the Riynea—Baii and Ilivi's people—nor the Chaese consumed animal flesh.

Individual plants, blooms, seeds and nuts had a place in nutrition, and the Chaese believed that the plant fulfilled its purpose by serving as a food source. Unlike the plants and insects that survived the cataclysm relatively unscathed due to the foresight of some scientists, many animals, some now extinct, suffered similar genetic mutations as the human population, that of dysgenesis of the reproductive organs, resulting in sterility.

"Was that created by chemicals?" Harry asked as he inspected an almost perfect leaf. "Pollutants?"

"Apart from the western continents, every territory had its industry," Baii told him. "There were agricultural regions, of course, and throughout their history, the many species, comprising the Chaese, the Cabit, the Esatopolorians and several others, were community oriented. The Chaese were indigenous to this planet, and although they were complicit in stripping the planet of its resources, some more enlightened Chaese scientists eventually realised they faced certain destruction. They alerted the governments of the dangers of experimenting with energy sources from the planet's core."

"And they didn't listen?" Darlen had seen this in Earth's future. That was a place where things would get worse before they got better. Baii dipped his head in acknowledgement.

"Nor did they learn, even as they sowed the seeds of their own destruction. Instead, they continued in stubborn ignorance, refusing to accept the legacy they would leave for their children. Only when the sunsets turned red did they look to Chaese scientists to lead them back."

"I'd be interested to know the nature of their research," Harry responded, genuinely fascinated.

"I will provide you with everything you wish to know," Baii said, "and also the benefit of one of the Chaese scholars, who will welcome the opportunity to discuss the cataclysm and reclamation of the planet with a fellow scientist."

"Onoth mentioned the sunsets remind them of their foolishness," Ava said.

"Hebre could not heal the western continents," Baii explained. "It is not part of the picot, so when the west turns to the sun at the end of the day, the dust in the atmosphere colours the sky red. The Chaese see it as a reminder; in truth, it is simply the limitations of the picot."

"That brings us to the size of the picot and how you have planetary events, sunrises, sunsets, a sky for that matter," Darlen said, looking upwards.

"The Hebre opened the picot to a time before the cataclysm," Baii told them, joining Darlen in looking up to the sky. "They took it back to when the world was fresh, the air pure. The soil is living history, and the weather is natural, filtered by the picot. The sun is real."

Baii stopped walking and took a deep breath, appreciating the purity of the air. He looked around. "The Hebre took this world back into its past, before science destroyed it, but we, the Chaese and the Riynea are of the present." He lifted his arm towards a green meadow. "Your friend rests here."

CHAPTER FORTY-FIVE _

Baii led them from the trees above a steep meadow massed with vibrant colours, green, gold, yellow grasses and tall poppy-like blossoms that bowed and danced in the breeze as far as the eye could see—an ideal backdrop for Xavier's final resting place.

"Is there a marker?" Harry asked. "A memorial?"

Baii pointed to the trees behind them. "He loved the gardens and grew these trees from seeds, so here is a fitting place for him to rest. We hold his memory in our hearts," he said. "We burn all mortal remains to return the ashes to the earth. Your friend lies here among his trees, the flowers and grasses, with my father and mother, and their mother and father before them, back to the age of the Hebre."

Laurel glanced up at Darlen. In his mind, he saw Helen's ashes lying here in this beautiful place, alongside Xavier's. Baii politely stayed out of the mental link, but he was ready to answer as soon as Laurel turned to him.

He bowed. "It would be our honour," he said, "and you need only say the word, and our artisans will fashion a jewel from the beloved's heart."

Laurel looked out over the field of red and gold to the

mountains beyond and reached out for Harry, who was thinking about his father, who would be dead after all this time. Harry hoped he was buried in as peaceful a place as this. Ava came to stand beside them, and Scarlett pulled Darlen's hand down onto her shoulder, staring up at the grown-ups in confusion. She recognized she should be quiet for a moment, while Auntie Laurel and Uncle Howie were thinking things she didn't understand, but to be almost four and having been cooped up in a spaceship all her young life and a big field just perfect for running, became too much. Breaking away, she ran squealing into the grass, leaving everyone else to their reverent contemplation.

The path to Xavier's resting place had taken them some time, but that allowed them plenty of opportunities to ask questions. Baii didn't tell them about the advent of the Hebre, smilingly telling them his sister insisted she wished to be present for a story that had enchanted her as a child. But they did learn about the intergalactic cultures that formerly populated the planet, the decline of the civilisation and the rise of disorder, greed and desire for power from each species' leaders. And Baii explained to them why Laurel saw her apartment from the ocean side of the palace when she had looked out over the valley.

"See this, Laurel?" He made the gentle scooping motion with his hand, manifesting a vision of the cliffside, filthy with pollution, devoid of any plant life and beneath, only dry dust where Laurel had looked over a beautiful scene across an archipelago. Laurel knew this was heading somewhere. Ava gave voice to her mother's thoughts. "This has something to do with time, hasn't it, Baii?"

Baii's face lit with amusement, but he didn't give them any more clues, enjoying their efforts in working out the puzzle.

Harry spoke up. "There is no palace," was the solution he submitted. "It's an illusion."

Baii shook his head. "There is a palace, my friend." He waited while his new friends gave the conundrum some thought.

"The question, I believe…" Laurel pointed towards the cliff face hovering above Baii's hand, "is not if there is a palace, but *when* is there a palace."

Baii scooped the hologram from sight, throwing Laurel a grin for her cleverness. Darlen made a face as if the penny had dropped. "I get it."

"I wish I did," Harry chimed in.

"I told you when we first arrived," Darlen said. "A picot is a kind of antechamber to a Transcender you can remain in for eternity. This planet's time progression…" Darlen sought tacit agreement from Baii, "for want of a better explanation, has been rewound."

"Darlen is correct," Baii said. "The Hebre opened the picot and restored the planet to an earlier time. They gave the people a second chance, but if they abuse their custodianship, the planet can die once more. All organic life within the picot, human, plant, and animal, is subject to the movement of time. They are born, they live, they die, and even after centuries have passed, these humans still struggle to recover from a self-made calamity."

"How does that explain the palace?" Interesting as all this might be, Harry couldn't connect the dots. "I understand that if the Hebre reset time, then the palace might not have existed. Did you build it on a transdimensional shift?"

"Where my ancestors come from, we can manifest many things we require." To demonstrate, Baii manifested, in rapid succession, a stream of various objects, ranging from a tiny jewel to a facsimile of a ship, which Baii hastily explained was not flightworthy and this merely a demonstration. "The Chaese's progression within the picot in the early days didn't proceed smoothly; they were without leadership, and they began to look on the Hebre as demigods, who would deliver them from every sickness, every crop failure, if they paid homage. The Hebre naturally rejected this worship, offering the fledgeling society an alternative; a race who would demonstrate a higher power, and who the new society believed would be worthy of their reverence. The leaders of their past displayed their status by building great houses. We merely created such a house, much of which remains fluid in time, thanks to the Hebre. It is there, but if we were to strip the need for the monument away, it is merely a cliff and our dwelling a humble house, the same as our Riynea brothers and sisters. My sister and I reside in such a place because we are descended from the first Riynea to be left here. Those with the power to manifest and to protect and lead the Chaese."

"Sounds exhausting!" Ava laughed. "Having to recreate an entire building and gardens whenever someone drops by."

Baii smiled. "It is a little like automatic pilot; we leave it to time, but I will say, the gardens are real."

"But we all agree on its appearance?" Harry said, looking for confirmation from the others.

"Laurel doesn't," Baii said. "She perceives the fluidic nature of the manifested part of the monument. I'm surprised you didn't, Darlen. I sense an ability to move through time equal to the Hebre."

"To be honest, it's as simple as the fact I wasn't looking," Darlen confessed without commenting on the second part of Baii's conjecture. "It looks like any other palace I've been in."

Both Harry and Laurel filed that nugget away for another time.

"Baii, you've answered so many questions," Laurel said, "even given us more to ask, but we want to know more about the Hebre, your people and the beings who came to your planet with the Hebre. You see Hebre in us," she looked at Ava, "but we know nothing about them."

"And we know little of our forebears or their lives," Baii admitted. "All these elements form part of the story Ilivi wishes you to hear. We will take time at sunset, now please, enjoy the day, food will be served when you wish, and I can arrange a guide for you to explore the local area."

"Are you able to manifest food? Is it possible for Laurel or Ava to do it?" Harry asked as the thought of hot SperelySour sticks made his mouth water. He hadn't had one in years. Darlen, in turn, had a brief vision of a Big Mac, his favourite food in any universe.

"It is easy to manifest that which appears to be food," Baii laughed, scooping up Darlen's vision to the astonishment of both Darlen and Laurel, the only two in the group who recognised the burger. "But manifested food has no nutritional value. As mortals, we require sustenance." Baii reconsidered the meat and bun construction hovering above his hand and wondered what fascination such a concoction would hold for Darlen. He closed his hand.

"Laurel, may I take Ava on a short trip? I will take good care of her." Laurel was a little surprised that the decision should include her, but she appreciated Baii's old-fashioned respect. She nodded her agreement.

Permission granted, Ava and Baii took off happily towards the base of the cliff, leaving Harry and Laurel to make their way up the winding path through the gardens to the portico. Darlen stayed in the garden with Scarlett to make the most of his time with her before he departed for the east the following morning.

Laurel looked over the balustrade down to the seashore. She knew now that she could look over any balustrade and see any view she wished, but it seemed more natural, more human to do it this way. She also knew now the bath was a manifestation of her desire to soak herself in deep, scented water, made possible by the picot. The fact that Harry could enjoy the manifestation made it doubly enticing.

Far below, Baii held a canoe steady for Ava. She'd changed from her silken robe into slacks and a shirt Laurel had never seen before, her long black hair lifted in the breeze, and Laurel could hear her laughter. Baii pushed out the canoe and jumped easily over the side to face Ava and take up the oars. They headed out towards the nest of tree-covered islands in the archipelago. Laurel smiled; her daughter would love the romance.

"You'd think they'd have an engine, wouldn't you?" Harry made a practical observation, seeing no romance in a boat trip. He hated any journeys involving water.

"It's a place of contradictions," Laurel replied. "We're standing on a cliffside in a palace that exists out of time. Here, thinking makes it so."

"Not for the Chaese. They live grateful lives in linear time."

"But the Riynea want to do everyday things. They enjoy eating, growing things, talking…" Laurel glanced at the tiny speck out on the water. They might not have an engine, but they'd made good headway with Baii at the oars. "And they appreciate the company of others."

"Laurel, where we are standing, do we see what we want to see, or is it what Baii and Ilivi have created?"

"They created it for us when we first arrived. What we see now would be coloured by our first impressions." Laurel leaned out, and sure enough, there was the terrace she and Harry shared above her. She pointed it out to Harry.

"So it is!" he spluttered, then eyed her suspiciously. "That's because you told me it was there."

Laurel nodded. "I don't think it matters, it's all perfectly lovely, and if it's an illusion, well, there's been lots of things in my life that were little more than that."

"How intriguing. Tell me more."

"Let's get some of that sweet tea, and we'll talk." Laurel sat Harry down on a few cushions scattered on the terrace. A flying tea jug appeared almost immediately, followed by an attendant, who set a steaming pot and cup before Harry.

Laurel pointed over the terrace balustrade to where, moments earlier they looked out over the sea. Now, they saw mountains and rolling hills.

CHAPTER FORTY-SIX _

Later that evening, Marcel and Ilivi returned and joined them on the terrace. Mer remained with the engineers for repair and helped them salvage vital systems from Darlen's ship.

Harry nudged Laurel. "If I can see the signs there, you can too." Laurel agreed. Marcel looked happy, and Ilivi stayed close to him, taking every excuse to touch his arm or lay a hand on his knee. "He worked pretty quickly; we've only been here a day."

Laurel gave him a chiding, sideways glance. "Well, I'm glad," she said. "To reach his age and not to ever have had a girlfriend…"

Harry spluttered. "What! Where were you when Shumuyi'beh was telling us about the string of broken hearts he left behind when he chose to come with us?"

She didn't know that, but the knowledge gladdened Laurel; she hated to think Marcel missed out on relationships. Beside her, Harry chuckled softly to himself, doing a double take when he realised she was still watching him. "He's a good-looking lad, Laurel," he said, "and she's a good-looking girl."

"I know." Laurel had to agree. Who knew how long they'd be here? "I'm more bothered about Ava. She's eighteen. I guess adolescence, young womanhood, and boys were another factor I didn't consider when I proposed this trip."

"I don't know. I think Ava may have made her first conquest." Harry jerked his head towards where Ava sat beside Baii. Laurel looked at her daughter, laughing and happy; her hair, thick and loose, tumbled down her back, her pale cream silk and lace gown clung to her body, revealing curves that, up to now, were always hidden under second-hand trader's garb. Ava had not yet told her mother about the boat trip with Baii, but it was clearly a success.

Even so, Laurel had doubts. "Baii would easily be the same age as Marcel, a little old for her, don't you think?"

"I don't think," Harry responded. "Look around you, Laurel. How many young men has she met? Baii is decent, and he respects her. Allow her to be reckless, exploratory, or romantic if she wants to be. She's spent most of her life with older people. Here, she can be a young girl, wear pretty things, let her hair down…" he smiled and tucked up one of Laurel's loose curls. "I haven't done that to your hair in ages."

Laurel nodded silently. Everything was geared to practicality on the ship, including her hair, her clothes, and it was the same for Ava, who'd never got to wear anything attractive or pretty or, dare she think it, sexy. In such a close environment, with all the responsibilities of space travel and ship's maintenance, such frivolities seemed pointless. But she liked Harry touching her hair, and she smiled back, knowing he loved her, but sad for him, for them both that romance had taken such a back seat.

Ilivi reported on the success of the trip to the eastern continents. Arrangements for Darlen for the next day were accomplished, and a plan was presented to the group while the Chaese built the new ship. Ilivi suggested Laurel and Harry might wish to accompany Darlen, but the alternative—remaining at the palace and enjoying an extended vacation held greater appeal. Darlen agreed to Scarlett receiving some education, and in anticipation, Ilivi engaged a Riynean educator. Ilivi explained the woman was not a fully developed telepath but an able tutor, and she was sure Scarlett would love her. In addition, the woman had two sons close to Scarlett's age who arrived with her and her partner—a botanist—who'd agreed to take a sabbatical to assist Baii in the gardens.

"Assist Baii?" Laurel asked, puzzled.

"Yes, Mom," Ava announced gleefully. "Baii's the gardener!"

This news came as a surprise. "The brother of the Empress is the gardener?"

Baii laughed. "As an 'unselected one,' I may choose a vocation which fits in with my duties as an aide to the sovereign. I have no lofty aspirations, and since boyhood, I have spent much time amongst the plants and flowers. Hence, I chose to be a gardener."

"Your gardens are a credit to you," Harry said. "On Mentelci, a place I always believed a paradise, no-one has a garden that belongs to them exclusively."

"Harry," Laurel suggested, "Why don't you show Ilivi

and Baii the images of where your father lives? It's so beautiful, and also share the story of his life on Earth and his sea voyage. I think they would love it."

Harry needed no more prompting, and indeed, Ilivi and Baii did love the story. Ava had heard it before, but Harry had overlooked relating it to Marcel, who was just as fascinated. The tale invited much discussion, some of which Laurel's knowledge of Earth answered. Even the attendants enjoyed the images, although for some, the language escaped their understanding.

"The telepathic ability of your people varies." Laurel glanced at an attendant. "Is it required to be in a position of leadership, like you Ilivi, and Onoth?"

"It is an inherited trait," Baii said. "But the power of manifestation is rarer, and those who possess it become sovereigns…" He grinned. "Or the brother of a sovereign. Advanced telepaths like Onoth become governors. We have never encountered a Chaese with telepathic or empathic powers. Unlike the Hebre, the Riynea cannot influence time nor govern dimensions."

"But the Hebre still ended up as hostages of the Farisee."

"I…" Baii seemed lost for words. Laurel sensed her remark startled the Empress and her brother.

"The Farisee delivered the Hebre from Eden," Ilivi said, opening her arms wide as if embracing an idea. "Your forebears, Laurel, not prisoners. Fugitives."

"Fugitives?"

Ilivi gestured about her, pausing as she chose her words. "You have worn your mortality for so long; your history has become indistinct, a mystery, as it had for your friend who rests in the meadow, but here, with us, we assumed the memories would return. Perhaps you need more time."

"I didn't know I had any telepathic nor empathic ability until Darlen brought me to this universe through the Transcender to take part in a war," Laurel told them. "It's how I met Marcel's father, who also became Ava's father. He was a whole soul, but his powers eclipsed mine."

"Tell us." Ilivi settled herself for another story, patted her knees and lifted her chin in anticipation.

Ilivi and Baii listened to the history of the whole souls forced into the League through the ages. They asked no questions nor made any interruptions as Laurel and Harry explained what they knew of whole souls, and Darlen described the role of the Soul Monger. Ilivi and Baii held no judgement and even telepathically did not comment to each other on the part of the story that would have included their ancestors. Laurel condensed her experience in the fortress to a few sentences, mainly covering Gabriel's extraordinary ability to conceal an entire army and his desire to free his family. The part of the story that included Canon Akkuh's treachery, breaking into the archives and the accidental discovery of the document relating to the whole soul's escape was of particular fascination, even drawing a ripple of applause at their daring. Only then, on hearing Laurel's halting translation of the ancient document, did Baii comment.

"These whole souls. It would seem they never found peace."

"Earth afforded them a kind of peace," Laurel said, "but at the expense of their abilities, at least until the Soul Monger's found us and brought us back."

Ilivi scooped up her hand, and a silver six-pointed star-like jewel appeared, so magnificently lustrous, Laurel, Harry and Ava blinked at its glory. The only one not to be dazzled was Darlen. Laurel sensed anxiety in him, and he deliberately pasted on an unreadable expression. He knew he couldn't hide it from Laurel, but he ignored her.

"The Chaese scientists detected a signature on your ship." Ilivi looked at Darlen. "A science unknown to this universe…"

"And to this time," Baii finished the sentence. "The Empress knows of this artefact; it is part of why we…" he took them all in with a sweep of his gentle eyes, "are all here." Baii's gaze lingered on Darlen, who sent him a dismissive shrug.

"What is the artefact, Darlen?" Harry demanded, but Darlen just shook his head.

"Do you even truly know? Remember?" Baii asked, gently encouraging Darlen to give them his knowledge. "You keep it close to you at all times."

"Of course, I know!" Darlen snapped. "Do *you?*"

Baii considered those words for a moment, then turned to his sister to link silently with her mind. Ilivi bowed her head as she contemplated Darlen's and her brother's words, then her mind met Laurel's.

"To understand how the Hebre came here, to understand at least part of their story, you need to know the power of the Magen. I will be silent if you wish to honour your friend's desire for secrecy. He fears the

Magen falling into the wrong hands. It makes him protective, suspicious, although I assure you, here, you are among friends. I ask you as the others look to your leadership in matters spiritual."

All eyes were trained on Laurel during the exchange. Ilivi even excluded Ava. Laurel wanted to honour Darlen's legacy secrets, but this journey was to learn the truth of the whole souls. Of all people, he would have known that exposing those secrets would carry a risk. He was part of the whole soul story, too.

"I'm sorry, Darlen. We need to know."

Laurel half expected Darlen to get to his feet and stalk out in a fury. Instead, he set his mouth in a hard line and cast down his eyes. A moment later, he raised his shirt and lifted his right arm. Between the sixth and seventh ribs, embedded for safekeeping, lay the six-pointed Magen star, tiny, brilliant and powerful.

"What are we looking at?" Harry peered at Darlen's side, and Marcel crawled closer to get a better view. They looked at each other in disbelief as Darlen dropped his shirt and sat up straight with an "are you satisfied?" expression thrown in Laurel's direction.

Ilivi allowed the facsimile above her hand to continue turning. "It has but one purpose," she said. "To cheat time."

Darlen suddenly laughed out loud. "Cheat time? Lady, you are deluded! It doesn't cheat time. Its real purpose is to fold spatial dimensions. It only seems like time is being manipulated." Darlen pointed at Laurel and Ava. "If you want time cheaters, there's the evidence!"

Laurel wasn't entirely sure if she was being insulted, but Ilivi inclined her head gracefully, accepting her knowledge of the Magen was incomplete.

"The Hebre stole the Magen, then fled into the corridor, thus stranding their tormentors on Eden for all time."

"If the oppressors were stranded," Marcel asked, "why were the Hebre fugitives?"

"The oppressors saved a single Magen," Baii said. "They used it to send their legions after the Hebre and those who had helped them escape, the Farisee. The legions took with them a detachment of the oppressors, although there was no way of them knowing to which dimension or time the Hebre fled unless they could trace the stolen Magens."

Baii looked over at the still stony-faced Darlen. "It seems they did find them."

"Do you know the details of this persecution? Our form before we became mortal? Who the oppressors were?" Ava tried to keep the disbelief from her voice. She'd travelled so far, seen so much, even seen her own abilities grow, but to know that somehow, she was not human, described by Uncle Darlen as a "time cheater" and had been "clothed in mortal flesh", stretched her belief systems to the limits. Laurel felt it too, but as each moment passed, it became less strange, and she understood what Darlen meant.

"We only have a record of my people," Baii said. "We come from the fourth planet in the Eden system. We also came under threat from the oppressors. The Farisee saved us."

Laurel could not recall seeing any of Baii's race in the vision showed her by the Diri wraiths. "The Diri wraiths showed us images of these Farisees, but I saw no one of your species."

"There were three Arks." Ilivi scooped up images of the vessels, the configuration precisely as the Diri wraith described. "The lead ship had already entered the corridor when our people were rescued."

The Diri wraith had only visited the one ship, so Laurel didn't have the full story. Those Arks would have transported hundreds of thousands of refugees.

Ilivi threw a diorama into the air above them, sending the ships to take their place in the scene that depicted graphically the events that led to the renewal of Isilia. "We have no history of the oppressors," she said, the colours of the diorama swirling between them, "their species or their crimes. We know only that the Hebre existed in a non-corporeal state, timeless, eternal, and they dwelt within the nebula. The Hebre would have remained here, within the picot, but they sensed the Magen legions and fled for fear of bringing the Chaese to the attention of the oppressors."

"And left you behind to face them?"

"The oppressors were interested in Hebre, Laurel, and in recovering the twenty-seven Magens taken. A single Magen for a single ship, and these oppressors numbered many. Without their jewels, they were abandoned on Eden. The picot did not give us up to the legion; they passed us by and continued to search for the Magens, so they may return them, and the Hebre to the oppressors."

"None of them went back, the oppressors, the legion. None of them," Darlen muttered under his breath.

Ilivi suspended the diorama.

"What did they do?" Marcel asked.

Darlen lifted his head. "They followed the whole souls to Canaa and started up the Soul Monger trade. My guess is it was the oppressors who followed the whole souls into the Transcender and got squashed because the Soul Monger's refused to give up the Magen and decided to get rid of them themselves."

"Why didn't you tell us this?" Harry demanded.

"I did, sort of."

The diorama hovered above them, and Ilivi waited for their silence before waving the story into motion once more. The nebula appeared, glorious and shining in the heavens.

Two Arks moved into the nebula to represent their position. The third struck orbit over Isilia, its sheer size turning day into night, and coupled with the polluted red atmosphere, instilled terror into the people's hearts. The diorama gave an excellent view of the vessel, the entire surface carved with elaborate symbols, some of which Laurel recognised from her studies in ancient languages.

A figure appeared in the diorama; a Chaese male, followed by a second, then a third. Three women completed the group, the six figures serving as conduits through which the Hebre spoke. As evangelists, they travelled among the remaining Chaese, imparting knowledge about what they must do to repair the planet. The people listened, and the Ark remained in orbit above the Western continent as the world renewed. Although the picot was not an instantaneous cure for the planet, it restored and stabilised. The people removed themselves to the safe areas and established communities where they set about rebuilding lives and questioning the miraculous events that saved them. The Hebre did not remove science and technology as these were tools to promote the restoration but cautioned the Chaese that what happened before could happen again. The picot ended at the western continent.

The Hebre remained above the planet, interacting with the fledgeling societies telepathically as they learned to thrive in their beautiful new environment.

Then the diorama turned darker, throwing up a scene of worrying anxiety and infighting among the people. From the image, Laurel sensed the stresses and strains underpinning the establishment of a new society and the realisation that past follies of their leaders deprived so many of them and even their animals the ability to reproduce. The people turned to the six enablers who laid the people's fears before the Hebre. In response, and for the first time, the Hebre left the ship to physically interact with the new civilisation. They looked human, and there were children among them. Laurel felt drawn to them, drawn to the knowledge and wisdom she knew became lost as the distance between the Hebre's pure form and their forced humanity grew.

A woman stepped forward, petite, dark, with startling energy that flowed through her physical form. She raised a hand towards the Hebre ships waiting out at the nebula and stretched her other hand towards the soil. Closing her vivid violet eyes, she inhaled deeply. As they watched, vapour appeared at the woman's fingertips, curling and advancing between the Arks and the earth. Her head dropped back, and a second form—unlike her physical body—lifted and separated from its mortal confines. Shining, fluidic, it rolled what appeared to be its head, then turned its face to the sky.

In seconds, several men and women materialised, bending at the knee before the violet eyed Hebre woman. The men and women were of Baii and Ilivi's kind. The Hebre woman reconnected with the entity and raised the Riynea from their homage.

"I've seen my friend Helen do this, not teleport people, but the vapour from her fingertips, a form lifting from her body, and she could cloak our ship," Laurel said, stunned.

"All Hebre have the power to manifest," Baii said. "This woman brought our forebears to the planet. Teleporting? Perhaps. It is the only record of such an event. I saw the vapour emerge from you and Ava at the tea ceremony." Baii's gaze lingered for a moment, and Helen's appearance came to Laurel's mind. Helen was not a ghost nor a spirit. She was a manifestation, an expression of Laurel's need. Helen said Laurel called her, but she didn't know where from. Laurel had brought her friend back into being at a moment when subconsciously, she needed her comfort. Baii was still watching her as she looked up and smiled at her realisation of her own power.

"What happened next?" Harry asked.

"The Hebre placed us here. For them to allow the picot to remain in a time before cataclysm was a simple manipulation, but ensuring the people didn't choose to misuse this gift? The Hebre have no power over free will; they took faith the Chaese would not abuse their new world. Then Hebre set us here to soothe the people."

"It seems to have worked," Marcel said. He turned to

Laurel, "You used this word—Arks, before. This is what you called the ships from the book on your world?"

"Yes," Laurel said, and for Baii and Ilivi's benefit, explained the story of Noah's Ark. "It's easy to draw similarities from the Hebre story," she continued. "They seem joined in some way but conflicted in another. Certain words, like Magen, the star-shaped stone for the matrix— these are all Hebrew symbols, significant in their language. Hebre? Hebrew?" She looked at Harry. "It can't be a coincidence."

"You speak of language?" Ilivi said, excited, her voice rising in her eagerness. "There are phrases, the Hebre left no translation, and none of our scholars can decipher the symbols." She manifested a short fragment of text, holding it aloft for them all to read. Laurel recognised the symbols from the tapestry, the word 'Sheerguhd', and the phrase, 'cast out from Eden,' but she had never felt entirely secure in her translations. Seeing them now brought a new meaning and consolidated her confidence. The single line, separated from the rest of the block of letters, held a poignancy that shot like a dart into Laurel's heart. A swift intake of breath from Ava showed Laurel she felt it too. A phrase of such sadness, of such humiliation and loss.

"Laurel?" Harry prompted, seeing her face change. "Do you need some time to translate it?"

Laurel gazed at those tragic words, an echo reached across the ages, and she raised a hand to her heart. "It's okay, Harry. I know what it says."

Ilivi leaned forward. Neither she nor Baii could read it in her mind; they saw only the image of a language lost to them for centuries.

"It is Hebrew," Laurel said and looked at her daughter. "It says, 'Let my people go'."

CHAPTER FORTY-SEVEN _

Harry lay with his back propped against one of Xavier's trees, looking over the meadow where Xavier, and just lately Helen, rested. The sun peeped over the mountains, spreading its morning rays across the gully. Over the weeks, a few blue flowers had lent their spectacular colour to the field, and in the early golden sunlight, the grasses glowed red and gold. Harry loved being here, admiring the view, Laurel tucked under his arm, her head against his chest. A place for them both to consider what the future might hold. Sure, this place was tranquil, but as the weeks went by and they'd had time to digest the information from Ilivi and Baii, Harry became unsettled and felt "tranquillitied-out". He was restless, perhaps to resume their journey or for at least a little more action. He and Laurel had seen a good deal of the planet over the weeks, experienced the hospitality of the Chaese, heard their history and given over many fascinating hours to studying with their physicians and engineers. They seldom saw Marcel and Ilivi outside of each other's company, and the same went for Ava and Baii. Scarlett was immersed in her education programme, and her overactive mind and body had settled into a routine. Darlen and the new ship were expected later in the day, and the decision to stay or leave was now upon them. He knew which way he would go if anyone asked for his opinion, but he would always support Laurel.

"I can hear you thinking," Laurel murmured against his chest.

"Just running the events of the past few months through my head," Harry responded, squeezing her. "It's quiet here, isn't it?"

Laurel didn't answer, just lay still for a further moment before wriggling around to kneel up and face him. He looked up at her with his trademark, toothy grin and angled his head to the side, a shaft of sunlight sparking up his ginger hair.

"Did you hear everything I thought?" he asked.

"Everything and…" Laurel drew in a deep breath and turned her face towards the meadow, "I feel like you. I wonder if it's time for us to leave."

"I hear a 'but' coming."

"Marcel and Ilivi, they're in love."

"So are Ava and Baii."

Laurel waived away the comment. "Ava's too young."

"We've had this conversation," Harry reminded her. "She isn't living a conventional life, so don't expect convention from her."

"Falling in love isn't conventional?"

"You know what I mean. Could you see yourself making a life here, becoming a grandmother to Ava's children, to Marcel's children and never finding out what took place before the Hebre arrived?"

Laurel made a few non-committal noises.

"Don't prevaricate, my darling," Harry laughed, "I know you too well! Ava and Marcel must make their own choices, but so do we. I don't doubt Darlen will want to leave, but if Ava chooses to stay, I suppose it sheds new light on things."

That was just it. Laurel wasn't sure she could leave Ava, and she loved Marcel as a son. Was uncovering her origins worth the risk she might not see her daughter for many years, if ever? How she wished there was a multi universal, multidimensional Ancestry.com to search it all for her. But there wasn't, and it was her choice to continue the journey or live without ever knowing the truth.

"I can't leave Ava," Laurel said honestly. "And I don't want to abandon the mission. I'm really confused, Harry."

Harry nodded. He knew she'd say that, but with a few adjustments, they could probably have a happy life on Isilia. He pulled her back against his chest. "We have a place as physicians with the Chaese. You can manifest a nice place for us to live..." he grinned as she grunted in self-deprecation of her abilities in that department. So far, she'd only manifested the bath and Helen. "You just need practice," Harry continued. "There, we have a plan."

It sounded upbeat, but Laurel felt Harry's forced optimism, lending support to whatever she chose to do. She felt torn.

Darlen, it seemed, suffered no such issue. He was at the palace when they returned. They'd called Scarlett from lessons, and even though she had given no real sign she'd missed him desperately, she now clung to him as if she would do anything to stop him from leaving again. Smiling and laughing, he held her in his arms, happy at their reunion.

He set her down the moment he saw Laurel and Harry, but the little girl didn't let go of his hand.

"Laurel! Harry!"

"Darlen, it's great to see you," Laurel smiled and nodded towards Scarlett. "Scarlett's happy to see you too."

Darlen laughed; it had been so long since Laurel and Harry had seen him so cheerful.

"The ship is to your satisfaction?" Harry enquired.

"It is, Harry, and it will be to yours. Come and see, Marcel and Ava are out there now. I just came to collect Scarlett."

"Are we going back to live on a ship, Darlen?" Scarlett said, urging her father to lift her up again.

Darlen laughed and swung her into his arms. "We sure are, sweetheart!"

Laurel and Harry followed them through the colonnade.

"Well, there's two of our group who won't be staying," Harry whispered to Laurel, and judging by Darlen's enthusiasm, she had to agree. She longed to reach out to Ava to gauge her feelings, but she had to admit Ava had developed a deep affection for Baii. They'd spent every waking moment together these past few weeks while the new ship was being built. They were both beautiful, good people; for love to blossom was inevitable. Laurel sighed. Her choice was simple, she wouldn't leave Ava, but Ava may not want her to abandon the mission. This would be difficult.

The new ship stood on a landing platform Laurel was confident had not existed prior. Twice the size of Darlen's old ship, the circular central section was supported by four wide struts, and a fifth strut held a snub-nosed forward area. Laurel always considered Darlen's ship ugly, but this ship, while not comparable because of its odd shape, still had little of the aesthetic about it. In trying to think of something positive to say regarding its design, she caught Ava's frank agreement with her evaluation. Darlen's enthusiastic admiration suggested the ship's design was a dream come true, but to Laurel, to Harry and Ava and Marcel, it looked like a metallic bug, poised to pounce, the sun reflecting off its dazzlingly white hull.

"It's very...white," Laurel said. "Did your engineers design the ship?" she asked Baii and Ilivi, knowing full well she couldn't hide her opinion but hoping her voice came across at least a little complimentary. Baii and Ilivi burst out laughing.

"You don't like it, Laurel? Of course, you don't! It's hideous!" Ilivi took a moment as Laurel recovered from her embarrassment. "But it is of a most functional design; wait and see. It has its landing gear down for now, but this ship is designed primarily for space travel. The Chaese call it an explorer-class vessel. In space, that's where its beauty will become evident."

"That's right." Baii scooped up his hand to show her an image of the ship in flight, no sign of the cumbersome legs, which lifted into the body of the ship, transforming it into a simple, elegant disc with only the viewing section interrupting the sleekness. "This ship is capable of withstanding the widespeed configuration that damaged Darlen's ship."

"It's better equipped as well," Darlen joined in with evident delight. "It's got decent quarters, a galley, several slots and a foolproof reservoir." Definitely a lot in its favour they all tacitly agreed, and from inside, you wouldn't have to witness its comical appearance.

"And can it withstand a Transcender?" Laurel asked. Darlen told them that in a picot of this size, it made sense that there would be a Transcender somewhere in the neighbourhood, although he was yet to test that theory. Laurel guessed that's where they'd be heading if they needed to cross a dimension or two, at least if they joined Darlen when he left.

Darlen smiled in triumph. "I reckon. I took it out to the nebula, and it flies like a dream."

"In that case," Ava said, heading towards a lowered access ramp, "you'd best give us the grand tour."

The interior of the ship was far more pleasing to the eye than the exterior. Several well-equipped cabins with proper beds and doors that locked were a welcome feature. Each cabin had its own slot, a single white pedestal that rose from a central stand, functional and clean looking. Although they didn't need to know, Darlen gave them a graphic explanation of the slots waste disposal, compaction, distillation, and recycling capability, all the while smiling his delight. The galley, a short narrow room with an anteroom for dining, sported state-of-the-art equipment that needed little space and automation of heating minerals for warming food.

The ship's central section had a two-person elevator in the heart of the room that raised to afford a three-hundred and sixty-degree view of the surrounding space. The room was furnished comfortably with an eye to leisure. The cockpit, called a flight cabin, was separate from the rest of the ship, an idea that they all thought would take some getting used to as on the old ship, whoever was piloting was never isolated. They found Mer in the flight cabin, clean but otherwise no different. He munched through a few sounds as Scarlett climbed all over him to welcome him, kissing his screen face and telling him she'd missed him. As he dodged some of Scarlett's attention, he advised Ava that he'd had a few upgrades to enhance compatibility with the ship.

"They could have taught him how to speak," Harry said.

"He can speak, Uncle Howie," Scarlett retorted. "He said he loves me too." She turned to Ava. "Didn't he, Ava?"

Ava nodded; she hadn't heard that, but Scarlett had obviously chosen to, so she humoured her.

A separate compartment housed upgraded stasis chambers. Darlen explained they were capable of variance should the need arise. A cargo bay was primarily taken up with the three axispods, but storage was well organised and not suffering from Darlen's haphazard idea of neatness. A medical alcove was well-equipped, and both Laurel and Harry were happy to see their familiar instrumentation returned, plus a few more they'd learned about since they arrived here. These would prove useful in maintaining health and for first-aid use.

Darlen proudly went through instrumentation, interfaces, infocharts and sensors. Control of the ship could even be transferred to the captain's quarters. Laurel had to admit it was streamlined and easy to understand. Flying the ship would be a breeze, and they all looked forward to the opportunity to take the helm.

"Is the ship ready to go?" Harry asked as they emerged back onto the landing pad. Darlen patted the hull as though the ship had become as beloved as his old vessel.

"I had a few components from the old ship installed, things that have been with me since forever," Darlen said. "But this one's got external cannons, and it's stocked with hand weapons—for defence of course—and the galley's stocked, medical bay stocked, pandroscope updated. She's as ready as she can be."

Their usual communal meal on the terrace was a subdued affair that evening. Ava and Baii sat together, as did Marcel and Ilivi, but Darlen made a few huffing sounds and fidgeted. Laurel knew that with the ship ready, he saw little point in staying.

"Come on, we have to talk," he said bluntly. "I don't need telepathy to see we're avoiding the issue of leaving. I think it's time we moved on. Your kindness—" he turned to Ilivi and Baii, "so freely given. Your generosity…" Darlen searched for words to express his thankfulness, but he just wasn't cut out for a sedentary life.

Marcel squeezed Ilivi's hand and stood. "We have made such special friends here," he said, smiling fondly down at Ilivi, "but first and foremost, we are a family of travellers who set out upon a journey that we have to see through to its end."

"Yes, Mom," Ava said. "I know it's worried you, but Baii and I—" she turned to smile at the handsome man at her side, "we've discussed this moment. We knew it would come, and we're okay, I promise."

All eyes turned to Laurel. It seemed she was the only one hesitating. Now the choosing was upon them, she feared leading them into further danger, of taking away Ava and Marcel's chances of happiness. On the other hand, she knew Ilivi and Baii had a duty to remain here and could not travel with them.

"It is the way of things," Ilivi said, her voice reassuring. "We will be here when you return."

CHAPTER FORTY-EIGHT _

"You should call Darlen, 'daddy', like your teacher's little boys call their father 'daddy, in their language," Ava said, lifting Scarlett onto her knee as she sat at the helm control in the flight cabin. They'd only been out from Isilia a few days and still not used to gathering in a separate common room, so there was more traffic in the flight cabin than needed. Fortunately, it was large enough to accommodate them all.

"You don't call Uncle Howie 'daddy'," Scarlett said, giving Ava the benefit of her wisdom.

"Howie isn't my daddy," Ava said, realising family dynamics weren't something often debated. Scarlett couldn't possibly know.

"Marcel is your brother, so Howie is his daddy, and he doesn't say 'daddy' and Marcel doesn't say 'Ava' either. He says, 'my lady sister'. Why?" Scarlett squirmed around to look Ava in the face, her blue eyes wide and questioning, demanding an answer. Scarlett was five now, the age when all things needed either prefixing or suffixing with that all-important, knowledge-building word, "why?"

Harry bit back a grin. Ava had dug herself into a hole.

"This ought to be good," he said.

"Okay," Ava said, flicking him a glance and taking a breath. "Howie isn't Marcel's daddy. But Marcel is my brother. We have the same daddy but different mommies."

"Who's Marcel's mommy?"

"We don't know."

"Auntie Laurel is your mommy."

"Yes."

"But Auntie Laurel and Uncle Howie do this," Scarlett made kissing sounds. "Mummies and daddy's kiss, and that makes Uncle Howie your daddy because Auntie Laurel is your mommy," she said, applying her child's logic in one breath. "If you call Uncle Howie 'daddy', I'll call Darlen 'daddy'."

Ava looked up. At nearly nineteen, it was pretty late in the day to make such a change. Harry had been simply "Howie" for as long as she could remember.

"Hmm," Ava grinned at the little girl who was taking this very seriously; she'd been to school and knew everything now. "How about I call him 'dad'?"

Scarlett thought for a moment. "Okay," she agreed, and from that day forward, Darlen and Harry got new titles.

The ship, as promised, performed like a dream. Despite the Chaese not having left the planet for centuries, Darlen had been impressed by their extraordinary technological expertise. He'd assumed they were simple folk, like those they saw in the town when they first arrived on Isilia, but that was merely their lifestyle choice. The Chaese were highly intelligent and creative engineers, able to interpret age-old schematics from their space-faring days to produce a ship capable of every level of security, manoeuvrability and comfort required of an explorer-class vessel. Darlen and Mer had a hand in the design, but after gauging Laurel and Ava's reaction, decided not to admit the hull shape had been to their specification.

The ship's helm control anticipatory module raised shields when any threat to the ship was detected. They hadn't yet entered the nebula's heart, as Ilivi and Baii assured them they could travel within normal space without fear and enjoy the beauty of this galaxy. They didn't rush, allowing the passing spacescape to distract them as they recovered from the sadness of leaving the people they cared so deeply about.

One night, a com message from Darlen woke Laurel. "Laurel, can you come down to the flight deck? Scarlett's here with me, and she's very unsettled."

Scarlett was crying in Darlen's arms. Laurel felt the child's face; she didn't feel warm and even taking her to the medical bay and running the pandroscope over her failed to reveal a problem.

"I'm at a loss, Darlen," Laurel frowned. "She's definitely distressed. I can get Harry. He might have some ideas."

"No, don't disturb him. We'll go back to the flight deck. Mer can take over, and perhaps I can distract her."

Laurel followed them back through the pleasantly furnished lounge area. She was fast warming to the ship now she didn't have to see the outside, and as the inside was comfortable and they all had privacy, she didn't care about its appearance. Laurel settled beside Darlen and looked out to where the nebula wove its glorious colours in the heavens. But something wasn't right. Darlen saw her frown at once.

"What is it?"

"The filaments have straightened out. They've dimmed."

"The filaments?" Darlen peered through the viewport. "Do you mean the nebula looks different?"

Laurel nodded, trying to gauge the sudden shift in her senses. Ava appeared in the doorway just as Scarlett sat up and pointed. "Look!" she said, giggling with excitement. "A flower!"

On what looked like a collision course, although the ship's sensors did not raise shields, the flower-like object headed towards them along the margin of the nebula. Ava stepped closer to the viewport.

"That's not moving towards us," she said. "It only looks like it is. It...it's *forming.*"

The five-sectioned corolla ahead built, intensified and fanned out its dense, swirling, smoky petals before them with terrifying rapidity. Darlen stared open-mouthed before speaking, his voice hoarse with emotion.

"I didn't sense it," he said, shaking his head in puzzlement and looking down at the recovered Scarlett. "But she did."

The corolla built exponentially until its smoky vortex filled all fields of vision. Slowly, it revolved. Each of the five sections was like a dark, brooding, colossal thunderhead, millions of kilometres across, with lightning sparking and flashing in their depths. The sheer size of the phenomenon blotted out the planets, the stars and the nebula. Still, the ship's sensors registered nothing. Marcel's voice, each syllable clipped in his amazement, came from behind them.

"What in heaven's name is *that?*"

"That, my friend," Darlen said, bringing the ship to a stop, "Is a Transcender."

A change in the ship's ambience also woke Harry, bringing him to the flight deck. Harry ran his hands through his hair.

"It looks like the gateway to hell."

"I think it's beautiful," Ava said, leaning close to the viewport.

"It would take forever to go around," Marcel turned to the sensors, which registered normal space and remained oblivious to the massive anomaly off their starboard bow.

"We won't be going around it," Darlen said, still reeling from the surprise Scarlett and not he sensed the Transcender. "We're going through it."

"Through it?" Marcel eyed the phenomenon in dismay.

"The Hebre came through here, Marcel," Laurel said, not taking her eyes from the slowly revolving tempest. "It's reasonable for us to go back the way they came."

"It's amazing." Harry was almost laughing. "I had no idea."

Laurel remembered the depiction of the Transcender as a flower opening and closing, although she suspected few had ever seen one. "It does look like a flower," she said, as the astonishing spectacle continued to grow before her eyes. "A very large, grey, terrifying flower. Harry, how did the

League isolate something they couldn't see?"

"We knew it had to be triggered." Harry looked at Darlen for confirmation. "And we knew its location, but as far as I know, no-one's ever seen one, except for the Soul Mongers."

"Did it respond to the Magen?" Ava asked.

"No," Darlen said. "Well, maybe, but Scarlett sensed it. You see that opening?" He pointed to a void in the centre of the petals that turned more slowly, its blackness frightening and hypnotic. "That is the dimensional portal, the Curlew; it will guide us in. When we enter, the Magen will fold the surrounding dimensions."

"Can you be sure it will take us where we want to go?" Marcel's voice hinted at his regret at leaving Isilia to enter an unknown maelstrom.

"We don't really know where that is now, do we?" Darlen pointed out, "but if the Hebre used this Transcender, the chances are that Ava will know which direction we need to take once we're inside. She's recognised their route so far. Once she knows, I'll know, and so will the Magen."

"So, do we just…" Harry made a scooting gesture, "dive in?"

"We can't." Darlen turned to Laurel. "I'm sorry, I can't take a chance. You and Harry need to go into variance, you too Marcel. Ava will be fine, and Scarlett…" he looked down with pride at the little girl, happily distracted by the immensity of the Transcender, "is a Soul Monger. It can't hurt her."

"Are you sure?" Marcel felt a surge of fear for his

beloved sister, for Scarlett and for everyone he thought of as his family.

"I'm sure, Marcel. Don't worry. Ava has never been through a Transcender, nor has she ever lived on Earth. Harry and you are human, and Laurel is now too human to survive the dimensional shifts, but we should get going." Darlen looked through the viewport and smiled as though he understood the Transcender's very thoughts. "It's waiting."

Once more, Laurel lay in a variance chamber; this time, some of the paraphernalia that gave her nightmares would be employed. Fortunately, the Chaese had made a few modifications in anticipation. An implant replaced the yawning stomach tube, but the collar probe essentially protected her lungs. The milky variance fluid also safeguarded and preserved her from the Transcender's effects. The Chaese didn't understand all of the technology well enough to improve upon it, declaring it to be of some 'otherworldly' nature. Laurel looked up at Harry as he kissed her goodbye, his own variance chamber placed next to hers.

"I wish Darlen had some way of knowing how long we are likely to be in here," Laurel said, unable to stop the few tears that slid down the side of her face and into her hair, which had to be cut short for this procedure.

She looked as she did when Harry first saw her on the Consular ship; he thought her beautiful then, and nothing had changed. She was still as beautiful, even with her glorious curls shorn.

"This time, he's going to be awake, and he'll navigate

the Transcender safely." Harry held her hand tightly. "Don't worry."

"If I keep going into stasis," Laurel said, making a weak attempt at humour, "I'll end up younger than Ava."

"No, you won't, Mom." Ava joined Harry and looked down at her mother. "You'll be asleep, and it'll pass like a dream."

"I've missed so much of your life." Laurel reached for Ava's hand, guilt overwhelming her that she'd allowed Ava to sacrifice a life with Baii only to now lose her parents and brother for goodness knows how long.

"We'll make up for it, I promise. I love you." Ava squeezed her hand, and Darlen closed the variance chamber. As her mother slid into sleep and the milky fluid bubbled up, Ava turned to Harry and sobbed in his arms.

Miran: adjective: /pəˈpɛtʃʊəl/ Perpetual, never ending.
Forin: noun: ˈfɒrɪn/ Demonic, devilish.
Nebula: noun: ˈnɛbjʊlə/ A cloud of dust and gas.
(Outdated): A galaxy.

Two figures stood on the domed observation platform of the sleek explorer-class vessel, "Canaa". The slender dark-haired woman, dressed in a trader's garb, her arms folded, watched through wide, violet eyes as the vividly coloured threads and filaments of the nebula faded, revealing, in every direction, normal space. She glanced up at her companion, a black robot with a silly smile drawn on the screen that served as a face, a black patch over an imaginary eye and a childish homemade pirate's hat stuck at a jaunty angle on its square head. It swivelled around to look at her and made a few munching sounds. The woman smiled.

"You're right. Let's go wake Mom and Dad."

TO BE CONTINUED...

Testimony: The Soul Monger Book Three is available on Amazon.

ACKNOWLEDGEMENTS

If you enjoyed the second part of Laurel's story, I would love for you to hop over to your Amazon orders page and leave a review. Good reviews are the lifeblood of Indie authors, and we thank you for your support. I would also like to thank my awesome editors, Amy and Jo, for all their hard work. I am so lucky to have them on the team.

If you would like me to keep you updated with my new releases, please subscribe to my (occasional) newsletter at
https://matildascotneybooks.com/

Or connect with me on Facebook:
https://www.facebook.com/Offtheplanetbooks

OTHER BOOKS BY MATILDA SCOTNEY

ABOUT THE AUTHOR

When my mind isn't off on galactic imaginings with my trusty chihuahua sidekick Oggie, I can be found in Australia, sand between my toes, collecting teapots and nerding about all things Star Wars.